Fools, Knaves and Heroes

Great Political Short Stories

JEFFREY ARCHER was born in England in 1940 and educated at Wellington School, Somerset, and Brasenose College, Oxford. He represented Great Britain in the 100 metres in the 1960s, and became the youngest member of the British Parliament in 1969. His bestselling books include *Not a Penny Less, Not a Penny More*; *Kane and Abel*; *First Among Equals*; *A Matter of Honour*; and most recently *A Twist in the Tale*, his latest collection of short stories.

SIMON BAINBRIDGE was born in Lancashire, England, in 1952, and educated at schools in England and the USA and at Oxford. After many years working as a bookseller in London, he is now a freelance writer and editor.

edited and introduced by

JEFFREY ARCHER
AND SIMON BAINBRIDGE

Fools, Knaves and Heroes

Great Political Short Stories

An M&S Paperback from
McClelland & Stewart Inc.
The Canadian Publishers

An M&S Paperback from McClelland & Stewart Inc.

First printing February 1991

This collection first published by
Bellew Publishing Company Limited, London

First paperback edition published 1990 by
Pan Books Ltd., London

Canadian Cataloguing in Publication Data

Main entry under title:

Fools, knaves, and heroes

(An M&S paperback)
ISBN 0-7710-0775-2

1. Short stories, English. 2. Short stories, American. I. Archer, Jeffrey, 1940- . II. Bainbridge, Simon, 1952- .

PR1309.S5F66 1991 823'.0108358 C90-095737-9

Cover illustration by Paul Slater

Printed and bound in Canada

McClelland & Stewart Inc.
The Canadian Publishers
481 University Avenue
Toronto, Ontario
M5G 2E9

Contents

Acknowledgements

Grateful acknowledgement is made to Kingsley Amis, Century Hutchinson Ltd and Jonathon Clewes Ltd for permission to reprint the story 'I Spy Strangers' from the *Collected Short Stories*; to the author, Hodder & Stoughton, and Simon & Schuster for the story 'The Coup' from *A Quiver Full of Arrows*; to Grafton Books, a division of William Collins & Sons Ltd, for the story 'The Bishop's Aunt' by L. E. Jones from the volume *The Bishop's Aunt and other Stories*; to the Executors of the James Joyce Estate and Jonathan Cape Ltd for the story 'Ivy Day in the Committee Room' from *Dubliners*; to Rosemary A. Thurber for the story 'The Greatest Man in the World'; copyright © 1935 James Thurber, copyright © 1963 Helen Thurber and Rosemary A. Thurber, from *The Middle-Aged Man on the Flying Trapeze*, published by Harper & Row, also to Hamish Hamilton Ltd from *Vintage Thurber*.

Introduction

To be invited to compile a collection of short stories with a political theme was an attractive challenge: there is a good deal of material to choose from, we believe no such anthology has been published before, and politics remains a subject of wide interest. But the anthologist's traditional introductory task of justifying his selections is made more difficult in our case by a problem of definition. What *is* a 'political' story? Perhaps only one of our eventual choices – Jack London's 'The Dream of Debs' – could be described in no other way. London constructs a convincing and vivid fantasy of the effects of a general strike in the USA. But not many short-story writers have had experience of political life to help them write circumstantially and knowledgeably; and while, particularly today, there are writers with political views as firmly held as was London's socialism, a collection made up only of stories written to make a political point would not make enjoyable reading.

Happily, writers without an insider's knowledge or a committed stance have used the world of politics for their own ends – usually as a setting in which a particular moral point can be made – and it is from these that our selection has been made. The earliest is Charles Dickens's 'The Election for Beadle', first published in the *Evening Chronicle* in 1835 and included in the First Series of 'Sketches by Boz' in the following year. Its inclusion reminds us that politics is not always a matter of important affairs of State: the orderly conduct of local government in a small town can be every bit as captivating. Dickens is very much alive to the humour of grandiloquence and takes pleasure in describing the issues at stake in the election as 'the great new beadle principles', while in reality each candidate bases his claim on the size of the family he has to support. This, perhaps, is mundane stuff, but Dickens's parodying of the oratorical styles on display at the election meeting would do the House of Commons proud. We can still hear their echoes today. Similarly, anyone with experience of local politics will understand that Dickens is right in stressing the importance of getting voters to the poll: on the day of the election, the crucial difference between Bung and Sproggins is the two hackney coaches and a cab supplied by Bung's chief supporter – 'the cab for the drunken voters and the two coaches for the old ladies'.

The only other product of the nineteenth century in this collection is Mark Twain's 'The Man that corrupted Hadleyburg', which once again is concerned with the life of a small town. It was first published in 1900, when Twain was sixty-five, after a sad and worrying time in his life was coming to an end. In 1894 he had been declared a bankrupt after the dual failure of his publishing house and of a new form of typesetter which he had helped to develop, finance and market; and far worse, in 1896 his favourite daughter, Susy, had died of meningitis. Twain had spent most of the 1890s abroad, undertaking vast lecture and recital tours to pay off his debts. In 1900 he returned to live in America, newly prosperous and again a celebrity, but it is impossible not to be aware of the bitterness and bleakness of this story and how much the experiences of debt and death had affected him. For 'The Man that corrupted Hadleyburg' is by no means a genial, cracker-barrel anecdote of the kind that had made Twain so popular: it is a relentlessly savage exposure of the moral pretensions of the self-appointed Nineteen (also known as the Symbols) who run Hadleyburg through their Committee on Propagation and Preservation of the Hadleyburg Reputation. It could be said that there is something artificial about Twain's use of a mysterious stranger who sets the plot in motion (Twain wrote another short story called 'The Mysterious Stranger', who turns out to be Satan), but the unstoppable power of Twain's depiction of the corrupting force of money is enough to dispel such objections. The end that he devises for old Mr and Mrs Richards, the only people in the story who have been allowed to engage the reader's affections, is proof of his ability to surprise.

There are some striking parallels between Twain's story and Rudyard Kipling's 'The Village that voted the Earth was Flat', which was written in 1913 and published four years later. Small-town life is again the target and again the story is one of an elaborate revenge being taken for a casual insult. The two authors' methods and manners, however, are very different. Where Twain is bleak and angry, Kipling is gleeful and mocking; where Twain's mysterious stranger works by stealth, Kipling's Woodhouse, Pallant, Ollyett and Maskerier (splendid, resonant names!) are attractively open in all they do to pour scorn on the village of Huckley – planting stories in newspapers, launching a popular song, asking questions in the House. It is this manipulation of public opinion which makes the story politically interesting just as much as the scenes in the House of Commons – a pity the House was not on television in those days. The way Kipling allows the final scene to take flight into something like fantasy is immensely skilful in view of the detailed authenticity of the rest of the story.

Unadulterated political fantasy is provided by Saki's 'Ministers of Grace'. Saki's carefully cultivated image of an Edwardian boulevardier who would coin epigrams until he had enough to make a story conceals the professionalism of a writer whose career had begun with political sketches for the *Westminster Gazette* and went on to include spells as a foreign correspondent in Europe. Not much of his experience in this world is perceptible in his work and the bulk of what there is, the pieces collected under the title of 'The Westminster Alice', is really only comprehensible to historians of the period, so specific and obscure are the contemporary references. 'Ministers of Grace' is rather different, because most of the politicians referred to under thinly disguised names (Quinston, Lord Kedzon and so on) are still known quantities today and there remains humour to be found in the idea of the haughty Lord Curzon – a man, in Saki's words, 'who had been Viceroy in the splendid East and who still reflected in his mien some of the cold dignity of the Himalayan snow-peaks' – treating a stranger to a bun and a glass of milk and discoursing genially on the subject of Indian birds.

The story, 'Ivy Day in the Committee Room', by Saki's younger contemporary James Joyce is as different from 'Ministers of Grace' as one would expect of these authors. It comes from Joyce's collection of short stories, *Dubliners*, which was first published in Ireland in 1912 in a small edition, nearly all of which was destroyed by the printer in a fit of censorious zeal. The book's English publication took place, after some difficulty, in 1914. Much of the controversy before publication centred on 'Ivy Day in the Committee Room', Joyce's publishers having two objections. The first, which applied to all the stories, was to Joyce's use of people's real names for his characters; and Joyce gave way on this point comparatively easily. The second objection was to the language in this exchange when the characters are discussing the impending visit to Dublin of King Edward VII:

'Now, here's the way I look at it. Here's this chap come to the throne after his old mother keeping him out of it till the man was grey. He's a man of the world, and he means well by us. He's a jolly fine, decent fellow, if you ask me, and no damn nonsense about him. He just says to himself: "The old one never went to see these wild Irish. By Christ, I'll go myself and see what they're like." And are we going to insult the man when he comes over here on a friendly visit? Eh? Isn't that right, Crofton?'

Crofton nodded his head.

'But after all now,' said Mr Lyons argumentatively, 'King Edward's life, you know is not the very . . .'

'Let bygones be bygones,' said Mr Henchy. 'I admire the man personally. He's just an ordinary knockabout like you and me. He's fond of his glass of grog and he's a bit of a rake, perhaps, and he's a good sportsman. Damn it, can't we Irish play fair?'

In Joyce's first version, the phrase is 'bloody owld bitch of a mother', which could raise eyebrows today in similar circumstances. But even the final version frightened the publishers into thinking that people might find such language and attitudes disrespectful to two late monarchs. Joyce, amazingly, went so far as to write to King George V on the matter, receiving a stiff note from the King's private secretary to the effect that His Majesty did not feel that he could take sides in a dispute of this sort. At this remove of time, Joyce's defence – that this is how the characters in this story would express themselves – seems watertight; and even at the time there were many who could not see the reason for all the fuss.

Perhaps the least known name in this collection is that of L. E. Jones, whose story, 'The Bishop's Aunt', is a splendidly witty and light-hearted fable about striking moral attitudes in public. The author's full name was Sir Lawrence Evelyn Jones, Bart., MC, TD, FRSL, a barrister and a prolific author: his three volumes of autobiography are most entertaining. He may be more familiar to some readers under his nickname, Jonah, by which he is constantly referred to throughout the six volumes of correspondence between George Lyttelton and Sir Rupert Hart-Davis. The story included here gave its name to a collection published in 1961.

By comparison with some of the stories in this book, which find time for quite lengthy examinations of a simply stated moral or political issue, James Thurber's 'The Greatest Man in the World' is concise. This brevity reflects the dilemma at the heart of the story; that is, what to do when it suddenly becomes apparent that your idol has feet of clay. As with his fellow American humorist Mark Twain, Thurber is here writing a very different kind of story from the childhood reminiscences and social comedies for which he is best known. Indeed, his skill and delight in depicting the completely unacceptable character of his 'hero' are the only humorous elements in what is otherwise a fairly sombre story.

Jack London's 'The Dream of Debs' was written in 1914 and is one of a handful of stories which explicitly reflect his strong political views. He was a member of America's Socialist Party for twenty years and because of his celebrity as a writer was almost as important a spokesman as Eugene V. Debs, the party leader and the man referred to in the story's title: this is *not* a story about well-born young girls being launched into society, as I suspect 'debs' was not a word London would have come across in Webster's. Much of the story's appeal comes from the relish with which London casts himself as narrator in the uncharacteristic role of the idle rich. It is possible to criticise the story's conclusion – capitulation by the employers and a return almost to the status quo – as simplistic, but not the stages by which London reaches that conclusion. The great set piece in which the narrator and his friends steal and slaughter a cow and the journey they make through an increasingly lawless California are both powerful evocations of a disintegrating society and show how even the most law-abiding citizen can break under stress.

The society in Kingsley Amis's 'I Spy Strangers' is not disintegrating so much as convulsing. Although the setting is military and the principal characters are dispirited members of a communications unit in Germany towards the end of the Second World War, the real subject of the story – Labour's huge and surprising General Election victory in 1945 and the changes it portended – is set off stage. It is made part of the fabric of the story in many ways. Most obviously, the mock Parliament, which the almost well-meaning commanding officer has arranged as an entertainment for the men, rehearses distorted versions of the arguments which featured in the election. More subtly, the characters' plans for their peacetime lives paint different pictures of postwar society and Major Raleigh begins to find in the behaviour and attitudes of his men hints that the new world will not be to his liking. The determination with which, at the end of the story, he faces the future, almost as if he were going to fight another war, is a strange mixture of the pathetic and the admirable.

I hope I can be forgiven for including one of my own stories, 'The Coup', based on my experiences when visiting Nigeria on business. Despite my love of politics, it is the only story of the twenty-four I have had published that could be described as political. This may be because I used up most of my ideas in a full-length novel, *First Among Equals*, some years ago.

It has to be said that the view of politics presented by all of us in these stories is not a sunny one. Perhaps only Jack London, for all the horrors of his tale, views politics as a positive force for good: most of the others choose to regard politicians as ruthless self-seekers and the world in which they move as a breeding-ground of corruption and interference with the life of the individual. This is probably no more than a fear of the unknown. Writing is famously a solitary task and most writers have not chosen to lead a public life: their suspicion of politicians has no more force than the politicians' view of all writers as subversives. But it makes a good story; and I suspect that a tale of service, honesty, probity and dedication to one's country would find few readers in the modern world.

The Man that corrupted Hadleyburg

Mark Twain

It was many years ago. Hadleyburg was the most honest and upright town in all the region around about. It had kept that reputation unsmirched during three generations, and was prouder of it than of any other of its possessions. It was so proud of it, and so anxious to ensure its perpetuation, that it began to teach the principles of honest dealing to its babies in the cradle, and made the like teachings the staple of their culture thenceforward through all the years devoted to their education. Also, throughout the formative years temptations were kept out of the way of the young people, so that their honesty could have every chance to harden and solidify, and become a part of their very bone. The neighboring towns were jealous of this honorable supremacy, and affected to sneer at Hadleyburg's pride in it and call it vanity; but all the same they were obliged to acknowledge that Hadleyburg was in reality an incorruptible town; and if pressed they would also acknowledge that the mere fact that a young man hailed from Hadleyburg was all the recommendation he needed when he went forth from his natal town to seek for responsible employment.

But at last, in the drift of time, Hadleyburg had the ill luck to offend a passing stranger – possibly without knowing it, certainly without caring, for Hadleyburg was sufficient unto itself, and cared not a rap for strangers or their opinions. Still, it would have been well to make an exception in this one's case, for he was a bitter man and revengeful. All through his wanderings during a whole year he kept his injury in mind, and gave all his leisure moments to trying to invent a compensating satisfaction for it. He contrived many plans, and all of them were good, but none of them was quite sweeping enough; the poorest of them would hurt a great many individuals, but what he wanted was a plan which would comprehend the entire town, and not let so much as one person escape unhurt. At last he had a fortunate idea, and when it fell into his brain it lit up his whole head with an evil joy. He began to form a plan at once, saying to himself, 'That is the thing to do – I will corrupt the town.'

Six months later he went to Hadleyburg, and arrived in a buggy at the house of the old cashier of the bank about ten at night. He got a sack out of the buggy, shouldered it, and staggered with it through the cottage yard, and knocked at the door. A woman's voice said 'Come in,' and he entered, and set his sack behind the stove in the parlor, saying politely to the old lady who sat reading the *Missionary Herald* by the lamp:

'Pray keep your seat, madam, I will not disturb you. There – now it is pretty well concealed; one would hardly know it was there. Can I see your husband a moment, madam?'

No, he was gone to Brixton, and might not return before morning.

'Very well, madam, it is no matter. I merely wanted to leave that sack in his care, to be delivered to the rightful owner when he shall be found. I am a stranger; he does not know me; I am merely passing through the town tonight to discharge a matter which has been long in my mind. My errand is now completed, and I go pleased and a little proud, and you will never see me again. There is a paper attached to the sack which will explain everything. Good night, madam.'

The old lady was afraid of the mysterious big stranger, and was glad to see him go. But her curiosity was roused, and she went straight to the sack and brought away the paper. It began as follows:

TO BE PUBLISHED; or, the right man sought out by private inquiry – either will answer. This sack contains gold coin weighing a hundred and sixty pounds four ounces—

'Mercy on us, and the door not locked!'

Mrs Richards flew to it all in a tremble and locked it, then pulled down the window-shades and stood frightened, worried, and wondering if there was anything else she could do toward making herself and the money more safe. She listened awhile for burglars, then surrendered to curiosity and went back to the lamp and finished reading the paper:

I am a foreigner, and am presently going back to my own country, to remain there permanently. I am grateful to America for what I have received at her hands during my long stay under her flag; and to one of her citizens – a citizen of Hadleyburg – I am especially grateful for a great kindness done me a year or two ago. Two great kindnesses, in fact. I will explain. I was a gambler. I say I *WAS*. I was a ruined gambler. I arrived in this village at night, hungry and without a penny. I asked for help – in the dark; I was ashamed to beg in the light. I begged of the right man. He gave me twenty dollars – that is to say, he gave me life, as I considered it. He also gave me fortune; for out of that money I have made myself rich at the gaming-table. And finally, a remark which he made to me has remained with me to this day, and has at last conquered me; and in conquering has saved the remnant of my morals; I shall gamble no more. Now I have no idea who that man was, but I want him found, and I want him to have this money, to give away, throw away, or keep, as he pleases. It is merely my way of testifying my gratitude to him. If I could stay, I would find him myself; but no matter, he will be found. This is an honest town, an incorruptible town, and I know I can trust it without fear. This man can be identified by the remark which he made to me; I feel persuaded that he will remember it.

And now my plan is this: If you prefer to conduct the inquiry privately, do so. Tell the contents of this present writing to any one who is likely to be the right man. If he shall answer, 'I am the man; the remark I made was so-and-so,' apply the test – to wit: open the sack, and in it you will find a sealed envelope containing that remark. If the remark mentioned by the candidate tallies with it, give him the money, and ask no further questions, for he is certainly the right man.

But if you shall prefer a public inquiry, then publish this present writing in the local paper – with these instructions added, to wit: Thirty days from now, let the candidate appear at the town-hall at eight in the evening (Friday), and hand his remark, in a sealed envelope, to the Revd Mr Burgess (if he will be kind enough to act); and let Mr Burgess there and then destroy the seals of the sack, open it, and see if the remark is correct; if correct, let the money be delivered, with my sincere gratitude, to my benefactor thus identified.

Mrs Richards sat down, gently quivering with excitement, and was soon lost in thinkings – after this pattern: 'What a strange thing it is! . . . And what a fortune for that kind man who set his bread afloat upon the waters! . . . If it had only been my husband that did it! – for we are so poor, so old and poor! . . .' Then, with a sigh – 'But it was not my Edward; no, it was not he that gave a stranger twenty dollars. It is a pity, too; I see it now. . . .' Then, with a shudder – 'But it is *gambler's* money! the wages of sin: we couldn't take it; we couldn't touch it. I don't like to be near it; it seems a defilement.' She moved to a farther chair. . . . 'I wish Edward would come and take it to the bank; a burglar might come at any moment; it is dreadful to be here all alone with it.'

At eleven Mr Richards arrived, and while his wife was saying, 'I am *so* glad you've come!' he was saying, 'I'm so tired – tired clear out; it is dreadful to be poor, and have to make these dismal journeys at my time of life. Always at the grind, grind, grind, on a salary – another man's slave, and he sitting at home in his slippers, rich and comfortable.'

'I am so sorry for you, Edward, you know that; but be comforted: we have our livelihood; we have our good name – '

'Yes, Mary, and that is everything. Don't mind my talk – it's just a moment's irritation and doesn't mean anything. Kiss me – there, it's all gone now, and I am not complaining any more. What have you been getting? What's in the sack?'

Then his wife told him the great secret. It dazed him for a moment; then he said:

'It weighs a hundred and sixty pounds? Why, Mary, it's for-ty thou-sand dollars – think of it – a whole fortune! Not ten men in this village are worth that much. Give me the paper.'

He skimmed through it and said:

'Isn't it an adventure! Why, it's a romance; it's like the impossible things one reads about in books, and never sees in life.' He was well stirred up now; cheerful, even gleeful. He tapped his old wife on the cheek, and said, humorously, 'Why, we're rich, Mary, rich; all we've got to do is to bury the money and burn the papers. If the gambler ever comes to inquire, we'll merely look coldly upon him and say: "What is this nonsense you are talking? We have never heard of you and your sack of gold before"; and then he would look foolish, and—'

'And in the mean time, while you are running on with your jokes, the money is still here, and it is fast getting along toward burglar-time.'

'True. Very well, what shall we do – make the inquiry private? No, not that: it would spoil the romance. The public method is better. Think what a noise it will make! And it will make all the other towns jealous; for no stranger would trust such a thing to any town but Hadleyburg, and they know it. It's a great card for us. I must get to the printing-office now, or I shall be too late.'

'But stop – stop – don't leave me here alone with it, Edward!'

But he was gone. For only a little while, however. Not far from his own house he met the editor-proprietor of the paper, and gave him the document, and said, 'Here is a good thing for you, Cox – put it in.'

'It may be too late, Mr Richards, but I'll see.'

At home again he and his wife sat down to talk the charming mystery over; they were in no condition for sleep. The first question was, Who could the citizen have been who gave the stranger the twenty dollars? It seemed a simple one; both answered it in the same breath:

'Barclay Goodson.'

'Yes,' said Richards, 'he could have done it, and it would have been like him, but there's not another in the town.'

'Everybody will grant that, Edward – grant it privately, anyway. For six months, now, the village has been its own proper self once more – honest, narrow, self-righteous, and stingy.'

'It is what he always called it, to the day of his death – said it right out publicly, too.'

'Yes, and he was hated for it.'

'Oh, of course; but he didn't care. I reckon he was the best-hated man among us, except the Reverend Burgess.'

'Well, Burgess deserves it – he will never get another congregation here. Mean as the town is, it knows how to estimate *him*. Edward, doesn't it seem odd that the stranger should appoint Burgess to deliver the money?'

'Well, yes – it does. That is – that is – '

'Why so much that-*is*-ing? Would *you* select him?'

'Mary, maybe the stranger knows him better than this village does.'

'Much *that* would help Burgess!'

The husband seemed perplexed for an answer; the wife kept a steady eye upon him, and waited. Finally Richards said, with the hesitancy of one who is making a statement which is likely to encounter doubt:

'Mary, Burgess is not a bad man.'

His wife was certainly surprised.

'Nonsense!' she exclaimed.

'He is not a bad man. I know. The whole of his unpopularity had its foundation in that one thing – the thing that made so much noise.'

'That "one thing", indeed! As if that "one thing" wasn't enough, all by itself.'

'Plenty. Plenty. Only he wasn't guilty of it.'

'How you talk! Not guilty of it! Everybody knows he *was* guilty.'

'Mary, I give you my word – he was innocent.'

'I can't believe it, and I don't. How do you know?'

'It is a confession. I am ashamed, but I will make it. I was the only man who knew he was innocent. I could have saved him, and – and – well, you know how the town was wrought up – I hadn't the pluck to do it. It would have turned everybody against me. I felt mean, ever so mean; but I didn't dare; I hadn't the manliness to face that.'

Mary looked troubled, and for a while was silent. Then she said, stammeringly:

'I – I don't think it would have done for you to – to – One mustn't – er – public opinion – one has to be so careful – so – ' It was a difficult road, and she got mired; but after a little she got started again. 'It was a great pity, but – Why, we couldn't afford it, Edward – we couldn't indeed. Oh, I wouldn't have had you do it for anything!'

'It would have lost us the good will of so many people, Mary; and then – and then—'

'What troubles me now is, what *he* thinks of us, Edward.'

'He? *He* doesn't suspect that I could have saved him.'

'Oh,' exclaimed the wife, in a tone of relief, 'I am glad of that! As long as he doesn't know that you could have saved him, he – he – well, that makes it a great deal better. Why, I might have known he didn't know, because he is always trying to be friendly with us, as little encouragement as we give him. More than once people have twitted me with it. There's the Wilsons, and the Wilcoxes, and the Harknesses, they take a mean pleasure in saying, "*Your friend* Burgess," because they know it pesters me. I wish he wouldn't persist in liking us so; I can't think why he keeps it up.'

'I can explain it. It's another confession. When the thing was new and hot, and the town made a plan to ride him on a rail, my conscience hurt me so that I couldn't stand it, and I went privately and gave him notice, and he got out of the town and stayed out till it was safe to come back.'

'Edward! If the town had found it out—'

'*Don't!* It scares me yet, to think of it. I repented of it the minute it was done; and I was even afraid to tell you, lest your face might betray it to somebody. I didn't sleep any that night, for worrying. But after a few days I saw that no one was going to suspect me, and after that I got to feeling glad I did it. And I feel glad yet, Mary – glad through and through.'

'So do I, now, for it would have been a dreadful way to treat him. Yes, I'm glad; for really you did owe him that, you know. But, Edward, suppose it should come out yet, some day!'

'It won't.'

'Why?'

'Because everybody thinks it was Goodson.'

'Of course they would!'

'Certainly. And of course *he* didn't care. They persuaded poor old Sawlsberry to go and charge it on him, and he went blustering over there and did it. Goodson looked him over, like as if he was hunting for a place on him that he could despise the most, then he says, "So you are the Committee of Inquiry, are you?" Sawlsberry said that was about what he was. "Hm. Do they require particulars, or do you reckon a kind of a *general* answer will do?" "If they require particulars, I will come back, Mr Goodson; I will take the general answer first." "Very well, then, tell them to go to hell – I reckon that's general enough. And I'll give you some advice, Sawlsberry; when you come back for the particulars, fetch a basket to carry the relics of yourself home in." '

'Just like Goodson; it's got all the marks. He had only one vanity: he thought he could give advice better than any other person.'

'It settled the business, and saved us, Mary. The subject was dropped.'

'Bless you, I'm not doubting *that*.'

Then they took up the gold-sack mystery again, with strong interest. Soon the conversation began to suffer breaks – interruptions caused by absorbed thinkings. The breaks grew more and more frequent. At last Richards lost himself wholly in thought. He sat long, gazing vacantly at the floor, and by and by he began to punctuate his thoughts with little nervous movements of his hands that seemed to indicate vexation. Meantime his wife too had relapsed into a thoughtful silence, and her movements were beginning to show a troubled discomfort. Finally Richards got up and strode aimlessly about the room, plowing his hands through his hair, much as a somnambulist might do who was having a bad dream. Then he seemed to arrive at a definite purpose; and without a word he put on his hat and passed quickly out of the house. His wife sat brooding, with a drawn face, and did not seem to be aware that she was alone. Now and then she murmured, 'Lead us not into t— . . . but – but – we are so poor, so poor! . . . Lead us not into . . . Ah, who would be hurt by it? – and no one would ever know. . . . Lead us . . .' The voice died out in mumblings. After a little she glanced up and muttered in a half-frightened, half-glad way:

'He is gone! But, oh dear, he may be too late – too late. . . . Maybe not – maybe there is still time.' She rose and stood thinking, nervously clasping and unclasping her hands. A slight shudder shook her frame, and she said, out of a dry throat, 'God forgive me – it's awful to think such things – but . . . Lord, how we are made – how strangely we are made!'

She turned the light low, and slipped stealthily over and kneeled down by the sack and felt of its ridgy sides with her hands, and fondled them lovingly; and there was a gloating light in her poor old eyes. She fell into fits of absence; and came half out of them at times to mutter, 'If we had only waited! – oh, if we had only waited a little, and not been in such a hurry!'

Meantime Cox had gone home from his office and told his wife all about the strange thing that had happened, and they had talked it over eagerly, and guessed that the late Goodson was the only man in the town who could have helped a suffering stranger with so noble a sum as twenty dollars. Then there was a pause, and the two became thoughtful and silent. And by and by nervous and fidgety. At last the wife said, as if to herself:

'Nobody knows this secret but the Richardses . . . and us . . . nobody.'

The husband came out of his thinkings with a slight start, and gazed wistfully at his wife, whose face was become very pale; then he hesitatingly rose, and glanced furtively at his hat, then at his wife – a sort of mute inquiry. Mrs Cox swallowed once or twice, with her hand at her throat, then in place of speech she nodded her head. In a moment she was alone, and mumbling to herself.

And now Richards and Cox were hurrying through the deserted streets, from opposite directions. They met, panting, at the foot of the printing-office stairs; by the night light there they read each other's face. Cox whispered:

'Nobody knows about this but us?'

The whispered answer was,

'Not a soul – on honor, not a soul!'

'If it isn't too late to – '

The men were starting upstairs; at this moment they were overtaken by a boy, and Cox asked:

'Is that you, Johnny?'

'Yes, sir.'

'You needn't ship the early mail – nor *any* mail; wait till I tell you.'

'It's already gone, sir.'

'*Gone?*' It had the sound of an unspeakable disappointment in it.

'Yes, sir. Timetable for Brixton and all the towns beyond changed today, sir – had to get the papers in twenty minutes earlier than common. I had to rush; if I had been two minutes later – '

The men turned and walked slowly away, not waiting to hear the rest. Neither of them spoke during ten minutes; then Cox said, in a vexed tone:

'What possessed you to be in such a hurry, *I* can't make out.'

The answer was humble enough:

'I see it now, but somehow I never thought, you know, until it was too late. But the next time—'

'Next time be hanged! It won't come in a thousand years.'

Then the friends separated without a good night, and dragged themselves home with the gait of mortally stricken men. At their homes their wives sprang up with an eager 'Well?' – then saw the answer with their eyes and sank down sorrowing, without waiting for it to come in words. In both houses a discussion followed of a heated sort – a new thing; there had been discussions before, but not heated ones, not ungentle ones. The discussions tonight were a sort of seeming plagiarisms of each other's. Mrs Richards said,

'If you had only waited, Edward – if you had only stopped to think; but no, you must run straight to the printing-office and spread it all over the world.'

'It *said* publish it.'

'That is nothing; it also said do it privately, if you liked. There, now – is that true, or not?'

'Why, yes – yes, it is true; but when I thought what a stir it would make, and what a compliment it was to Hadleyburg that a stranger should trust it so—'

'Oh, certainly, I know all that; but if you had only stopped to think, you would have seen that you *couldn't* find the right man, because he is in his grave, and hasn't left chick nor child nor relation behind him; and as long as the money went to somebody that awfully needed it, and nobody would be hurt by it, and – and—'

She broke down, crying. Her husband tried to think of some comforting thing to say, and presently came out with this:

'But after all, Mary, it must be for the best – it *must* be; we know that. And we must remember that it was so ordered—'

'Ordered! Oh, everything's *ordered*, when a person has to find some way out when he has been stupid. Just the same, it was *ordered* that the money should come to us in this special way, and it was you that must take it on yourself to go meddling with the designs of Providence – and who gave you the right? It was wicked, that is what it was – just blasphemous presumption, and no more becoming to a meek and humble professor of—'

'But, Mary, you know how we have been trained all our lives long, like the whole village, till it is absolutely second nature to us to stop not a single moment to think when there's an honest thing to be done—'

'Oh, I know it, I know it – it's been one everlasting training and training and training in honesty – honesty shielded, from the very cradle, against every possible temptation, and so it's *artificial* honesty, and weak as water when temptation comes, as we have seen this night. God knows I never had shade nor shadow of a doubt of my petrified and indestructible honesty until now – and now, under the very first big and real temptation, I – Edward, it is my belief that this town's honesty is as rotten as mine is; as rotten as yours is. It is a mean town, a hard, stingy town, and hasn't a virtue in the world but this honesty it is so celebrated for and so conceited about; and so help me, I do believe that if ever the day comes that its honesty falls under great temptation, its grand reputation will go to ruin like a house of cards. There, now, I've made confession, and I feel better; I am a humbug, and I've been one all my life, without knowing it. Let no man call me honest again – I will not have it.'

'I – well, Mary, I feel a good deal as you do; I certainly do. It seems strange, too, so strange. I never could have believed it – never.'

A long silence followed; both were sunk in thought. At last the wife looked up and said:

'I know what you are thinking, Edward.'

Richards had the embarrassed look of a person who is caught.

'I am ashamed to confess it, Mary, but—'

'It's no matter, Edward, I was thinking the same question myself.'

'I hope so. State it.'

'You were thinking, if a body could only guess out *what the remark was* that Goodson made to the stranger.'

'It's perfectly true. I feel guilty and ashamed. And you?'

'I'm past it. Let us make a pallet here; we've got to stand watch till the bank vault opens in the morning and admits the sack. . . . Oh dear, oh dear – if we hadn't made the mistake!'

The pallet was made, and Mary said:

'The open sesame – what could it have been? I do wonder what that remark could have been? But come; we will get to bed now.'

'And sleep?'

'No: think.'

'Yes, think.'

By this time the Coxes too had completed their spat and their reconciliation, and were turning in – to think, to think, and toss, and fret, and worry over what the remark could possibly have been which Goodson made to the stranded derelict; that golden remark; that remark worth forty thousand dollars, cash.

The reason that the village telegraph-office was open later than usual that night was this: The foreman of Cox's paper was the local representative of the Associated Press. One might say its honorary representative, for it wasn't four times a year that he could furnish thirty words that would be accepted. But this time it was different. His despatch stating what he had caught got an instant answer:

Send the whole thing – all the details – twelve hundred words.

A colossal order! The foreman filled the bill; and he was the proudest man in the State. By breakfast-time the next morning the name of Hadleyburg the Incorruptible was on every lip in America, from Montreal to the Gulf, from the glaciers of Alaska to the orange-groves of Florida; and millions and millions of people were discussing the stranger and his money-sack, and wondering if the right man would be found, and hoping some more news about the matter would come soon – right away.

Hadleyburg village woke up world-celebrated – astonished – happy – vain. Vain beyond imagination. Its nineteen principal citizens and their wives went about shaking hands with each other, and beaming, and smiling, and congratulating, and saying *this* thing adds a new word to the dictionary – *Hadleyburg*, synonym for *incorruptible* – destined to live in dictionaries forever! And the minor and unimportant citizens and their wives went around acting in much the same way. Everybody ran to the bank to see the gold-sack; and before noon grieved and envious crowds began to flock in from Brixton and all neighboring towns; and that afternoon and next day reporters began to arrive from everywhere to verify the sack and its history and write the whole thing up anew, and make dashing freehand pictures of the sack, and of Richards's house, and the bank, and the Presbyterian church, and the Baptist church, and the public square, and the town-hall where the test would be applied and the money delivered; and damnable portraits of the Richardses, and Pinkerton the banker, and Cox, and the foreman, and Reverend Burgess, and the postmaster – and even of Jack Halliday, who was the loafing, good-natured, no-account, irreverent fisherman, hunter, boys' friend, stray-dogs' friend, typical 'Sam Lawson' of the town. The little, mean, smirking, oily Pinkerton showed the sack to all comers, and rubbed his sleek palms together pleasantly, and enlarged upon the town's fine old reputation for honesty and upon this wonderful indorsement of it, and hoped and believed that the example would now spread far and wide over the American world, and be epoch-making in the matter of moral regeneration. And so on, and so on.

By the end of a week things had quieted down again; the wild intoxication of pride and joy had sobered to a soft, sweet, silent delight – a sort of deep, nameless, unutterable content. All faces bore a look of peaceful, holy happiness.

Then a change came. It was a gradual change: so gradual that its beginnings were hardly noticed; maybe were not noticed at all, except Jack Halliday, who always noticed everything; and always made fun of it, too, no matter what it was. He began to throw out chaffing remarks about people not looking quite so happy as they did a day or two ago; and next he claimed that the new aspect was deepening to positive sadness; next, that it was taking on a sick look; and finally he said that everybody was become so moody, thoughtful, and absent-minded that he could rob the meanest man in town of a cent out of the bottom of his breeches pocket and not disturb his revery.

At this stage – or at about this stage – a saying like this was dropped at bedtime – with a sigh, usually – by the head of each of the nineteen principal households: 'Ah, what *could* have been the remark that Goodson made?'

And straightway – with a shudder – came this, from the man's wife:

'Oh, *don't!* What horrible thing are you mulling in your mind? Put it away from you, for God's sake!'

But that question was wrung from those men again the next night – and got the same retort. But weaker.

And the third night the men uttered the question yet again – with anguish, and absently. This time – and the following night – the wives fidgeted feebly, and tried to say something. But didn't.

And the night after that they found their tongues and responded – longingly:

'Oh, if we *could* only guess!'

Halliday's comments grew daily more and more sparklingly disagreeable and disparaging. He went diligently about, laughing at the town, individually and in mass. But his laugh was the only one left in the village: it fell upon a hollow and mournful vacancy and emptiness. Not even a smile was findable anywhere. Halliday carried a cigar-box around on a tripod, playing that it was a camera, and halted all passers and aimed the thing and said, 'Ready! – now look pleasant, please,' but not even this capital joke could surprise the dreary faces into any softening.

So three weeks passed – one week was left. It was Saturday evening – after supper. Instead of the aforetime Saturday-evening flutter and bustle and shopping and larking, the streets were empty and desolate. Richards and his old wife sat apart in their little parlor – miserable and thinking. This was become their evening habit now: the lifelong habit which had preceded it, of reading, knitting, and contented chat, or receiving or paying neighborly calls, was dead and gone and forgotten, ages ago – two or three weeks ago; nobody talked now, nobody read, nobody visited – the whole village sat at home, sighing, worrying, silent. Trying to guess out that remark.

The postman left a letter. Richards glanced listlessly at the superscription and the postmark – unfamiliar, both – and tossed the letter on the table and resumed his might-have-beens and his hopeless dull miseries where he had left them off. Two or three hours later his wife got wearily up and was going away to bed without a good night – custom now – but she stopped near the letter and eyed it awhile with a dead interest, then broke it open, and began to skim it over. Richards, sitting there with his chair tilted back against the wall and his chin between his knees, heard something fall. It was his wife. He sprang to her side, but she cried out:

'Leave me alone, I am too happy. Read the letter – read it!'

He did. He devoured it, his brain reeling. The letter was from a distant state, and it said:

I am a stranger to you, but no matter: I have something to tell. I have just arrived home from Mexico, and learned about that episode. Of course you do not know who made that remark, but I know, and I am the only person living who does know. It was GOODSON. I knew him well, many years ago. I passed through your village that very night, and was his guest till the midnight train came along. I overheard him make that remark to the stranger in the dark – it was in Hale Alley. He and I talked of it the rest of the way home, and while smoking in his house. He mentioned many of your villagers in the course of his talk – most of them in a very uncomplimentary way, but two or three favorably; among these latter yourself. I say 'favorably' – nothing stronger. I remember his saying he did not actually LIKE any person in the town – not one; but that you – I THINK he said you – am almost sure – had done him a very great service once, possibly without knowing the full value of it, and he wished he had a fortune, he would leave it to you when he died, and a curse apiece for the rest of the citizens. Now, then, if it was you that did him that service, you are his legitimate heir, and entitled to the sack of gold. I know that I can trust to your honor and honesty, for in a citizen of Hadleyburg these virtues are an unfailing inheritance, and so I am going to reveal to you the remark, well satisfied that if you are not the right man you will seek and find the right one and see that poor Goodson's debt of gratitude for the service referred to is paid. This is the remark: 'YOU ARE FAR FROM BEING A BAD MAN: GO, AND REFORM.'

Howard L. Stephenson.

'Oh, Edward, the money is ours, and I am so grateful, *oh*, so grateful – kiss me, dear, it's forever since we kissed – and we needed it so – the money – and now you are free of Pinkerton and his bank, and nobody's slave any more; it seems to me I could fly for joy.'

It was a happy half-hour that the couple spent there on the settee caressing each other; it was the old days come again – days that had begun with their courtship and lasted without a break till the stranger brought the deadly money. By and by the wife said:

'Oh, Edward, how lucky it was you did him that grand service, poor Goodson! I never liked him, but I love him now. And it was fine and beautiful of you never to mention it or brag about it.' Then, with a touch of reproach, 'But you ought to have told *me*, Edward, you ought to have told your wife, you know.'

'Well, I – er – well, Mary, you see—'

'Now stop hemming and hawing, and tell me about it, Edward. I always loved you, and now I'm proud of you. Everybody believes there was only one good generous soul in this village, and now it turns out that you – Edward, why don't you tell me?'

'Well – er – er – Why, Mary, I can't!'

'You *can't*? *Why* can't you?'

'You see, he – well, he – he made me promise I wouldn't.'

The wife looked him over, and said, very slowly:

'Made – you – promise? Edward, what do you tell me that for?'

'Mary, do you think I would lie?'

She was troubled and silent for a moment, then she laid her hand within his and said:

'No . . . no. We have wandered far enough from our bearings – God spare us that! In all your life you have never uttered a lie. But now – now that the foundations of things seem to be crumbling from under us, we – we—' She lost her voice for a moment, then said, brokenly, 'Lead us not into temptation. . . . I think you made the promise, Edward. Let it rest so. Let us keep away from that ground. Now – that is all gone by; let us be happy again; it is no time for clouds.'

Edward found it something of an effort to comply, for his mind kept wandering – trying to remember what the service was that he had done Goodson.

The couple lay awake the most of the night, Mary happy and busy, Edward busy but not so happy. Mary was planning what she would do with the money. Edward was trying to recall that service. At first his conscience was sore on account of the lie he had told Mary – if it was a lie. After much reflection – suppose it *was* a lie? What then? Was it such a great matter? Aren't we always *acting* lies? Then why not *tell* them? Look at Mary – look what she had done. While he was hurrying off on his honest errand, what was she doing? Lamenting because the papers hadn't been destroyed and the money kept! Is theft better than lying?

That point lost its sting – the lie dropped into the background and left comfort behind it. The next point came to the front: *Had* he rendered that service? Well, here was Goodson's own evidence as reported in Stephenson's letter; there could be no better evidence than that – it was even *proof* that he had rendered it. Of course. So that point was settled. . . . No, not quite. He recalled with a wince that this unknown Mr Stephenson was just a trifle unsure as to whether the performer of it was Richards or some other – and, oh dear, he had put Richards on his honor! He must himself decide whither that money must go – and Mr Stephenson was not doubting that if he was the wrong man he would go honorably and find the right one. Oh, it was odious to put a man in such a situation – ah, why couldn't Stephenson have left out that doubt! What did he want to intrude that for?

Further reflection. How did it happen that *Richards*'s name remained in Stephenson's mind as indicating the right man, and not some other man's name? That looked good. Yes, that looked very good. In fact, it went on looking better and better, straight along – until by and by it grew into positive *proof*. And then Richards put the matter at once out of his mind, for he had a private instinct that a proof once established is better left so.

He was feeling reasonably comfortable now, but there was still one other detail that kept pushing itself on his notice: of course he had done that service – that was settled; but what *was* that service? He must recall it – he would not go to sleep till he had recalled it; it would make his peace of mind perfect. And so he thought and thought. He thought of a dozen things – possible services, even probable services – but none of them seemed adequate, none of them seemed large enough, none of them seemed worth the money – worth the fortune Goodson had wished he could leave in his will. And besides, he couldn't remember having done them, anyway. Now, then – now, then – what *kind* of a service would it be that would make a man so inordinately grateful? Ah – the saving of his soul! That must be it. Yes, he could remember, now, how he once set himself the task of converting Goodson, and labored at it as much as – he was going to say three months; but upon closer examination it shrank to a month, then to a week, then to a day, then to nothing. Yes, he remembered now, and with unwelcome vividness, that Goodson had told him to go to thunder and mind his own business – *he* wasn't hankering to follow Hadleyburg to heaven!

So that solution was a failure – he hadn't saved Goodson's soul. Richards was discouraged. Then after a little came another idea: had he saved Goodson's property? No, that wouldn't do – he hadn't any. His life? That is it! Of course. Why, he might have thought of it before. This time he was on the right track, sure. His imagination-mill was hard at work in a minute, now.

Thereafter during a stretch of two exhausting hours he was busy saving Goodson's life. He saved it in all kinds of difficult and perilous ways. In every case he got it saved satisfactorily up to a certain point; then, just as he was beginning to get well persuaded that it had really happened, a troublesome detail would turn up which made the whole thing impossible. As in the matter of drowning, for instance. In that case he had swum out and tugged Goodson ashore in an unconscious state with a great crowd looking on and applauding, but when he had got it all thought out and was just beginning to remember all about it, a whole swarm of disqualifying details arrived on the ground: the town would have known of the circumstance, Mary would have known of it, it would glare like a limelight in his own memory instead of being an inconspicuous service which he had possibly rendered 'without knowing its full value'. And at this point he remembered that he couldn't swim, anyway.

Ah – *there* was a point which he had been overlooking from the start: it had to be a service which he had rendered 'possibly without knowing the full value of it'. Why, really, that ought to be an easy hunt – much easier than those others. And sure enough, by and by he found it. Goodson, years and years ago, came near marrying a very sweet and pretty girl, named Nancy Hewitt, but in some way or other the match had been broken off; the girl died, Goodson remained a bachelor, and by and by became a soured one and frank despiser of the human species. Soon after the girl's death the village found out, or thought it had found out, that she carried a spoonful of negro blood in her veins. Richards worked at these details a good while, and in the end he thought he remembered things concerning them which must have gotten mislaid in his memory through long neglect. He seemed to dimly remember that it was *he* that found out about the negro blood; that it was he that told the village; that the village told Goodson where they got it; that he thus saved Goodson from marrying the tainted girl; that he had done him this great service 'without knowing the full value of it', in fact without knowing that he *was* doing it; but that Goodson knew the value of it, and what a narrow escape he had had, and so went to his grave grateful to his benefactor and wishing he had a fortune to leave him. It was all clear and simple now, and the more he went over it the more luminous and certain it grew; and at last, when he nestled to sleep satisfied and happy, he remembered the whole thing just as if it had been yesterday. In fact, he dimly remembered Goodson's *telling* him his gratitude once. Meantime Mary had spent six thousand dollars on a new house for herself and a pair of slippers for her pastor, and then had fallen peacefully to rest.

That same Saturday evening the postman had delivered a letter to each of the other principal citizens – nineteen letters in all. No two of the envelopes were alike, and no two of the superscriptions were in the same hand, but the letters inside were just like each other in every detail but one. They were exact copies of the letter received by Richards – handwriting and all – and were all signed by Stephenson, but in place of Richards's name each receiver's own name appeared.

All night long eighteen principal citizens did what their caste-brother Richards was doing at the same time – they put in their energies trying to remember what notable service it was that they had unconsciously done Barclay Goodson. In no case was it a holiday job; still they succeeded.

And while they were at this work, which was difficult,

their wives put in the night spending the money, which was easy. During that one night the nineteen wives spent an average of seven thousand dollars each out of the forty thousand in the sack – a hundred and thirty-three thousand altogether.

Next day there was a surprise for Jack Halliday. He noticed that the faces of the nineteen chief citizens and their wives bore that expression of peaceful and holy happiness again. He could not understand it, neither was he able to invent any remarks about it that could damage it or disturb it. And so it was his turn to be dissatisfied with life. His private guesses at the reasons for the happiness failed in all instances, upon examination. When he met Mrs Wilcox and noticed the placid ecstasy in her face, he said to himself, 'Her cat has had kittens' – and went and asked the cook: it was not so; the cook had detected the happiness, but did not know the cause. When Halliday found the duplicate ecstasy in the face of 'Shadbelly' Billson (village nickname), he was sure some neighbor of Billson's had broken his leg, but inquiry showed that this had not happened. The subdued ecstasy in Gregory Yates's face could mean but one thing – he was a mother-in-law short: it was another mistake. 'And Pinkerton – Pinkerton – he has collected ten cents that he thought he was going to lose.' And so on, and so on. In some cases the guesses had to remain in doubt, in the others they proved distinct errors. In the end Halliday said to himself, 'Anyway it foots up that there's nineteen Hadleyburg families temporarily in heaven: I don't know how it happened; I only know Providence is off duty today.'

An architect and builder from the next state had lately ventured to set up a small business in this unpromising village, and his sign had now been hanging out a week. Not a customer yet; he was a discouraged man, and sorry he had come. But his weather changed suddenly now. First one and then another chief citizen's wife said to him privately:

'Come to my house Monday week – but say nothing about it for the present. We think of building.'

He got eleven invitations that day. That night he wrote his daughter and broke off her match with her student. He said she could marry a mile higher than that.

Pinkerton the banker and two or three other well-to-do men planned country-seats – but waited. That kind don't count their chickens until they are hatched.

The Wilsons devised a grand new thing – a fancy-dress ball. They made no actual promises, but told all their acquaintanceship in confidence that they were thinking the matter over and thought they should give it – 'and if we do, you will be invited, of course'. People were surprised, and said, one to another, 'Why, they are crazy, those poor Wilsons, they can't afford it.' Several among the nineteen said privately to their husbands, 'It is a good idea: we will keep still till their cheap thing is over, then *we* will give one that will make it sick.'

The days drifted along, and the bill of future squanderings rose higher and higher, wilder and wilder, more and more foolish and reckless. It began to look as if every member of the nineteen would not only spend his whole forty thousand dollars before receiving-day, but be actually in debt by the time he got the money. In some cases light-headed people did not stop with planning to spend, they really spent – on credit. They bought land, mortgages, farms, speculative stocks, fine clothes, horses, and various other things, paid down the bonus, and made themselves liable for the rest – at ten days. Presently the sober second thought came, and Halliday noticed that a ghastly anxiety was beginning to show up in a good many faces. Again he was puzzled, and didn't know what to make of it. 'The Wilcox kittens aren't dead, for they weren't born; nobody's broken a leg; there's no shrinkage in mother-in-laws; *nothing* has happened – it is an unsolvable mystery.'

There was another puzzled man, too – the Revd Mr

Burgess. For days, wherever he went, people seemed to follow him or to be watching out for him; and if he ever found himself in a retired spot, a member of the nineteen would be sure to appear, thrust an envelope privately into his hand, whisper 'To be opened at the town-hall Friday evening,' then vanish away like a guilty thing. He was expecting that there might be one claimant for the sack – doubtful, however, Goodson being dead – but it never occurred to him that all this crowd might be claimants. When the great Friday came at last, he found that he had nineteen envelopes.

The town hall had never looked finer. The platform at the end of it was backed by a showy draping of flags; at intervals along the walls were festoons of flags; the gallery fronts were clothed in flags; the supporting columns were swathed in flags; all this was to impress the stranger, for he would be there in considerable force, and in a large degree he would be connected with the press. The house was full. The 412 fixed seats were occupied; also the 68 extra chairs which had been packed into the aisles; the steps of the platform were occupied; some distinguished strangers were given seats on the platform; at the horse-shoe of tables which fenced the front and sides of the platform sat a strong force of special correspondents who had come from everywhere. It was the best-dressed house the town had ever produced. There were some tolerably expensive toilets there, and in several cases the ladies who wore them had the look of being unfamiliar with that kind of clothes. At least the town thought they had that look, but the notion could have arisen from the town's knowledge of the fact that these ladies had never inhabited such clothes before.

The gold-sack stood on a little table at the front of the platform where all the house could see it. The bulk of the house gazed at it with a burning interest, a mouth-watering interest, a wistful and pathetic interest; a minority of nineteen couples gazed at it tenderly, lovingly, proprietarily, and the male half of this minority kept saying over to themselves the moving little impromptu speeches of thankfulness for the audience's applause and congratulations which they were presently going to get up and deliver. Every now and then one of these got a piece of paper out of his vest pocket and privately glanced at it to refresh his memory.

Of course there was a buzz of conversation going on – there always is; but at last when the Revd Mr Burgess rose and laid his hand on the sack he could hear his microbes gnaw, the place was so still. He related the curious history of the sack, then went on to speak in warm terms of Hadleyburg's old and well-earned reputation for spotless honesty, and of the town's just pride in this reputation. He said that this reputation was a treasure of priceless value; that under Providence its value had now become inestimably enhanced, for the recent episode had spread this fame far and wide, and thus had focused the eyes of the American world upon this village, and made its name for all time, as he hoped and believed, a synonym for commercial incorruptibility. [*Applause.*] 'And who is to be the guardian of this noble treasure – the community as a whole? No! The responsibility is individual, not communal. From this day forth each and every one of you is in his own person its special guardian, and individually responsible that no harm shall come to it. Do you – does each of you – accept this great trust? [*Tumultuous assent.*] Then all is well. Transmit it to your children and to your children's children. Today your purity is beyond reproach – see to it that it shall remain so. Today there is not a person in your community who could be beguiled to touch a penny not his own – see to it that you abide in this grace. ['*We will! We will!*'] This is not the place to make comparisons between ourselves and other communities – some of them ungracious toward us; they have their ways, we have ours; let us be content. [*Applause.*] I am done.

Under my hand, my friends, rests a stranger's eloquent recognition of what we are; through him the world will always henceforth know what we are. We do not know who he is, but in your name I utter your gratitude, and ask you to raise your voices in indorsement.'

The house rose in a body and made the walls quake with the thunders of its thankfulness for the space of a long minute. Then it sat down, and Mr Burgess took an envelope out of his pocket. The house held its breath while he slit the envelope open and took from it a slip of paper. He read its contents – slowly and impressively – the audience listening with tranced attention to this magic document, each of whose words stood for an ingot of gold:

' "*The remark which I made to the distressed stranger was this: 'You are very far from being a bad man: go, and reform.'* " ' Then he continued:

'We shall know in a moment now whether the remark here quoted corresponds with the one concealed in the sack; and if that shall prove to be so – and it undoubtedly will – this sack of gold belongs to a fellow-citizen who will henceforth stand before the nation as the symbol of the special virtue which has made our town famous throughout the land – Mr Billson!'

The house had gotten itself all ready to burst into the proper tornado of applause; but instead of doing it, it seemed stricken with a paralysis; there was a deep hush for a moment or two, then a wave of whispered murmurs swept the place – of about this tenor: '*Billson!* oh, come, this is *too* thin! Twenty dollars to a stranger – or *anybody* – *Billson!* tell it to the marines!' And now at this point the house caught its breath all of a sudden in a new access of astonishment, for it discovered that whereas in one part of the hall Deacon Billson was standing up with his head meekly bowed, in another part of it Lawyer Wilson was doing the same. There was a wondering silence now for a while.

Everybody was puzzled, and nineteen couples were surprised and indignant.

Billson and Wilson turned and stared at each other. Billson asked, bitingly:

'Why do *you* rise, Mr Wilson?'

'Because I have a right to. Perhaps you will be good enough to explain to the house why *you* rise?'

'With great pleasure. Because I wrote that paper.'

'It is an impudent falsity! I wrote it myself.'

It was Burgess's turn to be paralysed. He stood looking vacantly at first one of the men and then the other, and did not seem to know what to do. The house was stupefied. Lawyer Wilson spoke up, now, and said,

'I ask the Chair to read the name signed to that paper.'

That brought the Chair to itself, and it read out the name:

' "John Wharton *Billson*".'

'There!' shouted Billson, 'what have you got to say for yourself, now? And what kind of apology are you going to make to me and to this insulted house for the imposture which you have attempted to play here?'

'No apologies are due, sir; and as for the rest of it, I publicly charge you with pilfering my note from Mr Burgess and substituting a copy of it signed with your own name. There is no other way by which you could have gotten hold of the test-remark; I alone, of living men, possessed the secret of its wording.'

There was likely to be a scandalous state of things if this went on; everybody noticed with distress that the short-hand scribes were scribbling like mad; many people were crying 'Chair, Chair! Order! Order!' Burgess rapped with his gavel, and said:

'Let us not forget the proprieties due. There has evidently been a mistake somewhere, but surely that is all. If Mr Wilson gave me an envelope – and I remember now that he did – I still have it.'

He took one out of his pocket, opened it, glanced at

it, looked surprised and worried, and stood silent a few moments. Then he waved his hand in a wandering and mechanical way, and made an effort or two to say something, then gave it up, despondently. Several voices cried out:

'Read it! read it! What is it?'

So he began in a dazed and sleep-walker fashion:

' "*The remark which I made to the unhappy stranger was this: 'You are far from being a bad man.* [The house gazed at him, marveling.] *Go, and reform.*' " [*Murmurs:* 'Amazing! What can this mean?'] This one,' said the Chair, 'is signed Thurlow G. Wilson.'

'There!' cried Wilson. 'I reckon that settles it! I knew perfectly well my note was purloined.'

'Purloined!' retorted Billson. 'I'll let you know that neither you nor any man of your kidney must venture to—'

The Chair. 'Order, gentlemen, order! Take your seats, both of you, please.'

They obeyed, shaking their heads and grumbling angrily. The house was profoundly puzzled; it did not know what to do with this curious emergency. Presently Thompson got up. Thompson was the hatter. He would have liked to be a Nineteener; but such was not for him: his stock of hats was not considerable enough for the position. He said:

'Mr Chairman, if I may be permitted to make a suggestion, can both of these gentlemen be right? I put it to you, sir, can both have happened to say the very same words to the stranger? It seems to me – '

The tanner got up and interrupted him. The tanner was a disgruntled man; he believed himself entitled to be a Nineteener, but he couldn't get recognition. It made him a little unpleasant in his ways and speech. Said he:

'Sho, *that's* not the point! *That* could happen – twice in a hundred years – but not the other thing. *Neither* of them gave the twenty dollars!'

[*A ripple of applause.*]

Billson. '*I* did!'

Wilson. '*I* did!'

Then each accused the other of pilfering.

The Chair. 'Order! Sit down, if you please – both of you. Neither of the notes has been out of my possession at any moment.'

A Voice. 'Good – that settles *that!*'

The Tanner. 'Mr Chairman, one thing is now plain: one of these men has been eavesdropping under the other one's bed, and filching family secrets. If it is not unparliamentary to suggest it, I will remark that both are equal to it. [*The Chair.* 'Order! Order!'] I withdraw the remark, sir, and will confine myself to suggesting that *if* one of them has overheard the other reveal the test-remark to his wife, we shall catch him now.'

A Voice. 'How?'

The Tanner. 'Easily. The two have not quoted the remark in exactly the same words. You would have noticed that, if there hadn't been a considerable stretch of time and an exciting quarrel inserted between the two readings.'

A Voice. 'Name the difference.'

The Tanner. 'The word *very* is in Billson's note, and not in the other.'

Many Voices. 'That's so – he's right!'

The Tanner. 'And so, if the Chair will examine the test-remark in the sack, we shall know which of these two frauds – [*The Chair.* 'Order!'] – which of these two adventurers – [*The Chair.* 'Order! Order!'] – which of these two gentlemen – [*laughter and applause*] – is entitled to wear the belt as being the first dishonest blatherskite ever bred in this town – which he has dishonored, and which will be a sultry place for him from now out!' [*Vigorous applause.*]

Many Voices. 'Open it! – open the sack!'

Mr Burgess made a slit in the sack, slid his hand in and

brought out an envelope. In it were a couple of folded notes. He said:

'One of these is marked, "Not to be examined until all written communications which have been addressed to the Chair – if any – shall have been read." The other is marked "*The Test.*" It is worded – to wit:

' "I do not require that the first half of the remark which was made to me by my benefactor shall be quoted with exactness, for it was not striking, and could be forgotten; but its closing fifteen words are quite striking, and I think easily rememberable; unless *these* shall be accurately reproduced, let the applicant be regarded as an impostor. My benefactor began by saying he seldom gave advice to any one, but that it always bore the hallmark of high value when he did give it. Then he said this – and it has never faded from my memory: '*You are far from being a bad man –*' " '

Fifty Voices. 'That settles it – the money's Wilson's! Wilson! Wilson! Speech! Speech!'

People jumped up and crowded around Wilson, wringing his hand and congratulating fervently – meantime the Chair was hammering with the gavel and shouting:

'Order, gentlemen! Order! Order! Let me finish reading, please.' When quiet was restored, the reading was resumed – as follows:

' " '*Go, and reform – or, mark my words – some day, for your sins, you will die and go to hell or Hadleyburg* – TRY AND MAKE IT THE FORMER.' " '

A ghastly silence followed. First an angry cloud began to settle darkly upon the faces of the citizenship; after a pause the cloud began to rise, and a tickled expression tried to take its place; tried so hard that it was only kept under with great and painful difficulty; the reporters, the Brixtonites, and other strangers bent their heads down and shielded their faces with their hands, and managed to hold in by main strength and heroic courtesy. At this most inopportune time burst upon the stillness the roar of a solitary voice – Jack Halliday's:

'*That's* got the hallmark on it!'

Then the house let go, strangers and all. Even Mr Burgess's gravity broke down presently, then the audience considered itself officially absolved from all restraint, and it made the most of its privilege. It was a good long laugh, and a tempestuously whole-hearted one, but it ceased at last – long enough for Mr Burgess to try to resume, and for the people to get their eyes partially wiped; then it broke out again; and afterward yet again; then at last Burgess was able to get out these serious words:

'It is useless to try to disguise the fact – we find ourselves in the presence of a matter of grave import. It involves the honor of your town, it strikes at the town's good name. The difference of a single word between the test-remarks offered by Mr Wilson and Mr Billson was itself a serious thing, since it indicated that one or the other of these gentlemen had committed a theft—'

The two men were sitting limp, nerveless, crushed; but at these words both were electrified into movement, and started to get up—

'Sit down!' said the Chair, sharply, and they obeyed. 'That, as I have said, was a serious thing. And it was – but for only one of them. But the matter has become graver; for the honor of *both* is now in formidable peril. Shall I go even further, and say in inextricable peril? *Both* left out the crucial fifteen words.' He paused. During several moments he allowed the pervading stillness to gather and deepen its impressive effects, then added: 'There would seem to be but one way whereby this could happen. I ask these gentlemen – Was there *collusion*? – *agreement*?'

A low murmur sifted through the house; its import was, 'He's got them both.'

Billson was not used to emergencies; he sat in a helpless

collapse. But Wilson was a lawyer. He struggled to his feet, pale and worried, and said:

'I ask the indulgence of the house while I explain this most painful matter. I am sorry to say what I am about to say, since it must inflict irreparable injury upon Mr Billson, whom I have always esteemed and respected until now, and in whose invulnerability to temptation I entirely believed – as did you all. But for the preservation of my own honor I must speak – and with frankness. I confess with shame – and I now beseech your pardon for it – that I said to the ruined stranger all of the words contained in the test-remark, including the disparaging fifteen. [*Sensation.*] When the late publication was made I recalled them, and I resolved to claim the sack of coin, for by every right I was entitled to it. Now I will ask you to consider this point, and weigh it well: that stranger's gratitude to me that night knew no bounds; he said himself that he could find no words for it that were adequate, and that if he should ever be able he would repay me a thousandfold. Now, then, I ask you this: Could I expect – could I believe – could I even remotely imagine – that, feeling as he did, he would do so ungrateful a thing as to add those quite unnecessary fifteen words to his test? – set a trap for me? – expose me as a slanderer of my own town before my own people assembled in a public hall? It was preposterous; it was impossible. His test would contain only the kindly opening clause of my remark. Of that I had no shadow of doubt. You would have thought as I did. You would not have expected a base betrayal from one whom you had befriended and against whom you had committed no offense. And so, with perfect confidence, perfect trust, I wrote on a piece of paper the opening words – ending with "Go, and reform," – and signed it. When I was about to put it in an envelope I was called into my back office, and without thinking I left the paper lying open on my desk.' He stopped, turned his head slowly toward Billson, waited a moment, then added: 'I ask you to note this: when I returned, a little later, Mr Billson was retiring by my street door.' [*Sensation.*]

In a moment Billson was on his feet and shouting:

'It's a lie! It's an infamous lie!'

The Chair. 'Be seated, sir! Mr Wilson has the floor.'

Billson's friends pulled him into his seat and quieted him, and Wilson went on:

'Those are the simple facts. My note was now lying in a different place on the table from where I had left it. I noticed that, but attached no importance to it, thinking a draught had blown it there. That Mr Billson would read a private paper was a thing which could not occur to me; he was an honorable man, and he would be above that. If you will allow me to say it, I think his extra word "*very*" stands explained; it is attributable to a defect of memory. I was the only man in the world who could furnish here any detail of the test-remark – by *honorable* means. I have finished.'

There is nothing in the world like a persuasive speech to fuddle the mental apparatus and upset the convictions and debauch the emotions of an audience not practised in the tricks and delusions of oratory. Wilson sat down victorious. The house submerged him in tides of approving applause; friends swarmed to him and shook him by the hand and congratulated him, and Billson was shouted down and not allowed to say a word. The Chair hammered and hammered with its gavel, and kept shouting:

'But let us proceed, gentlemen, let us proceed!'

At last there was a measurable degree of quiet, and the hatter said:

'But what is there to proceed with, sir, but to deliver the money?'

Voices. 'That's it! That's it! Come forward, Wilson!'

The Hatter. 'I move three cheers for Mr Wilson, Symbol of the special virtue which—'

The cheers burst forth before he could finish; and in

the midst of them – and in the midst of the clamor of the gavel also – some enthusiasts mounted Wilson on a big friend's shoulder and were going to fetch him in triumph to the platform. The Chair's voice now rose above the noise—

'Order! To your places! You forget that there is still a document to be read.' When quiet had been restored he took up the document, and was going to read it, but laid it down again, saying, 'I forgot; this is not to be read until all written communications received by me have first been read.' He took an envelope out of his pocket, removed its enclosure, glanced at it – seemed astonished – held it out and gazed at it – stared at it.

Twenty or thirty voices cried out:

'What is it? Read it! read it!'

And he did – slowly, and wondering:

' "The remark which I made to the stranger – [*Voices.* 'Hello! how's this?'] – was this: 'You are far from being a bad man. [*Voices.* 'Great Scott!'] Go, and reform.' " [*Voice.* 'Oh, saw my leg off!'] Signed by Mr Pinkerton, the banker.'

The pandemonium of delight which turned itself loose now was of a sort to make the judicious weep. Those whose withers were unwrung laughed till the tears ran down; the reporters, in throes of laughter, set down disordered pot-hooks which would never in the world be decipherable; and a sleeping dog jumped up, scared out of its wits, and barked itself crazy at the turmoil. All manner of cries were scattered through the din: 'We're getting rich – *two* Symbols of Incorruptibility! – without counting Billson!' '*Three*! – count Shadbelly in – we can't have too many!' 'All right – Billson's elected!' 'Alas, poor Wilson – victim of *two* thieves!'

A Powerful Voice. 'Silence! The Chair's fished up something more out of its pocket.'

Voices. 'Hurrah! Is it something fresh? Read it! Read! Read!'

The Chair [reading]. ' "The remark which I made," etc.: 'You are far from being a bad man. Go,' etc. Signed, "Gregory Yates".'

Tornado of Voices. 'Four Symbols!' 'Rah for Yates!' 'Fish again!'

The house was in a roaring humor now, and ready to get all the fun out of the occasion that might be in it. Several Nineteeners, looking pale and distressed, got up and began to work their way toward the aisles, but a score of shouts went up:

'The doors, the doors – close the doors; no Incorruptible shall leave this place! Sit down, everybody!'

The mandate was obeyed.

'Fish again! Read! Read!'

The Chair fished again, and once more the familiar words began to fall from its lips – ' "You are far from being a bad man".'

'Name! Name! What's his name?'

' "L. Ingoldsby Sargent".'

'Five elected! Pile up the Symbols! Go on, go on!'

' "You are far from being a bad—" '

'Name! Name!'

' "Nicholas Whitworth".'

'Hooray! Hooray! It's a symbolical day!'

Somebody wailed in, and began to sing this rhyme (leaving out 'it's') to the lovely 'Mikado' tune of 'When a man's afraid, a beautiful maid – '; the audience joined in, with joy; then, just in time, somebody contributed another line—

And don't this you forget –

The house roared it out. A third line was at once furnished—

Corruptibles far from Hadleyburg are –

The house roared that one too. As the last note died, Jack

Halliday's voice rose high and clear, freighted with a final line—

But the Symbols are here, you bet!

That was sung, with booming enthusiasm. Then the happy house started in at the beginning and sang the four lines through twice, with immense swing and dash, and finished up with a crashing three-times-three and a tiger for 'Hadleyburg the Incorruptible and all Symbols of it which we shall find worthy to receive the hallmark to-night.'

Then the shoutings at the Chair began again, all over the place:

'Go on! Go on! Read! Read some more! Read all you've got!'

'That's it – go on! We are winning eternal celebrity!'

A dozen men got up now and began to protest. They said that this farce was the work of some abandoned joker, and was an insult to the whole community. Without a doubt these signatures were all forgeries –

'Sit down! Sit down! Shut up! You are confessing. We'll find *your* names in the lot.'

'Mr Chairman, how many of those envelopes have you got?'

The Chair counted.

'Together with those that have been already examined, there are nineteen.'

A storm of derisive applause broke out.

'Perhaps they all contain the secret. I move that you open them all and read every signature that is attached to a note of that sort – and read also the first eight words of the note.'

'Second the motion!'

It was put and carried – uproariously. Then poor old Richards got up, and his wife rose and stood at his side. Her head was bent down, so that none might see that she was crying. Her husband gave her his arm, and so supporting her, he began to speak in a quavering voice:

'My friends, you have known us two – Mary and me – all our lives, and I think you have liked us and respected us – '

The Chair interrupted him:

'Allow me. It is quite true – that which you are saying, Mr Richards: this town *does* know you two; it *does* like you; it *does* respect you; more – it honors you and *loves* you – '

Halliday's voice rang out:

'That's the hallmarked truth, too! If the Chair is right, let the house speak up and say it. Rise! Now, then – hip! hip! hip! – all together!'

The house rose in mass, faced toward the old couple eagerly, filled the air with a snowstorm of waving handkerchiefs, and delivered the cheers with all its affectionate heart.

The Chair then continued:

'What I was going to say is this: We know your good heart, Mr Richards, but this is not a time for the exercise of charity toward offenders. [*Shouts of* 'Right! Right!'] I see your generous purpose in your face, but I cannot allow you to plead for these men—'

'But I was going to—'

'Please take your seat, Mr Richards. We must examine the rest of these notes – simple fairness to the men who have already been exposed requires this. As soon as that has been done – I give you my word for this – you shall be heard.'

Many Voices. 'Right! – the Chair is right – no interruption can be permitted at this stage! Go on! – the names! the names! – according to the terms of the motion!'

The old couple sat reluctantly down, and the husband whispered to the wife, 'It is pitifully hard to have to wait; the shame will be greater than ever when they find we were only going to plead for *ourselves*.'

Straightway the jollity broke loose again with the reading of the names.

' "You are far from being a bad man – " Signature, "Robert J. Titmarsh."

' "You are far from being a bad man – " Signature, "Eliphalet Weeks."

' "You are far from being a bad man – " Signature, "Oscar B. Wilder".'

At this point the house lit upon the idea of taking the eight words out of the Chairman's hands. He was not unthankful for that. Thenceforward he held up each note in its turn, and waited. The house droned out the eight words in a massed and measured and musical deep volume of sound (with a daringly close resemblance to a well-known church chant) – ' "You are f-a-r from being a b-a-a-a-d man".' Then the Chair said, 'Signature, "Archibald Wilcox".' And so on, and so on, name after name, and everybody had an increasingly and gloriously good time except the wretched Nineteen. Now and then, when a particularly shining name was called, the house made the Chair wait while it chanted the whole of the test-remark from the beginning to the closing words, 'And go to hell or Hadleyburg – try and make it the for-or-m-e-r!' and in these special cases they added a grand and agonised and imposing 'A-a-a-a-*men*!'

The list dwindled, dwindled, dwindled, poor old Richards keeping tally of the count, wincing when a name resembling his own was pronounced, and waiting in miserable suspense for the time to come when it would be his humiliating privilege to rise with Mary and finish his plea, which he was intending to word thus: '. . . for until now we have never done any wrong thing, but have gone our humble way unreproached. We are very poor, we are old, and have no chick nor child to help us; we were sorely tempted, and we fell. It was my purpose when I got up before to make confession and beg that my name might not be read out in this public place, for it seemed to us that we could not bear it; but I was prevented. It was just; it was our place to suffer with the rest. It has been hard for us. It is the first time we have ever heard our name fall from anyone's lips – sullied. Be merciful – for the sake of the better days; make our shame as light to bear as in your charity you can.' At this point in his revery Mary nudged him, perceiving that his mind was absent. The house was chanting, 'You are f-a-r,' etc.

'Be ready,' Mary whispered. 'Your name comes now; he has read eighteen.'

The chant ended.

'Next! next! next!' came volleying from all over the house.

Burgess put his hand into his pocket. The old couple, trembling, began to rise. Burgess fumbled a moment, then said,

'I find I have read them all.'

Faint with joy and surprise, the couple sank into their seats, and Mary whispered:

'Oh, bless God, we are saved! – He has lost ours – I wouldn't give this for a hundred of those sacks!'

The house burst out with its 'Mikado' travesty, and sang it three times with ever-increasing enthusiasm, rising to its feet when it reached for the third time the closing line—

But the Symbols are here, you bet!

and finishing up with cheers and a tiger for 'Hadleyburg purity and our eighteen immortal representatives of it.'

Then Wingate, the saddler, got up and proposed cheers 'for the cleanest man in town, the one solitary important citizen in it who didn't try to steal that money – Edward Richards.'

They were given with great and moving heartiness; then somebody proposed that Richards be elected sole guardian and Symbol of the now Sacred Hadleyburg Tradition, with power and right to stand up and look the whole sarcastic world in the face.

Passed, by acclamation: then they sang the 'Mikado' again, and ended it with:

And there's *one* Symbol left, you bet!

There was a pause; then –

A Voice. 'Now, then, who's to get the sack?'

The Tanner (with bitter sarcasm). 'That's easy. The money has to be divided among the eighteen Incorruptibles. They gave the suffering stranger twenty dollars apiece – and that remark – each in his turn – it took twenty-two minutes for the procession to move past. Staked the stranger – total contribution, $360. All they want is just the loan back – and interest – forty thousand dollars altogether.'

Many Voices [derisively]. 'That's it! Divvy! Divvy! Be kind to the poor – don't keep them waiting!'

The Chair. 'Order! I now offer the stranger's remaining document. It says: "If no claimant shall appear [*grand chorus of groans*] I desire that you open the sack and count out the money to the principal citizens of your town, they to take it in trust [*cries of 'Oh! Oh! Oh!'*], and use it in such ways as to them shall seem best for the propagation and preservation of your community's noble reputation for incorruptible honesty [*more cries*] – a reputation to which their names and their efforts will add a new and far-reaching luster." [*Enthusiastic outburst of sarcastic applause.*] That seems to be all. No – here is a postscript:

' "P.S. – CITIZENS OF HADLEYBURG: There *is* no test-remark – nobody made one. [*Great sensation.*] There wasn't any pauper stranger, nor any twenty-dollar contribution, nor any accompanying benediction and compliment – these are all inventions. [*General buzz and hum of astonishment and delight.*] Allow me to tell my story – it will take but a word or two. I passed through your town at a certain time, and received a deep offense which I had not earned. Any other man would have been content to kill one or two of you and call it square, but to me that would have been a trivial revenge, and inadequate; for the dead do not *suffer*. Besides, I could not kill you all – and, anyway, made as I am, even that would not have satisfied me. I wanted to damage every man in the place, and every woman – and not in their bodies or in their estate, but in their vanity – the place where feeble and foolish people are most vulnerable. So I disguised myself and came back and studied you. You were easy game. You had an old and lofty reputation for honesty, and naturally you were proud of it – it was your treasure of treasures, the very apple of your eye. As soon as I found out that you carefully and vigilantly kept yourselves and your children *out of temptation*, I knew how to proceed. Why, you simple creatures, the weakest of all weak things is a virtue which has not been tested in the fire. I laid a plan, and gathered a list of names. My project was to corrupt Hadleyburg the Incorruptible. My idea was to make liars and thieves of nearly half a hundred smirchless men and women who had never in their lives uttered a lie or stolen a penny. I was afraid of Goodson. He was neither born nor reared in Hadleyburg. I was afraid that if I started to operate my scheme by getting my letter laid before you, you would say to yourselves, 'Goodson is the only man among us who would give away twenty dollars to a poor devil' – and then you might not bite at my bait. But Heaven took Goodson; then I knew I was safe, and I set my trap and baited it. It may be that I shall not catch all the men to whom I mailed the pretended test secret, but I shall catch the most of them, if I know Hadleyburg nature. [*Voices*. 'Right – he got every last one of them.'] I believe they will even steal ostensible *gamble*-money, rather than miss, poor, tempted, and mistrained fellows. I am hoping to eternally and everlastingly squelch your vanity and give Hadleyburg a new renown – one that will *stick* – and spread far. If I have succeeded, open the sack and summon the Committee on Propagation and Preservation of the Hadleyburg Reputation." '

A Cyclone of Voices. 'Open it! Open it! The Eighteen to the front! Committee on Propagation of the Tradition! Forward – the Incorruptibles!'

The Chair ripped the sack wide, and gathered up a handful of bright, broad, yellow coins, shook them together, then examined them –

'Friends, they are only gilded disks of lead!'

There was a crashing outbreak of delight over this news, and when the noise had subsided, the tanner called out:

'By right of apparent seniority in this business, Mr Wilson is Chairman of the Committee on Propagation of the Tradition. I suggest that he step forward on behalf of his pals, and receive in trust the money.'

A Hundred Voices. 'Wilson! Wilson! Wilson! Speech! Speech!'

Wilson [in a voice trembling with anger]. 'You will allow me to say, and without apologies for my language, *damn* the money!'

A Voice. 'Oh, and him a Baptist!'

A Voice. 'Seventeen Symbols left! Step up, gentlemen, and assume your trust!'

There was a pause – no response.

The Saddler. 'Mr Chairman, we've got *one* clean man left, anyway, out of the late aristocracy; and he needs money, and deserves it. I move that you appoint Jack Halliday to get up there and auction off that sack of gilt twenty-dollar pieces, and give the result to the right man – the man whom Hadleyburg delights to honor – Edward Richards.'

This was received with great enthusiasm, the dog taking a hand again; the saddler started the bids at a dollar, the Brixton folk and Barnum's representative fought hard for it, the people cheered every jump that the bids made, the excitement climbed moment by moment higher and higher, the bidders got on their mettle and grew steadily more and more daring, more and more determined, the jumps went from a dollar up to five, then to ten, then to twenty, then fifty, then to a hundred, then –

At the beginning of the auction Richards whispered in distress to his wife: 'O Mary, can we allow it? It – it – you see, it is an honor-reward, a testimonial to purity of character, and – and – can we allow it? Hadn't I better get up and – O Mary, what ought we to do? – what do you think we – [*Halliday's voice. 'Fifteen I'm bid! – fifteen for the sack! – twenty! – ah, thanks! – thirty – thanks again! Thirty, thirty, thirty! – do I hear forty? – forty it is! Keep the ball rolling, gentlemen, keep it rolling! – fifty! thanks, noble Roman! going at fifty, fifty, fifty! – seventy! – ninety! – splendid! – a hundred! – pile it up, pile it up! – hundred and twenty – forty! – just in time! – hundred and fifty! –* TWO *hundred! – superb! Do I hear two h – thanks! – two hundred and fifty! –* ']

'It is another temptation, Edward – I'm all in a tremble – but, oh, we've escaped *one* temptation, and that ought to warn us to – ['*Six did I hear! – thanks! – six-fifty, six-f* – SEVEN *hundred!*'] And yet, Edward, when you think – nobody susp – ['*Eight hundred dollars! – hurrah! – make it nine! – Mr Parsons, did I hear you say – thanks – nine! – this noble sack of virgin lead going at only nine hundred dollars, gilding and all – come! do I hear – a thousand! – gratefully yours! – did some one say eleven? – a sack which is going to be the most celebrated in the whole Uni* – '] O Edward' (beginning to sob), 'we are *so* poor! – but – but – do as you think best – do as you think best.'

Edward fell – that is, he sat still; sat with a conscience which was not satisfied, but which was overpowered by circumstances.

Meantime a stranger, who looked like an amateur detective gotten up as an impossible English earl, had been watching the evening's proceedings with manifest interest, and with a contented expression on his face; and he had been privately commenting to himself. He was now soliloquising somewhat like this: 'None of the Eighteen are bidding; that is not satisfactory; I must change that – the dramatic unities require it; they must buy the sack they tried to steal; they must pay a heavy price, too – some of them are rich. And another thing, when I make a mistake in Hadleyburg nature the man that puts that error upon me is entitled to a high honorarium, and some one must pay it. This poor old Richards has brought my judgment to shame; he is an honest man: – I don't understand it, but I acknowledge it. Yes, he saw my deuces *and* with a straight flush, and by rights the pot is his. And it shall be a jackpot, too, if I can manage it. He disappointed me, but let that pass.'

He was watching the bidding. At a thousand, the market broke; the prices tumbled swiftly. He waited – and still watched. One competitor dropped out; then another, and another. He put in a bid or two, now. When the bids had sunk to ten dollars, he added a five; some one raised him a three; he waited a moment, then flung in a fifty-dollar jump, and the sack was his – at $1,282. The house broke out in cheers – then stopped; for he was on his feet, and had lifted his hand. He began to speak.

'I desire to say a word, and ask a favor. I am a speculator in rarities, and I have dealings with persons interested in numismatics all over the world. I can make a profit on this purchase, just as it stands; but there is a way, if I can get your approval, whereby I can make every one of these leaden twenty-dollar pieces worth its face in gold, and perhaps more. Grant me that approval, and I will give part of my gains to your Mr Richards, whose invulnerable probity you have so justly and so cordially recognised tonight; his share shall be ten thousand dollars, and I will hand him the money tomorrow. [*Great applause from the house*. But the 'invulnerable probity' made the Richardses blush prettily; however, it went for modesty, and did no harm.] If you will pass my proposition by a good majority – I would like a two-thirds vote – I will regard that as the town's consent, and that is all I ask. Rarities are always helped by any device which will rouse curiosity and compel remark. Now if I may have your permission to stamp upon the faces of each of these ostensible coins the names of the eighteen gentlemen who—'

Nine-tenths of the audience were on their feet in a moment – dog and all – and the proposition was carried with a whirlwind of approving applause and laughter.

They sat down, and all the Symbols except 'Dr' Clay Harkness got up, violently protesting against the proposed outrage, and threatening to –

'I beg you not to threaten me,' said the stranger, calmly. 'I know my legal rights, and am not accustomed to being frightened at bluster.' [*Applause.*] He sat down. 'Dr' Harkness saw an opportunity here. He was one of the two very rich men of the place, and Pinkerton was the other. Harkness was proprietor of a mint; that is to say, a popular patent medicine. He was running for the legislature on one ticket, and Pinkerton on the other. It was a close race and a hot one, and getting hotter every day. Both had strong appetites for money; each had bought a great tract of land, with a purpose; there was going to be a new railway, and each wanted to be in the legislature and help locate the route to his own advantage; a single vote might make the decision, and with it two or three fortunes. The stake was large, and Harkness was a daring speculator. He was sitting close to the stranger. He leaned over while one or another of the other Symbols was entertaining the house with protests and appeals, and asked, in a whisper:

'What is your price for the sack?'

'Forty thousand dollars.'

'I'll give you twenty.'

'No.'

'Twenty-five.'

'No.'

'Say thirty.'

'The price is forty thousand dollars; not a penny less.'

'All right, I'll give it. I will come to the hotel at ten in the morning. I don't want it known: will see you privately.'

'Very good.' Then the stranger got up and said to the house:

'I find it late. The speeches of these gentlemen are not without merit, not without interest, not without grace; yet if I may be excused I will take my leave. I thank you for the great favor which you have shown me in granting my petition. I ask the Chair to keep the sack for me until tomorrow, and to hand these three five-hundred-dollar notes to Mr Richards.' They were passed up to the Chair. 'At nine I will call for the sack, and at eleven will deliver the rest of the ten thousand to Mr Richards in person, at his home. Good night.'

Then he slipped out, and left the audience making a vast noise, which was composed of a mixture of cheers, the 'Mikado' song, dog-disapproval, and the chant, 'You are f-a-r from being a b-a-a-d man – a-a-a-a-men!'

At home the Richardses had to endure congratulations and compliments until midnight. Then they were left to themselves. They looked a little sad, and they sat silent and thinking. Finally Mary sighed and said,

'Do you think we are to blame, Edward – *much* to blame?' and her eyes wandered to the accusing triplet of big bank-notes lying on the table, where the congratulators had been gloating over them and reverently fingering them. Edward did not answer at once; then he brought out a sigh and said, hesitatingly:

'We – we couldn't help it, Mary. It – well, it was ordered. *All* things are.'

Mary glanced up and looked at him steadily, but he didn't return the look. Presently she said:

'I thought congratulations and praises always tasted good. But – it seems to me, now – Edward?'

'Well?'

'Are you going to stay in the bank?'

'N-no.'

'Resign?'

'In the morning – by note.'

'It does seem best.'

Richards bowed his head in his hands and muttered:

'Before, I was not afraid to let oceans of people's money pour through my hands, but – Mary, I am so tired, so tired—'

'We will go to bed.'

At nine in the morning the stranger called for the sack and took it to the hotel in a cab. At ten Harkness had a talk with him privately. The stranger asked for and got five checks on a metropolitan bank – drawn to 'Bearer' – four for $1,500 each, and one for $34,000. He put one of the former in his pocketbook, and the remainder, representing $38,500, he put in an envelope, and with these he added a note, which he wrote after Harkness was gone. At eleven he called at the Richards house and knocked. Mrs Richards peeped through the shutters, then went and received the envelope, and the stranger disappeared without a word. She came back flushed and a little unsteady on her legs, and gasped out:

'I am sure I recognised him! Last night it seemed to me that maybe I had seen him somewhere before.'

'He is the man that brought the sack here?'

'I am almost sure of it.'

'Then he is the ostensible Stephenson, too, and sold every important citizen in this town with his bogus secret. Now if he has sent checks instead of money, we are sold, too, after we thought we had escaped. I was beginning to feel fairly comfortable once more, after my night's rest, but the look of that envelope makes me sick. It isn't fat enough; $8,500 in even the largest bank-notes makes more bulk than that.'

'Edward, why do you object to checks?'

'Checks signed by Stephenson! I am resigned to take

the $8,500 if it could come in bank-notes – for it does seem that it was so ordered. Mary – but I have never had much courage, and I have not the pluck to try to market a check signed with that disastrous name. It would be a trap. That man tried to catch me; we escaped somehow or other; and now he is trying a new way. If it is checks—'

'Oh, Edward, it is *too* bad!' and she held up the checks and began to cry.

'Put them in the fire! Quick! We mustn't be tempted. It is a trick to make the world laugh at *us*, along with the rest, and – Give them to *me*, since you can't do it!' He snatched them and tried to hold his grip till he could get to the stove; but he was human, he was a cashier, and he stopped a moment to make sure of the signature. Then he came near to fainting.

'Fan me, Mary, fan me! They are the same as gold!'

'Oh, how lovely, Edward! Why?'

'Signed by Harkness. What can the mystery of that be, Mary?'

'Edward, do you think – '

'Look here – look at this! Fifteen – fifteen – fifteen – thirty-four. Thirty-eight thousand five hundred! Mary, the sack isn't worth twelve dollars, and Harkness – apparently – has paid about par for it.'

'And does it all come to us, do you think – instead of the ten thousand?'

'Why, it looks like it. And the checks are made to "Bearer", too.'

'Is that good, Edward? What is it for?'

'A hint to collect them at some distant bank, I reckon. Perhaps Harkness doesn't want the matter known. What is that – a note?'

'Yes. It was with the checks.'

It was in the 'Stephenson' handwriting, but there was no signature. It said:

'I am a disappointed man. Your honesty is beyond the reach of temptation. I had a different idea about it, but I wronged you in that, and I beg pardon, and do it sincerely. I honor you – and that is sincere, too. This town is not worthy to kiss the hem of your garment. Dear sir, I made a square bet with myself that there were nineteen debauchable men in your self-righteous community. I have lost. Take the whole pot, you are entitled to it.'

Richards drew a deep sigh, and said:

'It seems written with fire – it burns so. Mary – I am miserable again.'

'I, too. Ah, dear, I wish—'

'To think, Mary – he *believes* in me.'

'Oh, don't, Edward – I can't bear it.'

'If those beautiful words were deserved, Mary – and God knows I believed I deserved them once – I think I could give the forty thousand dollars for them. And I would put that paper away, as representing more than gold and jewels, and keep it always. But now – We could not live in the shadow of its accusing presence, Mary.'

He put it in the fire.

A messenger arrived and delivered an envelope.

Richards took from it a note and read it; it was from Burgess.

'You saved me, in a difficult time. I saved you last night. It was at cost of a lie, but I made the sacrifice freely, and out of a grateful heart. None in this village knows so well as I know how brave and good and noble you are. At bottom you cannot respect me, knowing as you do of that matter of which I am accused, and by the general voice condemned; but I beg that you will at least believe that I am a grateful man; it will help me to bear my burden.'

[signed] 'Burgess'

'Saved, once more. And on such terms!' He put the note in the fire. 'I – I wish I were dead, Mary, I wish I were out of it all.'

'Oh, these are bitter, bitter days, Edward. The stabs,

through their very generosity, are so deep – and they come so fast!'

Three days before the election each of two thousand voters suddenly found himself in possession of a prized memento – one of the renowned bogus double-eagles. Around one of its faces was stamped these words: 'THE REMARK I MADE TO THE POOR STRANGER WAS – ' Around the other face was stamped these: 'GO, AND REFORM. [SIGNED] PINKERTON.' Thus the entire remaining refuse of the renowned joke was emptied upon a single head, and with calamitous effect. It revived the recent vast laugh and concentrated it upon Pinkerton; and Harkness's election was a walkover.

Within twenty-four hours after the Richardses had received their checks their consciences were quieting down, discouraged; the old couple were learning to reconcile themselves to the sin which they had committed. But they were to learn, now, that a sin takes on new and real terrors when there seems a chance that it is going to be found out. This gives it a fresh and most substantial and important aspect. At church the morning sermon was of the usual pattern; it was the same old things said in the same old way; they had heard them a thousand times and found them innocuous, next to meaningless, and easy to sleep under; but now it was different: the sermon seemed to bristle with accusations; it seemed aimed straight and specially at people who were concealing deadly sins. After church they got away from the mob of congratulators as soon as they could, and hurried homeward, chilled to the bone at they did not know what – vague, shadowy, indefinite fears. And by chance they caught a glimpse of Mr Burgess as he turned a corner. He paid no attention to their nod of recognition! He hadn't seen it; but they did not know that. What could his conduct mean? It might mean – it might mean – oh, a dozen dreadful things. Was it possible that he knew that Richards could have cleared him of guilt in that bygone time, and had been silently waiting for a chance to even up accounts? At home, in their distress they got to imagining that their servant might have been in the next room listening when Richards revealed the secret to his wife that he knew of Burgess's innocence; next, Richards began to imagine that he had heard the swish of a gown in there at that time; next, he was sure he *had* heard it. They would call Sarah in, on a pretext, and watch her face; if she had been betraying them to Mr Burgess, it would show in her manner. They asked her some questions – questions which were so random and incoherent and seemingly purposeless that the girl felt sure that the old people's minds had been affected by their sudden good fortune; the sharp and watchful gaze which they bent upon her frightened her, and that completed the business. She blushed, she became nervous and confused, and to the old people these were plain signs of guilt – guilt of some fearful sort or other – without doubt she was a spy and a traitor. When they were alone again they began to piece many unrelated things together and get horrible results out of the combination. When things had got about to the worst, Richards was delivered of a sudden gasp, and his wife asked:

'Oh, what is it? – what is it?'

'The note – Burgess's note! Its language was sarcastic, I see it now.' He quoted: ' "At bottom you cannot respect me, *knowing*, as you do, of *that matter* of which I am accused" – oh, it is perfectly plain, now, God help me! He knows that I know! You see the ingenuity of the phrasing. It was a trap – and like a fool, I walked into it. And Mary—?'

'Oh, it is dreadful – I know what you are going to say – he didn't return your transcript of the pretended test-remark.'

'No – kept it to destroy us with. Mary, he has exposed us to some already. I know it – I know it well. I saw it in a dozen faces after church. Ah, he wouldn't answer our nod of recognition – *he* knew what he had been doing!'

In the night the doctor was called. The news went around in the morning that the old couple were rather seriously ill – prostrated by the exhausting excitement growing out of their great windfall, the congratulations, and the late hours, the doctor said. The town was sincerely distressed; for these old people were about all it had left to be proud of, now.

Two days later the news was worse. The old couple were delirious, and were doing strange things. By witness of the nurses, Richards had exhibited checks – for $8,500? No – for an amazing sum – $38,500! What could be the explanation of this gigantic piece of luck?

The following day the nurses had more news – and wonderful. They had concluded to hide the checks, lest harm come to them; but when they searched they were gone from under the patient's pillow – vanished away. The patient said:

'Let the pillow alone; what do you want?'

'We thought it best that the checks—'

'You will never see them again – they are destroyed. They came from Satan. I saw the hell-brand on them, and I knew they were sent to betray me to sin.' Then he fell to gabbling strange and dreadful things which were not clearly understandable, and which the doctor admonished them to keep to themselves.

Richards was right; the checks were never seen again.

A nurse must have talked in her sleep, for within two days the forbidden gabblings were the property of the town; and they were of a surprising sort. They seemed to indicate that Richards had been a claimant for the sack himself, and that Burgess had concealed that fact and then maliciously betrayed it.

Burgess was taxed with this and stoutly denied it. And he said it was not fair to attach weight to the chatter of a sick old man who was out of his mind. Still, suspicion was in the air, and there was much talk.

After a day or two it was reported that Mrs Richards's delirious deliveries were getting to be duplicates of her husband's. Suspicion flamed up into conviction, now, and the town's pride in the purity of its one undiscredited important citizen began to dim down and flicker toward extinction.

Six days passed, then came more news. The old couple were dying. Richards's mind cleared in his latest hour, and he sent for Burgess. Burgess said:

'Let the room be cleared. I think he wishes to say something in privacy.'

'No!' said Richards: 'I want witnesses. I want you all to hear my confession, so that I may die a man, and not a dog. I was clean – artificially – like the rest; and like the rest I fell when temptation came. I signed a lie, and claimed the miserable sack. Mr Burgess remembered that I had done him a service, and in gratitude (and ignorance) he suppressed my claim and saved me. You know the thing that was charged against Burgess years ago. My testimony, and mine alone, could have cleared him, and I was a coward, and left him to suffer disgrace—'

'No – no – Mr Richards, you—'

'My servant betrayed my secret to him—'

'No one has betrayed anything to me—'

'—and then he did a natural and justifiable thing, he repented of the saving kindness which he had done me, and he *exposed* me – as I deserved—'

'Never! – I make oath—'

'Out of my heart I forgive him.'

Burgess's impassioned protestations fell upon deaf ears; the dying man passed away without knowing that once more he had done poor Burgess a wrong. The old wife died that night.

The last of the sacred Nineteen had fallen a prey to the fiendish sack; the town was stripped of the last rag of its ancient glory. Its mourning was not showy, but it was deep.

By act of the Legislature – upon prayer and petition – Hadleyburg was allowed to change its name to (never mind what – I will not give it away), and leave one word out of the motto that for many generations had graced the town's official seal.

It is an honest town once more, and the man will have to rise early that catches it napping again.

The Election for Beadle

Charles Dickens

A great event has recently occurred in our parish. A contest of paramount interest has just terminated; a parochial convulsion has taken place. It has been succeeded by a glorious triumph, which the country – or at least the parish – it is all the same – will long remember. We have had an election; an election of beadle. The supporters of the old beadle system have been defeated in their stronghold, and the advocates of the great new beadle principles have achieved a proud victory.

Our parish, which, like all other parishes, is a little world of its own, has long been divided into two parties, whose contentions, slumbering for a while, have never failed to burst forth with unabated vigour, on any occasion on which they could by possibility be renewed. Watching-rates, lighting-rates, paving-rates, sewer's-rates, church-rates, poor's-rates – all sorts of rates, have been in their turns the subjects of a grand struggle; and as to questions of patronage, the asperity and determination with which they have been contested is scarcely credible.

The leader of the official party – the steady advocate of the churchwardens, and the unflinching supporter of the overseers – is an old gentleman who lives in our row. He owns some half a dozen houses in it, and always walks on the opposite side of the way, so that he may be able to take in a view of the whole of his property at once. He is a tall, thin, bony man, with an interrogative nose, and little restless perking eyes, which appear to have been given him for the sole purpose of peeping into other people's affairs with. He is deeply impressed with the importance of our parish business, and prides himself, not a little, on his style of addressing the parishioners in vestry assembled. His views are rather confined than extensive; his principles more narrow than liberal. He has been heard to declaim very loudly in favour of the liberty of the press, and advocates the repeal of the stamp duty on newspapers, because the daily journals who now have a monopoly of the public, never give *verbatim* reports of vestry meetings. He would not appear egotistical for the world, but at the same time he must say, that there *are* speeches – that celebrated speech of his own, on the emoluments of the sexton, and the duties of the office, for instance – which might be communicated to the public, greatly to their improvement and advantage.

His great opponent in public life is Captain Purday, the old naval officer on half-pay, to whom we have already introduced our readers. The captain being a determined opponent of the constituted authorities, whoever they may chance to be, and our other friend being their steady supporter, with an equal disregard of their individual merits, it will readily be supposed, that occasions for their coming into direct collision are neither few nor far between. They divided the vestry fourteen times on a motion for heating the church with warm water instead of coals: and made speeches about liberty and expenditure, and prodigality and hot water, which threw the whole parish into a state of excitement. Then the captain, when he was on the visiting committee, and his opponent overseer, brought forward certain distinct and specific charges relative to the management of the workhouse, boldly expressed his total want of confidence in the existing authorities, and moved for 'a copy of the recipe by which the paupers' soup was prepared, together with any documents relating thereto'. This the overseer steadily resisted; he fortified himself by precedent, appealed to the established usage, and declined to produce the papers, on the ground of the injury that would be done to the public service, if documents of a strictly private nature, passing between the master of the workhouse and the cook, were to be thus dragged to light on the motion of any individual member of the vestry. The motion was lost by a majority of two; and then the captain, who never allows himself to be defeated, moved for a committee of inquiry into the whole subject. The affair grew serious: the question was discussed at meeting after meeting, and vestry after vestry; speeches were made, attacks repudiated, personal defiances exchanged, explanations received, and the greatest excitement prevailed, until at last, just as the question was going to be finally decided, the vestry found that somehow or other, they had become entangled in a point of form, from which it was impossible to escape with propriety. So, the motion was dropped, and everybody looked extremely important, and seemed quite satisfied with the meritorious nature of the whole proceeding.

This was the state of affairs in our parish a week or two since, when Simmons, the beadle, suddenly died. The lamented deceased had over-exerted himself, a day or two previously, in conveying an aged female, highly intoxicated, to the strong room of the workhouse. The excitement thus occasioned, added to a severe cold, which this indefatigable officer had caught in his capacity of director of the parish engine, by inadvertently playing over himself instead of a fire, proved too much for a constitution already enfeebled by age; and the intelligence was conveyed to the Board one evening that Simmons had died, and left his respects.

The breath was scarcely out of the body of the deceased functionary, when the field was filled with competitors for the vacant office, each of whom rested his claims to public support, entirely on the number and extent of his family, as if the office of beadle were originally instituted as an encouragement for the propagation of the human species. 'Bung for Beadle. Five small children!' – 'Hopkins for Beadle. Seven small children!!' – 'Timkins for Beadle. Nine small children!!!' Such were the placards in large black letters on a white ground, which were plentifully pasted on the walls, and posted in the windows of the principal shops. Timkins's success was considered certain: several mothers of families half promised their votes, and the nine small children would have run over the course, but for the production of another placard, announcing the appearance of a still more meritorious candidate. 'Spruggins for Beadle. Ten small children (two of them twins), and a wife!!!' There was no resisting this; ten small children would have been almost irresistible in themselves, without the twins, but the touching parenthesis about that interesting production of nature, and the still more touching allusion to Mrs Spruggins, must ensure success. Spruggins was the favourite at once, and the appearance of his lady, as she went about to solicit votes (which encouraged confident hopes of a still further addition to the house of Spruggins at no remote period), increased the general prepossession in his favour. The other candidates, Bung alone excepted, resigned in despair. The day of election was fixed; and the canvass proceeded with briskness and perseverance on both sides.

The members of the vestry could not be supposed to escape the contagious excitement inseparable from the occasion. The majority of the lady inhabitants of the parish declared at once for Spruggins; and the *quondam* overseer took the same side, on the ground that men with large families always had been elected to the office, and that although he must admit, that, in other respects, Spruggins was the least qualified candidate of the two, still it was an old practice, and he saw no reason why an old practice should be departed from. This was enough for the captain. He immediately sided with Bung, canvassed for him personally in all directions, wrote squibs on Spruggins, and got his butcher to skewer them up on conspicuous joints in his shop-front; frightened his neighbour, the old lady, into a palpitation of the heart, by his awful denunciations of Spruggins's party; and bounced in and out, and up and down, and backwards and forwards, until all the sober inhabitants of the parish thought it inevitable that he must die of a brain fever, long before the election began.

The day of election arrived. It was no longer an individual struggle, but a party contest between the ins and outs. The question was, whether the withering influence of the overseers, the domination of the churchwardens, and the blighting despotism of the vestry-clerk, should be allowed to render the election of beadle a form – a nullity: whether they should impose a vestry-elected beadle on the parish, to do their bidding and forward their views, or whether the parishioners, fearlessly asserting their undoubted rights, should elect an independent beadle of their own.

The nomination was fixed to take place in the vestry, but so great was the throng of anxious spectators, that it was found necessary to adjourn to the church, where the ceremony commenced with due solemnity. The appearance of the churchwardens and overseers, and the ex-churchwardens and ex-overseers, with Spruggins in the rear, excited general attention. Spruggins was a little thin man, in rusty black, with a long pale face, and a countenance expressive of care and fatigue, which might either be attributed to the extent of his family or the anxiety of his feelings. His opponent appeared in a cast-off coat of the captain's – a blue coat with bright buttons: white trousers, and that description of shoes familiarly known by the appellation of 'high-lows'. There was a serenity in the open countenance of Bung – a kind of moral dignity in his confident air – an 'I wish you may get it' sort of expression in his eye – which infused animation into his supporters, and evidently dispirited his opponents.

The ex-churchwarden rose to propose Thomas Spruggins for beadle. He had known him long. He had had his eye upon him closely for years; he had watched him with twofold vigilance for months. (A parishioner here suggested that this might be termed 'taking a double sight', but the observation was drowned in loud cries of 'Order!') He would repeat that he had had his eye upon him for years, and this he would say, that a more well-conducted, a more well-behaved, a more sober, a more quiet man, with a more well-regulated mind, he had never met with. A man with a larger family he had never known (cheers). The parish required a man who could be depended on ('Hear!' from the Spruggins side, answered by ironical cheers from the Bung party). Such a man he now proposed ('No', 'Yes'). He would not allude to individuals (the ex-churchwarden continued, in the celebrated negative style adopted by great speakers). He would not advert to a gentleman who had once held a high rank in the service of his majesty; he would not say, that that gentleman was no gentleman; he would not assert, that that man was no man; he would not say, that he was a turbulent parishioner; he would not say, that he had grossly misbehaved himself, not only on this, but on all former occasions; he would not say, that he was one of those discontented and treasonable spirits, who carried confusion and disorder wherever they went; he would not say, that he harboured in his heart envy, and hatred, and malice, and all uncharitableness. No! He wished to have everything comfortable and pleasant, and therefore, he would say – nothing about him (cheers).

The captain replied in a similar parliamentary style. He would not say, he was astonished at the speech they had just heard; he would not say, he was disgusted (cheers). He would not retort the epithets which had been hurled against him (renewed cheering); he would not allude to men once in office, but now happily out of it, who had mismanaged the workhouse, ground the paupers, diluted the beer, slack-baked the bread, boned the meat, heightened the work, and lowered the soup (tremendous cheers). He would not ask what such men deserved (a voice, 'Nothing a-day, and find themselves!'). He would not say, that one burst of general indignation should drive them from the parish they polluted with their presence ('Give it him!'). He would not allude to the unfortunate man who had been proposed – he would not say, as the vestry's tool, but as Beadle. He would not advert to that individual's family; he would not say, that nine children, twins, and a wife, were very bad examples of pauper imitation (loud cheers). He would not advert in detail to the qualifications of Bung. The man stood before him, and he would not say in his presence, what he might be disposed to say of him, if he were absent. (Here Mr Bung telegraphed to a friend near him, under cover of his hat, by contracting his left eye, and applying his right thumb to the tip of his nose). It had been objected to Bung that he had only five children ('Hear, hear!' from the opposition). Well; he had yet to learn that the legislature had affixed any precise amount of infantine qualification to the office of beadle; but taking it for granted that an extensive family were a great requisite, he entreated them to look to facts, and compare *data*, about which there could be no mistake. Bung was thirty-five years of age. Spruggins – of whom he wished to speak with all possible respect – was fifty. Was it not more than possible – was it not very probable – that by the time Bung attained the latter age, he might see around him a family, even exceeding in number and extent, that to which Spruggins at present laid claim (deafening cheers and waving of handkerchiefs)? The captain concluded, amidst loud applause, by calling upon the parishioners to sound the tocsin, rush to the poll, free themselves from dictation, or be slaves for ever.

On the following day the polling began, and we never have had such a bustle in our parish since we got up our famous anti-slavery petition, which was such an important one, that the House of Commons ordered it to be printed, on the motion of the member for the district. The captain engaged two hackney-coaches and a cab for Bung's people – the cab for the drunken voters, and the two coaches for the old ladies, the greater portion of whom, owing to the captain's impetuosity, were driven up to the poll and home again, before they recovered from their flurry sufficiently to know, with any degree of clearness, what they had been doing. The opposite party wholly neglected these precautions, and the consequence was, that a great many ladies who were walking leisurely up to the church – for it was a very hot day – to vote for Spruggins, were artfully decoyed into the coaches, and voted for Bung. The captain's arguments, too, had produced considerable effect: the attempted influence of the vestry produced a greater. A threat of exclusive dealing was clearly established against the vestry-clerk – a case of heartless and profligate atrocity. It appeared that the delinquent had been in the habit of purchasing six penn'orth of muffins, weekly, from an old woman who rents a small house in the parish, and resides among the original settlers; on her last weekly visit, a message was conveyed to her through the medium of the cook, couched in mysterious terms, but indicating with sufficient clearness, that the vestry-clerk's appetite for muffins, in future, depended entirely on her vote on the beadleship. This was sufficient: the stream had been turning previously, and the impulse thus administered directed its final course. The Bung party ordered one shilling's-worth of muffins weekly for the remainder of the old woman's natural life; the parishioners were loud in their exclamations; and the fate of Spruggins was sealed.

It was in vain that the twins were exhibited in dresses of the same pattern, and night-caps to match, at the church door: the boy in Mrs Spruggins's right arm, and the girl in her left – even Mrs Spruggins herself failed to be an object of sympathy any longer. The majority attained by Bung on the gross poll was four hundred and twenty-eight, and the cause of the parishioners triumphed.

The Village that voted the Earth was Flat

Rudyard Kipling

Our drive till then had been quite a success. The other men in the car were my friend Woodhouse, young Ollyett, a distant connection of his, and Pallant, the MP. Woodhouse's business was the treatment and cure of sick journals. He knew by instinct the precise moment in a newspaper's life when the impetus of past good management is exhausted and it fetches up on the deadcentre between slow and expensive collapse and the new start which can be given by gold injections – and genius. He was wisely ignorant of journalism; but when he stooped on a carcase there was sure to be meat. He had that week added a half-dead, halfpenny evening paper to his collection, which consisted of a prosperous London daily, one provincial ditto, and a limp-bodied weekly of commercial leanings. He had also, that very hour, planted me with a large block of the evening paper's common shares, and was explaining the whole art of editorship to Ollyett, a young man three years from Oxford, with coir-matting-coloured hair and a face harshly modelled by harsh experiences, who, I understood, was assisting in the new venture. Pallant, the long, wrinkled MP, whose voice is more like a crane's than a peacock's, took no shares, but gave us all advice.

'You'll find it rather a knacker's yard,' Woodhouse was saying. 'Yes, I know they call me The Knacker; but it will pay inside a year. All my papers do. I've only one motto: Back your luck and back your staff. It'll come out all right.'

Then the car stopped, and a policeman asked our names and addresses for exceeding the speed-limit. We pointed out that the road ran absolutely straight for half a mile ahead without even a side-lane. 'That's just what we depend on,' said the policeman unpleasantly.

'The usual swindle,' said Woodhouse under his breath. 'What's the name of this place?'

'Huckley,' said the policeman. 'H-u-c-k-l-e-y,' and wrote something in his note-book at which young Ollyett protested. A large red man on a grey horse who had been watching us from the other side of the hedge shouted an order we could not catch. The policeman laid his hand on the rim of the right driving-door (Woodhouse carries his spares tyres aft), and it closed on the button of the electric horn. The grey horse at once bolted, and we could hear the rider swearing all across the landscape.

'Damn it, man, you've got your silly fist on it! Take it off!' Woodhouse shouted.

'Ho!' said the constable, looking carefully at his fingers as though we had trapped them. 'That won't do you any good either,' and he wrote once more in his note-book before he allowed us to go.

This was Woodhouse's first brush with motor law, and since I expected no ill consequences to myself, I pointed out that it was very serious. I took the same view myself when in due time I found that I, too, was summonsed on charges ranging from the use of obscene language to endangering traffic.

Judgement was done in a little pale-yellow market-town with a small, Jubilee clock-tower and a large corn-exchange. Woodhouse drove us there in his car. Pallant, who had not been included in the summons, came with us as moral support. While we waited outside, the fat man on the grey horse rode up and entered into loud talk with his brother magistrates. He said to one of them – for I took the trouble to note it down – 'It falls away from my lodge-gates, dead straight, three-quarters of a mile. I'd defy any one to resist it. We rooked seventy pounds out of 'em last month. No car can resist the temptation. You ought to have one your side of the county, Mike. They simply can't resist it.'

'Whew!' said Woodhouse. 'We're in for trouble. Don't you say a word – or Ollyett either! I'll pay the fines and we'll get it over as soon as possible. Where's Pallant?'

'At the back of the court somewhere,' said Ollyett. 'I saw him slip in just now.'

The fat man then took his seat on the Bench, of which he was chairman, and I gathered from a bystander that his name was Sir Thomas Ingell, Bart., MP, of Ingell Park, Huckley. He began with an allocution pitched in a tone that would have justified revolt throughout empires. Evidence, when the crowded little court did not drown it with applause, was given in the pauses of the address. They were all very proud of their Sir Thomas, and looked from him to us, wondering why we did not applaud too.

Taking its time from the chairman, the Bench rollicked with us for seventeen minutes. Sir Thomas explained that he was sick and tired of processions of cads of our type, who would be better employed breaking stones on the road than in frightening horses worth more than themselves or their ancestors. This was after it had been proved that Woodhouse's man had turned on the horn purposely to annoy Sir Thomas, who 'happened to be riding by'! There were other remarks too – primitive enough – but it was the unspeakable brutality of the tone, even more than the quality of the justice, or the laughter of the audience that stung our souls out of all reason. When we were dismissed – to the tune of twenty-three pounds, twelve shillings and sixpence – we waited for Pallant to join us, while we listened to the next case – one of driving without a licence. Ollyett with an eye to his evening paper, had already taken very full notes of our own, but we did not wish to seem prejudiced.

'It's all right,' said the reporter of the local paper soothingly. 'We never report Sir Thomas *in extenso*. Only the fines and charges.'

'Oh, thank you,' Ollyett replied, and I heard him ask who everyone in court might be. The local reporter was very communicative.

The new victim, a large, flaxen-haired man in somewhat striking clothes, to which Sir Thomas, now thoroughly warmed, drew public attention, said that he had left his licence at home. Sir Thomas asked him if he expected the police to go to his home address at Jerusalem to find it for him; and the court roared. Nor did Sir Thomas approve of the man's name, but insisted on calling him 'Mr Masquerader', and every time he did so, all his people shouted. Evidently this was their established *auto-da-fé*.

'He didn't summons me – because I'm in the House, I suppose. I think I shall have to ask a Question,' said Pallant, reappearing at the close of the case.

'I think *I* shall have to give it a little publicity too,' said Woodhouse. 'We can't have this kind of thing going on, you know.' His face was set and quite white. Pallant's, on the other hand, was black, and I know that my very stomach had turned with rage. Ollyett was dumb.

'Well, let's have lunch,' Woodhouse said at last. 'Then we can get away before the show breaks up.'

We drew Ollyett from the arms of the local reporter, crossed the Market Square to the Red Lion and found Sir Thomas's 'Mr Masquerader' just sitting down to beer, beef and pickles.

'Ah!' said he, in a large voice. 'Companions in misfortune. Won't you gentlemen join me?'

'Delighted,' said Woodhouse. 'What did you get?'

'I haven't decided. It might make a good turn, but – the public aren't educated up to it yet. It's beyond 'em. If it wasn't, that red dub on the Bench would be worth fifty a week.'

'Where?' said Woodhouse. The man looked at him with unaffected surprise.

'At any one of My places,' he replied. 'But perhaps you live here?'

'Good heavens!' cried young Ollyett suddenly. 'You *are* Masquerier, then? I thought you were!'

'Bat Masquerier.' He let the words fall with the weight of an international ultimatum. 'Yes, that's all I am. But you have the advantage of me, gentlemen.'

For the moment, while we were introducing ourselves, I was puzzled. Then I recalled prismatic music-hall posters – of enormous acreage – that had been the unnoticed background of my visits to London for years past. Posters of men and women, singers, jongleurs, impersonators and audacities of every draped and undraped brand, all moved on and off in London and the Provinces by Bat Masquerier – with the long wedge-tailed flourish following the final 'r'.

'*I* knew you at once,' said Pallant, the trained MP, and I promptly backed the lie. Woodhouse mumbled excuses. Bat Masquerier was not moved for or against us any more than the frontage of one of his own palaces.

'I always tell My people there's a limit to the size of the lettering,' he said. 'Overdo that and the ret'na doesn't take it in. Advertisin' is the most delicate of all the sciences.'

'There's one man in the world who is going to get a little of it if I live for the next twenty-four hours,' said Woodhouse, and explained how this would come about.

Masquerier stared at him lengthily with gun-metal-blue eyes.

'You mean it?' he drawled; the voice was as magnetic as the look.

'*I* do,' said Ollyett. 'That business of the horn alone ought to have him off the Bench in three months.' Masquerier looked at him even longer than he had looked at Woodhouse.

'He told *me*,' he said suddenly, 'that my home-address was Jerusalem. You heard that?'

'But it was the tone – the tone,' Ollyett cried.

'You noticed that, too, did you?' said Masquerier.

'That's the artistic temperament. You can do a lot with it. And I'm Bat Masquerier,' he went on. He dropped his chin in his fists and scowled straight in front of him . . . 'I made the Silhouettes – I made the Trefoil and the Jocunda. I made 'Dal Benzaguen.' Here Ollyett sat straight up, for in common with the youth of that year he worshipped Miss Vidal Benzaguen of the Trefoil immensely and unreservedly. ' "*Is* that a dressing-gown or an ulster you're supposed to be wearing?" You heard *that*? . . . "And I suppose you hadn't time to brush your hair either?" You heard *that*? . . . Now, you hear *me*!' His voice filled the coffee-room, then dropped to a whisper as dreadful as a surgeon's before an operation. He spoke for several minutes. Pallant muttered 'Hear! hear!' I saw Ollyett's eye flash – it was to Ollyett that Masquerier addressed himself chiefly – and Woodhouse leaned forward with joined hands.

'Are you *with* me?' he went on, gathering us all up in one sweep of the arm. 'When I begin a thing I see it through, gentlemen. What Bat can't break, breaks him! But I haven't struck that thing yet. This is no one-turn turn-it-down show. This is business to the dead finish. Are you with me, gentlemen? Good! Now, we'll pool our assets. One London morning, and one provincial daily, didn't you say? One weekly commercial ditto and one MP.'

'Not much use, I'm afraid,' Pallant smirked.

'But privileged. *But* privileged,' he returned. 'And we have also my little team – London, Blackburn, Liverpool, Leeds – I'll tell you about Manchester later – and Me! Bat Masquerier.' He breathed the name reverently into his tankard. 'Gentlemen, when our combination has finished with Sir Thomas Ingell, Bart., MP, and everything else that is his, Sodom and Gomorrah will be a winsome bit of Merrie England beside 'em. I must go back to town now, but I trust you gentlemen will give me the pleasure of your company at dinner tonight at the Chop Suey –

the Red Amber Room – and we'll block out the scenario.' He laid his hand on young Ollyett's shoulder and added: 'It's your brains I want.' Then he left, in a good deal of astrakhan collar and nickel-plated limousine, and the place felt less crowded.

We ordered our car a few minutes later. As Woodhouse, Ollyett and I were getting in, Sir Thomas Ingell, Bart., MP, came out of the Hall of Justice across the square and mounted his horse. I have sometime thought that if he had gone in silence he might even then have been saved, but as he settled himself in the saddle he caught sight of us and must needs shout: 'Not off yet? You'd better get away and you'd better be careful.' At that moment Pallant, who had been buying picture-postcards, came out of the inn, took Sir Thomas's eye and very leisurely entered the car. It seemed to me that for one instant there was a shade of uneasiness on the baronet's grey-whiskered face.

'I hope,' said Woodhouse after several miles, 'I hope he's a widower.'

'Yes,' said Pallant. 'For his poor, dear wife's sake I hope that, very much indeed. I suppose he didn't see me in Court. Oh, here's the parish history of Huckley written by the Rector and here's your share of the picture-postcards. Are we all dining with this Mr Masquerier tonight?'

'Yes!' said we all.

If Woodhouse knew nothing of journalism, young Ollyett, who had graduated in a hard school, knew a good deal. Our halfpenny evening paper, which we will call *The Bun* to distinguish her from her prosperous morning sister, *The Cake*, was not only diseased but corrupt. We found this out when a man brought us the prospectus of a new oil-field and demanded sub-leaders on its prosperity. Ollyett talked pure Brasenose to him for three minutes. Otherwise he spoke and wrote trade-English – a toothsome amalgam of Americanisms and epigrams. But though the slang changes the game never alters, and Ollyett and I and, in the end, some others enjoyed it immensely. It was weeks ere we could see the wood for the trees, but so soon as the staff realised that they had proprietors who backed them right or wrong, and specially when they were wrong (which is the sole secret of journalism), and that their fate did not hang on any passing owner's passing mood, they did miracles.

But we did not neglect Huckley. As Ollyett said our first care was to create an 'arresting atmosphere' round it. He used to visit the village of week-ends, on a motor-bicycle with a side-car; for which reason I left the actual place alone and dealt with it in the abstract. Yet it was I who drew first blood. Two inhabitants of Huckley wrote to contradict a small, quite solid paragraph in *The Bun* that a hoopoe had been seen at Huckley and had, 'of course, been shot by the local sportsmen'. There was some heat in their letters, both of which we published. Our version of how the hoopoe got his crest from King Solomon was, I grieve to say, so inaccurate that the Rector himself – no sportsman as he pointed out, but a lover of accuracy – wrote to us to correct it. We gave his letter good space and thanked him.

'This priest is going to be useful,' said Ollyett. 'He has the impartial mind. I shall vitalise him.'

Forthwith he created M. L. Sigden, a recluse of refined tastes who in *The Bun* demanded to know whether this Huckley-of-the-Hoopoe was the Hugly of his boyhood and whether, by any chance, the fell change of name had been wrought by collusion between a local magnate and the railway, in the mistaken interests of spurious refinement. 'For I knew it and loved it with the maidens of my day – *eheu ab angulo!* – as Hugly,' wrote M. L. Sigden from Oxford.

Though other papers scoffed, *The Bun* was gravely sympathetic. Several people wrote to deny that Huckley had been changed at birth. Only the Rector – no philosopher as he pointed out, but a lover of accuracy – had his doubts, which he laid publicly before Mr M. L. Sigden, who suggested, through *The Bun*, that the little place might have begun life in Anglo-Saxon days as 'Hogslea' or among the Normans as 'Argilé', on account of its much clay. The Rector had his own ideas too (he said it was mostly gravel), and M. L. Sigden had a fund of reminiscences. Oddly enough – which is seldom the case with free reading-matter – our subscribers rather relished the correspondence, and contemporaries quoted freely.

'The secret of power,' said Ollyett, 'is not the big stick. It's the liftable stick.' (This means the 'arresting' quotation of six or seven lines.) 'Did you see the *Spec.* had a middle on "Rural Tenacities" last week. That was all Huckley. I'm doing a "Mobiquity" on Huckley next week.'

Our 'Mobiquities' were Friday evening accounts of easy motor-bike-*cum*-side-car trips round London, illustrated (we could never get that machine to work properly) by smudgy maps. Ollyett wrote the stuff with a fervour and a delicacy which I always ascribed to the side-car. His account of Epping Forest, for instance, was simply young love with its soul at its lips. But his Huckley 'Mobiquity' would have sickened a soap-boiler. It chemically combined loathsome familiarity, leering suggestion, slimy piety and rancid 'social service' in one fuming compost that fairly lifted me off my feet.

'Yes,' said he, after compliments. 'It's the most vital, arresting and dynamic bit of tump I've done up to date. *Non nobis gloria!* I met Sir Thomas Ingell in his own park. He talked to me again. He inspired most of it.'

'Which? The "glutinous native drawl", or "the neglected adenoids of the village children"?' I demanded.

'Oh, no! That's only to bring in the panel doctor. It's the last flight we – I'm proudest of.'

This dealt with 'the crepuscular penumbra spreading her dim limbs over the boskage'; with 'jolly rabbits'; with a herd of 'gravid polled Angus'; and with the 'arresting, gipsy-like face of their swart, scholarly owner – as well known at the Royal Agricultural Shows as that of our late King-Emperor.'

' "Swart" is good and so's "gravid",' said I, 'but the panel doctor will be annoyed about the adenoids.'

'Not half as much as Sir Thomas will about his face,' said Ollyett. 'And if you only knew what I've left out!'

He was right. The panel doctor spent his week-end (this is the advantage of Friday articles) in overwhelming us with a professional counterblast of no interest whatever to our subscribers. We told him so, and he, then and there, battered his way with it into the *Lancet* where they are keen on glands, and forgot us altogether. But Sir Thomas Ingell was of sterner stuff. He must have spent a happy week-end too. The letter which we received from him on Monday proved him to be a kinless loon of upright life, for no woman, however remotely interested in a man, would have let it pass the home wastepaper basket. He objected to our references to his own herd, to his own labours in his own village, which he said was a Model Village, and to our infernal insolence; but he objected most to our invoice of his features. We wrote him courteously to ask whether the letter was meant for publication. He, remembering, I presume, the Duke of Wellington, wrote back, 'publish and be damned'.

'Oh! This is too easy,' Ollyett said as he began heading the letter.

'Stop a minute,' I said. 'The game is getting a little beyond us. Tonight's the Bat dinner.' (I may have forgotten to tell you that our dinner with Bat Masquerier in the Red Amber Room of the Chop Suey House had come to be a weekly affair.) 'Hold it over till they've all seen it.'

'Perhaps you're right,' he said. 'You might waste it.'

At dinner, then, Sir Thomas's letter was handed round. Bat seemed to be thinking of other matters, but Pallant was very interested.

'I've got an idea,' he said presently. 'Could you put

something into *The Bun* tomorrow about foot-and-mouth disease in that fellow's herd?'

'Oh, plague if you like,' Ollyett replied. 'They're only five measly Shorthorns. I saw one lying down in the park. She'll serve as a substratum of fact.'

'Then, do that; and hold the letter over meanwhile. I think *I* come in here,' said Pallant.

'Why?' said I.

'Because there's something coming up in the House about foot-and-mouth, and because he wrote me a letter after that little affair when he fined you. Took ten days to think it over. Here you are,' said Pallant. 'House of Commons paper, you see.' We read:

Dear Pallant –

Although in the past our paths have not lain much together, I am sure you will agree with me that on the floor of the House all members are on a footing of equality. I make bold, therefore, to approach you in a matter which I think capable of a very different interpretation from that which perhaps was put upon it by your friends. Will you let them know that that was the case and that I was in no way swayed by animus in the exercise of my magisterial duties, which you, as a brother magistrate, can imagine are frequently very distasteful to –

Yours very sincerely,
T. Ingell

P.S. – I have seen to it that the motor vigilance to which your friends took exception has been considerably relaxed in my district.

'What did you answer,' said Ollyett, when all our opinions had been expressed.

'I told him I couldn't do anything in the matter. And I couldn't – then. But you'll remember to put in that foot-and-mouth paragraph. I want something to work upon.'

'It seems to me *The Bun* has done all the work up to date,' I suggested. 'When does *The Cake* come in?'

'*The Cake*,' said Woodhouse, and I remembered afterwards that he spoke like a Cabinet Minister on the eve of a Budget, 'reserves to itself the fullest right to deal with situations as they arise.'

'Ye-eh!' Bat Masquerier shook himself out of his thoughts. ' "Situations as they arise." I ain't idle either. But there's no use fishing till the swim's baited. You' – he turned to Ollyett – 'manufacture very good groundbait . . . I always tell *My* people – What the deuce is that?'

There was a burst of song from another private dining-room across the landing. 'It ees some ladies from the Trefoil,' the waiter began.

'Oh, I know that. What are they singing, though?'

He rose and went out, to be greeted by shouts of applause from that merry company. Then there was silence, such as one hears in the form-room after a master's entry. Then a voice that we loved began again: 'Here we go gathering nuts in May – nuts in May – nuts in May!'

'It's only 'Dal – and some nuts,' he explained when he returned. 'She says she's coming in to dessert.' He sat down, humming the old tune to himself, and till Miss Vidal Benzaguen entered, he held us speechless with tales of the artistic temperament.

We obeyed Pallant to the extent of slipping into *The Bun* a wary paragraph about cows lying down and dripping at the mouth, which might be read either as an unkind libel or, in the hands of a capable lawyer, as a piece of faithful nature-study.

'And besides,' said Ollyett, 'we allude to "gravid polled Angus". I am advised that no action can lie in respect of virgin Shorthorns. Pallant wants us to come to the House tonight. He's got us places for the Strangers' Gallery. I'm beginning to like Pallant.'

'Masquerier seems to like you,' I said.

'Yes, but I'm afraid of him,' Ollyett answered with perfect sincerity. 'I am. He's the Absolutely Amoral Soul. I've never met one yet.'

We went to the House together. It happened to be an Irish afternoon, and as soon as I had got the cries and the faces a little sorted out, I gathered there were grievances in the air, but how many of them was beyond me.

'It's all right,' said Ollyett of the trained ear. 'They've shut their ports against – oh yes – export of Irish cattle! Foot-and-mouth disease at Ballyhellion. *I* see Pallant's idea!'

The House was certainly all mouth for the moment, but, as I could feel, quite in earnest. A Minister with a piece of typewritten paper seemed to be fending off volleys of insults. He reminded me somehow of a nervous huntsman breaking up a fox in the face of rabid hounds.

'It's question-time. They're asking questions,' said Ollyett. 'Look! Pallant's up.'

There was no mistaking it. His voice, which his enemies said was his one parliamentary asset, silenced the hubbub as toothache silences mere singing in the ears. He said:

'Arising out of that, may I ask if any special consideration has recently been shown in regard to any suspected outbreak of this disease on *this* side of the Channel?'

He raised his hand; it held a noon edition of *The Bun*. We had thought it best to drop the paragraph out of the later ones. He would have continued, but something in a grey frock-coat roared and bounded on a bench opposite, and waved another *Bun*. It was Sir Thomas Ingell.

'As the owner of the herd so dastardly implicated—' His voice was drowned in shouts of 'Order!' – the Irish leading.

'What's wrong?' I asked Ollyett. 'He's got his hat on his head, hasn't he?'

'Yes, but his wrath should have been put as a question.'

'Arising out of that, Mr Speaker, Sirrr!' Sir Thomas bellowed through a lull, 'are you aware that – that all this is a conspiracy – part of a dastardly conspiracy to make Huckley ridiculous – to make *us* ridiculous? Part of a deep-laid plot to make *me* ridiculous, Mr Speaker, Sir!'

The man's face showed almost black against his white whiskers, and he struck out swimmingly with his arms. His vehemence puzzled and held the House for an instant, and the Speaker took advantage of it to lift his pack from Ireland to a new scent. He addressed Sir Thomas Ingell in tones of measured rebuke, meant also, I imagine, for the whole House, which lowered its hackles at the word. Then Pallant, shocked and pained: 'I can only express my profound surprise that in response to my simple question the honourable member should have thought fit to indulge in a personal attack. If I have in any way offended—'

Again the Speaker intervened, for it appeared that he regulated these matters.

He, too, expressed surprise, and Sir Thomas sat back in a hush of reprobation that seemed to have the chill of the centuries behind it. The Empire's work was resumed.

'Beautiful!' said I, and I felt hot and cold up my back.

'And now we'll publish his letter,' said Ollyett.

We did – on the heels of his carefully reported outburst. We made no comment. With that rare instinct for grasping the heart of a situation which is the mark of the Anglo-Saxon, all our contemporaries and, I should say, two-thirds of our correspondents demanded how such a person could be made more ridiculous than he had already proved himself to be. But beyond spelling his name 'Injle', we alone refused to hit a man when he was down.

'There's no need,' said Ollyett. 'The whole press is on the huckle from end to end.'

Even Woodhouse was a little astonished at the ease with which it had come about, and said as much.

'Rot!' said Ollyett. 'We haven't really begun. Huckley isn't news yet.'

'What do you mean?' said Woodhouse, who had grown to have great respect for his young but by no means distant connection.

'Mean? By the grace of God, Master Ridley, I mean to have it so that when Huckley turns over in its sleep,

Reuters and the Press Association jump out of bed to cable.' Then he went off at score about certain restorations in Huckley Church which, he said – and he seemed to spend his every week-end there – had been perpetrated by the Rector's predecessor, who had abolished a 'leper-window' or a 'squinch-hole' (whatever these may be) to institute a lavatory in the vestry. It did not strike me as stuff for which Reuters or the Press Association would lose much sleep, and I left him declaiming to Woodhouse about a fourteenth-century font which, he said, he had unearthed in the sexton's tool-shed.

My methods were more on the lines of peaceful penetration. An odd copy, in *The Bun*'s rag-and-bone library, of Hone's *Every-Day Book* had revealed to me the existence of a village dance founded, like all village dances, on Druidical mysteries connected with the Solar Solstice (which is always unchallengeable) and Midsummer Morning, which is dewy and refreshing to the London eye. For this I take no credit – Hone being a mine any one can work – but that I rechristened that dance, after I had revised it, 'The Gubby' is my title to immortal fame. It was still to be witnessed, I wrote, 'in all its poignant purity at Huckley, the last home of significant medieval survivals'; and I fell so in love with my creation that I kept it back for days, enamelling and burnishing.

'You'd better put it in,' said Ollyett at last. 'It's time we asserted ourselves again. The other fellows are beginning to poach. You saw that thing in the *Pinnacle* about Sir Thomas's Model Village? He must have got one of their chaps down to do it.'

''Nothing like the wounds of a friend,' I said. 'That account of the non-alcoholic pub alone was—'

'I liked the bit best about the white-tiled laundry and the Fallen Virgins who wash Sir Thomas's dress shirts. Our side couldn't come within a mile of that, you know. We haven't the proper flair for sexual slobber.'

'That's what I'm always saying,' I retorted. 'Leave 'em

alone. The other fellows are doing our work for us now. Besides I want to touch up my "Gubby Dance" a little more.'

'No. You'll spoil it. Let's shove it in today. For one thing it's Literature. I don't go in for compliments as you know, but, etc. etc.'

I had a healthy suspicion of young Ollyett in every aspect, but though I knew that I should have to pay for it, I fell to his flattery, and my priceless article on the 'Gubby Dance' appeared. Next Saturday he asked me to to bring out *The Bun* in his absence, which I naturally assumed would be connected with the little maroon side-car. I was wrong.

On the following Monday I glanced at *The Cake* at breakfast-time to make sure, as usual, of her inferiority to my beloved but unremunerative *Bun*. I opened on a heading: 'The Village that Voted the Earth was Flat'. I read . . . I read that the Geoplanarian Society – a society devoted to the proposition that the earth is flat – had held its Annual Banquet and Exercises at Huckley on Saturday, when after convincing addresses, amid scenes of the greatest enthusiasm, Huckley village had decided by an unanimous vote of 438 that the earth was flat. I do not remember that I breathed again till I had finished the two columns of description that followed. Only one man could have written them. They were flawless – crisp, nervous, austere yet human, poignant, vital, arresting – most distinctly arresting – dynamic enough to shift a city – and quotable by whole sticks at a time. And there was a leader, a grave and poised leader, which tore me in two with mirth, until I remembered that I had been left out – infamously and unjustifiably dropped. I went to Ollyett's rooms. He was breakfasting, and, to do him justice, looked conscience-stricken.

'It wasn't my fault,' he began. 'It was Bat Masquerier. I swear *I* would have asked you to come if—'

'Never mind that,' I said. 'It's the best bit of work you've ever done or will do. Did any of it happen?'

'Happen? Heavens! D'you think even *I* could have invented it?'

'Is it exclusive to *The Cake*?' I cried.

'It cost Bat Masquerier two thousand,' Ollyett replied. 'D'you think he'd let anyone else in on that? But I give you my sacred word I knew nothing about it till he asked me to come down and cover it. He had Huckley posted in three colours, "The Geoplanarians' Annual Banquet and Exercises". Yes, he invented "Geoplanarians". He wanted Huckley to think it meant aeroplanes. Yes, I know that there is a real Society that thinks the world's flat – they ought to be grateful for the lift – but Bat made his own. He did! He created the whole show, I tell you. He swept out half his Halls for the job. Think of that – on a Saturday! They – we went down in motor char-à-bancs – three of 'em – one pink, one primrose, and one forget-me-not blue – twenty people in each one and "The Earth *is* Flat" on each side and across the back. I went with Teddy Rickets and Lafone from the Trefoil, and both the Silhouette Sisters, and – wait a minute! – the Crossleigh Trio. You know the Every-Day Dramas Trio at the Jocunda – Ada Crossleigh, "Bunt" Crossleigh, and little Victorine? Them. And there was Hoke Ramsden, the lightning-change chap in *Morgiana and Drexel* – and there was Billy Turpeen. Yes, you know him! The North London Star. "I'm the Referee that got himself disliked at Blackheath." *That* chap! And there was Mackaye – that one-eyed Scotch fellow that all Glasgow is crazy about. Talk of subordinating yourself for Art's sake! Mackaye was the earnest inquirer who got converted at the end of the meeting. And there was quite a lot of girls I didn't know, and – oh, yes – there was 'Dal! 'Dal Benzaguen herself! We sat together, going and coming. She's all the darling there ever was. She sent you her love, and she told me to tell you that she won't forget about Nellie

Farren. She says you've given her an ideal to work for. She? Oh, she was the Lady Secretary to the Geoplanarians, of course. I forget who were in the other brakes – provincial stars mostly – but they played up gorgeously. The art of the music-hall's changed since your day. They didn't overdo it a bit. You see, people who believe the earth is flat don't dress quite like other people. You may have noted that I hinted at that in my account. It's a rather flat-fronted Ionic style – neo-Victorian, except for the bustles, 'Dal told me – but 'Dal looked heavenly in it! So did little Victorine. And there was a girl in the blue brake – she's a provincial – but she's coming to town this winter and she'll knock 'em – Winnie Deans. Remember that! She told Huckley how she had suffered for the Cause as a governess in a rich family where they believed that the world is round, and how she threw up her job sooner than teach immoral geography. That was at the overflow meeting outside the Baptist chapel. She knocked 'em to sawdust! We must look out for Winnie . . . But Lafone! Lafone was beyond everything. Impact, personality – conviction – the whole bag o'tricks! He sweated conviction. Gad, he convinced *me* while he was speaking! (Him? He was President of the Geoplanarians, of course. Haven't you read my account?) It *is* an infernally plausible theory. After all, no one has actually proved the earth is round, have they?'

'Never mind the earth. What about Huckley?'

'Oh, Huckley got tight. That's the worst of these model villages if you let 'em smell fire-water. There's one alcoholic pub in the place that Sir Thomas can't get rid of. Bat made it his base. He sent down the banquet in two motor lorries – dinner for five hundred and drinks for ten thousand. Huckley voted all right. Don't you make any mistake about that. No vote, no dinner. An unanimous vote – exactly as I've said. At least, the Rector and the Doctor were the only dissentients. We didn't count them. Oh yes, Sir Thomas was there. He came and grinned at us through his park gates. He'll grin worse today. There's an aniline dye that you rub through a stencil-plate that eats about a foot into any stone and wears good to the last. Bat had both the lodge-gates stencilled "The Earth *is* flat!" and all the barns and walls they could get at . . . Oh Lord, but Huckley was drunk! We had to fill 'em up to make 'em forgive us for not being aeroplanes. Unthankful yokels! D'you realise that Emperors couldn't have commanded the talent Bat decanted on 'em? Why, 'Dal alone was . . . And by eight o'clock not even a bit of paper left! The whole show packed up and gone, and Huckley hoo-raying for the earth being flat.'

'Very good,' I began. 'I am, as you know, a one-third proprietor of *The Bun*.'

'I didn't forget that,' Ollyett interrupted. 'That was uppermost in my mind all the time. I've got a special account for *The Bun* today – it's an idyll – and just to show how I thought of you, I told 'Dal, coming home, about your Gubby Dance, and she told Winnie. Winnie came back in our char-à-banc. After a bit we had to get out and dance it in a field. It's quite a dance the way we did it – and Lafone invented a sort of gorilla lockstep procession at the end. Bat had sent down a film-chap on the chance of getting something. He was the son of a clergyman – a most dynamic personality. He said there isn't anything for the cinema in meetings *qua* meetings – they lack action. Films are a branch of art by themselves. But he went wild over the Gubby. He said it was like Peter's vision at Joppa. He took about a million feet of it. Then I photoed it exclusive for *The Bun*. I've sent 'em in already, only remember we must eliminate Winnie's left leg in the first figure. It's too arresting . . . And there you are! But I tell you I'm afraid of Bat. That man's the Personal Devil. He did it all. He didn't even come down himself. He said he'd distract his people.'

'Why didn't he ask me to come?' I persisted.

'Because he said you'd distract me. He said he wanted

my brains on ice. He got 'em. I believe it's the best thing I've ever done.' He reached for *The Cake* and re-read it luxuriously. 'Yes, out and away the best – supremely quotable,' he concluded, and – after another survey – 'By God, what a genius I was yesterday!'

I would have been angry, but I had not the time. That morning, Press agencies grovelled to me in *The Bun* office for leave to use certain photos, which, they understood, I controlled, of a certain village dance. When I had sent the fifth man away on the edge of tears, my self-respect came back a little. Then there was *The Bun*'s poster to get out. Art being elimination, I fined it down to two words (one too many, as it proved) – 'The Gubby!' in red, at which our manager protested; but by five o'clock he told me that I was *the* Napoleon of Fleet Street. Ollyett's account in *The Bun* of the Geoplanarians' Exercises and Love Feast lacked the supreme shock of his version in *The Cake*, but it bruised more; while the photos of 'The Gubby' (which, with Winnie's left leg, was why I had set the doubtful press to work so early) were beyond praise and, next day, beyond price. But even then I did not understand.

A week later, I think it was, Bat Masquerier telephoned me to come to the Trefoil.

'It's your turn now,' he said. 'I'm not asking Ollyett. Come to the stage-box.'

I went, and, as Bat's guest, was received as Royalty is not. We sat well back and looked out on the packed thousands. It was *Morgiana and Drexel*, that fluid and electric review which Bat – though he gave Lafone the credit – really created.

'Ye-es.' said Bat dreamily, after Morgiana had given 'the nasty jar' to the Forty Thieves in their forty oil 'combinations'. 'As you say, I've got 'em and I can hold 'em. What a man does doesn't matter much; and how he does it don't matter either. It's the *when* – the psychological moment. 'Press can't make up for it; money can't;

brains can't. A lot's luck, but all the rest is genius. I'm not speaking about *My* people now. I'm talking of myself.'

Then 'Dal – she was the only one who dared – knocked at the door and stood behind us all alive and panting as Morgiana. Lafone was carrying the police-court scene, and the house was ripped up crossways with laughter.

'Ah! Tell a fellow now,' she asked me for the twentieth time, 'did you love Nellie Farren when you were young?'

'Did we love her?' I answered. ' "If the earth and the sky and the sea" – There were three million of us, 'Dal, and we worshipped her.'

'How did she get it across?' 'Dal went on.

'She was Nellie. The houses used to coo over her when she came on.'

'I've had a good deal, but I've never been cooed over yet,' said 'Dal wistfully.

'It isn't the how, it's the when,' Bat repeated. 'Ah!'

He leaned forward as the house began to rock and peal full-throatedly. 'Dal fled. A sinuous and silent procession was filing into the police-court to a scarcely audible accompaniment. It was dressed – but the world and all its picture-palaces know how it was dressed. It danced and it danced, and it danced the dance which bit all humanity in the leg for half a year, and it wound up with the lockstep finale that mowed the house down in swathes, sobbing and aching. Somebody in the gallery moaned, 'Oh Gord, the Gubby!' and we heard the word run like a shudder, for they had not a full breath left among them. Then 'Dal came on, an electric star in her dark hair, the diamonds flashing in her three-inch heels – a vision that made no sign for thirty counted seconds while the police-court scene dissolved behind her into Morgiana's Manicure Palace, and they recovered themselves. The star on her forehead went out and a soft light bathed her as she took – slowly, slowly to the croon of adoring strings – the eighteen paces forward. We saw her first as a queen alone; next as a queen for the first time conscious of her subjects, and at the end, when her hands fluttered, as a woman delighted, awed not a little, but transfigured and illuminated with sheer, compelling affection and goodwill. I caught the broken mutter of welcome – the coo which is more than tornadoes of applause. It died and rose and died again lovingly.

'She's got it across,' Bat whispered. 'I've never seen her like this. I told her to light up the star, but I was wrong, and she knew it. She's an artist.'

''Dal, you darling!' someone spoke, not loudly but it carried through the house.

'Thank *you*!' 'Dal answered, and in that broken tone one heard the last fetter riveted. 'Good evening, boys! I've just come from – now – where the dooce was it I have come from?' She turned to the impassive files of the Gubby dancers, and went on: 'Ah, so good of you to remind me, you dear, bun-faced things. I've just come from the village – The Village that Voted the Earth was Flat.'

She swept into that song with the full orchestra. It devastated the habitable earth for the next six months. Imagine, then, what its rage and pulse must have been at the incandescent hour of its birth! She only gave the chorus once. At the end of the second verse 'Are you *with* me, boys?' she cried, and the house tore it clean away from her – '*Earth* was flat – *Earth* was flat. Flat as my hat – Flatter than that' – drowning all but the bassoons and double-basses that marked the word.

'Wonderful,' I said to Bat. 'And it's only "Nuts in May" with variations.'

'Yes – but *I* did the variations,' he replied.

At the last verse she gestured to Carlini the conductor, who threw her up his baton. She caught it with a boy's ease. 'Are you *with* me?' she cried once more, and – the maddened house behind her – abolished all the instruments except the guttural belch of the double-basses on '*Earth*'- 'The village that voted the *Earth* was flat – *Earth* was flat!' It was delirium. Then she picked up the Gubby dancers and led them in a clattering improvised lockstep thrice round the stage till her last kick sent her diamond-hilted shoe catherine-wheeling to the electrolier.

I saw the forest of hands raised to catch it, heard the roaring and stamping pass through hurricanes to full typhoon; heard the song, pinned down by the faithful double-basses as the bull-dog pins down the bellowing bull, overbear even those; till at last the curtain fell and Bat took me round to her dressing-room, where she lay spent after her seventh call. Still the song, through all those white-washed walls, shook the reinforced concrete of the Trefoil as steam pile-drivers shake the flanks of a dock.

'I'm all out – first time in my life. Ah! Tell a fellow now, did I get it across?' she whispered huskily.

'You know you did,' I replied as she dipped her nose deep in a beaker of barley-water. 'They cooed over you.'

Bat nodded. 'And poor Nellie's dead – in Africa, ain't it?'

'I hope I'll die before they stop cooing,' said 'Dal.

' "*Earth* was flat – *Earth* was flat!" ' Now it was more like mine-pumps in flood.

'They'll have the house down if you don't take another,' someone called.

'Bless 'em!' said 'Dal, and went out for her eighth, when in the face of that cataract she said yawning, 'I don't know how *you* feel, children, but *I*'m dead. You be quiet.'

'Hold a minute,' said Bat to me. 'I've got to hear how it went in the provinces. Winnie Deans had it in Manchester, and Ramsden at Glasgow – and there are all the films too. I had rather a heavy week-end.'

The telephones presently reassured him.

'It'll do,' said he. 'And *he* said my home address was Jerusalem.' He left me humming the refrain of 'The Holy City'. Like Ollyett I found myself afraid of that man.

When I got out into the street and met the disgorging picture-palaces capering on the pavements and humming it (for he had put the gramophones on with the films), and when I saw far to the south the red electrics flash 'Gubby' across the Thames, I feared more than ever.

A few days passed which were like nothing except, perhaps, a suspense of fever in which the sick man perceives the search-lights of the world's assembled navies in act to converge on one minute fragment of wreckage – one only in all the black and agony-strewn sea. Then those beams focused themselves. Earth as we knew it – the full circuit of our orb – laid the weight of its impersonal and searing curiosity on this Huckley which had voted that it was flat. It asked for news about Huckley – where and what it might be, and how it talked – it knew how it danced – and how it thought in its wonderful soul. And then, in all the zealous, merciless press, Huckley was laid out for it to look at, as a drop of pond water is exposed on the sheet of a magic-lantern show. But Huckley's sheet was only coterminous with the use of type among mankind. For the precise moment that was necessary, Fate ruled it that there should be nothing of first importance in the world's idle eye. One atrocious murder, a political crisis, an incautious or heady continental statesman, the mere catarrh of a king, would have wiped out the significance of our message, as a passing cloud annuls the urgent helio. But it was halcyon weather in every respect. Ollyett and I did not need to lift our little fingers any more than the Alpine climber whose last sentence has unkeyed the arch of the avalanche. The thing roared and pulverised and swept beyond eyesight all by itself – all by itself. And once well away, the fall of kingdoms could not have diverted it.

Ours is, after all, a kindly earth. While The Song ran and raped it with the cataleptic kick of 'Ta-ra-ra-boom-de-ay', multiplied by the West African significance of 'Everybody's doing it', plus twice the infernal elementality of a certain tune in *Dona et Gamma*; when for all practical purposes, literary, dramatic, artistic, social, municipal, political, commercial, and administrative, the Earth *was* flat, the Rector of Huckley wrote to us – again as a lover of accuracy – to point out that the Huckley vote on 'the alleged flatness of this scene of our labours here below' was *not* unanimous; he and the doctor having voted against it. And the great Baron Reuter himself (I am sure it could have been none other) flashed that letter in full to the front, back, and both wings of this scene of our labours. For Huckley was News. *The Bun* also contributed a photograph which cost me some trouble to fake.

'We are a vital nation,' said Ollyett while we were discussing affairs at a Bat dinner. 'Only an Englishman could have written that letter at this present juncture.'

'It reminded me of a tourist in the Cave of the Winds under Niagara. Just one figure in a mackintosh. But perhaps you saw our photo?' I said proudly.

'Yes,' Bat replied. 'I've been to Niagara, too. And how's Huckley taking it?'

'They don't quite understand, of course,' said Ollyett. 'But it's bringing pots of money into the place. Ever since the motor-bus excursions were started—'

'I didn't know they had been,' said Pallant.

'Oh yes. Motor char-à-bancs – uniformed guides and key-bugles included. They're getting a bit fed up with the tune there nowadays,' Ollyett added.

'They play it under his windows, don't they?' Bat asked. 'He can't stop the right of way across his park.'

'He cannot,' Ollyett answered. 'By the way, Woodhouse, I've bought that font for you from the sexton. I paid fifteen pounds for it.'

'What am I supposed to do with it?' asked Woodhouse.

'You give it to the Victoria and Albert Museum. It is fourteenth-century work all right. You can trust me.'

'Is it worth it – now?' said Pallant. 'Not that I'm weakening, but merely as a matter of tactics?'

'But this is true,' said Ollyett. 'Besides, it is my hobby, I always wanted to be an architect. I'll attend to it myself.

It's too serious for *The Bun* and miles too good for *The Cake*.'

He broke ground in a ponderous architectural weekly, which had never heard of Huckley. There was no passion in his statement, but mere fact backed by a wide range of authorities. He established beyond doubt that the old font at Huckley had been thrown out, on Sir Thomas's instigation, twenty years ago, to make room for a new one of Bath stone adorned with Limoges enamels; and that it had lain ever since in a corner of the sexton's shed. He proved, with learned men to support him, that there was only one other font in all England to compare with it. So Woodhouse bought it and presented it to a grateful South Kensington which said it would see the earth still flatter before it returned the treasure to purblind Huckley. Bishops by the benchful and most of the Royal Academy, not to mention 'Margaritas ante Porcos', wrote fervently to the papers. *Punch* based a political cartoon on it; the *Times* a third leader, 'The Lust of Newness'; and the *Spectator* a scholarly and delightful middle, 'Village Hausmania.' The vast amused outside world said in all its tongues and types: 'Of course! This is just what Huckley would do!' And neither Sir Thomas nor the Rector nor the sexton nor any one else wrote to deny it.

'You see,' said Ollyett, 'this is much more of a blow to Huckley than it looks – because every word of it's true. Your Gubby dance was inspiration, I admit, but it hadn't its roots in—'

'Two hemispheres and four continents so far,' I pointed out.

'Its roots in the hearts of Huckley was what I was going to say. Why don't you ever come down and look at the place? You've never seen it since we were stopped there.'

'I've only my week-ends free,' I said, 'and you seem to spend yours there pretty regularly – with the side-car. I was afraid—'

'Oh, *that's* all right,' he said cheerily. 'We're quite an

old engaged couple now. As a matter of fact, it happened after "the gravid polled Angus" business. Come along this Saturday. Woodhouse says he'll run us down after lunch. He wants to see Huckley too.'

Pallant could not accompany us, but Bat took his place.

'It's odd,' said Bat, 'that none of us except Ollyett has ever set eyes on Huckley since that time. That's what I always tell My people. Local colour is all right after you've got your idea. Before that, it's a mere nuisance.' He regaled us on the way down with panoramic views of the success – geographical and financial – of 'The Gubby' and The Song.

'By the way,' said he, 'I've assigned 'Dal all the gramophone rights of "The Earth". She's a born artist. 'Hadn't sense enough to hit me for triple-dubs the morning after. She'd have taken it out in coos.'

'Bless her! And what'll she make out of the gramophone rights?' I asked.

'Lord knows!' he replied. 'I've made fifty-four thousand my little end of the business, and it's only just beginning. Hear *that*!'

A shell-pink motor-brake roared up behind us to the music on a key-bugle of 'The Village that Voted the Earth was Flat'. In a few minutes we overtook another, in natural wood, whose occupants were singing it through their noses.

'I don't know that agency. It must be Cook's,' said Ollyett. 'They *do* suffer.' We were never out of ear-shot of the tune the rest of the way to Huckley.

Though I knew it would be so, I was disappointed with the actual aspect of the spot we had – it is not too much to say – created in the face of the nations. The alcoholic pub; the village green; the Baptist chapel; the church; the sexton's shed; the Rectory whence the so-wonderful letters had come; Sir Thomas's park gate-pillars still violently declaring 'The Earth *is* flat', were as mean, as average, as ordinary as the photograph of a room where a murder has been committed. Ollyett, who, of course, knew the place specially well, made the most of it to us. Bat, who had employed it as a back-cloth to one of his own dramas, dismissed it as a thing used and emptied, but Woodhouse expressed my feelings when he said: 'Is that all – after all we've done?'

'*I* know,' said Ollyett soothingly. ' "Like that strange song I heard Apollo sing: When Ilion like a mist rose into towers." I've felt the same sometimes, though it has been paradise for me. But they *do* suffer.'

The fourth brake in thirty minutes had just turned into Sir Thomas's park to tell the Hall that 'The *Earth* was flat'; a knot of obviously American tourists were kodaking his lodge gates; while the tea-shop opposite the lych-gate was full of people buying postcards of the old font as it had lain twenty years in the sexton's shed. We went to the alcoholic pub and congratulated the proprietor.

'It's bringin' money to the place,' said he. 'But in a sense you can buy money too dear. It isn't doin' us any good. People are laughin' at us. That's what they're doin' . . . Now, with regard to that Vote of ours you may have heard talk about . . .'

'For Gorze sake, chuck that votin' business,' cried an elderly man at the door. 'Money-gettin' or no money-gettin', we're fed up with it.'

'Well, I do think,' said the publican, shifting his ground, 'I do think Sir Thomas might ha' managed better in some things.'

'He tole me,' – the elderly man shouldered his way to the bar – 'he tole me twenty years ago to take an' lay that font in my tool-shed. He *tole* me so himself. An' now, after twenty years, me own wife makin' me out little better than the common 'angman!'

'That's the sexton,' the publican explained. 'His good lady sells the postcards – if you 'aven't already got some. But we feel Sir Thomas might ha' done better.'

'What's he got to do with it?' said Woodhouse.

'There's nothin' we can trace 'ome to 'im in so many words, but we think he might 'ave saved us the font business. Now, in regard to that votin' business—'

'Chuck it! Oh, chuck it!' the sexton roared, 'or you'll 'ave me cuttin' my throat at cock-crow. 'Ere's another parcel of fun-makers!'

A motor-brake had pulled up at the door and a multitude of men and women immediately descended. We went out to look. They bore rolled banners, a reading-desk in three pieces, and, I specially noticed, a collapsible harmonium, such as is used on ships at sea.

'Salvation Army?' I said, though I saw no uniforms.

Two of them unfurled a banner between poles which bore the legend: 'The Earth *is* flat'. Woodhouse and I turned to Bat. He shook his head. 'No, no! Not me . . . If I had only seen their costumes in advance!'

'Good Lord!' said Ollyett. 'It's the genuine Society!'

The company advanced on the green with the precision of people well broke to these movements. Scene-shifters could not have been quicker with the three-piece rostrum, nor stewards with the harmonium. Almost before its cross-legs had been kicked into their catches, certainly before the tourists by the lodge-gates had begun to move over, a woman sat down to it and struck up a hymn:

Hear ther truth our tongues are telling,
  Spread ther light from shore to shore,
God hath given man a dwelling
  Flat and flat for evermore.

When ther Primal Dark retreated,
  When ther deeps were undesigned,
He with rule and level meted
  Habitation for mankind!

I saw sick envy on Bat's face. 'Curse Nature,' he muttered. 'She gets ahead of you every time. To think *I* forgot hymns and a harmonium!'

Then came the chorus:

Hear ther truth our tongues are telling,
  Spread ther light from shore to shore –
Oh, be faithful! Oh, be truthful!
  Earth is flat for evermore.

They sang several verses with the fervour of Christians awaiting their lions. Then there were growlings in the air. The sexton, embraced by the landlord, two-stepped out of the pub door. Each was trying to outroar the other. 'Apologising in advance for what he says,' the landlord shouted: 'You'd better go away' (here the sexton began to speak words). 'This isn't the time nor yet the place for – for any more o' this chat.'

The crowd thickened. I saw the village police-sergeant come out of his cottage buckling his belt.

'But surely,' said the woman at the harmonium, 'there must be some mistake. We are not suffragettes.'

'Damn it! They'd be a change,' cried the sexton. 'You get out of this! Don't talk! *I* can't stand it for one! Get right out, or we'll font you!'

The crowd which was being recruited from every house in sight echoed the invitation. The sergeant pushed forward. A man beside the reading-desk said: 'But surely we are among dear friends and sympathisers. Listen to me for a moment.'

It was the moment that a passing char-à-banc chose to strike into The Song. The effect was instantaneous. Bat, Ollyett, and I, who by divers roads have learned the psychology of crowds, retreated towards the tavern door. Woodhouse, the newspaper proprietor, anxious, I presume, to keep touch with the public, dived into the thick of it. Everyone else told the Society to go away at once. When the lady at the harmonium (I began to understand why it is sometimes necessary to kill women) pointed at the stencilled park pillars and called them 'the cromlechs of our common faith', there was a snarl and a rush. The police-sergeant checked it, but advised the Society to keep on going. The Society withdrew into the brake fighting, as it were, a rearguard action of oratory up each step. The collapsed harmonium was hauled in last, and with the perfect unreason of crowds, they cheered it loudly, till the chauffeur slipped in his clutch and sped away. Then the crowd broke up, congratulating all concerned except the sexton, who was held to have disgraced his office by having sworn at ladies. We strolled across the green towards Woodhouse, who was talking to the police-sergeant near the park-gates. We were not twenty yards from him when we saw Sir Thomas Ingell emerge from the lodge and rush furiously at Woodhouse with an uplifted stick, at the same time shrieking: 'I'll teach you to laugh, you—' but Ollyett has the record of the language. By the time we reached them, Sir Thomas was on the ground; Woodhouse, very white, held the walking-stick and was saying to the sergeant:

'I give this person in charge for assault.'

'But, good Lord!' said the sergeant, whiter than Woodhouse. 'It's Sir Thomas.'

'Whoever it is, it isn't fit to be at large,' said Woodhouse. The crowd suspecting something wrong began to reassemble, and all the English horror of a row in public moved us, headed by the sergeant, inside the lodge. We shut both park-gates and lodge-door.

'You saw the assault, sergeant,' Woodhouse went on. 'You can testify I used no more force than was necessary to protect myself. You can testify that I have not even damaged this person's property. (Here! take your stick, you!) You heard the filthy language he used.'

'I – I can't say I did,' the sergeant stammered.

'Oh, but *we* did!' said Ollyett, and repeated it, to the apron-veiled horror of the lodge-keeper's wife.

Sir Thomas on a hard kitchen chair began to talk. He said he had 'stood enough of being photographed like a wild beast', and expressed loud regret that he had not killed 'that man', who was 'conspiring with the sergeant to laugh at him'.

''Ad you ever seen 'im before, Sir Thomas?' the sergeant asked.

'No! But it's time an example was made here. I've never seen the sweep in my life.'

I think it was Bat Masquerier's magnetic eye that recalled the past to him, for his face changed and his jaw dropped. 'But I have!' he groaned. 'I remember now.'

Here a writhing man entered by the back door. He was, he said, the village solicitor. I do not assert that he licked Woodhouse's boots, but we should have respected him more if he had and been done with it. His notion was that the matter could be accommodated, arranged and compromised for gold, and yet more gold. The sergeant thought so too. Woodhouse undeceived them both. To the sergeant he said, 'Will you or will you not enter the charge!' To the village solicitor he gave the name of his lawyers, at which the man wrung his hands and cried, 'Oh, Sir T., Sir T.!' in a miserable falsetto, for it was a Bat Masquerier of a firm. They conferred together in tragic whispers.

'I don't dive after Dickens,' said Ollyett to Bat and me by the window, 'but every time *I* get into a row I notice the police-court always fills up with his characters.'

'I've noticed that too,' said Bat. 'But the odd thing is you mustn't give the public straight Dickens – not in My business. I wonder why that is.'

Then Sir Thomas got his second wind and cursed the day that he, or it may have been we, were born. I feared that though he was a Radical he might apologise and, since he was an M.P., might lie his way out of the difficulty. But he was utterly and truthfully beside himself. He asked foolish questions – such as what we were doing in the village at all, and how much blackmail Woodhouse expected to make out of him. But neither Woodhouse nor the sergeant nor the writhing solicitor listened. The upshot of their talk, in the chimney-corner, was that Sir Thomas stood engaged to appear next Monday before his brother magistrates on charges of assault, disorderly conduct, and language calculated, etc. Ollyett was specially careful about the language.

Then we left. The village looked very pretty in the late light – pretty and tuneful as a nest of nightingales.

'You'll turn up on Monday, I hope,' said Woodhouse, when we reached town. That was his only allusion to the affair.

So we turned up – through a world still singing that the Earth was flat – at the little clay-coloured market-town with the large Corn Exchange and the small Jubilee memorial. We had some difficulty in getting seats in the court. Woodhouse's imported London lawyer was a man of commanding personality, with a voice trained to convey blasting imputations by tone. When the case was called, he rose and stated his client's intention not to proceed with the charge. His client, he went on to say, had not entertained, and, of course, in the circumstances could not have entertained, any suggestion of accepting on behalf of public charities any moneys that might have been offered to him on the part of Sir Thomas's estate. At the same time, no one acknowledged more sincerely than his client the spirit in which those offers had been made by those entitled to make them. But, as a matter of fact – here he became the man of the world colloguing with his equals – certain – er – details had come to his client's knowledge *since* the lamentable outburst, which . . . He shrugged his shoulders. Nothing was served by going into them, but he ventured to say that, had those painful circumstances only been known earlier, his client would – again 'of course' – never have dreamed – A gesture concluded the sentence, and the ensnared Bench looked at Sir Thomas with new and withdrawing eyes. Frankly, as they could see, it would be nothing less than cruelty to proceed further with this – er – unfortunate affair. He asked leave, therefore, to withdraw the charge *in toto*, and at the same time to express his client's deepest sympathy with all who had been in any way distressed, as his client had been, by the fact and the publicity of proceedings which he could, of course, again assure them that his client would never have dreamed of instituting if, as he hoped he had made plain, certain facts had been before his client at the time when . . . But he had said enough. For his fee it seemed to me that he had.

Heaven inspired Sir Thomas's lawyer – all of a sweat lest his client's language should come out – to rise up and thank him. Then, Sir Thomas – not yet aware what leprosy had been laid upon him, but grateful to escape on any terms – followed suit. He was heard in interested silence, and people drew back a pace as Gehazi passed forth.

'You hit hard,' said Bat to Woodhouse afterwards. 'His own people think he's mad.'

'You don't say so? I'll show you some of his letters tonight at dinner,' he replied.

He brought them to the Red Amber Room of the Chop Suey. We forgot to be amazed, as till then we had been amazed, over the Song or 'The Gubby', or the full tide of Fate that seemed to run only for our sakes. It did not even interest Ollyett that the verb 'to huckle' had passed into the English leader-writers' language. We were studying the interior of a soul, flash-lighted to its grimiest corner by the dread of 'losing its position'.

'And then it thanked you, didn't it, for dropping the case?' said Pallant.

'Yes, and it sent me a telegram to confirm.' Woodhouse turned to Bat. 'Now d'you think I hit too hard?' he asked.

'No-o!' said Bat. 'After all – I'm talking of every one's business now – one can't ever do anything in Art that comes up to nature in any game in life. Just think how this thing has—'

'Just let me run through that little case of yours again,'

said Pallant, and picked up *The Bun* which had it set out in full.

'Any chance of 'Dal looking in on us tonight?' Ollyett began.

'She's occupied with her Art too,' Bat answered bitterly. 'What's the use of Art! Tell me, someone!' A barrel-organ outside promptly pointed out that the *Earth* was flat. 'The gramophone's killing street organs, but I let loose a hundred-and-seventy-four of those hurdygurdys twelve hours after The Song,' said Bat. 'Not counting the Provinces.' His face brightened a little.

'Look here!' said Pallant over the paper. 'I don't suppose you or those asinine JP's knew it – but your lawyer ought to have known that you've all put your foot in it most confoundedly over this assault case.'

'What's the matter?' said Woodhouse.

'It's ludicrous. It's insane. There isn't two penn'orth of legality in the whole thing. Of course, you could have withdrawn the charge, but the way you went about it is childish – besides being illegal. What on earth was the Chief Constable thinking of?'

'Oh, he was a friend of Sir Thomas's. They all were for that matter,' I replied.

'He ought to be hanged. So ought the Chairman of the Bench. I'm talking as a lawyer now.'

'Why, what have we been guilty of? Misprision of treason or compounding a felony – or what?' said Ollyett.

'I'll tell you later,' Pallant went back to the paper with knitted brows, smiling unpleasantly from time to time. At last he laughed.

'Thank you!' he said to Woodhouse. 'It ought to be pretty useful – for us.'

'What d'you mean?' said Ollyett.

'For our side. They are all Rads who are mixed up in this – from the Chief Constable down. There must be a Question. There must be a Question.'

'Yes, but I wanted the charge withdrawn in my own way,' Woodhouse insisted.

'That's nothing to do with the case. It's the legality of your silly methods. You wouldn't understand if I talked till morning.' He began to pace the room, his hands behind him. 'I wonder if I can get it through our Whip's thick head that it's a chance . . . That comes of stuffing the Bench with radical thinkers,' he muttered.

'Oh, sit down!' said Woodhouse.

'Where's your lawyer to be found now?' he jerked out.

'At the Trefoil,' said Bat promptly. 'I gave him the stage-box for tonight. He's an artist too.'

'Then I'm going to see him,' said Pallant. 'Properly handled this ought to be a godsend for our side.' He withdrew without apology.

'Certainly, this thing keeps on opening up, and up,' I remarked inanely.

'It's beyond me!' said Bat. 'I don't think if I'd known I'd have ever . . . Yes, I would, though. He said my home address was—'

'It was his tone – his tone!' Ollyett almost shouted. Woodhouse said nothing, but his face whitened as he brooded.

'Well, any way,' Bat went on, 'I'm glad I always believed in God and Providence and all those things. Else I should lose my nerve. We've put it over the whole world – the full extent of the geographical globe. We couldn't stop it if we wanted to now. It's got to burn itself out. I'm not in charge any more. What d'you expect'll happen next. Angels?'

I expected nothing. Nothing that I expected approached what I got. Politics are not my concern, but, for the moment, since it seemed that they were going to 'huckle' with the rest, I took an interest in them. They impressed me as a dog's life without a dog's decencies, and I was confirmed in this when an unshaven and unwashen Pallant called on me at ten o'clock one morning, begging for a bath and a couch.

'Bail too?' I asked. He was in evening dress and his eyes were sunk feet in his head.

'No,' he said hoarsely. 'All night sitting. Fifteen divisions. 'Nother tonight. Your place was nearer than mine, so—' He began to undress in the hall.

When he awoke at one o'clock he gave me lurid accounts of what he said was history, but which was obviously collective hysteria. There had been a political crisis. He and his fellow MPs had 'done things' – I never quite got at the things – for eighteen hours on end, and the pitiless Whips were even then at the telephones to herd 'em up to another dog-fight. So he snorted and grew hot all over again while he might have been resting.

'I'm going to pitch in my question about that miscarriage of justice at Huckley this afternoon, if you care to listen to it,' he said. 'It'll be absolutely thrown away – in our present state. I told 'em so; but it's my only chance for weeks. P'raps Woodhouse would like to come.'

'I'm sure he would. Anything to do with Huckley interests us,' I said.

'It'll miss fire, I'm afraid. Both sides are absolutely cooked. The present situation has been working up for some time. You see the row was bound to come, etc. etc.,' and he flew off the handle once more.

I telephoned to Woodhouse, and we went to the House together. It was a dull, sticky afternoon with thunder in the air. For some reason or other, each side was determined to prove its virtue and endurance to the utmost. I heard men snarling about it all round me. 'If they won't spare us, we'll show 'em no mercy.' 'Break the brutes up from the start. They can't stand late hours.' 'Come on! No shirking! I know *you*'ve had a Turkish bath,' were some of the sentences I caught on our way. The House was packed already, and one could feel the negative electricity of a jaded crowd wrenching at one's own nerves, and depressing the afternoon soul.

'This is bad!' Woodhouse whispered. 'There'll be a row before they've finished. Look at the Front Benches!' And he pointed out little personal signs by which I was to know that each man was on edge. He might have spared himself. The House was ready to snap before a bone had been thrown. A sullen minister rose to reply to a staccato question. His supporters cheered defiantly. 'None o' that! None o' that!' came from the Back Benches. I saw the Speaker's face stiffen like the face of a helmsman as he humours a hard-mouthed yacht after a sudden following sea. The trouble was barely met in time. There came a fresh, apparently causeless gust a few minutes later – savage, threatening, but futile. It died out – one could hear the sigh – in sudden wrathful realisation of the dreary hours ahead, and the ship of state drifted on.

Then Pallant – and the raw House winced at the torture of his voice – rose. It was a twenty-line question, studded with legal technicalities. The gist of it was that he wished to know whether the appropriate Minister was aware that there had been a grave miscarriage of justice on such and such a date, at such and such a place, before such and such justices of the peace, in regard to a case which arose—

I heard one desperate, weary 'damn!' float up from the pit of that torment. Pallant sawed on '—out of certain events which occurred at the village of Huckley.'

The House came to attention with a parting of the lips like a hiccough, and it flashed through my mind . . . Pallant repeated, 'Huckley. The village—'

'That voted the *Earth* was flat.' A single voice from a Back Bench sang it once like a lone frog in a far pool.

'*Earth* was flat,' croaked another voice opposite.

'*Earth* was flat.' There were several. Then several more.

It was, you understand, the collective, over-strained nerve of the House, snapping, strand by strand to various notes, as the hawser parts from its moorings.

'The Village that voted the *Earth* was flat.' The tune was beginning to shape itself. More voices were raised and feet began to beat time. Even so it did not occur to me that the thing would—

'The Village that voted the *Earth* was flat!' It was easier now to see who were not singing. There were still a few. Of a sudden (and this proves the fundamental instability of the cross-bench mind) a cross-bencher leaped on to his seat and there played an imaginary double-bass with tremendous maestro-like wagglings of the elbow.

The last strand parted. The ship of state drifted out helpless on the rocking tide of melody.

'The Village that voted the *Earth* was flat!
The Village that voted the *Earth* was flat!'

The Irish first conceived the idea of using their order-papers as funnels wherewith to reach the correct '*vroom – vroom*' on '*Earth*'. Labour, always conservative and respectable at a crisis, stood out longer than any other section, but when it came in it was howling syndicalism. Then, without distinction of Party, fear of constituents, desire for office, or hope of emolument, the House sang at the tops and at the bottoms of their voices, swaying their stale bodies and epileptically beating with their swelled feet. They sang 'The Village that voted the *Earth* was flat': first, because they wanted to, and secondly – which is the terror of that song – because they could not stop. For no consideration could they stop.

Pallant was still standing up. Someone pointed at him and they laughed. Others began to point, lunging, as it were, in time with the tune. At this moment two persons came in practically abreast from behind the Speaker's chair, and halted appalled. One happened to be the Prime Minister and the other a messenger. The House, with tears running down their cheeks, transferred their attention to the paralysed couple. They pointed six hundred fore-fingers at them. They rocked, they waved, and they rolled while they pointed, but still they sang. When they weakened for an instant, Ireland would yell: 'Are ye *with* me, bhoys?' and they all renewed their strength like Antaeus. No man could say afterwards what happened in the Press or the Strangers' Gallery. It was the House, the hysterical and abandoned House of Commons that held all eyes, as it deafened all ears. I saw both Front Benches bend forward, some with their foreheads on their dispatch-boxes, the rest with their faces in their hands; and their moving shoulders jolted the House out of its last rag of decency. Only the Speaker remained unmoved. The entire press of Great Britain bore witness next day that he had not even bowed his head. The Angel of the Constitution, for vain was the help of man, foretold him the exact moment at which the House would have broken into 'The Gubby'. He is reported to have said: 'I heard the Irish beginning to shuffle it. So I adjourned.' Pallant's version is that he added: 'And I was never so grateful to a private member in all my life as I was to Mr Pallant.'

He made no explanation. He did not refer to orders or disorders. He simply adjourned the House till six that evening. And the House adjourned – some of it nearly on all fours.

I was not correct when I said that the Speaker was the only man who did not laugh. Woodhouse was beside me all the time. His face was set and quite white – as white, they told me, as Sir Thomas Ingell's when he went, by request, to a private interview with his Chief Whip.

The Coup

Jeffrey Archer

The blue and silver jet, displaying a large 'P' on its tail plane, taxied to a halt at the north end of Lagos International Airport. A fleet of six black Mercedes drove up to the side of the aircraft and waited in a line resembling a land-bound crocodile. Six sweating, uniformed drivers leaped out and stood to attention. When the driver of the front car opened his rear door, Colonel Usman of the Federal Guard stepped out, and walked quickly to the bottom of the passenger steps which had been hurriedly pushed into place by four of the airport staff.

The front section cabin door swung back and the colonel stared up into the gap, to see, framed against the dark interior of the cabin, a slim, attractive hostess dressed in a blue suit with silver piping. On her jacket lapel was a large 'P'. She turned and nodded in the direction of the cabin. A few seconds later, an immaculately dressed tall man with thick black hair and deep brown eyes replaced her in the doorway. The man had an air of effortless style about him which self-made millionaires would have paid a considerable part of their fortune to possess. The colonel saluted as Senhor Eduardo Francisco de Silveira, head of the Prentino empire, gave a curt nod.

De Silveira emerged from the coolness of his air-conditioned 707 into the burning Nigerian sun without showing the slightest sign of discomfort. The colonel guided the tall, elegant Brazilian, who was accompanied only by his private secretary, to the front Mercedes while the rest of the Prentino staff filed down the back stairway of the aircraft and filled the other five cars. The driver, a corporal who had been detailed to be available night and day for the honoured guest, opened the rear door of the front car and saluted. Eduardo de Silveira showed no sign of acknowledgement. The corporal smiled nervously, revealing the largest set of white teeth the Brazilian had ever seen.

'Welcome to Lagos,' the corporal volunteered. 'Hope you make very big deal while you are in Nigeria.'

Eduardo did not comment as he settled back into his seat and stared out of the tinted window to watch some passengers of a British Airways 707 that had landed just before him form a long queue on the hot tarmac as they waited patiently to clear customs. The driver put the car into first gear and the black crocodile proceeded on its journey. Colonel Usman, who was now in the front seat beside the corporal, soon discovered that the Brazilian guest did not care for small talk, and the secretary who was seated by his employer's side never once opened his mouth. The colonel, used to doing things by example, remained silent, leaving de Silveira to consider his plan of campaign.

Eduardo Francisco de Silveira had been born in the small village of Rebeti, a hundred miles north of Rio de Janeiro, heir to one of the two most powerful family fortunes in Brazil. He had been educated privately in Switzerland before attending the University of California in Los Angeles. He went on to complete his education at the Harvard Business School. After Harvard he returned from America to work in Brazil where he started neither at the top or the bottom of the firm but in the middle, managing his family's mining interests in Minas Gerais. He quickly worked his way to the top, even faster than his father had planned, but then the boy turned out to be not so much a chip as a chunk off the old block. At twenty-nine he married Maria, eldest daughter of his father's closest friend, and when twelve years later his father died Eduardo succeeded to the Prentino throne. There were seven sons in all: the second son, Alfredo, was now in charge of banking; João ran shipping; Carlos organised construction; Manoel arranged food and supplies; Jaime managed the family newspapers, and little Antonio, the last – and certainly the least – ran the family farms. All the brothers reported to Eduardo before making any major decision, for he was still chairman of the largest private company in Brazil, despite the boastful claims of his old family enemy, Manuel Rodrigues.

When General Castelo Branco's military regime overthrew the civilian government in 1964 the generals agreed that they could not kill off all the de Silveiras or the Rodrigues so they had better learn to live with the two rival families. The de Silveiras for their part had always had enough sense never to involve themselves in politics other than by making payments to every government official, military or civilian, according to his rank. This ensured that the Prentino empire grew alongside whatever faction came to power. One of the reasons Eduardo de Silveira had allocated three days in his crowded schedule for a visit to Lagos was that the Nigerian system of government seemed to resemble so closely that of Brazil, and at least on this project he had cut the ground from under Manuel Rodrigues' feet, which would more than make up for losing the Rio airport tender to him. Eduardo smiled at the thought of Rodrigues' not realising that he was in Nigeria to close a deal that could make him twice the size of his rival.

As the black Mercedes moved slowly through the teeming noisy streets paying no attention to traffic lights, red or green, Eduardo thought back to his first meeting with General Mohammed, the Nigerian Head of State, on the occasion of the President's official visit to Brazil. Speaking at the dinner given in General Mohammed's honour, President Ernesto Geisel declared a hope that the two countries would move towards closer co-operation in politics and commerce. Eduardo agreed with his unelected leader and was happy to leave the politics to the President if he allowed him to get on with the commerce. General Mohammed made his reply, on behalf of the guests, in an English accent that normally would only be associated with Oxford. The general talked at length of the project that was most dear to his heart, the building of a new Nigerian capital in Abuja, a city which he considered might even rival Brasilia. After the speeches were over, the general took de Silveira on one side and spoke in greater detail of the Abuja city project asking him if he might consider a private tender. Eduardo smiled and only wished that his enemy, Rodrigues, could hear the intimate conversation he was having with the Nigerian Head of State.

Eduardo studied carefully the outline proposal sent to him a week later, after the general had returned to Nigeria, and agreed to his first request by despatching a research team of seven men to fly to Lagos and complete a feasibility study on Abuja.

One month later, the team's detailed report was in de Silveira's hands. Eduardo came to the conclusion that the potential profitability of the project was worthy of a full proposal to the Nigerian government. He contacted General Mohammed personally to find that he was in full agreement and authorised the go-ahead. This time twenty-three men were despatched to Lagos and three months and one hundred and seventy pages later, Eduardo signed and sealed the proposal designated as, 'A New Capital for Nigeria'. He made only one alteration to the final document. The cover of the proposal was in blue and silver with the Prentino logo in the centre: Eduardo had that changed to green and white, the national colours of Nigeria, with the national emblem of an eagle astride two horses: he realised it was the little things that impressed generals and often tipped the scales. He sent ten copies of the feasibility study to Nigeria's Head of State with an invoice for one million dollars.

When General Mohammed had studied the proposal he invited Eduardo de Silveira to visit Nigeria as his guest, in order to discuss the next stage of the project. De Silveira telexed back, provisionally accepting the invitation, and pointing out politely but firmly that he had not yet received reimbursement for the one million dollars spent on the initial feasibility study. The money was telexed by return from the Central Bank of Nigeria and de Silveira managed to find four consecutive days in his diary for 'The New Federal Capital project': his schedule demanded that he arrive in Lagos on a Monday morning because he had to be in Paris at the latest by the Thursday night.

While these thoughts were going through Eduardo's mind, the Mercedes drew up outside Dodan Barracks. The iron gates swung open and a full armed guard gave the general salute, an honour normally afforded only to a visiting Head of State. The black Mercedes drove slowly through the gates and came to a halt outside the President's private residence. A brigadier waited on the steps to escort de Silveira through to the President.

The two men had lunch together in a small room that closely resembled a British officers' mess. The meal consisted of a steak, that would not have been acceptable to any South American cowhand, surrounded by vegetables that reminded Eduardo of his schooldays. Still, Eduardo had never yet met a soldier who understood that a good chef was every bit as important as a good batman. During the lunch they talked in overall terms about the problems of building a whole new city in the middle of an equatorial jungle.

The provisional estimate of the cost of the project had been one thousand million dollars but de Silveira warned the President that the final outcome might well end up nearer three thousand million dollars – the President's jaw dropped slightly. De Silveira had to admit that the project would be the most ambitious that Prentino International had ever tackled, but he was quick to point out to the

President that the same would be true of any construction company in the world.

De Silveira, not a man to play his best card early, waited until the coffee to slip into the conversation that he had just been awarded, against heavy opposition (that had included Rodrigues), the contract to build an eight-lane highway through the Amazonian jungle, which would eventually link up with the Pan-American highway, a contract second in size only to the one they were now contemplating in Nigeria. The President was impressed and inquired if the venture would not prevent de Silveira involving himself in the new capital project.

'I'll know the answer to that question in three days' time,' replied the Brazilian, and undertook to have a further discussion with the Head of State at the end of his visit when he would let him know if he was prepared to continue with the scheme.

After lunch Eduardo was driven to the Federal Palace Hotel where the entire sixth floor had been placed at his disposal. Several complaining guests who had come to Nigeria to close deals involving mere millions had been asked to vacate their rooms at short notice to make way for de Silveira and his staff. Eduardo knew nothing of these goings on, as there was always a room available for him wherever he arrived in the world.

The six Mercedes drew up outside the hotel and the colonel guided his charge through the swing doors and past reception. Eduardo had not checked himself into a hotel for the past fourteen years except on those occasions when he chose to register under an assumed name, not wanting anyone to know the identity of the woman he was with.

The chairman of Prentino International walked down the centre of the hotel's main corridor and stepped into a waiting lift. His legs went weak and he suddenly felt sick. In the corner of the lift stood a stubby, balding, overweight man, who was dressed in a pair of old jeans and a tee-shirt, his mouth continually opening and closing as he chewed gum. The two men stood as far apart as possible, neither showing any sign of recognition. The lift stopped at the fifth floor and Manuel Rodrigues, chairman of Rodrigues International S.A., stepped out, leaving behind him the man who had been his bitter rival for thirty years.

Eduardo held on to the rail in the lift to steady himself as he still felt dizzy. How he despised that uneducated self-made upstart whose family of four half-brothers, all by different fathers, claimed they now ran the largest construction company in Brazil. Both men were as interested in the other's failure as they were in their own success.

Eduardo was somewhat puzzled to know what Rodrigues could possibly be doing in Lagos as he felt certain that his rival had not come into contact with the Nigerian President. After all, Eduardo had never collected the rent on a small house in Rio that was occupied by the mistress of a very senior official in the government's protocol department. And the man's only task was to be certain that Rodrigues was never invited to any function attended by a visiting dignitary when in Brazil. The continual absence of Rodrigues from these state occasions ensured the absent-mindedness of Eduardo's rent collector in Rio.

Eduardo would never have admitted to anyone that Rodrigues' presence worried him, but he nevertheless resolved to find out immediately what had brought his old enemy to Nigeria. Once he reached his suite de Silveira instructed his private secretary to check what Manuel Rodrigues was up to. Eduardo was prepared to return to Brazil immediately if Rodrigues turned out to be involved in any way with the new capital project, while one young lady in Rio would suddenly find herself looking for alternative accommodation.

Within an hour, his private secretary returned with the information that his chairman had requested. Rodrigues, he had discovered, was in Nigeria to tender for the contract to construct a new port in Lagos and was apparently not involved in any way with the new capital, and in fact was still trying to arrange a meeting with the President.

'Which minister is in charge of the ports and when am I due to see him?' asked de Silveira.

The secretary delved into his appointments file. 'The Minister of Transport,' the secretary said. 'You have an appointment with him at nine o'clock on Thursday morning.' The Nigerian Civil Service had mapped out a four-day schedule of meetings for de Silveira that included every cabinet minister involved in the new city project. 'It's the last meeting before your final discussion with the President. You then fly on to Paris.'

'Excellent. Remind me of this conversation five minutes before I see the minister and again when I talk to the President.'

The secretary made a note in the file and left.

Eduardo sat alone in his suite, going over the reports on the new capital project submitted by his experts. Some of his team were already showing signs of nervousness. One particular anxiety that always came up with a large construction contract was the principal's ability to pay, and pay on time. Failure to do so was the quickest route to bankruptcy, but since the discovery of oil in Nigeria there seemed to be no shortage of income and certainly no shortage of people willing to spend that money on behalf of the government. These anxieties did not worry de Silveira as he always insisted on a substantial payment in advance; otherwise he wouldn't move himself or his vast staff one centimetre out of Brazil. However, the massive scope of this particular contract made the circumstances somewhat unusual. Eduardo realised that it would be most damaging to his international reputation if he started the assignment and then was seen not to complete it. He re-read the reports over a quiet dinner in his room and retired to bed early, having wasted an hour in vainly trying to place a call through to his wife.

De Silveira's first appointment the next morning was with the Governor of the Central Bank of Nigeria. Eduardo wore a newly pressed suit, fresh shirt and highly polished shoes: for four days no one would see him in the same clothes. At eight-forty-five there was a quiet knock on the door of his suite and the secretary opened it to find Colonel Usman standing to attention, waiting to escort Eduardo to the bank. As they were leaving the hotel Eduardo again saw Manuel Rodrigues, wearing the same pair of jeans, the same crumpled tee-shirt, and probably chewing the same gum as he stepped into a BMW in front of him. De Silveira only stopped scowling at the disappearing BMW when he remembered his Thursday morning appointment with the minister in charge of ports, followed by a meeting with the President.

The Governor of the Central Bank of Nigeria was in the habit of proposing how payment schedules would be met and completion orders would be guaranteed. He had never been told by anyone that if the payment was seven days overdue he could consider the contract null and void, and they could take it or leave it. The minister would have made some comment if Abuja had not been the President's pet project. That position established, de Silveira went on to check the bank's reserves, long-term deposits, overseas commitments, and estimated oil revenues for the next five years. He left the Governor in what could only be be described as a jelly-like state. Glistening and wobbling. Eduardo's next appointment was an unavoidable courtesy call on the Brazilian Ambassador for lunch. He hated these functions as he believed embassies to be fit only for cocktail parties and discussion of out-of-date trivia, neither of which he cared for. The food in such establishments was invariably bad and the company worse. It turned out to be no different on this occasion and the only profit (Eduardo considered everything in terms of profit and loss) to be derived from the encounter was the information that Manuel Rodrigues was on a short list of three for the building of the new port in Lagos, and was expecting to have an audience with the President on Friday if he was awarded the contract. By Thursday morning that will be a short list of two and there will be no meeting with the President, de Silveira promised himself, and considered that was the most he was likely to gain from the lunch until the Ambassador added:

'Rodrigues seems most keen on you being awarded the new city contract at Abuja. He's singing your praises to every minister he meets. Funny,' the Ambassador continued, 'I always thought you two didn't see eye to eye.'

Eduardo made no reply as he tried to fathom out what trick Rodrigues could be up to by promoting his cause.

Eduardo spent the afternoon with the Minister of Finance and confirmed the provisional arrangements he had made with the Governor of the bank. The Minister of Finance had been forewarned by the Governor what he was to expect from an encounter with Eduardo de Silveira and that he was not to be taken aback by the Brazilian's curt demands. De Silveira, aware that this warning would have taken place, let the poor man bargain a little and even gave way on a few minor points that he would be able to tell the President about at the next meeting of the Supreme Military Council. Eduardo left the smiling minister believing that he had scored a point or two against the formidable South American.

That evening, Eduardo dined privately with his senior advisers who themselves were already dealing with the ministers' officials. Each was now coming up with daily reports about the problems that would have to be faced if they worked in Nigeria. His chief engineer was quick to emphasise that skilled labour could not be hired at any price as the Germans had already cornered the market for their extensive road projects. The financial advisers also presented a gloomy report, of international companies waiting six months or more for their cheques to be cleared by the central bank. Eduardo made notes on the views they expressed but never ventured an opinion himself. His staff left him a little after eleven and he decided to take a stroll around the hotel grounds before retiring to bed. On his walk through the luxuriant tropical gardens he only just avoided a face-to-face confrontation with Manuel Rodrigues by darting behind a large Iroko plant. The little man passed by champing away at his gum, oblivious to Eduardo's baleful glare. Eduardo informed a chattering grey parrot of his most secret thoughts: by Thursday afternoon, Rodrigues, you will be on your way back to Brazil with a suitcase full of plans that can be filed under 'abortive projects'. The parrot cocked his head and screeched at him as if he had been let in on his secret. Eduardo allowed himself a smile and returned to his room.

Colonel Usman arrived on the dot of eight forty-five again the next day and Eduardo spent the morning with the Minister of Supplies and Co-operatives – or lack of them, as he commented to his private secretary afterwards. The afternoon was spent with the Minister of Labour checking over the availability of unskilled workers and the total lack of skilled operatives. Eduardo was fast reaching the conclusion that, despite the professed optimism of the ministers concerned, this was going to be the toughest contract he had ever tackled. There was more to be lost than money if the whole international business world stood watching him fall flat on his face. In the evening his staff reported to him once again, having solved a few old problems and unearthed some new ones. Tentatively, they had come to the conclusion that if the present regime stayed in power, there need be no serious concern over payment, as the President had earmarked the new city as a priority project. They had even heard a rumour that the army would be willing to lend-lease part of the Service Corps if there turned out to be a shortage of skilled labour. Eduardo made a note to have this point confirmed in writing by the Head of State during their final meeting the next day. But the labour problem was not what was occupying Eduardo's thoughts as he put on his silk pyjamas that night. He was chuckling at the idea of Manuel Rodrigues' imminent and sudden departure for Brazil. Eduardo slept well.

He rose with renewed vigour the next morning, showered and put on a fresh suit. The four days were turning out to be well worth while and a single stone might yet kill two birds. By eight forty-five, he was waiting impatiently for the previously punctual colonel. The colonel did not show up at eight forty-five and had still not appeared when the clock on his mantelpiece struck nine. De Silveira sent his private secretary off to find out where he was while he paced angrily backwards and forwards through the hotel suite. His secretary returned a few minutes later in a panic with the information that the hotel was surrounded by armed guards. Eduardo did not panic. He had been through eight coups in his life from which he had learnt one golden rule: the new regime never kills visiting foreigners as it needs their money every bit as much as the last government. Eduardo picked up the telephone but no one answered him so he switched on the radio. A tape recording was playing.

'This is Radio Nigeria, this is Radio Nigeria. There has been a coup. General Mohammed has been overthrown and Lieutenant Colonel Dimka has assumed leadership of the new revolutionary government. Do not be afraid; remain at home and everything will be back to normal in a few hours. This is Radio Nigeria, this is Radio Nigeria. There has been a . . .'

Eduardo switched off the radio as two thoughts flashed through his mind. Coups always held up everything and caused chaos, so undoubtedly he had wasted the four days. But worse, would it be possible for him even to get out of Nigeria and carry on his normal business with the rest of the world?

By lunchtime, the radio was playing martial music interspersed with the tape recorded message he now knew off by heart. Eduardo detailed all his staff to find out anything they could and to report back to him direct. They all returned with the same story; that it was impossible to get past the soldiers surrounding the hotel so no new information could be unearthed. Eduardo swore for the first time in months. To add to his inconvenience, the hotel manager rang through to say that regretfully Mr de Silveira would have to eat in the main dining room as there would be no room service until further notice. Eduardo went down to the dining room somewhat reluctantly only to discover that the head waiter showed no interest in who he was and placed him unceremoniously at a small table already occupied by three Italians. Manuel Rodrigues was seated only two tables away: Eduardo stiffened at the thought of the other man enjoying his discomfiture and then remembered it was that morning he was supposed to have seen the Minister of Ports. He ate his meal quickly despite being served slowly and when the Italians tried to make conversation with him he waved them away with his hand, feigning lack of understanding, despite the fact that he spoke their language fluently. As soon as he had finished the second course he returned to his room. His staff had only gossip to pass on and they had been unable to make contact with the Brazilian Embassy to lodge an official protest. 'A lot of good an official protest will do us,' said Eduardo, slumping down in his chair. 'Who do you send it to, the new regime or the old one?'

He sat alone in his room for the rest of the day, interrupted only by what he thought was the sound of gunfire in the distance. He read the new Federal Capital project proposal and his advisers' reports for a third time.

The next morning Eduardo, dressed in the same suit as he had worn on the day of his arrival, was greeted by his secretary with the news that the coup had been crushed; after fierce street fighting, he informed his unusually attentive chairman, the old regime had regained power but not without losses; among those killed in the uprising had been General Mohammed, the Head of State. The secretary's news was officially confirmed on Radio Nigeria later that morning. The ringleader of the abortive coup had been one Lieutenant Colonel Dimka: Dimka, along with one or two junior officers, had escaped, and the government had ordered a dusk to dawn curfew until the evil criminals were apprehended.

Pull off a coup and you're a national hero, fail and you're an evil criminal; in business it's the same difference between bankruptcy and making a fortune, considered Eduardo as he listened to the news report. He was beginning to form plans in his mind for an early departure from Nigeria when the newscaster made an announcement that chilled him to the very marrow.

'While Lieutenant Colonel Dimka and his accomplices remain on the run, airports throughout the country will be closed until further notice.'

When the newscaster had finished his report, martial music was played in memory of the late General Mohammed.

Eduardo went downstairs in a flaming temper. The hotel was still surrounded by armed guards. He stared at the fleet of six empty Mercedes which was parked only ten yards beyond the soldier's rifles. He marched back into the foyer, irritated by the babble of different tongues coming at him from every direction. Eduardo looked around him: it was obvious that many people had been stranded in the hotel overnight and had ended up sleeping in the lounge or the bar. He checked the paperback rack in the lobby for something to read but there were only four copies left of a tourist guide to Lagos; everything had been sold. Authors who had not been read for years were now changing hands at a premium. Eduardo returned to his room, which was fast assuming the character of a prison, and balked at reading the New Federal Capital project for a fourth time. He tried again to make contact with the Brazilian Ambassador to discover if he could obtain special permission to leave the country as he had his own aircraft. No one answered the Embassy phone. He went down for an early lunch only to find the dining room was once again packed to capacity. Eduardo was placed at a table with some Germans who were worrying about a contract that had been signed by the government the previous week, before the abortive coup. They were wondering if it would still be honoured. Manuel Rodrigues entered the room a few minutes later and was placed at the next table.

During the afternoon, de Silveira ruefully examined his schedule for the next seven days. He had been due in Paris that morning to see the Minister of the Interior, and from there should have flown on to London to confer with the chairman of the Steel Board. His calendar was fully booked for the next ninety-two days until his family holiday in May. 'I'm having this year's holiday in Nigeria,' he commented wryly to an assistant.

What annoyed Eduardo most about the coup was the lack of communication it afforded with the outside world. He wondered what was going on in Brazil and he hated not being able to telephone or telex Paris or London to explain his absence personally. He listened addictively to Radio Nigeria on the hour every hour for any new scrap of information. At five o'clock, he learned that the Supreme Military Council had elected a new President who would address the nation on television and radio at nine o'clock that night.

Eduardo de Silveira switched on the television at eight forty-five; normally an assistant would have put it on for him at one minute to nine. He sat watching a Nigerian lady giving a talk on dressmaking, followed by the weather forecast man who supplied Eduardo with the revealing information that the temperature would continue to be hot for the next month. Eduardo's knee was twitching up and down nervously as he waited for the address by the new President. At nine o'clock, after the national anthem had been played, the new Head of State, General Obasanjo, appeared on the screen in full dress uniform. He spoke first of the tragic death and sad loss for the nation of the late President, and went on to say that his government would continue to work in the best interest of Nigeria. He looked ill at ease as he apologised to all foreign visitors who were inconvenienced by the attempted coup but went on to make it clear that the dusk to dawn curfew would continue until the rebel leaders were tracked down and brought to justice. He confirmed that all airports would remain closed until Lieutenant Colonel Dimka was in safe custody. The new President ended his statement by saying that all other forms of communication would be opened up again as soon as possible. The national anthem was played for a second time, while Eduardo thought of the millions of dollars that might be lost to him by his incarceration in that hotel room, while his private plane sat idly on the tarmac only a few miles away. One of his senior managers opened a book as to how long it would take for the authorities to capture Lieutenant Colonel Dimka; he did not tell de Silveira how short the odds were on a month.

Eduardo went down to the dining room in the suit he had worn the day before. A junior waiter placed him at a table with some Frenchmen who had been hoping to win a contract to drill bore holes in the Niger state. Again Eduardo waved a languid hand when they tried to include him in their conversation. At that very moment he was meant to be with the French Minister of the Interior, not with some French hole-borers. He tried to concentrate on his watered-down soup, wondering how much longer it would be before it would be just water. The head waiter appeared by his side, gesturing to the one remaining seat at the table, in which he placed Manuel Rodrigues. Still neither man gave any sign of recognising the other. Eduardo debated with himself whether he should leave the table or carry on as if his oldest rival was still in Brazil. He decided the latter was more dignified. The Frenchmen began an argument among themselves as to when they would be able to get out of Lagos. One of them declared emphatically that he had heard on the highest authority that the government intended to track down every last one of those involved in the coup before they opened the airports and that might take up to a month.

'What?' said the two Brazilians together, in English.

'I can't stay here for a month,' said Eduardo.

'Neither can I,' said Manuel Rodrigues.

'You'll have to, at least until Dimka is captured,' said one of the Frenchmen, breaking into English. 'So you must both relax yourselves, yes?'

The two Brazilians continued their meal in silence. When Eduardo had finished he rose from the table and without looking directly at Rodrigues said good night in Portuguese. The old rival inclined his head in reply to the salutation.

The next day brought forth no new information. The hotel remained surrounded with soldiers and by the evening Eduardo had lost his temper with every member of staff with whom he had come into contact. He went down to dinner on his own and as he entered the dining room he saw Manuel Rodrigues sitting alone at a table in the corner. Rodrigues looked up, seemed to hesitate for a moment, and then beckoned to Eduardo. Eduardo himself hesitated before walking slowly towards Rodrigues and taking the seat opposite him. Rodrigues poured him a glass of wine. Eduardo, who rarely drank, drank it. Their conversation was stilted to begin with, but as both men consumed more wine so they each began to relax in the other's company. By the time coffee had arrived, Manuel was telling Eduardo what he could do with this god-forsaken country.

'You will not stay on, if you are awarded the ports contract?' inquired Eduardo.

'Not a hope,' said Rodrigues, who showed no surprise that de Silveira knew of his interest in the ports contract. 'I withdrew from the short list the day before the coup. I had intended to fly back to Brazil that Thursday morning.'

'Can you say why you withdrew?'

'Labour problems mainly, and then the congestion of the ports.'

'I am not sure I understand,' said Eduardo, understanding full well but curious to learn if Rodrigues had picked up some tiny detail his own staff had missed.

Manuel Rodrigues paused to ingest the fact that the man he had viewed as his most dangerous enemy for over thirty years was now listening to his own inside information. He considered the situation for a moment while he sipped his coffee. Eduardo didn't speak.

'To begin with, there's a terrible shortage of skilled labour, and on top of that there's this mad quota system.'

'Quota system?' said Eduardo innocently.

'The percentage of people from the contractor's country which the government will allow to work in Nigeria.'

'Why should that be a problem?' said Eduardo, leaning forward.

'By law, you have to employ at a ratio of fifty nationals to one foreigner so I could only have brought over twenty-five of my top men to organise a fifty million dollar contract, and I'd have had to make do with Nigerians at every other level. The government are cutting their own throats with the wretched system; they can't expect unskilled men, black or white, to become experienced engineers overnight. It's all to do with their national pride. Someone must tell them they can't afford that sort of pride if they want to complete the job at a sensible price. That path is the surest route to bankruptcy. On top of that, the Germans have already rounded up all the best skilled labour for their road projects.'

'But surely,' said Eduardo, 'you charge according to the rules, however stupid, thus covering all eventualities, and as long as you're certain that payment is guaranteed . . .'

Manuel raised his hand to stop Eduardo's flow: 'That's another problem. You can't be certain. The government reneged on a major steel contract only last month. In so doing,' he explained, 'they had bankrupted a distinguished international company. So they are perfectly capable of trying the same trick with me. And if they don't pay up, who do you sue? The Supreme Military Council?'

'And the ports problem?'

'The port is totally congested. There are one hundred and seventy ships desperate to unload their cargo with a waiting time of anything up to six months. On top of that, there is a demurrage charge of five thousand dollars a day and only perishable foods are given any priority.'

'But there's always a way round that sort of problem,' said Eduardo, rubbing a thumb twice across the top of his fingers.

'Bribery? It doesn't work, Eduardo. How can you possibly jump the queue when all one hundred and seventy ships have already bribed the harbour master? And don't imagine that fixing the rent on a flat for one of his mistresses would help either,' said Rodrigues grinning. 'With that man you will have to supply the mistress as well.'

Eduardo held his breath but said nothing.

'Come to think of it,' continued Rodrigues, 'if the situation becomes any worse, the harbour master will be the one man in the country who is richer than you.'

Eduardo laughed for the first time in three days.

'I tell you, Eduardo, we could make a bigger profit building a salt mine in Siberia.'

Eduardo laughed again and some of the Prentino and Rodrigues staff dining at other tables stared in disbelief at their masters.

'You were in for the big one, the new city of Abuja?' said Manuel.

'That's right,' admitted Eduardo.

'I have done everything in my power to make sure you were awarded that contract,' said the other quietly.

'What?' said Eduardo in disbelief. 'Why?'

'I thought Abuja would give the Prentino empire more headaches than even you could cope with, Eduardo, and that might possibly leave the field wide open for me at home. Think about it. Every time there's a cutback in Nigeria, what will be the first head to roll off the chopping block? "The unnecessary city" as the locals call it.'

'The unnecessary city?' repeated Eduardo.

'Yes, and it doesn't help when you say you won't move without advance payment. You know as well as I do, you will need one hundred of your best men here full time to organise such a massive enterprise. They'll need feeding, salaries, housing, perhaps even a school and a hospital. Once they were settled down here, you can't just pull them off the job every two weeks because the government is running late clearing the cheques. It's not practical and you know it.' Rodrigues poured Eduardo de Silveira another glass of wine.

'I had already taken that into consideration,' Eduardo said as he sipped the wine, 'but I thought that with the support of the Head of State . . .'

'The late Head of State—'

'I take your point, Manuel.'

'Maybe the next Head of State will also back you, but what about the one after that? Nigeria has had three coups in the past three years.'

Eduardo remained silent for a moment.

'Do you play backgammon?'

'Yes. Why do you ask?'

'I must make *some* money while I'm here.' Manuel laughed.

'Why don't you come to my room,' continued de Silveira. 'Though I must warn you I always manage to beat my staff.'

'Perhaps they always manage to lose,' said Manuel, as he rose and grabbed the half empty bottle of wine by its neck. Both men were laughing as they left the dining room.

After that, the two chairmen had lunch and dinner together every day. Within a week, their staff were eating at the same tables. Eduardo could be seen in the dining room without a tie while Manuel wore a shirt for the first time in years. By the end of a fortnight, the two rivals had played each other at table tennis, backgammon and bridge with the stakes set at one hundred dollars a point. At the end of each day Eduardo always seemed to end up owing Manuel about a million dollars which Manuel happily traded for the best bottle of wine left in the hotel's cellar.

Although Lieutenant Colonel Dimka had been sighted by about forty thousand Nigerians in about as many different places, he still remained resolutely uncaptured. As the new President had insisted, airports remained closed but communications were opened which at least allowed Eduardo to telephone and telex Brazil. His brothers and wife were sending replies by the hour, imploring Eduardo to return home at any cost: decisions on major contracts throughout the world were being held up by his absence. But Eduardo's message back to Brazil was always the same: as long as Dimka is on the loose, the airports will remain closed.

It was on a Tuesday night during dinner that Eduardo took the trouble to explain to Manuel why Brazil had lost the World Cup. Manuel dismissed Eduardo's outrageous claims as ill-informed and prejudiced. It was the only subject on which they hadn't agreed in the past three weeks.

'I blame the whole fiasco on Zagalo,' said Eduardo.

'No, no, you cannot blame the manager,' said Manuel. 'The fault lies with our stupid selectors who know even less about football then you do. They should never have dropped Leao from goal and in any case we should have learned from the Argentinian defeat last year that our methods are now out of date. You must attack, attack, if you want to score goals.'

'Rubbish. We still have the surest defence in the world.'

'Which means the best result you can hope for is a 0–0 draw.'

'Never . . .' began Eduardo.

'Excuse me, sir.'

Eduardo looked up to see his private secretary standing by his side looking anxiously down at him.

'Yes, what's the problem?'

'An urgent telex from Brazil, sir.'

Eduardo read the first paragraph and then asked Manuel if he would be kind enough to excuse him for a few minutes. The latter nodded politely. Eduardo left the table and as he marched through the dining room seventeen other guests left unfinished meals and followed him quickly to his suite on the top floor, where the rest of his staff were already assembled. He sat down in the corner of the room on his own. No one spoke as he read through the telex carefully, suddenly realising how many days he had been imprisoned in Lagos.

The telex was from his brother Carlos and the contents concerned the Pan-American road project, an eight-lane highway that would stretch from Brazil to Mexico. Prentinos had tendered for the section that ran through the middle of the Amazon jungle and had to have the bank guarantees signed and certified by midday tomorrow; Tuesday. But Eduardo had quite forgotten which Tuesday it was and the document he was committed to sign by the following day's deadline.

'What's the problem?' Eduardo asked his private secretary. 'The Banco do Brasil have already agreed with Alfredo to act as guarantors. What's stopping Carlos signing the agreement in my absence?'

'The Mexicans are now demanding that responsibility

for the contract be shared because of the insurance problems: Lloyd's of London will not cover the entire risk if only one company is involved. The details are all on page seven of the telex.'

Eduardo flicked quickly through the pages. He read that his brothers had already tried to put pressure on Lloyd's, but to no avail. That's like trying to bribe a maiden aunt into taking part in a public orgy, thought Eduardo, and he would have told them as much if he had been back in Brazil. The Mexican government was therefore insisting that the contract be shared with an international construction company acceptable to Lloyd's if the legal documents were to be signed by the midday deadline the following day.

'Stay put,' said Eduardo to his staff, and he returned to the dining room alone, trailing the long telex behind him. Rodrigues watched him as he scurried back to their table.

'You look like a man with a problem.'

'I am,' said Eduardo. 'Read that.'

Manuel's experienced eye ran down the telex, picking out the salient points. He had tendered for the Amazon road project himself and could still recall the details. At Eduardo's insistence, he re-read page seven.

'Mexican bandits,' he said as he returned the telex to Eduardo. 'Who do they think they are, telling Eduardo de Silveira how he must conduct his business. Telex them back immediately and inform them you're chairman of the greatest construction company in the world and they can roast in hell before you will agree to their pathetic terms. You know it's far too late for them to go out to tender again with every other section of the highway ready to begin work. They would lose millions. Call their bluff, Eduardo.'

'I think you may be right, Manuel, but any hold-up now can only waste my time and money, so I intend to agree to their demand and look for a partner.'

'You'll never find one at such short notice.'

'I will.'

'Who?'

Eduardo de Silveira hesitated only for a second. 'You, Manuel. I want to offer Rodrigues International S.A. fifty per cent of the Amazon road contract.'

Manuel Rodrigues looked up at Eduardo. It was the first time that he had not anticipated his old rival's move. 'I suppose it might help cover the millions you owe me in table tennis debts.'

The two men laughed, then Rodrigues stood up and they shook hands gravely. De Silveira left the dining room on the run and wrote out a telex for his manager to transmit.

'Sign, accept terms, fifty per cent partner will be Rodrigues International Construction SA, Brazil.'

'If I telex that message, sir, you do realise that it's legally binding?'

'Send it,' said Eduardo.

Eduardo returned once again to the dining room where Manuel had ordered the finest bottle of champagne in the hotel. Just as they were calling for a second bottle, and singing a spirited version of *Esta Cheganda a hora*, Eduardo's private secretary appeared by his side again, this time with two telexes, one from the President of the Banco do Brasil and a second from his brother Carlos. Both wanted confirmation of the agreed partner for the Amazon road project. Eduardo uncorked the second bottle of champagne without looking up at his private secretary.

'Confirm Rodrigues International Construction to the President of the bank and my brother,' he said as he filled Manuel's empty glass. 'And don't bother me again tonight.'

'Yes, sir,' said the private secretary and left without another word.

Neither man could recall what time he climbed into bed that night but de Silveira was abruptly awakened from a deep sleep by his secretary early the next morning. Eduardo took a few minutes to digest the news. Lieutenant Colonel Dimka had been caught in Kano at three o'clock that morning, and all the airports were now open again. Eduardo picked up the phone and dialled three digits.

'Manuel, you've heard the news? . . . Good . . . Then you must fly back with me in my 707 or it may be days before you get out . . . One hour's time in the lobby . . . See you then.'

At eight forty-five there was a quiet knock on the door and Eduardo's secretary opened it to find Colonel Usman standing to attention, just as he had done in the days before the coup. He held a note in his hand. Eduardo tore open the envelope to find an invitation to lunch that day with the new Head of State, General Obasanjo.

'Please convey my apologies to your President,' said Eduardo, 'and be kind enough to explain that I have pressing commitments to attend to in my own country.'

The colonel retired reluctantly. Eduardo dressed in the suit, shirt and tie he had worn on his first day in Nigeria and took the lift downstairs to the lobby where he joined Manuel who was once more wearing jeans and a tee-shirt. The two chairmen left the hotel and climbed into the back of the leading Mercedes and the motorcade of six began its journey to the airport. The colonel, who now sat in front with the driver, did not venture to speak to either of the distinguished Brazilians for the entire journey. The two men, he would be able to tell the new President later, seemed to be preoccupied with a discussion on an Amazon road project and how the responsibility should be divided between their two companies.

Customs were bypassed as neither man had anything they wanted to take out of the country other than themselves, and the fleet of cars came to a halt at the side of Eduardo's blue and silver 707. The staff of both companies climbed aboard the rear section of the aircraft, also engrossed in discussion on the Amazon road project.

A corporal jumped out of the lead car and opened the back door, to allow the two chairmen to walk straight up the steps and board the front section of the aircraft.

As Eduardo stepped out of the Mercedes, the Nigerian driver saluted smartly. 'Goodbye, sir,' he said, revealing the large set of white teeth once again.

Eduardo said nothing.

'I hope,' said the corporal politely, 'you made very big deal while you were in Nigeria.'

The Greatest Man in the World

James Thurber

Looking back on it now, from the vantage point of 1940, one can only marvel that it hadn't happened long before it did. The United States of America had been, ever since Kitty Hawk, blindly constructing the elaborate petard by which, sooner or later, it must be hoist. It was inevitable that some day there would come roaring out of the skies a national hero of insufficient intelligence, background and character successfully to endure the mounting orgies of glory prepared for aviators who stayed up a long time or flew a great distance. Both Lindbergh and Byrd, fortunately for national decorum and international amity, had been gentlemen; so had our other famous aviators. They wore their laurels gracefully, withstood the awful weather of publicity, married excellent women, usually of fine family, and quietly retired to private life and the enjoyment of their varying fortunes. No untoward incidents, on a worldwide scale, marred the perfection of their conduct on the perilous heights of fame. The exception to the rule was, however, bound to occur and it did, in July, 1937, when Jack ('Pal') Smurch, erstwhile mechanic's helper in a small garage in Westfield, Iowa, flew a second-hand, single-motored Bresthaven Dragon-Fly III monoplane all the way around the world, without stopping.

Never before in the history of aviation had such a flight as Smurch's ever been dreamed of. No one had even taken seriously the weird floating auxiliary gas tanks, invention of the mad New Hampshire professor of astronomy, Dr Charles Lewis Gresham, upon which Smurch placed full reliance. When the garage worker, a slightly built, surly, unprepossessing young man of twenty-two, appeared at Roosevelt Field early in July, 1937, slowly chewing a great quid of scrap tobacco, and announced 'Nobody ain't seen no flyin' yet,' the newspapers touched briefly and satirically upon his projected twenty-five-thousand-mile flight. Aeronautical and automotive experts dismissed the idea curtly, implying that it was a hoax, a publicity stunt. The rusty, battered, second-hand plane wouldn't go. The Gresham auxiliary tanks wouldn't work. It was simply a cheap joke.

Smurch, however, after calling on a girl in Brooklyn who worked in the flap-folding department of a large paper-box factory, a girl whom he later described as his 'sweet patootie', climbed nonchalantly into his ridiculous plane at dawn of the memorable seventh of July, 1937, spat a curve of tobacco juice into the still air, and took off, carrying with him only a gallon of bootleg gin and six pounds of salami.

When the garage boy thundered out over the ocean the papers were forced to record, in all seriousness, that a mad, unknown young man – his name was variously misspelled – had actually set out upon a preposterous attempt to span the world in a rickety, one-engined contraption, trusting to the long-distance refuelling device of a crazy schoolmaster. When, nine days later, without having stopped once, the tiny plane appeared above San Francisco Bay, headed for New York, spluttering and choking, to be sure, but still magnificently and miraculously aloft, the headlines, which long since had crowded everything else off the front page – even the shooting of the Governor of Illinois by the Vileti gang – swelled to unprecedented size, and the news stories began to run to twenty-five and thirty columns. It was noticeable, however, that the accounts of the epoch-making flight touched rather lightly upon the aviator himself. This was not because facts about the hero as a man were too meagre, but because they were too complete.

Reporters, who had been rushed out to Iowa when Smurch's plane was first sighted over the little French coast town of Serly-le-Mer, to dig up the story of the great man's life, had promptly discovered that the story of his life could not be printed. His mother, a sullen short-order cook in a shack restaurant on the edge of a tourists' camping ground near Westfield, met all enquiries as to her son with an angry 'Ah, the hell with him; I hope he drowns.' His father appeared to be in gaol somewhere for stealing spotlights and laprobes from tourists' automobiles; his young brother, a weak-minded lad, had but recently escaped from the Preston, Iowa, Reformatory and was already wanted in several Western towns for the theft of money-order blanks from post offices. These alarming discoveries were still piling up at the very time that Pal Smurch, the greatest hero of the twentieth century, blear-eyed, dead for sleep, half-starved, was piloting his crazy junk-heap high above the region in which the lamentable story of his private life was being unearthed, headed for New York and a greater glory than any man of his time had ever known.

The necessity for printing some account in the papers of the young man's career and personality had led to a remarkable predicament. It was of course impossible to reveal the facts, for a tremendous popular feeling in favour of the young hero had sprung up, like a grass fire, when he was half-way across Europe on his flight around the globe. He was, therefore, described as a modest chap, taciturn, blond, popular with his friends, popular with girls. The only available snapshot of Smurch, taken at the wheel of a phoney automobile in a cheap photo studio at an amusement park, was touched up so that the little vulgarian looked quite handsome. His twisted leer was smoothed into a pleasant smile. The truth was, in this way, kept from the youth's ecstatic compatriots; they did not dream that the Smurch family was despised and feared by its neighbours in the obscure Iowa town, nor that the hero himself, because of numerous unsavoury exploits, had come to be regarded in Westfield as a nuisance and a menace. He had, the reporters discovered, once knifed the principal of his high school – not mortally, to be sure, but he had knifed him; and on another occasion, surprised in the act of stealing an altarcloth from a church, he had bashed the sacristan over the head with a pot of Easter lilies; for each of these offences he had served a sentence in the reformatory.

Inwardly, the authorities, both in New York and in Washington, prayed that an understanding Providence might, however awful such a thing seemed, bring disaster to the rusty, battered plane and its illustrious pilot, whose unheard-of flight had aroused the civilised world to hosannas of hysterical praise. The authorities were convinced that the character of the renowned aviator was such that the limelight of adulation was bound to reveal him, to all the world, as a congenital hooligan mentally and morally unequipped to cope with his own prodigious fame. 'I trust,' said the Secretary of State, at one of many secret Cabinet meetings called to consider the national dilemma, 'I trust that his mother's prayer will be answered,' by which he referred to Mrs Emma Smurch's wish that her son might be drowned. It was, however, too late for that – Smurch had leaped the Atlantic and then the Pacific as if they were millponds. At three minutes after two o'clock on the afternoon of July 17, 1937, the garage boy brought his idiotic plane into Roosevelt Field for a perfect three-point landing.

It had, of course, been out of the question to arrange a modest little reception for the greatest flier in the history of the world. He was received at Roosevelt Field with such elaborate and pretentious ceremonies as rocked the world. Fortunately, however, the worn and spent hero promptly swooned, had to be removed bodily from his plane, and was spirited from the field without having opened his mouth once. Thus he did not jeopardise the dignity of this first reception, a reception illumined by the presence of the Secretaries of War and the Navy, Mayor Michael J. Moriarity of New York, the Premier of Canada, Governors Fanniman, Groves, McFeely and Critchfield, and a brilliant array of European diplomats. Smurch did not, in fact, come to in time to take part in the gigantic hullabaloo arranged at City Hall for the next day. He was rushed to a secluded nursing home and confined in bed.It was nine days before he was able to get up, or to be more exact, before he was permitted to get up. Meanwhile the greatest minds in the country, in solemn assembly, had arranged a secret conference of city, state and government officials, which Smurch was to attend for the purpose of being instructed in the ethics and behaviour of heroism.

On the day that the little mechanic was finally allowed to get up and dress and, for the first time in two weeks, took a great chew of tobacco, he was permitted to receive the newspapermen – this by way of testing him out. Smurch did not wait for questions. 'Youse guys,' he said – and the *Times* man winced – 'youse guys can tell the cock-eyed world dat I put it over on Lindbergh, see? Yeh – an' made an ass o' them two frogs.' The 'two frogs' was a reference to a pair of gallant French fliers who, in attempting a flight only halfway round the world, had, two weeks before, unhappily been lost at sea. The *Times* man was bold enough, at this point, to sketch out for Smurch the accepted formula for interviews in cases of this kind; he explained that there should be no arrogant statements belittling the achievements of other heroes, particularly heroes of foreign nations. 'Ah, the hell with that,' said Smurch. 'I did it, see? I did it, an' I'm talkin' about it.' And he did talk about it.

None of this extraordinary interview, was of course, printed. On the contrary, the newspapers, already under the disciplined direction of a secret directorate created for the occasion and composed of statesmen and editors, gave out to a panting and restless world that 'Jacky', as he had been arbitrarily nicknamed, would consent to say only that he was very happy and that anyone could have done what he did. 'My achievement has been, I fear, slightly exaggerated,' the *Times* man's article had him protest, with a modest smile. These newspaper stories were kept from the hero, a restriction which did not serve to abate the rising malevolence of his temper. The situation was, indeed, extremely grave, for Pal Smurch was, as he kept insisting, 'rarin' to go'. He could not much longer be kept from a nation clamorous to lionise him. It was the most desperate crisis the United States of America had faced since the sinking of the *Lusitania*.

On the afternoon of the twenty-seventh of July, Smurch was spirited away to a conference-room in which were gathered mayors, governors, government officials, behaviourist psychologists, and editors. He gave them each a limp, moist paw and a brief unlovely grin. 'Hah ya?' he said. When Smurch was seated, the Mayor of New York arose and, with obvious pessimism, attempted to explain what he must say and how he must act when presented to the world, ending his talk with a high tribute to the hero's courage and integrity. The Mayor was followed by Governor Fanniman of New York, who, after a touching declaration of faith, introduced Cameron Spottiswood, Second Secretary of the American Embassy in Paris, the gentleman selected to coach Smurch in the amenities of public ceremonies. Sitting in a chair, with a soiled yellow tie in his hand and his shirt open at the throat, unshaved, smoking a rolled cigarette, Jack Smurch listened with a leer on his lips. 'I get ya, I get ya,' he cut in, nastily. 'Ya want me to ack like a softy, huh? Ya want me to ack like that – baby-face Lindbergh, huh? Well, nuts to that, see?' Everyone took in his breath sharply; it was a sigh and a hiss. 'Mr Lindbergh,' began a United States Senator, purple with rage, 'and Mr Byrd – ' Smurch, who was paring his nails with a jackknife, cut in again. 'Byrd!' he exclaimed. 'Aw fa God's sake, *dat* big—' Somebody shut off his blasphemies with a sharp word. A newcomer had entered the room. Everyone stood up, except Smurch, who, still busy with his nails, did not even glance up. 'Mr Smurch,' said someone, sternly, 'the President of the United States!' It had been thought that the presence of the Chief Executive might have a chastening effect upon the young hero, and the former had been, thanks to the remarkable co-operation of the press, secretly brought to the obscure conference-room.

A great, painful silence fell. Smurch looked up, waved a hand at the President. 'How ya comin'?' he asked, and began rolling a fresh cigarette. The silence deepened. Someone coughed in a strained way. 'Geez, it's hot, ain't it?' said Smurch. He loosened two more shirt buttons, revealing a hairy chest and the tattooed word 'Sadie' enclosed in a stencilled heart. The great and important men in the room, faced by the most serious crisis in recent American history, exchanged worried frowns. Nobody seemed to know how to proceed. 'Come awn, come awn,' said Smurch. 'Let's get the hell out of here! When do I start cuttin' in on de parties, huh? And what's they goin' to be *in* it?' He rubbed a thumb and forefinger together meaningly. 'Money!' exclaimed a state senator, shocked, pale. 'Yeh, money,' said Pal, flipping his cigarette out of a window. 'An' big money.' He began rolling a fresh cigarette. 'Big money,' he repeated, frowning over the rice paper. He tilted back in his chair, and leered at each gentleman, separately, the leer of an animal that knows its power, the leer of a leopard loose in a bird-and-dog shop. 'Aw fa God's sake, let's get some place where it's cooler,' he said. 'I been cooped up plenty for three weeks!'

Smurch stood up and walked over to an open window, where he stood staring down into the street, nine floors below. The faint shouting of newsboys floated up to him. He made out his name. 'Hot dog!' he cried, grinning, ecstatic. He leaned out over the sill. 'You tell 'em, babies!' he shouted down. 'Hot diggity dog!' In the tense little knot of men standing behind him, a quick mad impulse flared up. An unspoken word of appeal, of command, seemed to ring through the room. Yet it was deadly silent. Charles K. L. Brand, secretary to the Mayor of New York City, happened to be standing nearest Smurch; he looked inquiringly at the President of the United States. The President, pale, grim, nodded shortly. Brand, a tall, powerfully built man, once a tackle at Rutgers, stepped forward, seized the greatest man in the world by his left shoulder and the seat of his pants, and pushed him out of the window.

'My God, he's fallen out the window!' cried a quick-witted editor.

'Get me out of here!' cried the President. Several men sprang to his side and he was hurriedly escorted out of a door toward a side-entrance of the building. The editor of the Associated Press took charge, being used to such things. Crisply he ordered certain men to leave, others to stay; quickly he outlined a story which all the papers were to agree on, sent two men to the street to handle that end of the tragedy, commanded a Senator to sob and two Congressmen to go to pieces nervously. In a word, he skilfully set the stage for the gigantic task that was to follow, the task of breaking to a grief-stricken world the sad story of the untimely, accidental death of its most illustrious and spectacular figure.

The funeral was, as you know, the most elaborate, the finest, the solemnest, and the saddest ever held in the United States of America. The monument in Arlington Cemetery, with its clean white shaft of marble and the simple device of a tiny plane carved on its base, is a place for pilgrims, in deep reverence, to visit. The nations of the world paid lofty tributes to little Jacky Smurch, America's greatest hero. At a given hour there were two minutes of silence throughout the nation. Even the inhabitants of the small, bewildered town of Westfield, Iowa, observed this touching ceremony; agents of the Department of Justice saw to that. One of them was especially assigned to stand grimly in the doorway of a little shack restaurant on the edge of the tourists' camping ground just outside the town. There, under his stern scrutiny, Mrs Emma Smurch bowed her head above two hamburger steaks sizzling on her grill – bowed her head and turned away, so that the Secret Service men could not see the twisted, strangely familiar, leer on her lips.

The Bishop's Aunt

L. E. Jones

A picture of peace and happiness. That is how most of us, who are inclined to think in simple terms, would have described the appearance of the compact and ancient town of P. had we been gazing at it, on a May day in the year 1946, from the café terrace across the river. The warm brown roofs hung in folds, as if a massive rug had been thrown across the descending ridge; at the top of the town rose the castle and the thin flêche of the little cathedral (for P. was an old Catholic see), round which the swifts swooped and shrilled; between the river and the town a row of chestnut trees, still in full bloom, drew, with their continuous shadows, a bold, dark line. The May sunshine, bright and beneficent, lay over all.

But in the town itself was neither peace nor happiness. For P. was in Eastern Europe; the Red Army was occupying the country, and tragedy had come to this quiet little place.

Two days earlier a Russian soldier, sitting unarmed in a café on the small cobbled square, had been assassinated, stabbed in the back by an assailant who had escaped. Even today the edges of a thin, paper-like crust of dried blood and dust lifted and fell in the breeze below the iron chair in which the dead soldier had been sitting. The general of the Division occupying the district had immediately arrested twenty of the leading citizens, including the Catholic Bishop and the Mayor, and had issued a proclamation announcing that, unless the assassin surrendered, or was given up, within forty-eight hours, the twenty hostages would be shot. That period had expired at eleven o'clock on this lovely May morning. At half-past eleven the Bishop and the Mayor were brought, under guard, from the Castle to the small Gothic town hall. Here, in the Mayor's parlour, sat the General, with a list of the hostages upon the table before him. There was nothing typical of Russian generals – if photographs can be trusted – in his appearance. His face could have been that of a thoughtful, energetic and efficient senior officer in any Western army; it was strong, but not hard; and he had the air, uncommon in generals, of being capable of listening as well as of speaking. All the same, he could shut his mouth tightly indeed. At the moment his expression was stern, but his grey eyes were not happy.

The two prisoners who now stood before him, the Bishop and the Mayor, had nothing, so far as appearances go, in common. The Bishop, who was in cassock and skull-cap, was a slight wisp of a man in his fifties, with a touch of the peasant about him; his thin face was unremarkable except for the candour, the trustfulness of his wide-open blue eyes. He stood there very much at his ease; even if born a peasant, he moved, stood and spoke like a bishop. The Mayor, on the contrary, was a great bull of a man with angry eyes. His stiff black hair was *en brosse* over a creased forehead; he had a habit of jerking back his head and moving his heavy shoulders under his loose alpaca jacket, that came from his habitual impatience with stupid people – among whom he placed the Bishop. For the Mayor was an aggressive infidel.

When the guards had finished with all those noisy stampings and time-markings, ending with the thump, as they grounded arms, which punctuates military justice everywhere, the General spoke:

'Well, gentlemen, I am sorry it has come to this. The time is up: you have not given up your man: you know the consequences.'

'Naturally we have not given anybody up,' said the Bishop, with a touch of indignation in his rather flat voice.

'Firstly because we do not betray one another, and secondly because we don't know who he is.'

'I know who he is,' said the Mayor.

'Oh you do, do you?' said the General, but before he could say more the Bishop had turned on the Mayor, red in the face.

'In that case, Mr Mayor, you should have persuaded him to give himself up.'

'I beg your pardon?' The Mayor swung round, genuinely surprised.

'Murder,' said the Bishop, 'is always a sin, and a deadly one.' The Mayor turned to the General, putting, for the Bishop's benefit, a weary note into his voice.

'There he goes again, General.' He turned once more to the Bishop. 'As I have wasted far too much of the public's time on telling you and them, Bishop, you always get things mixed up. Murder is a sin: all right. But killing a lance-corporal in the General's army is not murder. It's an act of war. You yourself used to appoint days of prayer for Victory—'

'But the war is over,' interrupted the Bishop. 'We capitulated. And the man was unarmed – stabbed to death, while drinking coffee. It was a cowardly, as well as a wicked, murder.'

'Cowardly!' The Mayor began to shout. 'My dear Bishop, I should like to know if *you* would have the guts to allow twenty of your fellow-citizens, including my worshipful self, to be executed, rather than let the General here get away with this futile game of hostages? The man's a hero!'

The Bishop smiled. 'I agree that I might never have had the nerve to let *you* be shot, my son. The thought of your almost certain fate in the next world would be too much for me. But when your man assassinated that poor fellow in the café—'

The General cut him short.

'You can save your sympathy for the "poor" fellow,

Bishop. His CO tells me he was suspected of Trotskyism, and is better dead. And of course the Mayor is right. If you are going to have a Resistance movement, there can be no rules. But my business, gentlemen, is to suppress the Resistance movement—'

'Which remains unsuppressed,' said the Mayor. 'Our man has beaten you.'

'Don't be too sure, Mr Mayor,' said the General. 'For one hero, as you call him, there will be fifty others who will think twice before sending a Bishop to Paradise and a Mayor to – where did you hint that the Mayor may be before six o'clock, Bishop?'

'I never claimed Paradise, General,' said the Bishop hastily. 'I shall be fortunate if, by Divine Grace, it proves to be Purgatory.'

'I'm in Purgatory now, General,' said the Mayor. 'It's this sentry of yours – I can't abide garlic – could he stand a little farther off?'

'But of course,' said the General, with a glance at the NCO in charge of the guard. There was a bark; a rattle; some more stamping, and the sentry retreated two paces.

'Thank you,' said the Mayor.

'Don't mention it,' said the General. 'No, Mr Mayor,' he continued, 'I cannot admit that my system of hostages has failed. At the same time I agree that in this particular case things might have gone better. Perhaps I arrested the wrong people. In a town like this there are bound to be individuals whom public opinion would like to see shot.'

'Our Mayor,' said the Bishop, 'is enormously – and from my point of view I must add deplorably – popular.'

'Our Bishop,' said the Mayor, 'muddle-headed though he is, is universally beloved.'

'Were some of the other hostages thought to be expendable, perhaps?' asked the General.

'They are all most highly respected,' said the Bishop.

'It may have been a mistake to include the Inspector of Taxes,' said the Mayor.

'I see,' said the General. 'Do you think that if I released the Inspector of Taxes your man would surrender to save the rest?'

'Not a hope,' said the Mayor. 'Actually he raised the point with me last night.'

The General, for a second or so, looked more startled than a General should.

'Are you telling me,' he replied, 'that you have been in touch with this man since your arrest?'

The Mayor spoke soothingly. 'Our Resistance is not an amateur movement, General. As I was saying, he did mention the Inspector of Taxes. It's one grain of comfort to him in his heroic unhappiness.'

'Aha. So he is unhappy?'

'Undoubtedly,' said the Mayor. 'But then he's a very sensitive type. For most of us these shootings of yours have become just a thing that happens. If I may say, you make them too common, General.'

'It is interesting that you should say that,' said the General, 'because it is exactly what I have been thinking myself. An announcement that so many notables have been executed at dawn in a prison-yard – it has become rather *vieux-jeu*. Our capacity for being horrified is strangely limited, don't you agree, Bishop?'

'Alas, it is only too true,' said the Bishop. 'Compassion, the most divine of virtues, is also by far the most fatiguing. It is perhaps the supreme horror of atrocities – that in the end they cease to excite horror.'

'Then it looks,' said the General, 'as if you may both feel at any rate an intellectual sympathy with my decision – a decision which I have come to since it appeared pretty certain that the murderer was not going to be given up. It seemed to me that I must do something more horrifying, more spectacular, better calculated to impress than a mere routine execution. So I am going to make you an offer, Bishop. I shall not insist upon it, if you refuse: but if you will volunteer to be publicly crucified in the market-place tomorrow, I will let the other nineteen go free, including your admirable Mayor.'

'Never!' shouted the Mayor, on whose great neck two veins were swelling.

'Silence, sir!' rapped out the General, 'I am speaking.' He turned to the Bishop. 'I think a crucifixion should make a decided impression. The mere announcement of it might cause your man to surrender at the eleventh hour. What do you say?'

'Never!' yelled the Mayor once more. 'It's an outrageous suggestion. It shall never be allowed. Never!'

'I am speaking to the Bishop, Mr Mayor,' the General shouted back. 'He can allow it, or he can refuse it. Well, Bishop?'

'What time, tomorrow?' inquired the Bishop.

The General looked a little puzzled. 'Whenever I order it, of course. But what has the time got to do with it?'

'It has a great deal to do with it,' said the Bishop. 'How could I possibly face the sublime honour of crucifixion without due preparation? I must make my Confession, I must get shaved and bathed. I must choose the proper vestments in which to approach the Cross; above all, I must have time for prayer and meditation. I cannot be rushed. This is not a small thing you offer me, General. And you must let me go home tonight – under guard, of course.'

'That will be quite in order, Bishop,' said the General. 'You may go home now, under guard, and the crucifixion will be at noon tomorrow.'

'Then I accept your offer,' said the Bishop.

The Mayor, who had been listening to the Bishop's words with his mouth as wide open as his eyes, again broke in.

'It can't be allowed! It's too utterly horrible!'

The Bishop looked shocked.

'Hush, my son. That is not the way to speak of a crucifixion.'

'Of course it's horrible,' said the General, 'but I thought we were agreed that, from my point of view, a little more horror is indicated. And *I* am the one who allows things in this town, Mr Mayor.'

'There is just one question, General,' said the Bishop, 'that I should like to ask. Why don't you crucify the Mayor, instead of me?'

'A very good idea,' said the Mayor, turning eagerly towards the General. 'Why don't you?'

'Common sense, I suppose,' said the General. 'If one is compelled, unhappily, to destroy, one destroys the most dangerous man first.'

The Mayor actually laughed.

'Dangerous? Our good Bishop is the most harmless person alive. Why, he even wanted our brave Resistance fighter to give himself up to you.'

'That,' said the General, 'is the reason why he is so formidable compared to you, with your rather crude belief in violence. We can always beat you at that game – provided, that is, that the Bishop's fifth column is not permitted to corrupt us.'

The Bishop's face suddenly shone.

'Is it your meaning, General, that you chose me and not the Mayor for this great honour because of the Faith I hold?'

'It could be put like that, I suppose,' said the General.

'Then God be praised for His great goodness!' exclaimed the Bishop, radiant, 'I shall, after all, die for the Faith.' He held out a hand to the Mayor. 'Congratulate me, my son.'

The Mayor took his hand.

'You're a hero, Bishop.'

The Bishop laughed. 'Who's muddle-headed now?' he said. He turned to the General. 'What can we do, General, with a man so uninstructed that he confuses martyrs with heroes?'

The General looked puzzled.

'Is he so far wrong? I agree a hero need not be a martyr, but surely a martyr is a hero?'

'I see that I must pray for your brains too,' said the Bishop. 'If all goes well, I hope by tomorrow night to be in a position to do something substantial for both of you. Till then, goodbye, gentlemen, and once again my thanks, General.'

'Don't mention it,' said the General.

The General rose from his seat; the corporal of the guard barked out another order; there was stamping and banging and turning about, and the Bishop with his escort reached the door. The General called out to him.

'Won't you take my car, Bishop?'

'No, thank you,' said the Bishop, 'I shall enjoy the walk.'

And he went out tranquilly, but with care to keep in step with his guards, up the narrow cobbled street to his home in the cathedral square.

The General turned to the Mayor. 'I expect you will wish to be the first to tell the good news to your friends, Mr Mayor.'

'Send your own man,' said the Mayor. 'I haven't the courage to break it to them.'

It was past noon, an hour when the people went home to their dinners, and nobody noticed the Mayor as he walked, heavily and with his chin on his chest, to his house a few doors away from the town hall. But in less than half an hour the people were out in the streets again, for a military car equipped with a loudspeaker was going at a foot's pace through the town, blaring out the news that the hostages had been released, all but the Bishop who, at his own free choice, would, unless the assassin was delivered up, be crucified at noon tomorrow in the market-square. Upon which there arose a murmuring and a buzz of talk which kept the town pigeons restless and uneasy for an hour or more.

At five o'clock that same afternoon a little old lady, all

in black and carrying a shopping-bag with no bulge in it, slipped out of a postern door in the Cathedral and crossed the little square to the Bishop's house. The square was almost deserted, since the people still thought the Bishop to be a prisoner in the Castle, and it was before the great doors of the inner keep that they had gathered to cheer him. The old lady's eyes were red, but her mouth was firm and her chin in the air. She paused for a moment on the doorstep, and stared at the familiar, nail-studded door as if it had turned suddenly into something strange and hostile; then, visibly pulling herself together, she twisted the heavy iron stirrup-handle and went into the house. Inside she paused again; again made an effort, and opened the door of the Bishop's study. In it sat the Bishop, reading, in his easy chair. On a hard chair by the empty grate sat a Russian soldier. The little old lady appeared thunderstruck.

'Joseph! What on earth are you doing here? I thought you were dead.'

'I am reading the fifteenth chapter of the Gospel according to St Mark, Aunt.'

'But why haven't you been shot? Here I've been wasting half the day in church, praying for your soul and weeping my old eyes out, and all for nothing! Besides, I've only brought home enough food for one supper. Have you seen to the kitchen fire? And have you been reprieved? What's that man doing here? Don't you stand up for a lady?'

The soldier, who understood nothing but Russian, remained seated.

'He's a sentry,' said the Bishop. 'He's guarding me. But haven't they told you the news?'

'I tell you, I've been in the Cathedral since ten this morning. Are you really reprieved, dear Joseph?'

'Better than that, far better,' said the Bishop.

'Has he given himself up?'

The Bishop shook his head. 'No. But I – your nephew,

dear Aunt – am to win a martyr's crown. I can still hardly believe it.'

'You a martyr? Don't be foolish, Joseph. You're a good man, but we don't have martyrs in our family. What have they been doing to you? Would you like a drop of cognac?'

'I know it sounds impossible,' said the Bishop, 'and nobody knows better than I do how unworthy I am. But God in His great goodness has willed it. Tomorrow I am to share the fate of my Blessed Lord. And only because of my Faith – the General made that perfectly clear.'

'Hush, Joseph – you mustn't talk like that – what's come over you?' She moved quickly to his side, full of concern. 'Have they been hitting you over the head? If so, you must not on any account have cognac.'

The Bishop took her hand.

'Please listen, dear Aunt,' he said. 'It's the General's decision but God must have put it into his head. The other hostages are to be released, but I, because of my Faith – although unworthy – am to be publicly crucified in the market-place tomorrow at noon.'

'Crucified?' said his aunt, drawing away her hand. 'Don't be blasphemous, Joseph. How can *you* be crucified?' Suddenly her hands flew to her temples. 'Mother of God! You don't mean that those devils, these filthy heathen Communists, are going to dare to—'

'No, no,' said the Bishop, 'nothing of the sort. I freely chose it. There was no compulsion at all. The General could not have been fairer. Either we were all shot together, or I was to be crucified alone. He left it entirely to me.'

His aunt's face took on a look of blank incredulity.

'And you chose the – the *cross*, Joseph?'

'But of course,' said the Bishop.

'Then I'm ashamed of you,' said his aunt bitterly. 'I wouldn't have believed it of you! You were always a bit of a simpleton – but to walk into that trap! and you a Bishop! You'll go back to the General this minute, and tell him that you've changed your mind. Really, Joseph, there are times when one would take you for a small boy. Martyr indeed!'

It was the Bishop's turn to look blank.

'I don't understand. A trap? What do you mean by "walking into a trap"?'

'Oh, you noodle,' said his aunt. 'Can't you see their wicked thoughts? How could they better belittle and make a mock of our Blessed Saviour than by crucifying a little man like you, Joseph? What will your Master's Sacrifice and Passion mean to your people after they have watched *you* being tortured on a cross? Who do you suppose is going to have their prayers and adoration for the next hundred years – our Blessed Lord, or their own little St Joseph, Bishop and Martyr? Aren't you always complaining that your flock seem to think more of our local saints than of the Christ? And who's going to be their favourite saint, do you imagine – when they've seen you, their own dear Bishop, martyred before their eyes?'

'Perhaps they won't come to the – er – market-place,' said the Bishop. 'They may not want to see me – it will be painful, of course.'

'Not come? Of course they'll come. It will be the day of their lives. No, my poor Joseph, you've been made a fool of, and the sooner you put things right the better.'

For thirty years the Bishop, although he did not know it, had been ruled by his aunt, and he had lost the capacity, through long disuse, of thinking her mistaken. He looked very downcast indeed.

'This is – this is rather a shock to me,' he said. 'I confess I had not looked at it from that point of view. It's all very difficult. I suppose, in a way, it does seem rather presumptuous—'

'It's downright blasphemy.'

'But since it was to save the lives of so many good men—'

His aunt snorted. 'The Inspector of Taxes, for instance?'

'Our Saviour died for him,' said the Bishop.

'All the less reason why you should. You've been altogether above yourself, Joseph.'

The Bishop sighed heartily. 'It's a terrible responsibility to go back now and ask for those men to be shot. Think of their families, Aunt.'

'I've been praying for their families for the last forty-eight hours – when I wasn't housekeeping. And it's not your responsibility, it's the General's. Besides, better a thousand men shot than let the Cross be mocked.'

The Bishop sighed again.

'You're a good woman, Aunt. And I'm afraid you are right. I didn't think, or worse, I was thinking of myself.'

'You were dazzled, Joseph. That's the plain truth of it.'

'Yes,' said the Bishop, 'I'm afraid I was dazzled. And now, oh dear, the thing must be undone. How shall I ever explain it to the Mayor?'

'Explain it?' said his aunt. 'Have you no sense, Joseph? Of course you can't explain it. Are you going to tell that atheist and his friends that the glory and holiness of our dear Lord's Crucifixion are not safe in the keeping of your own flock? That you can't trust Christians to know the difference between the Cross of Christ and the murder of a hostage? You know you are not.'

'No, I suppose not,' said the Bishop. 'No, I shall say nothing. They must just think me a coward.'

'Then they'll think wrong,' said his aunt. 'It won't be the first time. And now be off with you. You'd better go by the back lane, and avoid the crowds.'

'On the contrary, there is something I have got to say to the crowds. I'm afraid it will be bitter news to some of them.'

'Then I shall come with you,' said his aunt.

'Don't you trust me?'

'I don't trust crowds,' said his aunt.

'I am their Bishop. What are you afraid of?'

'Mightn't they,' said his aunt, ' – oh, dear God, now it's my turn to be blasphemous – mightn't they cry: Crucify him! Crucify him!'

'Nonsense,' said the Bishop. But she was not far wrong.

The Bishop, who knew a word or two of Russian, spoke to the sentry on the chair, and explained that he wished to be taken back to the town hall. The rest of the guard tramped in from the kitchen, but the Corporal made difficulties. The news had spread that the Bishop was now in his own house, and there was a big crowd gathering in the Cathedral square, he said, in a highly excitable state. Women in tears, men crying: 'Long live our Bishop.' He had only six men; if a rescue were attempted, he would have to fire on the crowd.

The Bishop's aunt tried to explain to him that by 'Long live our Bishop' they did not mean that they wished their Bishop to live longer than noon tomorrow, and that an attempt at rescue was the last thing to be feared. She did not add that she herself was more afraid of an attempt on his life, but she did point out to the Corporal that the back lane, which avoided the Square altogether, would probably be deserted.

'I've only six men,' said the Corporal doubtfully.

'Only five,' said the Bishop. 'One of them must go to the General to tell him I wish to see him immediately in the town hall.'

'But I,' said his aunt, 'will be worth another six men at the least.'

'I must speak to the people first,' said the Bishop.

'Then you must speak from a window,' said the aunt. 'We will then slip out by the back door.'

The Bishop went to the formal parlour at the front of the house, a soldier on one side of him, his aunt on the other, and stood at an open window. A great roar went up from the crowd, and the town pigeons rose as one bird from the roofs. The Bishop put up his hand for silence. All sounds died away, for the Bishop's authority, always great, had become absolute by reason of his proclaimed martyrdom.

The Bishop's voice, when he spoke, was high and clear.

'My people,' he said, 'I have sad news for you. You have been told that, by my own free choice, I was to have been crucified tomorrow. Well, I have changed my mind. There will be no crucifixion. Together with my fellow-hostages, I shall be shot instead.'

He held up two fingers in sign of benediction and withdrew from the window.

For a few seconds the crowd was dumb. Then it began to murmur; the murmur turned to a growl; a man shouted something, and was answered by a roar; in no time the frightening 'rhubarb, rhubarb' noise of stage tradition filled the little square.

Inside the Bishop's house, the Corporal was hustling his captive out into the back lane which, as the aunt had guessed, was entirely deserted. Down it the little party marched briskly to the town hall. Only the Bishop's aunt failed to keep step; she trotted.

In the Mayor's parlour they had not long to wait. As the General strode in, spurs jingling, with a tight mouth, the noise of distant booing came through the open window.

'Shut that window, Corporal,' snapped the General. He turned to the Bishop as he took his seat.

'So a prisoner, Bishop, sends a peremptory summons to his captor? This is something new. Who is this lady?'

'Allow me to present to you my aunt, General,' said the Bishop.

The General made the slightest inclination of his head.

'I wish I could bid you welcome, madam. But this is highly irregular – may I ask to what I owe this honour?'

'Can't you hear them howling?' said the aunt. 'My nephew needed an escort.'

'He had my guards,' said the General.

'They would have eaten up your guards. But they still respect a woman – in this country,' said the aunt.

The General turned to the Bishop.

'What has happened to your people, Bishop? A little while ago they were cheering for you like—'

He was interrupted by a clatter of feet outside; the bursting open of the parlour door, and the bull-like rush of the Mayor, head down, angry, pushing a soldier out of his path. He ignored the General altogether.

'What the devil's the meaning of this, Bishop? The town's completely out of hand. There's a rumour going round that you've ratted – absurd, of course, but you'll have to come and speak to them yourself, at once.'

The General used his parade voice.

'Mr Mayor, you forget yourself. *I* happen to be present.'

The Mayor took a pull at himself.

'I'm sorry, General. I apologise, but there's no time to be lost. You haven't a loudspeaker ready, have you?'

'I have already spoken to them,' said the Bishop.

'The devil you have! Then why the – what have you been telling them?'

'I told them that I had changed my mind. There will be no crucifixion tomorrow,' said the Bishop.

The Mayor stared at him. He had an air of never having seen the Bishop before. His eyes, for an instant, were full of curiosity. Then his great face flushed red.

'You – you bloody coward!' he cried.

'A lady present, Mr Mayor,' said the General. 'This is news to me, Bishop.'

'Yes,' said the Bishop, 'I asked for this meeting in order to tell you.'

'You little rat,' said the Mayor.

'And you wish the previous arrangement to stand?' said the General. 'Mr Mayor here and the other hostages are to be shot?'

'I'm afraid that follows,' said the Bishop. 'And me, of course.'

'Shooting hurts less, eh?' said the Mayor.

'Silence, sir,' said the General to the Mayor. 'You have no right yet to assume anything. Perhaps, Bishop, as you have put me to a good deal of trouble in arranging for your crucifixion, you will tell me your reasons for this sudden change of plan?'

'Careful, Joseph,' said the Bishop's aunt.

'I'm sorry, I have no reason to give,' said the Bishop.

'Aha!' said the Mayor.

'No explanation at all?' said the General. 'There's the people to be considered as well, you know, not to speak of your fellow-hostages and their families.'

'No explanation at all,' said the Bishop.

'So we draw our own conclusions,' said the Mayor.

The General looked grave. 'We draw our own conclusions,' he said.

The Mayor swung round to face the General.

'Then let me tell you, General, that there will be a crucifixion tomorrow. Your arrangements can stand.'

'I fail to understand,' said the General.

'You will crucify *me*,' said the Mayor. 'Better tell the people now, I think. It may quieten them.'

The Bishop, for the first time in the affair, lost his serenity. He all but shouted.

'No, no, no, General. You can't do that! It was to me you gave the chance, not to him.' He turned to the Mayor, speaking gently once more. 'You are a brave man, all the same.'

'Pray don't excite yourself, Bishop,' said the General. 'I have no intention of crucifying the Mayor. I don't believe in torture – if I did, I should have tortured him long ago. Doesn't he know all the names I am looking for? Not that he would have disclosed them.'

'Thank you, General. I wish I was as sure of that. But look here, you were quite ready to torture the Bishop. If him, why not me? It's so unfair on the other hostages. If you were ready to let them be ransomed by a crucifixion, what difference can it make whose crucifixion it is?'

'It makes the whole difference,' said the General. 'The Bishop represents a Faith which is one of the major obstacles, in this benighted country, to the spread of our own enlightened doctrines. I had hoped, by publicly crucifying him, to cheapen one of the central mysteries of the Faith. Your case is quite different. Like me, you are an atheist. To crucify instead of shooting you would be mere pointless savagery.'

The Mayor rubbed the back of his great head. 'You're an artful one, I must say, General. I should never have thought of it myself. So the failure of that wretched man's nerve has cheated you of your little game. It's almost funny in a way.'

'I don't think the Bishop's nerve failed him,' said the General. 'I believe he saw through my little game, as you call it. Am I right, Bishop?'

The Bishop shook his head mournfully.

'No, General, to my shame, I did not see through you. I have always been a bit simple. Fortunately my aunt here did see through you.'

The General turned to the aunt with an ironical inclination of the head.

'You did, madam? I congratulate you.'

'It was sticking out a mile,' said the aunt. 'I certainly can't congratulate *you*, General. And you, Mr Mayor, will now kindly apologise for your disgraceful abuse of my nephew. He may be a simpleton – but he's certainly a hero.'

'I agree with you, madam,' said the General. 'It takes a brave man to choose crucifixion, but it takes a braver one still to send you, Mr Mayor, and eighteen others to the firing squad, knowing that he will be branded for ever as a coward for doing so.'

The Mayor nodded.

'And perhaps you realise now,' continued the General, 'why I am so much opposed to the Bishop's Faith. It has qualities which, I am very much afraid, are almost invincible.'

The Mayor held out his hand to the Bishop.

'Bishop, I apologise. Forgive me.'

'You had every excuse, my son,' said the Bishop. 'There is nothing to forgive.'

'And you, Joseph,' said his aunt, 'must not let your head be turned. Brave as you have been, you are not in the same street for courage as the Mayor.'

'Right again, madam,' said the General.

'What nonsense is this?' said the Mayor.

'It's quite simple,' said the aunt. 'My nephew, crucified or not, dies with a sure and certain hope of his reward in Heaven. You, Mr Mayor, are prepared to undergo the same sufferings with no hope at all. If there's to be a prize for sheer courage, you win hands down.'

'We must all agree there,' said the General.

'There can be no question,' said the Bishop.

'And it's a thousand pities, if you ask me,' said the aunt, still addressing the Mayor, 'that you should have to suffer eternal torment.'

'My dear aunt!' said the Bishop, 'God's mercy is infinite.'

'That may be, but He knows the Mayor,' said the aunt.

The General held up his hand.

'If I may interrupt these interesting conjectures, I would like to say that, if the Bishop – or perhaps I should say his lady aunt – has beaten me, you, Mr Mayor, are also of an invincible type. What can I do against men who, without hope or faith, will face torture? Luckily such men are rare. If I get rid of you and the Bishop, I think I can afford to let the other hostages go free. I admit I did not realise at first what a valuable catch I had made. Would dawn tomorrow suit you, gentlemen?'

'Perfectly,' said the Bishop.

'Whenever you like,' said the Mayor.

'Don't be absurd, General,' said the Bishop's aunt. 'You have just admitted that the Mayor is invincible, and that such men are rare. But if you shoot him, you will be making them common. There's nothing like example to make men brave. For every one invincible you shoot, you will make fifty more invincibles. Heroism is catching. The dear God knows it's not for me to save you from weakening yourself, but I never could hold my tongue when I see stupidity, and to shoot the Mayor would be grossly stupid.'

The General looked hard at her. He blinked once or twice.

'Upon my word,' he said, 'you're a very intelligent person, madam. I wish I had you on my staff. I am greatly obliged to you. You have saved me from a blunder. Mr Mayor, you are free.'

'I would rather you released the Bishop,' said the Mayor.

'I'm sorry,' said the General, 'but the Bishop's case is, as I told you, different. He is the product of a Faith. By shooting him I shall neither weaken nor strengthen this Faith. Besides, I must shoot somebody.'

'May I open the window, General?' said the aunt. Without waiting for his permission she crossed the room and opened it. Once more the sounds of booing were heard. She closed the window and resumed her position. 'Did you hear that?' she said. 'They are out for the Bishop's blood. Are you going to oblige them?'

'I shall of course explain to them that, so far from being the coward they think, the Bishop is a hero.'

'You can't make sense of that without giving away your own little plot, and how he beat you.'

'How *you* beat him, dear Aunt,' said the Bishop.

'Is that story going to be good for your prestige?' said the aunt. 'The attempt to crucify a Bishop which failed? Will Moscow think it funny?'

The General stroked his chin.

'They might not. You may be right. It would be difficult to explain to a mob, in any case. No, I'm sorry, Bishop, but I'm afraid it's not practical to explain. You must be content, as you were just now, with your own conscience being clear.'

The Bishop nodded.

'Then, General,' said his aunt, 'you will be shooting at dawn tomorrow the one man the people will be willing to see shot – the cowardly Bishop who ratted. As I said, I ought not to want to save you from yourself, but the pointlessness of it! It's so downright silly.'

For the first time the General looked savage.

'I know who I should *like* to shoot – madam!'

'Nobody but Joseph here would care a hoot if you did,' said the aunt.

'I imagine you are not popular,' said the General. 'People who are always in the right seldom are.' He made a gesture of annoyance. 'Very well, you can go, Bishop.'

'Into that howling mob?' said the aunt, 'with the stain of cowardice on him? You will stay here, Joseph, while I go and explain to the people.'

'Explain what?' said the Bishop.

'That the crucifixion was planned by the General as an insult to our Faith, and that you – that we saw through it. Goodbye, General. Good-night, Mr Mayor.'

The General was a man of resource.

'Wait a moment, madam,' he said; 'I will save you any further trouble. I propose to send out my loudspeaker to inform the crowd that the crucifixion had been already cancelled, not by the Bishop, but by myself, and that the hostages have been released since it has come to light that the murdered man was the aggressor in a brawl.'

'And our man killed him in self-defence?' said the Mayor.

'Exactly,' said the General.

'A dreadful lie, General,' said the Bishop. 'I have misjudged you, I fear. I thought you were at least a man of truth.'

'And whose fault is it that I am not, I should like to know? Who has driven me into a corner from which only a falsehood can extricate me? There she stands, gentlemen – and she a Bishop's aunt!'

'There's another thing,' said the Mayor. 'Your announcement does not clear the Bishop. 'Unfortunately he himself told his people that he had changed his mind.'

'His aunt will clear him, you'll see,' said the General.

The Bishop shook his head.

'What I have said, I have said. My people may think me a coward; they will never believe I could tell an untruth.'

'My dear Joseph,' said his aunt, 'I shall merely tell them that you were acting under my orders. I shall take the full responsibility.'

The Bishop smiled at her.

'You'll never convince them of that,' he said.

'I shan't have to convince anybody,' said his aunt. 'They've known it for thirty years.'

Twenty minutes later the military car with the loud-speaker was again patrolling the streets, blaring out the General's announcement. And while the crowds were cheering for the release of the hostages, a little old lady in black, with her chin in the air, was passing from group to group, button-holing the most talkative of the citizens. Within the hour a crowd was in the Cathedral Square, cheering for the Bishop. The swifts continued to swoop and shrill round the Cathedral spire, and had you been seated on the café terrace across the river, you would have thought the old town, now bathed in the yellow evening light, the very picture of peace and happiness. And this time you would have been right.

Ministers of Grace

Saki

Although he was scarcely yet out of his teens, the Duke of Scaw was already marked out as a personality widely differing from others of his caste and period. Not in externals; therein he conformed correctly to type. His hair was faintly reminiscent of Houbigant, and at the other end of him his shoes exhaled the right *soupçon* of harness-room; his socks compelled one's attention without losing one's respect; and his attitude in repose had just that suggestion of Whistler's mother, so becoming in the really young. It was within that the trouble lay, if trouble it could be accounted, which marked him apart from his fellows. The Duke was religious. Not in any of the ordinary senses of the word; he took small heed of High Church or Evangelical standpoints, he stood outside of all the movements and missions and cults and crusades of the day, uncaring and uninterested. Yet in a mystical-practical way of his own, which had served him unscathed and unshaken through the fickle years of boyhood, he was intensely and intensively religious. His family were naturally, though unobtrusively, distressed about it. 'I am so afraid it may affect his bridge,' said his mother.

The Duke sat in a pennyworth of chair in St James's Park, listening to the pessimisms of Belturbet, who reviewed the existing political situation from the gloomiest of standpoints.

'Where I think you political spade-workers are so silly,' said the Duke, 'is in the misdirection of your efforts. You spend thousands of pounds of money, and Heaven knows how much dynamic force of brain power and personal energy, in trying to elect or displace this or that man, whereas you could gain your ends so much more simply by making use of the men as you find them. If they don't suit your purpose as they are, transform them into something more satisfactory.'

'Do you refer to hypnotic suggestion?' asked Belturbet, with the air of one who is being trifled with.

'Nothing of the sort. Do you understand what I mean by the verb to koepenick? That is to say, to replace an authority by a spurious imitation that would carry just as much weight for the moment as the displaced original; the advantage, of course, being that the koepenick replica would do what you wanted, whereas the original does what seems best in its own eyes.'

'I suppose every public man has a double, if not two or three,' said Belturbet; 'but it would be a pretty hard task to koepenick a whole bunch of them and keep the originals out of the way.'

'There have been instances in European history of highly successful koepenickery,' said the Duke dreamily.

'Oh, of course, there have been False Dimitris and Perkin Warbecks, who imposed on the world for a time,' assented Belturbet, 'but they personated people who were dead or safely out of the way. That was a comparatively simple matter. It would be far easier to pass oneself off as dead Hannibal than as living Haldane, for instance.'

'I was thinking,' said the Duke, 'of the most famous case of all, the angel who koepenicked King Robert of Sicily with such brilliant results. Just imagine what an advantage it would be to have angels deputising, to use a horrible but convenient word, for Quinston and Lord Hugo Sizzle, for example. How much smoother the Parliamentary machine would work than at present!'

'Now you're talking nonsense,' said Belturbet; 'angels don't exist nowadays, at least, not in that way, so what is the use of dragging them into a serious discussion? It's merely silly.'

'If you talk to me like that I shall just *do* it,' said the Duke.

'Do what?' asked Belturbet. There were times when his young friend's uncanny remarks rather frightened him.

'I shall summon angelic forces to take over some of the more troublesome personalities of our public life, and I shall send the ousted originals into temporary retirement in suitable animal organisms. It's not every one who would have the knowledge or the power necessary to bring such a thing off—'

'Oh, stop that inane rubbish,' said Belturbet angrily; 'it's getting wearisome. Here's Quinston coming,' he added, as there approached along the almost deserted path the well-known figure of a young Cabinet Minister, whose personality evoked a curious mixture of public interest and unpopularity.

'Hurry along, my dear man,' said the young Duke to the Minister, who had given him a condescending nod; 'your time is running short,' he continued in a provocative strain; 'the whole inept crowd of you will shortly be swept away into the world's wastepaper basket.'

'You poor little strawberry-leafed nonentity,' said the Minister, checking himself for a moment in his stride and rolling out his words spasmodically; 'who is going to sweep us away, I should like to know? The voting masses are on our side, and all the ability and administrative talent is on our side too. No power of earth or Heaven is going to move us from our place till we choose to quit it. No power of earth or—'

Belturbet saw, with bulging eyes, a sudden void where a moment earlier had been a Cabinet Minister; a void emphasised rather than relieved by the presence of a puffed-out bewildered-looking sparrow, which hopped about for a moment in a dazed fashion and then fell to a violent cheeping and scolding.

'If we could understand sparrow-language,' said the

Duke serenely, 'I fancy we should hear something infinitely worse than "strawberry-leafed nonentity".'

'But good Heavens, Eugène,' said Belturbet hoarsely, 'what has become of – Why, there he is! How on earth did he get there?' And he pointed with a shaking finger towards a semblance of the vanished Minister, which approached once more along the unfrequented path.

The Duke laughed.

'It is Quinston to all outward appearance,' he said composedly, 'but I fancy you will find, on closer investigation, that it is an angel understudy of the real article.'

The Angel-Quinston greeted them with a friendly smile.

'How beastly happy you two look sitting there!' he said wistfully.

'I don't suppose you'd care to change places with poor little us,' replied the Duke chaffingly.

'How about poor little me?' said the Angel modestly. 'I've got to run about behind the wheels of popularity, like a spotted dog behind a carriage, getting all the dust and trying to look as if I was an important part of the machine. I must seem a perfect fool to you onlookers sometimes.'

'I think you are a perfect angel,' said the Duke.

The Angel-that-had-been-Quinston smiled and passed on his way, pursued across the breadth of the Horse Guards Parade by a tiresome little sparrow that cheeped incessantly and furiously at him.

'That's only the beginning,' said the Duke complacently; 'I've made it operative with all of them, irrespective of parties.'

Belturbet made no coherent reply; he was engaged in feeling his pulse. The Duke fixed his attention with some interest on a black swan that was swimming with haughty, stiff-necked aloofness amid the crowd of lesser water-fowl that dotted the ornamental water. For all its pride of bearing, something was evidently ruffling and enraging it;

in its way it seemed as angry and amazed as the sparrow had been.

At the same moment a human figure came along the pathway. Belturbet looked up apprehensively.

'Kedzon,' he whispered briefly.

'An Angel-Kedzon, if I am not mistaken,' said the Duke. 'Look, he is talking affably to a human being. That settles it.'

A shabbily dressed lounger had accosted the man who had been Viceroy in the splendid East, and who still reflected in his mien some of the cold dignity of the Himalayan snow-peaks.

'Could you tell me, sir, if them white birds is storks or halbatrosses? I had an argument—'

The cold dignity thawed at once into genial friendliness.

'Those are pelicans, my dear sir. Are you interested in birds? If you would join me in a bun and a glass of milk at the stall yonder, I could tell you some interesting things about Indian birds. Right oh! Now the hill-mynah, for instance—'

The two men disappeared in the direction of the bun stall, chatting volubly as they went, and shadowed from the other side of the railed enclosure by a black swan, whose temper seemed to have reached the limit of inarticulate rage.

Belturbet gazed in an open-mouthed wonder after the retreating couple, then transferred his attention to the infuriated swan, and finally turned with a look of scared comprehension at his young friend lolling unconcernedly in his chair. There was no longer any room to doubt what was happening. The 'silly talk' had been translated into terrifying action.

'I think a prairie oyster on the top of a stiffish brandy-and-soda might save my reason,' said Belturbet weakly, as he limped towards his club.

It was late in the day before he could steady his nerves sufficiently to glance at the evening papers. The Parliamentary report proved significant reading, and confirmed the fears that he had been trying to shake off. Mr Ap Dave, the Chancellor, whose lively controversial style endeared him to his supporters and embittered him, politically speaking, to his opponents, had risen in his place to make an unprovoked apology for having alluded in a recent speech to certain protesting taxpayers as 'skulkers'. He had realised on reflection that they were in all probability perfectly honest in their inability to understand certain legal technicalities of the new finance laws. The House had scarcely recovered from this sensation when Lord Hugo Sizzle caused a further flutter of astonishment by going out of his way to indulge in an outspoken appreciation of the fairness, loyalty and straightforwardness not only of the Chancellor, but of all the members of the Cabinet. A wit had gravely suggested moving the adjournment of the House in view of the unexpected circumstances that had arisen.

Belturbet anxiously skimmed over a further item of news printed immediately below the Parliamentary report: 'Wild cat found in an exhausted condition in Palace Yard.'

'Now I wonder which of them—' he mused, and then an appalling idea came to him. 'Supposing he's put them both into the same beast!' He hurriedly ordered another prairie oyster.

Belturbet was known in his club as a strictly moderate drinker; his consumption of alcoholic stimulants that day gave rise to considerable comment.

The events of the next few days were piquantly bewildering to the world at large; to Belturbet, who knew dimly what was happening, the situation was fraught with recurring alarms. The old saying that in politics it's the unexpected that always happens received a justification that it had hitherto somewhat lacked, and the epidemic of startling personal changes of front was not wholly confined to the realm of actual politics. The eminent chocolate magnate, Sadbury, whose antipathy to the Turf and everything connected with it was a matter of general knowledge, had evidently been replaced by an Angel-Sadbury, who proceeded to electrify the public by blossoming forth as an owner of racehorses, giving as a reason his matured conviction that the sport was, after all, one which gave healthy open-air recreation to large numbers of people drawn from all classes of the community, and incidentally stimulated the important industry of horse-breeding. His colours, chocolate and cream hoops spangled with pink stars, promised to become as popular as any on the Turf. At the same time, in order to give effect to his condemnation of the evils resulting from the spread of the gambling habit among wage-earning classes, who lived for the most part from hand to mouth, he suppressed all betting news and tipsters' forecasts in the popular evening paper that was under his control. His action received instant recognition and support from the Angel-proprietor of the *Evening Views*, the principal rival evening halfpenny paper, who forthwith issued an ukase decreeing a similar ban on betting news, and in a short while the regular evening Press was purged of all mention of starting prices and probable winners. A considerable drop in the circulation of all these papers was the immediate result, accompanied, of course, by a falling-off in advertisement value, while a crop of special betting broadsheets sprang up to supply the newly created want. Under their influence the betting habit became if anything rather more widely diffused than before. The Duke had possibly overlooked the futility of koepenicking the leaders of the nation with excellently intentioned angel understudies, while leaving the mass of the people in its original condition.

Further sensation and dislocation was caused in the Press world by the sudden and dramatic *rapprochement* which took place between the Angel-Editor of the *Scrutator* and the Angel-Editor of the *Anglian Review*, who not only ceased to criticize and disparage the tone and tendencies of each other's publication, but agreed to exchange editorships for alternating periods. Here again public support was not on the side of the angels; constant readers of the *Scrutator* complained bitterly of the strong meat which was thrust upon them at fitful intervals in place of the almost vegetarian diet to which they had become confidently accustomed; even those who were not mentally averse to strong meat as a separate course were pardonably annoyed at being supplied with it in the pages of the *Scrutator*. To be suddenly confronted with a pungent herring salad when one had attuned oneself to tea and toast, or to discover a richly truffled segment of *pâté de foie* dissembled in a bowl of bread and milk, would be an experience that might upset the equanimity of the most placidly disposed mortal. An equally vehement outcry arose from the regular subscribers of the *Anglian Review*, who protested against being served from time to time with literary fare which no young person of sixteen could possibly want to devour in secret. To take infinite precautions, they complained, against the juvenile perusal of such eminently innocuous literature was like reading the Riot Act on an uninhabited island. Both reviews suffered a serious falling-off in circulation and influence. Peace hath its devastations as well as war.

The wives of noted public men formed another element of discomfiture which the young Duke had almost entirely left out of his calculations. It is sufficiently embarrassing to keep abreast of the possible wobblings and veerings-round of a human husband, who, from the strength or weakness of his personal character, may leap over or slip through the barriers which divide the parties; for this reason a merciful politician usually marries late in life, when he has definitely made up his mind on which side he wishes his wife to be socially valuable. But these trials were as nothing compared to the bewilderment caused by the Angel-husbands who seemed in some cases to have revolutionised their outlook on life in the interval between breakfast and dinner, without premonition or preparation of any kind, and apparently without realising the least need for subsequent explanation. The temporary peace which brooded over the Parliamentary situation was by no means reproduced in the home circles of the leading statesmen and politicians. It had been frequently and extensively remarked of Mrs Exe that she would try the patience of an angel; now the tables were reversed, and she unwittingly had an opportunity for discovering that the capacity for exasperating behaviour was not all on one side.

And then, with the introduction of the Navy Estimates, Parliamentary peace suddenly dissolved. It was the old quarrel between Ministers and the Opposition as to the adequacy or the reverse of the Government's naval programme. The Angel-Quinston and the Angel-Hugo-Sizzle contrived to keep the debates free from personalities and pinpricks, but an enormous sensation was created when the elegant lackadaisical Halfan Halfour threatened to bring up fifty thousand stalwarts to wreck the House if the Estimates were not forthwith revised on a Two-Power basis. It was a memorable scene when he rose in his place, in response to the scandalised shouts of his opponents, and thundered forth, 'Gentlemen, I glory in the name of Apache.'

Belturbet, who had made several fruitless attempts to ring up his young friend since the fateful morning in St James's Park, ran him to earth one afternoon at his club, smooth and spruce and unruffled as ever.

'Tell me, what on earth have you turned Cocksley Coxon into!' Belturbet asked anxiously, mentioning the name of one of the pillars of unorthodoxy in the Anglican Church. 'I don't fancy he *believes* in angels, and if he finds an angel preaching orthodox sermons from his pulpit while he's been turned into a fox-terrier, he'll develop rabies in less than no time.'

'I rather think it was a fox-terrier,' said the Duke lazily.

Belturbet groaned heavily, and sank into a chair.

'Look here, Eugène,' he whispered hoarsely, having first looked well round to see that no one was within hearing range, 'you've got to stop it. Consols are jumping up and down like bronchos, and that speech of Halfour's in the House last night has simply startled everybody out of their wits. And then on the top of it, Thistlebery—'

'What has he been saying?' asked the Duke quickly.

'Nothing. That's just what's so disturbing. Everyone thought it was simply inevitable that he should come out with a great epoch-making speech at this juncture, and I've just seen on the tape that he has refused to address any meetings at present, giving as a reason his opinion that something more than mere speech-making was wanted.'

The young Duke said nothing, but his eyes shone with quiet exultation.

'It's so unlike Thistlebery,' continued Belturbet; 'at least,' he said suspiciously, 'it's unlike the *real* Thistlebery—'

'The real Thistlebery is flying about somewhere as a vocally industrious lapwing,' said the Duke calmly; 'I expect great things of the Angel-Thistlebery,' he added.

At this moment there was a magnetic stampede of members towards the lobby, where the tape-machines were ticking out some news of more than ordinary import.

'*Coup d'état* in the North. Thistlebery seizes Edinburgh Castle. Threatens civil war unless Government expands naval programme.'

In the babel which ensued Belturbet lost sight of his young friend. For the best part of the afternoon he searched one likely haunt after another, spurred on by the sensational posters which the evening papers were displaying broadcast over the West End. 'General Baden-Baden mobilises Boy Scouts. Another *coup d'état* feared. Is Windsor Castle safe?' This was one of the earlier posters, and was followed by one of even more sinister purport: 'Will the Test match have to be postponed?' It was this disquieting question which brought home the real seriousness of the situation to the London public, and made people wonder whether one might not pay too high a price for the advantages of party government. Belturbet, questing round in the hope of finding the originator of the trouble, with a vague idea of being able to induce him to restore matters to their normal human footing, came across an elderly club acquaintance who dabbled extensively in some of the more sensitive market securities. He was pale with indignation, and his pallor deepened as a breathless newsboy dashed past with a poster inscribed: 'Premier's constituency harried by moss-troopers. Halfour sends encouraging telegram to rioters. Letchworth Garden City threatens reprisals. Foreigners taking refuge in Embassies and National Liberal Club.'

'This is devils' work!' he said angrily.

Belturbet knew otherwise.

At the bottom of St James's Street a newspaper motor-cart, which had just come rapidly along Pall Mall, was surrounded by a knot of eagerly talking people, and for the first time that afternoon Belturbet heard expressions of relief and congratulation.

It displayed a placard with the welcome announcement: 'Crisis ended. Government gives way. Important expansion of naval programme.'

There seemed to be no immediate necessity for pursuing the quest of the errant Duke, and Belturbet turned to make his way homeward through St James's Park. His mind, attuned to the alarms and excursions of the afternoon, became dimly aware that some excitement of a detached nature was going on around him. In spite of the political ferment which reigned in the streets, quite a large crowd had gathered to watch the unfolding of a tragedy that had taken place on the shore of the ornamental water. A large black swan, which had recently shown signs of a savage and dangerous disposition, had suddenly attacked a young gentleman who was walking by the water's edge, dragged him down under the surface, and drowned him before any one could come to his assistance. At the moment when Belturbet arrived on the spot several park-keepers were engaged in lifting the corpse into a punt. Belturbet stooped to pick up a hat that lay near the scene of the struggle. It was a smart soft felt hat, faintly reminiscent of Houbigant.

More than a month elapsed before Belturbet had sufficiently recovered from his attack of nervous prostration to take an interest once more in what was going on in the world of politics. The Parliamentary Session was still in full swing, and a General Election was looming in the near future. He called for a batch of morning papers and skimmed rapidly through the speeches of the Chancellor, Quinston, and other Ministerial leaders, as well as those of the principal Opposition champions, and then sank back in his chair with a sigh of relief. Evidently the spell had ceased to act after the tragedy which had overtaken its invoker. There was no trace of angel anywhere.

The Dream of Debs

Jack London

I awoke fully an hour before my customary time. This in itself was remarkable, and I lay very wide awake, pondering over it. Something was the matter, something was wrong – I knew not what. I was oppressed by a premonition of something terrible that had happened or was about to happen. But what was it? I strove to orient myself. I remembered that at the time of the Great Earthquake of 1906 many claimed that they awakened some moments before the first shock and that during these moments they experienced strange feelings of dread. Was San Francisco again to be visited by earthquake?

I lay there for a full minute, numbly expectant, but there occurred no reeling of walls nor shock and grind of falling masonry. All was quiet. That was it! The silence! No wonder I had been perturbed. The hum of the great live city was strangely absent. The surface cars passed along my street, at that time of day, on an average of one every three minutes; but in the ten succeeding minutes not a car passed. Perhaps it was a street-railway strike, was my thought; or perhaps there had been an accident and the power was shut off. But no, the silence was too profound. I heard no jar and rattle of wagon wheels, nor stamp of iron-shod hoofs straining up the street cobblestones.

Pressing the push-button beside my bed, I strove to hear the sound of the bell, though I well knew it was impossible for the sound to rise three storeys to me even if the bell did ring. It rang all right, for a few minutes later Brown entered with the tray and morning paper. Though his features were impassive as ever, I noted a startled, apprehensive light in his eyes. I noted, also, that there was no cream on the tray.

'The creamery did not deliver this morning,' he explained; 'nor did the bakery.'

I glanced again at the tray. There were no fresh French rolls – only slices of stale graham bread from yesterday, the most detestable of bread so far as I was concerned.

'Nothing was delivered this morning, sir,' Brown started to explain apologetically; but I interrupted him.

'The paper?'

'Yes, sir, it was delivered, but it was the only thing, and it is the last time, too. There won't be any paper tomorrow. The paper says so. Can I send out and get you some condensed milk?'

I shook my head, accepted the coffee black, and spread open the paper. The headlines explained everything – explained too much, in fact, for the lengths of pessimism to which the journal went were ridiculous. A general strike, it said, had been called all over the United States; and most foreboding anxieties were expressed concerning the provisioning of the great cities.

I read on hastily, skimming much and remembering much of labour troubles in the past. For a generation the general strike had been the dream of organized labour, which dream had arisen originally in the mind of Debs, one of the great labour leaders of thirty years before. I recollected that in my young college-settlement days I had even written an article on the subject for one of the magazines and that I had entitled it 'The Dream of Debs'. And I must confess that I had treated the idea very cavalierly and academically as a dream and nothing more. Time and the world had rolled on, Gompers was gone, the American Federation of Labour was gone, and gone was Debs with all his wild revolutionary ideas; but the dream had persisted, and here it was at last realized in fact. But I laughed, as I read, at the journal's gloomy outlook. I knew better. I had seen organized labour worsted in too many conflicts. It would be a matter only of days when the thing would be settled. This was a national strike, and it wouldn't take the Government long to break it.

I threw the paper down and proceeded to dress. It would certainly be interesting to be out in the streets of San Francisco when not a wheel was turning and the whole city was taking an enforced vacation.

'I beg your pardon, sir,' Brown said, as he handed me my cigar-case, 'but Mr Harmmed has asked to see you before you go out.'

'Send him in right away,' I answered.

Harmmed was the butler. When he entered I could see he was labouring under controlled excitement. He came at once to the point.

'What shall I do, sir? There will be needed provisions, and the delivery drivers are on strike. And the electricity is shut off – I guess they're on strike, too.'

'Are the shops open?' I asked.

'Only the small ones, sir. The retail clerks are out, and the big ones can't open; but the owners and their families are running the little ones themselves.'

'Then take the machine,' I said, 'and go the rounds and make your purchases. Buy plenty of everything you need or may need. Get a box of candles – no, get half a dozen boxes. And, when you're done, tell Harrison to bring the machine around to the club for me – not later than eleven.'

Harmmed shook his head gravely. 'Mr Harrison has struck along with the Chauffeurs' Union, and I don't know how to run the machine myself.'

'Oh, ho, he has, has he?' I said. 'Well, when next *Mister* Harrison happens around you tell him that he can look elsewhere for a position.'

'Yes, sir.'

'You don't happen to belong to a Butlers' Union, do you, Harmmed?'

'No, sir,' was the answer. 'And even if I did I'd not desert my employer in a crisis like this. No, sir, I would—'

'All right, thank you,' I said. 'Now you get ready to accompany me. I'll run the machine myself, and we'll lay in a stock of provisions to stand a siege.'

It was a beautiful first of May, even as May days go. The sky was cloudless, there was no wind, and the air was warm – almost balmy. Many autos were out, but the owners were driving them themselves. The streets were crowded but quiet. The working class, dressed in its Sunday best, was out taking the air and observing the effects of the strike. It was all so unusual, and withal so peaceful, that I found myself enjoying it. My nerves were tingling with mild excitement. It was a sort of placid adventure. I passed Miss Chickering. She was at the helm of her little runabout. She swung around and came after me, catching me at the corner.

'Oh, Mr Corf!' she hailed. 'Do you know where I can buy candles? I've been to a dozen shops, and they're all sold out. It's dreadfully awful, isn't it?'

But her sparkling eyes gave the lie to her words. Like the rest of us, she was enjoying it hugely. Quite an adventure it was, getting those candles. It was not until we went across the city and down into the working-class quarter south of Market Street that we found small corner groceries that had not yet sold out. Miss Chickering thought one box was sufficient, but I persuaded her into taking four. My car was large, and I laid in a dozen boxes. There was no telling what delays might arise in the settlement of the strike. Also, I filled the car with sacks of flour, baking-powder, tinned goods, and all the ordinary necessaries of life suggested by Harmmed, who fussed around and clucked over the purchases like an anxious old hen.

The remarkable thing, that first day of the strike, was that no one really apprehended anything serious. The announcement of organized labour in the morning papers that it was prepared to stay out a month or three months was laughed at. And yet that very first day we might have guessed as much from the fact that the working class took practically no part in the great rush to buy provisions. Of course not. For weeks and months, craftily and secretly, the whole working class had been laying in private stocks of provisions. That was why we were permitted to go down and buy out the little groceries in the working-class neighbourhoods.

It was not until I arrived at the club that afternoon that I began to feel the first alarm. Everything was in confusion. There were no olives for the cocktails, and the service was by hitches and jerks. Most of the men were angry, and all were worried. A babel of voices greeted me as I entered. General Folsom, nursing his capacious paunch in a window-seat in the smoking-room, was defending himself against half a dozen excited gentlemen who were demanding that he should do something.

'What can I do more than I have done?' he was saying. 'There are no orders from Washington. If you gentlemen will get a wire through I'll do anything I am commanded to do. But I don't see what can be done. The first thing I did this morning, as soon as I learned of the strike, was to order in the troops from the Presidio – three thousand of them. They're guarding the banks, the Mint, the post office, and all the public buildings. There is no disorder whatever. The strikers are keeping the peace perfectly. You can't expect me to shoot them down as they walk along the streets with wives and children all in their best bib and tucker.'

'I'd like to know what's happening on Wall Street,' I heard Jimmy Wombold say as I passed along. I could imagine his anxiety, for I knew that he was deep in the big Consolidated-Western deal.

'Say, Corf,' Atkinson bustled up to me, 'is your machine running?'

'Yes,' I answered, 'but what's the matter with your own?'

'Broken down, and the garages are all closed. And my wife's somewhere around Truckee, I think, stalled on the overland. Can't get a wire to her for love or money. She should have arrived this evening. She may be starving. Lend me your machine.'

'Can't get it across the bay,' Halstead spoke up. 'The ferries aren't running. But I tell you what you can do. There's Rollinson – oh, Rollinson, come here a moment. Atkinson wants to get a machine across the bay. His wife is stuck on the overland at Truckee. Can't you bring the *Lurlette* across from Tiburon and carry the machine over for him?'

The *Lurlette* was a two-hundred-ton, ocean-going schooner-yacht.

Rollinson shook his head. 'You couldn't get a longshoreman to land the machine on board, even if I could get the *Lurlette* over, which I can't, for the crew are members of the Coast Seamen's union, and they're on strike along with the rest.'

'But my wife may be starving,' I could hear Atkinson wailing as I moved on.

At the other end of the smoking-room I ran into a group of men bunched excitedly and angrily around Bertie Messener. And Bertie was stirring them up and prodding them in his cool, cynical way. Bertie didn't care about the strike. He didn't care much about anything. He was blasé – at least in all the clean things of life; the nasty things had no attraction for him. He was worth twenty millions, all of it in safe investments, and he had never done a tap of productive work in his life – inherited it all from his father and two uncles. He had been everywhere, seen everything, and done everything except get married, and this last in the face of the grim and determined attack of a few hundred ambitious mammas. For years he had been the greatest catch, and as yet he had avoided being caught. He was disgracefully eligible. On top of his wealth he was young, handsome, and, as I said before, clean. He was a great athlete, a young blond god that did everything perfectly and admirably with the solitary exception of matrimony. And he didn't care about anything, had no ambitions, no passions, no desire to do the very things he did so much better than other men.

'This is sedition!' one man in the group was crying. Another called it revolt and revolution, and another called it anarchy.

'I can't see it,' Bertie said. 'I have been out in the streets all morning. Perfect order reigns. I never saw a more law-abiding populace. There's no use calling it names. It's not any of those things. It's just what it claims to be, a general strike, and it's your turn to play, gentlemen.'

'And we'll play all right!' cried Garfield, one of the traction millionaires. 'We'll show this dirt where its place is – the beasts! Wait till the Government takes a hand.'

'But where is the Government?' Bertie interposed. 'It might as well be at the bottom of the sea so far as you're concerned. You don't know what's happening at Washington. You don't know whether you've got a Government or not.'

'Don't you worry about that,' Garfield blurted out.

'I assure you I'm not worrying,' Bertie smiled languidly. 'But it seems to me it's what you fellows are doing. Look in the glass, Garfield.'

Garfield did not look, but had he looked he would have seen a very excited gentleman with rumpled, iron-grey hair, a flushed face, mouth sullen and vindictive, and eyes wildly gleaming.

'It's not right, I tell you,' little Hanover said; and from his tone I was sure that he had already said it a number of times.

'Now that's going too far, Hanover,' Bertie replied. 'You fellows make me tired. You're all open-shop men. You've eroded my eardrums with your endless gabble for the open shop and the right of a man to work. You've harangued along those lines for years. Labour is doing nothing wrong in going out on this general strike. It is violating no law of God nor man. Don't you talk, Hanover. You've been ringing the changes too long on the God-given right to work . . . or not to work; you can't escape the corollary. It's a dirty little sordid scrap, that's all the whole thing is. You've got labour down and gouged it, and now labour's got you down and is gouging you, that's all, and you're squealing.'

Every man in the group broke out in indignant denials that labour had ever been gouged.

'No, sir!' Garfield was shouting. 'We've done the best for labour. Instead of gouging it, we've given it a chance to live. We've made work for it. Where would labour be if it hadn't been for us?'

'A whole lot better off,' Bertie sneered. 'You've got labour down and gouged it every time you got a chance, and you went out of your way to make chances.'

'No! No!' were the cries.

'There was the teamsters' strike, right here in San Francisco,' Bertie went on imperturbably. 'The Employers' Association precipitated that strike. You know that. And you know I know it, too, for I've sat in these very rooms and heard the inside talk and news of the fight. First you precipitated the strike, then you bought the Mayor and the Chief of Police and broke the strike. A pretty spectacle, you philanthropists getting the teamsters down and gouging them.

'Hold on, I'm not through with you. It's only last year that the labour ticket of Colorado elected a governor. He was never seated. You know why. You know how your brother philanthropists and capitalists of Colorado worked it. It was a case of getting labour down and gouging it. You kept the president of the South-western Amalgamated Association of Miners in jail for three years on trumped-up murder charges, and with him out of the way you broke up the association. That was gouging labour, you'll admit. The third time the graduated income tax was declared unconstitutional was a gouge. So was the eight-hour Bill you killed in the last Congress.

'And of all unmitigated immoral gouges, your destruction of the closed-shop principle was the limit. You know how it was done. You bought out Farburg, the last president of the old American Federation of Labour. He was your creature – or the creature of all the trusts and employers' associations, which is the same thing. You precipitated the big closed-shop strike. Farburg betrayed that strike. You won, and the old American Federation of Labour crumbled to pieces. You fellows destroyed it, and by so doing undid yourselves; for right on top of it began the organization of the ILW – the biggest and solidest organization of labour the United States has ever seen, and you are responsible for its existence and for the present general strike. You smashed all the old federations and drove labour into the ILW, and the ILW called the general strike – still fighting for the closed shop. And then you have the effrontery to stand here face to face and tell me that you never got labour down and gouged it. Bah!'

This time there were no denials. Garfield broke out in self-defence:

'We've done nothing we were not compelled to do, if we were to win.'

'I'm not saying anything about that,' Bertie answered. 'What I am complaining about is your squealing now that you're getting a taste of your own medicine. How many strikes have you won by starving labour into submission? Well, labour's worked out a scheme whereby to starve you into submission. It wants the closed shop, and, if it can get it by starving you, why, starve you shall.'

'I notice that you have profited in the past by those very labour gouges you mention,' insinuated Brentwood, one of the wiliest and most astute of our corporation lawyers. 'The receiver is as bad as the thief,' he sneered. 'You had no hand in the gouging, but you took your whack out of the gouge.'

'That is quite beside the question, Brentwood,' Bertie drawled. 'You're as bad as Hanover, intruding the moral element. I haven't said that anything is right or wrong. It's all a rotten game, I know; and my sole kick is that you fellows are squealing now that you're down and labour's taking a gouge out of you. Of course I've taken the profits from the gouging and, thanks to you, gentlemen, without having personally to do the dirty work. You did that for me – oh, believe me, not because I am more virtuous than you, but because my good father and his various brothers left me a lot of money with which to pay for the dirty work.'

'If you mean to insinuate—' Brentwood began hotly.

'Hold on, don't get all – ruffled up,' Bertie interposed insolently. 'There's no use in playing hypocrites in this thieves' den. The high and lofty is all right for the newspapers, boys' clubs, and Sunday schools – that's part of the game; but for heaven's sake don't let's play it on one another. You know, and you know that I know, just what jobbery was done in the building trades' strike last fall, who put up the money, who did the work, and who profited by it.' (Brentwood flushed darkly.) 'But we are all tarred with the same brush, and the best thing for us to do is to leave morality out of it. Again I repeat, play the game, play it to the last finish, but for goodness' sake don't squeal when you get hurt.'

When I left the group Bertie was off on a new tack tormenting them with the more serious aspects of the situation, pointing out the shortage of supplies that was already making itself felt, and asking them what they were going to do about it. A little later I met him in the cloakroom, leaving, and gave him a lift home in my machine.

'It's a great stroke, this general strike,' he said, as we bowled along through the crowded but orderly streets. 'It's a smashing body-blow. Labour caught us napping and struck at our weakest place, the stomach. I'm going to get out of San Francisco, Corf. Take my advice and get out, too. Head for the country, anywhere. You'll have more chance. Buy up a stock of supplies and get into a tent or a cabin somewhere. Soon there'll be nothing but starvation in this city for such as we.'

How correct Bertie Messener was I never dreamed. I decided that he was an alarmist. As for myself, I was content to remain and watch the fun. After I dropped him, instead of going directly home, I went on in a hunt for more food. To my surprise, I learned that the small groceries where I had bought in the morning were sold out. I extended my search to the Potrero, and by good luck managed to pick up another box of candles, two sacks of wheat flour, ten pounds of graham flour (which would do for the servants), a case of tinned corn, and two cases of tinned tomatoes. It did look as though there was going to be at least a temporary food shortage, and I hugged myself over the goodly stock of provisions I had laid in.

The next morning I had my coffee in bed as usual, and, more than the cream, I missed the daily paper. It was this absence of knowledge of what was going on in the world that I found the chief hardship. Down at the club there was little news. Rider had crossed from Oakland in his launch, and Halstead had been down to San Jose and back in his machine. They reported the same conditions in those places as in San Francisco. Everything was tied up by the strike. All grocery stocks had been bought out by the upper classes. And perfect order reigned. But what was happening over the rest of the country – in Chicago? New York? Washington? Most probably the same things that were happening with us, we concluded; but the fact that we did not know with absolute surety was irritating.

General Folsom had a bit of news. An attempt had been made to place army telegraphers in the telegraph offices, but the wires had been cut in every direction. This was, so far, the one unlawful act committed by labour, and that it was a concerted act he was fully convinced. He had communicated by wireless with the army post at Benicia, the telegraph lines were even then being patrolled by soldiers all the way to Sacramento. Once, for one short instant, they had got the Sacramento call, then the wires, somewhere, were cut again. General Folsom reasoned that similar attempts to open communication were being made by the authorities all the way across the continent, but he was non-committal as to whether or not he thought the attempt would succeed. What worried him was the wire-cutting; he could not but believe that it was an important part of the deep-laid labour conspiracy. Also, he regretted that the Government had not long since established its projected chain of wireless stations.

The days came and went, and for a while it was a humdrum time. Nothing happened. The edge of excitement had become blunted. The streets were not so crowded. The working class did not come uptown any more to see how we were taking the strike. And there were not so many automobiles running around. The repair-shops and garages were closed, and whenever a machine broke down it went out of commission. The clutch on mine broke, and neither love nor money could get it repaired. Like the rest, I was now walking. San Francisco lay dead, and we did not know what was happening over the rest of the country. But from the very fact that we did not know we could conclude only that the rest of the country lay as dead as San Francisco. From time to time the city was placarded with the proclamations of organized labour – these had been printed months before, and evidenced how thoroughly the ILW had prepared for the strike. Every detail had been worked out long in advance. No violence had occurred as yet, with the exception of the shooting of a few wire-cutters by the soldiers, but the people of the slums were starving and growing ominously restless.

The business men, the millionaires and the professional class held meetings and passed resolutions, but there was no way of making the proclamations public. They could not even get them printed. One result of these meetings, however, was that General Folsom was persuaded into taking military possession of the wholesale houses and of all the flour, grain, and food warehouses. It was high time, for suffering was becoming acute in the homes of the rich, and bread-lines were necessary. I knew that my servants were beginning to draw long faces, and it was amazing – the hole they made in my stock of provisions. In fact, as I afterwards surmised, each servant was stealing from me and secreting a private stock of provisions for himself.

But with the formation of the bread-lines came new troubles. There was only so much of a food reserve in San Francisco, and at the best it could not last long. Organized labour, we knew, had its private supplies; nevertheless, the whole working class joined the bread-lines. As a result, the provisions General Folsom had taken possession of diminished with perilous rapidity. How were the soldiers to distinguish between a shabby middle-class man, a member of the ILW, or a slum dweller? The first and the last had to be fed, but the soldiers did not know all the ILW men in the city, much less the wives and sons and daughters of the ILW men. The employers helping, a few of the known union men were flung out of the bread-lines; but that amounted to nothing. To make matters worse, the Government tugs that had been hauling food from the army depots on Mare Island to Angel Island found no more food to haul. The soldiers now received their rations from the confiscated provisions, and they received them first.

The beginning of the end was in sight. Violence was beginning to show its face. Law and order were passing away, and passing away, I must confess, among the slum people and the upper classes. Organized labour still maintained perfect order. It could well afford to – it had plenty to eat. I remember the afternoon at the club when I caught Halstead and Brentwood whispering in a corner. They took me in on the venture. Brentwood's machine was still in running order, and they were going out cow-stealing. Halstead had a long butcher knife and a cleaver. We went out to the outskirts of the city. Here and there were cows grazing, but always they were guarded by their owners. We pursued our quest, following along the fringe of the city to the east, and on the hills near Hunter's Point we came upon a cow guarded by a little girl. There was also a young calf with the cow. We wasted no time on preliminaries. The little girl ran away screaming, while we slaughtered the cow. I omit the details, for they are not nice – we were unaccustomed to such work, and we bungled it.

But in the midst of it, working with the haste of fear, we heard cries, and we saw a number of men running towards us. We abandoned the spoils and took to our heels. To our surprise we were not pursued. Looking back, we saw the men hurriedly cutting up the cow. They had been on the same lay as ourselves. We argued that there was plenty for all, and ran back. The scene that followed beggars description. We fought and squabbled over the division like savages. Brentwood, I remember, was a perfect brute, snarling and snapping and threatening that murder would be done if we did not get our proper share.

And we were getting our share when there occurred a new irruption on the scene. This time it was the dreaded peace officers of the ILW. The little girl had brought them. They were armed with whips and clubs, and there were a score of them. The little girl danced up and down in anger, the tears streaming down her cheeks, crying: 'Give it to 'em! Give it to 'em! That guy with the specs – he did it! Mash his face for him! Mash his face!' That guy with the specs was I, and I got my face mashed, too, though I had the presence of mind to take off my glasses at the first. My! but we did receive a trouncing as we scattered in all directions. Brentwood, Halstead and I fled away for the machine. Brentwood's nose was bleeding, while Halstead's cheek was cut across with the scarlet slash of a black-snake whip.

And lo, when the pursuit ceased and we had gained the machine, there, hiding behind it, was the frightened calf. Brentwood warned us to be cautious, and crept up on it like a wolf or a tiger. Knife and cleaver had been left behind, but Brentwood still had his hands, and over and over on the ground he rolled with the poor little calf as he throttled it. We threw the carcass into the machine, covered it over with a robe, and started for home. But our misfortunes had only begun. We blew out a tyre. There was no way of fixing it and twilight was coming on. We abandoned the machine, Brentwood puffing and staggering along in advance, the calf, covered by the robe, slung across his shoulders. We took turn about carrying that calf, and it nearly killed us. Also, we lost our way. And then, after hours of wandering and toil, we encountered a gang of hoodlums. They were not ILW men, and I guess they were as hungry as we. At any rate, they got the calf and we got the thrashing. Brentwood raged like a madman the rest of the way home, and he looked like one, with his torn clothes, swollen nose and blackened eyes.

There wasn't any more cow-stealing after that. General Folsom sent his troopers out and confiscated all the cows, and his troopers, aided by the militia, ate most of the meat. General Folsom was not to be blamed; it was his duty to maintain law and order, and he maintained it by means of the soldiers, wherefore he was compelled to feed them first of all.

It was about this time that the great panic occurred. The wealthy classes precipitated the fight, and then the slum people caught the contagion and stampeded wildly out of the city. General Folsom was pleased. It was estimated that at least 200,000 had deserted San Francisco, and by that much was his food problem solved. Well do I remember that day. In the morning I had eaten a crust of bread. Half the afternoon I had stood in the bread-line; and after dark I returned home, tired and miserable, carrying a quart of rice and a slice of bacon. Brown met me at the door. His face was worn and terrified. All the servants had fled, he informed me. He alone remained. I was touched by his faithfulness and, when I learned that he had eaten nothing all day, I divided my food with him. We cooked half the rice and half the bacon, sharing it equally and reserving the other half for morning. I went to bed with my hunger, and tossed restlessly all night. In the morning I found Brown had deserted me, and, greater misfortune still, he had stolen what remained of the rice and bacon.

It was a gloomy handful of men that came together at the club that morning. There was no service at all. The last servant was gone. I noticed, too, that the silver was gone, and I learned where it had gone. The servants had not taken it, for the reason, I presume, that the club members got to it first. Their method of disposing of it was simple. Down south of Market Street, in the dwellings of the ILW, the housewives had given square meals in exchange for it. I went back to my house. Yes, my silver was gone – all but a massive pitcher. This I wrapped up and carried down south of Market Street.

I felt better after the meal, and returned to the club to learn if there was anything new in the situation. Hanover, Collins and Dakon were just leaving. There was no one inside, they told me, and they invited me to come along with them. They were leaving the city, they said, on Dakon's horses, and there was a spare one for me. Dakon had four magnificent carriage horses that he wanted to save, and General Folsom had given him the tip that next morning all the horses that remained in the city were to be confiscated for food. There were not many horses left, for tens of thousands of them had been turned loose into the country when the hay and grain gave out during the first days. Birdall, I remember, who had great draying interests, had turned loose three hundred dray horses. At an average value of five hundred dollars, this had amounted to $150,000. He had hoped, at first, to recover most of the horses after the strike was over, but in the end he never recovered one of them. They were all eaten by the people that fled from San Francisco. For that matter, the killing of the army mules and horses for food had already begun.

Fortunately for Dakon, he had had a plentiful supply of hay and grain stored in his stable. We managed to raise four saddles, and we found the animals in good condition and spirited, withal unused to being ridden. I remembered the San Francisco of the great earthquake as we rode through the streets, but this San Francisco was vastly more pitiable. No cataclysm of nature had caused this, but, rather, the tyranny of the labour unions. We rode down past Union Square and through the theatre, hotel and shopping districts. The streets were deserted. Here and there stood automobiles, abandoned where they had broken down or when the gasoline had given out. There was no sign of life, save for the occasional policeman and the soldiers guarding the banks and public buildings. Once we came upon an ILW man pasting up the latest proclamation. We stopped to read. 'We have maintained an orderly strike,' it ran; 'and we shall maintain order to the end. The end will come when our demands are satisfied, and our demands will be satisfied when we have starved our employers into submission, as we ourselves in the past have often been starved into submission.'

'Messener's very words,' Collins said. 'And I, for one, am ready to submit, only they won't give me a chance to submit. I haven't had a full meal in an age. I wonder what horse-meat tastes like?'

We stopped to read another proclamation: 'When we think our employers are ready to submit we shall open up the telegraphs and place the employers' associations of the United States in communication. But only messages relating to peace terms shall be permitted over the wires.'

We rode on, crossed Market Street, and a little later were passing through the working-class district. Here the streets were not deserted. Leaning over the gates or standing in groups were the ILW men. Happy, well-fed children were playing games, and stout housewives sat on the front steps gossiping. One and all cast amused glances at us. Little children ran after us, crying: 'Hey, mister, ain't you hungry?' And one woman, nursing a child at her breast, called to Dakon: 'Say, Fatty, I'll give you a meal for your skate – ham and potatoes, currant jelly, white bread, canned butter, and two cups of coffee.'

'Have you noticed, the last few days,' Hanover remarked to me, 'that there's not been a stray dog in the streets?'

I had noticed, but I had not thought about it before. It was high time to leave the unfortunate city. We at last managed to connect with the San Bruno Road, along which we headed south. I had a country place near Menlo, and it was our objective. But soon we began to discover that the country was worse off and far more dangerous than the city. There the soldiers and the ILW kept order; but the country had been turned over to anarchy. Two hundred thousand people had fled from San Francisco, and we had countless evidences that their flight had been like that of an army of locusts.

They had swept everything clean. There had been robbery and fighting. Here and there we passed bodies by the roadside and saw the blackened ruins of farmhouses. The fences were down, and the crops had been trampled by the feet of a multitude. All the vegetable patches had been rooted up by the famished hordes. All the chickens and farm animals had been slaughtered. This was true of all the main roads that led out of San Francisco. Here and there, away from the roads, farmers had held their own with shotguns and revolvers, and were still holding their own. They warned us away and refused to parley with us. And all the destruction and violence had been done by the slum dwellers and the upper classes. The ILW men, with plentiful food supplies, remained quietly in their homes in the cities.

Early in the ride we received concrete proof of how desperate was the situation. To the right of us we heard cries and rifle-shots. Bullets whistled dangerously near. There was a crashing in the underbrush; then a magnificent black truck-horse broke across the road in front of us and was gone. We had barely time to notice that he was bleeding and lame. He was followed by three soldiers. The chase went on among the trees on the left. We could hear the soldiers calling to one another. A fourth soldier limped out upon the road from the right, sat down on a boulder, and mopped the sweat from his face.

'Militia,' Dakon whispered. 'Deserters.'

The man grinned up at us and asked for a match. In reply to Dakon's 'What's the word?' he informed us that the militiamen were deserting. 'No grub,' he explained. 'They're feedin' it all to the regulars.' We also learned from him that the military prisoners had been released from Alcatraz Island because they could no longer be fed.

I shall never forget the next sight we encountered. We came upon it abruptly around a turn of the road. Overhead arched the trees. The sunshine was filtering down through the branches. Butterflies were fluttering by, and from the fields came the song of larks. And there it stood, a powerful touring car. About it and in it lay a number of corpses. It told its own tale. Its occupants, fleeing from the city, had been attacked and dragged down by a gang of slum dwellers – hoodlums. The thing had occurred within twenty-four hours. Freshly opened meat and fruit tins explained the reason for the attack. Dakon examined the bodies.

'I thought so,' he reported. 'I've ridden in that car. It

was Perriton – the whole family. We've got to watch out for ourselves from now on.'

'But we have no food with which to invite attack,' I objected.

Dakon pointed to the horse I rode, and I understood.

Early in the day Dakon's horse had cast a shoe. The delicate hoof had split, and by noon the animal was limping. Dakon refused to ride it farther, and refused to desert it. So, on his solicitation, we went on. He would lead the horse and join us at my place. That was the last we saw of him; nor did we ever learn his end.

By one o'clock we arrived at the town of Menlo, or, rather, at the site of Menlo, for it was in ruins. Corpses lay everywhere. The business part of the town, as well as part of the residences, had been gutted by fire. Here and there a residence still held out; but there was no getting near them. When we approached too closely we were fired upon. We met a woman who was poking about in the smoking ruins of her cottage. The first attack, she told us, had been on the stores, and as she talked we could picture that raging, roaring, hungry mob flinging itself on the handful of townspeople. Millionaires and paupers had fought side by side for the food, and then fought with one another after they got it. The town of Palo Alto and Stanford University had been sacked in similar fashion, we learned. Ahead of us lay a desolate, wasted land; and we thought we were wise in turning off to my place. It lay three miles to the west, snuggling among the first rolling swells of the foothills.

But as we rode along we saw that the devastation was not confined to the main roads. The van of the flight had kept to the roads, sacking the small towns as it went; while those that followed had scattered out and swept the whole countryside like a great broom. My place was built of concrete, masonry and tiles, and so had escaped being burned, but it was gutted clean. We found the gardener's body in the windmill, littered around with empty shotgun shells. He had put up a good fight. But no trace could we find of the two Italian labourers, nor of the housekeeper and her husband. Not a live thing remained. The calves, the colts, all the fancy poultry and thoroughbred stock, everything, was gone. The kitchen and the fireplaces, where the mob had cooked, were a mess, while many campfires outside bore witness to the large number that had fed and spent the night. What they had not eaten they had carried away. There was not a bite for us.

We spent the rest of the night vainly waiting for Dakon, and in the morning, with our revolvers, fought off half a dozen marauders. Then we killed one of Dakon's horses, hiding for the future what meat we did not immediately eat. In the afternoon Collins went out for a walk, but failed to return. This was the last straw to Hanover. He was for flight there and then, and I had great difficulty in persuading him to wait for daylight. As for myself, I was convinced that the end of the general strike was near, and I was resolved to return to San Francisco. So, in the morning, we parted company, Hanover heading south, fifty pounds of horse-meat strapped to his saddle, while I, similarly loaded, headed north. Little Hanover pulled through all right, and to the end of his life he will persist, I know, in boring everybody with the narrative of his subsequent adventures.

I got as far as Belmont, on the main road back, when I was robbed of my horse-meat by three militiamen. There was no change in the situation, they said, except that it was going from bad to worse. The ILW had plenty of provisions hidden away and could last out for months. I managed to get as far as Baden, when my horse was taken away from me by a dozen men. Two of them were San Francisco policemen, and the remainder were regular soldiers. This was ominous. The situation was certainly extreme when the regulars were beginning to desert. When I continued my way on foot, they already had the fire started, and the last of Dakon's horses lay slaughtered on the ground.

As luck would have it, I sprained my ankle, and succeeded in getting no farther than South San Francisco. I lay there that night in an outhouse, shivering with the cold and at the same time burning with fever. Two days I lay there, too sick to move, and on the third, reeling and giddy, supporting myself on an extemporised crutch, I tottered on towards San Francisco. I was weak as well, for it was the third day since food had passed my lips. It was a day of nightmare and torment. As in a dream I passed hundreds of regular soldiers drifting along in the opposite direction, and many policemen, with their families, organized in large groups for mutual protection.

As I entered the city I remembered the workman's house at which I had traded the silver pitcher, and in that direction my hunger drove me. Twilight was falling when I came to the place. I passed around by the alleyway and crawled up the back steps, on which I collapsed. I managed to reach out with the crutch and knock on the door. Then I must have fainted, for I came to in the kitchen, my face wet with water, and whisky being poured down my throat. I choked and spluttered and tried to talk. I began saying something about not having any more silver pitchers, but that I would make it up to them afterwards if they would only give me something to eat. But the housewife interrupted me.

'Why, you poor man,' she said, 'haven't you heard? The strike was called off this afternoon. Of course we'll give you something to eat.'

She bustled around, opening a tin of breakfast bacon and preparing to fry it.

'Let me have some now, please,' I begged; and I ate the raw bacon on a slice of bread, while her husband explained that the demands of the ILW had been granted. The wires had been opened up in the early afternoon, and everywhere the employers' associations had given in.

There hadn't been any employers left in San Francisco, but General Folsom had spoken for them. The trains and steamers would start running in the morning, and so would everything else just as soon as system could be established.

And that was the end of the general strike. I never want to see another one. It was worse than a war. A general strike is a cruel and immoral thing, and the brain of man should be capable of running industry in a more rational way. Harrison is still my chauffeur. It was part of the conditions of the ILW that all of its members should be reinstated in their old positions. Brown never came back, but the rest of the servants are with me. I hadn't the heart to discharge them – poor creatures, they were pretty hard-pressed when they deserted with the food and silver. And now I can't discharge them. They have all been unionized by the ILW. The tyranny of organized labour is getting beyond endurance. Something must be done.

I Spy Strangers

Kingsley Amis

'Doing what's right, that's going to be the keynote of our policy. Honouring our obligations. Loyalty before self-interest. None of this letting our friends down when we think it's going to serve our turn. Not that it ever does in the end, of course, that type of thing. We can all see that from what happened pre-war. It was greed and selfishness got us into that mess. Anyway, coming down to details a bit now. First, Europe.'

The Foreign Secretary, a tall young man whose schoolmasterly and rather slovenly air did not rob him of a certain impressiveness, glanced over at the tanned, neatly moustached face of the Opposition's spokesman on Defence questions. It was from this quarter that real difficulty was to be expected, not from the Foreign Affairs spokesman, let alone from the Leader of the Opposition. For a moment the Foreign Secretary quailed. More than one member of the Government, he knew, found his policies absurd or extravagant rather than extremist and would gladly see him humiliated. He knew too that other, less overtly political reasons for this attitude were widespread on both sides of the House (and in the Visitors' Gallery). The temptation to play safe was strong. But he must resist it. He could not have it said that he had covered up his real programme with comfortable platitude. That was what They had always done.

'In Europe,' he went steadily on, 'we're going to go all out for co-operation and friendship with the Soviet Union. France too, naturally, but the state France is in these days, it'll be a long time before she's ready to play her full part in world affairs. It's obvious the lead's got to come from ourselves and the Russians. So first of all we have a system of guarantees of small countries, done between us. That is, Britain and the Soviet Union get together and say they'll clobber anyone who tries to walk into Austria and Czechoslovakia and Poland and Greece and Albania and all those places. And really clobber him, not just notes and protests and sanctions. We're not going to have it like it was last time.

'Then there's self-determination. That means everybody's got to have their own country and their own government. Nobody under foreign domination. Now I'll just take one example and show the type of thing I have in mind.'

He took his one example. It was Poland, not because he thought it was an example, good or bad, of anything in particular, but because he had not long ago read a short book on recent Polish history and, as was his habit, made notes on it. These supplied him now with many an unfamiliar name and obscure fact, made him sound like a bit of an expert on Poland, and by implication, he hoped, on politics in general. After an account of post-1918 events in Eastern Europe, he leant heavily on Poland's outmoded system of land tenure, the anti-democratic utterances of its government in exile and the Warsaw workers' resistance in 1939 and since.

He had got a lot of this off by heart and was able to look round the debating chamber. Two Opposition backbenchers were ostentatiously playing cards, conversations were muttering away here and there, and the Chancellor of the Exchequer was apparently asleep, but on the whole there seemed to be the right kind of semi-attentiveness. At least two people were taking everything in. They were the Speaker, whom the Foreign Secretary instinctively distrusted but of whose basic progressivism there could be little real doubt, and the Parliamentary Under-Secretary to the Home Office, whose brilliant brown eyes stared disconcertingly into his.

Did anything ever happen as it should? For months he had been wishing with all his heart that the Under-Secretary would look at him like that one day. But now that it seemed to have come about he felt none of the sudden joy and confidence he had expected. All he got was a jolt in the nerves which caused his mind to skip a groove or two, so that he found himself implying pretty unambiguously, in the next sentence he uttered, that the building of the Rożnów Dam had been an act of irresponsible provocation justifying to the hilt the Russian invasion of Finland.

This evidently went unnoticed. The Foreign Secretary, judging his audience to be adequately softened up by abstruse information, modulated to an account, statistically supported, of German atrocities in Poland. This led to a more lyrical passage on the theme of Russo-Polish brotherhood in arms, followed by a carefully worded suggestion that Russia had earned the right to get things set up her way at her end of Europe. Next, a designedly short paragraph on the Americans, in which protestations of admiring gratitude – meant to fool nobody – introduced the message that to have fought for the liberation of a continent brought with it no automatic right to a say in its future, and that the sooner the Yanks realized this and cleared off back to their own half of the world the better for everyone.

There was some show of applause here on both sides of the House, and a voice from the Visitors' Gallery was heard to say that the fellow was talking a bit of sense at last. Mildly encouraged, trying not to look at the Under-Secretary to the Home Office, the Foreign Secretary turned to a fresh page of his notes. 'Next, the Middle East,' he said.

Immediate uproar broke out in all parts of the chamber. Those who had managed without apparent protest to sit through a deluge of information about the Silesian coalfields found they could not contemplate further lessons on the break-up of the Ottoman Empire or, it might be, the average weekly take-home pay of the Egyptian *fellaheen*. The Prime Minister felt it his duty to intervene. 'Turn it up, Hargy,' he called. 'You've had nearly twenty minutes now. Give the other lot a go, eh?'

The Foreign Secretary addressed the Speaker. 'What do you say, Mr Archer?'

'Well,' – the Speaker glanced to and fro – 'I think we might split this up a bit, don't you? Sort of debate parts of it at a time? How much more stuff have you got there?'

'About as much again, sir.'

There was a general groan and some shouts of 'Shame!'

'Order, order,' the Speaker said, blushing slightly. 'I think if you don't mind, Hargreaves, we might hold the rest of your speech for now. Let's hear from Sergeant – sorry: I now call upon the Leader of the Opposition.'

This personage, the left breast of whose uniform bore several campaign-medal ribbons, turned and exchanged energetic whispers with his colleagues. After a time he stopped shaking his head violently and started nodding it feebly.

Like many another political leader, he owed his position less to talent or even ambition than to a group of deficiencies: lack of general unpopularity, of immoderate enthusiasms, of firm views about anything. Sergeant Fleming helped his officers without taking their part in their absence, fiddled the stores inventory but not the leave roster, never stood the Company Quartermaster-Sergeant more than one extra drink an evening, helped to carry his passed-out mates to their billets and then dropped them on the floor. A natural middle-of-the-road man, Fleming, and equally naturally a Tory through and through, or perhaps just through. Nobody had thought of questioning his nomination as titular head of the alternative to a Government that extended, Popular Front fashion, from the Trotskyist at the Colonial Office to the Moral Rearmament International Christian Democrat who had found himself Chancellor of the Duchy of Lancaster.

Fleming's head was nodding faster now, though no less feebly, in fact slightly more so. He got up and said loudly and indistinctly: 'Well, we've heard what my learned friend, that is the Foreign Secretary, what he's had to say about what he thinks ought to be done about foreign countries and that. And I must say I've never heard such a load of rubbish in all my born days. It beats me that a so-called educated man with all his intelligence can talk all that rubbish. What do we care about all these Poles and French? They let us down, didn't they? No, we've got to look after ourselves because there's nobody else will. Break them all up into small states so's they can't start anything, that's the only way. Eh? All right, Bert. Well, I'm going to give you our military expert now because you've got to keep the peace, haven't you? That's the first thing, so I'll hand you over now to Sergeant Doll.'

The military expert's military aspect was half misleading. He was in the Army all right, but the shape and condition of his moustache, the unnecessary presence round his waist of a splendidly furbished webbing belt, the very knot of his khaki necktie suggested the Officers' Mess at some exclusive armoured-car regiment of incessantly invoked lancer or hussar ancestry, rather than the Orderly Room at an unemployed half-unit of the Royal Corps of Signals. Doll's extreme efficiency behind the sergeant's desk in that Orderly Room was perhaps what had led him, in compensation, to adopt this heavily martial persona. If so, he would only have been acting out on an individual and more symbolic scale the compulsion (born of the inferiority feelings common to all technical troops) that had afflicted his superiors during the period of training in England. All present could very well remember the cross-country runs, the musketry competitions, the three-day infantry-tactics schemes with smoke-bombs and a real barrage, the twelve-mile route-marches in respirators, which had seemed in retrospect to show such a curious power of inverted prophecy when the unit finally completed its role in the European theatre of war without having had to walk a step or fire a shot.

One of the most convinced proponents of these early rehearsals for death or glory was at the moment sitting in the Visitors' Gallery with a hard expression on his soft face. He was Major R. W. Raleigh, the commander of a communications company until just after the German surrender, and now, the bulk of the unit having departed to help furnish signal facilities at the Potsdam Conference, the overlord of a sort of dispirited rump. This, originally comprising most of his old company with the addition of a spare section from the cable-laying company, had been swollen by successive injections administered by higher authority. In the chaos of disbandments, postings, re-formations and moves to the United Kingdom that characterized the aftermath of the campaign, a command like the major's represented a handy point of stabilization, a nucleus for any sort of drifting particle.

Expansion, once begun, had been rapid. Daily erosions took place as a corporal with one set of qualifications or three signalmen with another suffered removal for eventual use in the Far East, but these were far more than redressed by reinforcements. At one time or another, and with or without warning, there had arrived a further cable-laying section that had proved superfluous at Potsdam, most of the small but variegated Signals formation lately serving a now demolished independent parachute regiment, half a Base company without any officers or sergeants, an entire technical-maintenance section without any transport or stores, and two or three dozen teleprinter-operators, lineman-mechanics, drivers, electricians and fitters who had turned up individually or in little groups. All this amounted to a ration strength of something like twelve officers and four hundred other ranks, a total quite impressive enough to justify such gestures as renaming the original company office the Orderly Room and starting to refer to Sergeant Doll, the chief clerk in that office, as the Orderly Room Sergeant.

The major thought of Doll as a useful lad, and never more so than this evening. A certain amount of undisciplined behaviour, of affected intellectual nonsense, even of actual hints of disloyalty to the country – these were to be expected of a mock parliament, but there was surely no need for the thing to turn out quite so mock as it had. The blokes seemed to think that they could simply get up and say whatever they liked. Where that sort of attitude got you had been made all too clear at the previous sitting, when the bunch of jokers who called themselves the Government had brought in their Nationalization Bill. This meant, apparently, that they were in favour of collaring the coal-mines, the steel industry, transport, public services – everything that created wealth and employment – and running them as they saw fit. That could never happen in the real world, in England, but the major could not agree with his friends in the Officers' Mess that the passing of that Bill merely showed how idiotic the whole issue had become – he wished he could. No, it was far more serious than that: the indication of a really ugly mood. He had too much sense of responsibility not to have come along tonight to keep an eye on things, use his influence to stop them getting out of hand. He hoped he would not have to intervene. It would not be necessary if Doll did his stuff properly, and Doll surely would. Reliable fellow, Doll, even if he was a bit of a puzzle. That perpetual parade-ground appearance and manner – what was it all in aid of?

Whatever the complications of Doll's internal drives, he was not a middle-of-the-road man; indeed, to extend the image a trifle, he was brushing up against the wall on the right-hand side. In the melodious voice that had served him so well as Complaints Supervisor at a large store in Leeds, he was saying: 'I shan't waste much time in destroying the dangerous nonsense we've just been exposed to. Russia has always been an aggressive power and always will be unless we stop her. All that restrained the Reds until 1939 was weakness. Then they went for the Baltic republics, Poland, Finland, plus various Balkan adventures. Their only interest in self-determination is to prevent it. Desertions to the Nazis included . . . I beg your pardon?'

'Facts!' the Foreign Secretary was shouting above the Speaker's half-hearted appeals for order. 'This is all just . . . insinuation. You haven't—'

'Facts?' The spokesman on Defence questions brought out his own notebook, then went on as mellifluously as before: 'All right, facts. From *The Times* of 29 June. Czechoslovakia signed Ruthenia over to Russia. Why? Because the Czechs wanted to get rid of it? From a BBC broadcast this morning. Russia is putting pressure on Turkey to revise their Black Sea Straits treaty and cede two territories to her. Why? Because the Turks are planning to blockade her? From another broadcast. Three hundred more Poles shot by the order of People's—'

'They were traitors, collaborators, there've been—'

'I've no doubt many of them were. But we shall never know now, shall we? These people should have been tried by an international court, as we've said we—'

'It was the heat of the moment. You always get—'

'As I started to tell you, these were executions carried out under sentences passed by People's Courts, there wasn't just a mob blazing away in the streets. But I really must appeal to you, Mr Speaker, to quell these interruptions. I managed to keep quiet while all that Red propaganda was going on, so I don't see why—'

'All right, Sergeant Doll. Hargreaves, I must warn you to keep quiet.' There was reluctance and a half-buried sympathy in the Speaker's tone.

'Sorry, sir. But I've simply got to ask him about the Polish elections. Surely that proves—'

'*Order*, Hargreaves. You'll have to shut up or leave.'

'Yes, sir.'

The House resettled itself rather sulkily, feeling, and muttering, that it was always the bloody same: the moment you got a decent row going, some pernickety sod piped up with some moan about order. Might as well be sitting in the billet reading last week's paper.

'Thank you, Mr Speaker.' Doll stared across at Hargreaves. 'As a matter of fact I welcome the opportunity of saying something about those elections. I find it rather odd that the Reds should be so keen to get those elections held at this stage, with the country still in turmoil – but then it'll be all right really, won't it? – with the Reds everywhere to see fair play. No undemocratic interference from us or the French or the Yanks that might result in free elections, because the wrong people might get elected then, mightn't they? Can't have that, can we? Comrade Stalin wouldn't like that.

'I should like to round off this question with a few words on the Warsaw rising and the Reds' unfortunate inability to come to the aid of their Polish brothers in arms. In the spring of this year—'

Hargreaves had lost all the poise that might have been expected of a Foreign Secretary, even a mock one. He leant forward on the heavy, scarred wooden bench and put his head in his hands. If only he knew more and could think faster; if only he had at his side, as living proof that Doll was wrong, one or other of the fine men and women he knew on his local Labour Party branch committee, people who had grown up in the service of Socialism and given it all their spare energy, fighting in Spain, leading hunger marches, canvassing in hopelessly impregnable Tory strongholds . . . He tried not to think of all that going to waste, failing ever to find its way to power. His almost continuous excitement over the results of the British General Election, due to be announced the following week, froze momentarily into despair. Contrary to what everyone thought, he had never been a member of the Communist Party. He was suspicious of the one-party system and his doubts about the Russian labour camps still lingered. But if Doll's ideas carried the day at home there was only one logical step to take. Hargreaves was enough of a Marxist to recognize a situation in which the Left must combine against the main enemy. To have taken this half-decision brought him no relief: on tonight's showing he was politically useless.

His obvious dejection was not lost on Major Raleigh, whose soft face had softened somewhat since Doll began to put things in the right perspective and who was now leaning back in his chair in search of what degree of comfort it could provide. This was not great. Like everything else in the room it seemed to have been made without reference to human use. Typical German unimaginativeness, the major thought to himself. The small oblong windows, through which a strong late-evening sun was pouring, were set too high in the wall to be properly seen out of, certainly by most of the children who until recently had attended prayers here, sung Nazi songs or whatever it was they did in their school hall. Two rows of flat-topped desks had been dragged out of an adjacent store-room to form the Government and Opposition front benches. It would have taken a long-torsoed boy or girl to work at one with any ease or even see fairly over it, and the design demonstrably called for a far shorter-legged man than the average mock parliamentarian currently in occupation.

The major brooded for a time upon Hargreaves and the many things that could be done with or to him to make him less all-embracingly unsatisfactory – failing which, some positive enactment of how the world in general felt about him would do him good. The things available to the major ranged from giving Hargreaves an extra duty for being unshaven (any and every day would do) to getting him transferred elsewhere. An influential contact in the relevant department at General HQ was in the habit of seeing to it that, to a large extent, the major was able to decide who should and who should not be posted out of his command. There was only one place where, after a brief break in the United Kingdom, Hargreaves would finally be sent: a very hot and distant place, full of stuff which would interest him and which, as a budding expert on world affairs, he could not afford not to know about.

In one his rare moments of self-contemplation, brought on by slight uneasiness over the impending Election result, the major had started wondering about the morality of dispatching jungleward anybody under his authority who had happened to annoy him. The moment had sped harmlessly by when he remembered that, to an experienced and conscientious officer such as he trusted he was, men who annoyed him were certain to be, corresponded one hundred per cent with, men who were bad soldiers. It did not worry him that he was thus filling the relevant units of South-East Asia Command with drunks, incompetents, homosexuals, Communists, ration-vendors and madmen. His first duty was to the formation he led.

Thoughts of the Japanese campaign naturally led him to consider another person who was going the right way about getting to it soon. Lieutenant F. N. Archer, sometime defendant in a celebrated unconstitutional court of inquiry staged by the major in an only half-successful attempt to humiliate him, was now scowling openly at what Doll was saying. Archer sat in a tall ecclesiastical-looking throne affair, much carved with Gothic lettering, at the far end of the room from the Visitors' Gallery. This was no gallery, but a simple row of hard chairs at floor level. The real gallery over the oak doorway had not suited the major, who still resented Archer's original attempt to make him and his friends sit up there as if they were nothing to do with the proceedings. It had been just like Archer not to see that it was absurd to try and reproduce the House of Commons set-up in details like that. Not seeing the obvious was his speciality, as his regimental work showed. To have appointed him Speaker of this fandango had probably been a mistake, but then he was the one who was always showing off his political knowledge in the Mess. A fat lot that had amounted to.

His voice sounding hollow in the barely furnished room, Doll said: 'But before that we must immediately negotiate a peace with Japan, while she still has some sort of military machine left. We're going to need every ship and plane and man they have. A settlement wouldn't be difficult. They're talking about peace already. Nobody really cares who owns those islands – it's the bases that count. And with a common enemy that'd soon sort itself out.'

'What about the Chinese?' the Postmaster-General asked. He was a corporal of dispatch-riders from the parachute formation, one of the few recent arrivals who had taken part in the parliament.

Doll never smiled, but cordiality enhanced his tones when he answered: 'An excellent question. I think the Japs with their reduced bargaining-power could probably be bullied into making enough concessions to the Chinks to keep them quiet. Certainly the Yanks have got quite enough cash to bribe the Nationalist Chinks – Chiang's lot – into selling their little yellow souls. The Red Chinks are more of a problem, though they won't amount to much for a good while yet. I think there's a fair chance they could be bought off too, into some sort of tacit neutrality anyway.

'But the real problem is Europe. The thing there is to advance until we're stopped. We stop wherever they start shooting. And they won't do that for a bit. We push into Czechoslovakia and Hungary and the Balkans and southern Poland if we can get there, until we're stopped. Then we dig in. They can't have troops everywhere. Later on we straighten the line by agreement with the Reds. It's our only chance of saving any of these people – to fight on our side later, if necessary.

'We'll need troops for that, of course. To dig in and stay there. Demobilization must be halted at once. Twenty-eight days' leave in the UK for everybody we can spare, then back on the job. No Yanks are going home if I have anything to do with it; they're all needed here. Re-form the French, Dutch, Belgian and Italian armies. And the Germans, as many of those boys as we can get. It does seem a pity we spent so much energy killing so many of them, doesn't it? When if we'd gone in with them when they asked us in 1941 we'd have smashed the Reds between us by now? But we'll leave that for the time being. We'll have to put the Nazi Party back on its feet, by the way. They understand these things. Perhaps old Adolf will turn up from wherever he is and give us a hand. We could use him.

'Well, that's about it. Keep them nattering away in Potsdam as long as possible and move like hell meanwhile. I think it would probably work. Everybody's exhausted, but our manpower and resources are superior. What we almost certainly haven't got is the will. That's their strong suit. In conclusion, let me just say formally that in foreign affairs the first policy of my party is resistance to Communism.'

Doll sat down, having finished his speech, a rare achievement in this chamber. There was a lot of applause, most of it based on close attention to what had been said. Nodding his head to the pair of gloomy subalterns who sat beside him, the major joined judicially in. He knew he was supposed to be impartial, but really there could be no question but that the whole thing was on the right lines, except perhaps for the bit about the Nazi Party, which was premature to say the least. His speculations why Doll had never put in for a commission were interrupted by the Foreign Secretary, who clattered to his feet and cleared his throat in a long bellow. Hargreaves's normally mottled face was flushed; parts of his scrubby hair stuck out horizontally; his chest rose and fell.

'Could I ask first of all,' he said in a trembling voice, 'if the Honourable Member imagines that any British Government would put the policy he outlines, put into effect the policy he outlines?'

Doll's stare was not unfriendly. 'Oh no. That's to say almost certainly not. They'd be turned out as soon as the electorate realized what they'd let themselves in for. You'd be asking people to admit in effect that they'd been fighting on the wrong side, you see, and having their relatives killed doing it. And they're tired too. No, I'd say the chances—'

'Then what . . . what the hell . . . ? I mean what's the point of—?'

'The point? The point of what we're doing as I see it is to work out what we think we *should* do, not what the Government we elect *probably will* do. If we're all just playing a guessing game, then I think I'm with you. You'll very likely get what you want, especially if the country's fool enough to elect those Socialist prigs. I only hope you enjoy it when you find out what it's really like.'

'Mr Speaker, sir,' Hargreaves cried, and he was looking directly at Archer, 'I never thought to sit in this House, which is a, which exists only with the traditions of that other House across the sea, sir, and hear an Honourable Member admit to an admiration for the Nazi Party, which has been responsible for so many dreadful crimes, and which, the German Army I mean, we've been fighting it all these years and now I hear this said, or perhaps he now wishes to—'

'I didn't admit to an admiration for the Nazi Party, and I would never do so. Their racial policy was against reason and their appeal was based on mass hysteria. No, I was only arguing that in a desperate situation like ours you need all the allies you can get, especially if they can organize and fight. That we all know the Nazis can do.'

'No wonder you want the Nazis. You're an aggressor, you want to aggress – you want to attack the Russians.

The people who've died in their millions to stop the Nazis from conquering the world – honestly, how insane can you—'

The Foreign Secretary's voice tailed off. The House was perfectly silent, crossing its fingers with the wish that no pernickety sod was going to invoke order. Doll said efficiently: 'The Nazis could never have conquered the world. There were too few of them and they were confined to one country. The Reds are an international conspiracy. And my proposals were entirely defensive. What interests me is resistance to Communism, as I said, not an assault on it. It's too early for that, or too late. There's only been one assault on it in our lifetime, and it failed because we were too stupid to join in. And now perhaps somebody else might care to—'

'Fascist!' Hargreaves screamed. 'The strong arm, that's the thing for you, isn't it? The jackboot. The good old truncheon. I know your sort, Doll. There are people like you in England, all over, in the bloody Empire, Africa and India, smooth as buggery in the club with the old brandy and soda and then off to break a strike or flog a wog or . . . You're all the same. And everybody who clapped you . . .' His unblinking glance swept the chamber, meeting the major's eyes for a moment. 'Ought to be ashamed of yourselves. Black-and-Tan material. You're going to lose. You're on the side of death. History'll get you. Auden warned you but you never listened. I won't even sit in the same room with you.'

Sincere emotion enforces a hearing. Hargreaves had almost reached the impressive exit doorway – no more than twenty years old but, to an English eye, redolent of weighty Teutonic medievalism – before comment and protest got properly going. Doll smoothed his abundant straight dark hair. Archer and the Parliamentary Under-Secretary to the Home Office gazed with similar expressions after the retreating Hargreaves. The major blew his nose and tucked the pale tan silk handkerchief into the sleeve of his battledress blouse. His soft face concealed emotion at the hardly won memory (he did not care to blur with too much detail his faculty for making quick decisions) that Archer was Hargreaves's section officer and, as such, responsible for everything he did.

'Anything special for me this morning, Wilf?' Major Raleigh hung up his service-dress hat – which, in defiance of his own edict, he regularly wore with battledress – on the fist-sized bronze knob of the bookcase door. Behind the glass of this, apart from a couple of dozen battered books in a foreign language or two, there huddled a heap of painted china vases and ewers which the major thought might be eighteenth century or nineteenth century or one of those. He had collected them from various houses and shops in the area and sometimes wondered what to do with them.

Captain Cleaver looked listlessly at a pad on his table. 'I don't think so, Major. There's the pay to collect.'

'Get one of the cable wallahs to go. Time they did something to earn their living.'

'Well, it's a trip, you know, Major.'

'So much the better.'

'No, I was thinking somebody might like to go. Get out of the place for a bit.'

'Oh, I see what you mean. Go yourself if you like, Wilf.'

'Well, actually I was hoping to look in at the Officers' Shop if you're not going to need me here. That's in the opposite direction to the cashier.'

'Ask that parachute chap, then, Pinch or Finch or whatever his name is. He's been looking a bit down in the mouth.'

'Winch. Yes, he has, hasn't he? He must feel a bit of a fish out of water here. Nothing going on. It must have been a bit different at Arnhem. All that excitement. Pretty hectic too, though. I expect he misses that, don't you?'

'What?' The major, at his in-tray, stared up over his reading-glasses. They made him look ineffectively studious, like a neglected schoolboy at a crammer's. 'Misses what?'

'You know, the excitement and the big bangs and so on at Arnhem. I was asking you if you thought he was missing it.'

'Who?'

'Winch, the parachute chap.'

'How the hell should I know what he's missing and what he isn't missing? And he wasn't at Arnhem, I asked him. Got taken off the drop at the last minute because of dysentery.'

'I understood him to say—'

'He wasn't on the Normandy drop, either.'

'Well, he wouldn't have been, would he? Normandy was Sixth Airborne. Arnhem was First.'

'Yes. Look, Wilf, if you're going to the Officers' Shop there are a couple of things you might pick up for me, if you would.'

'Certainly, Major, of course.' Cleaver turned to a fresh page of his pad, pleased at the chance of writing something down, and poised his pencil devotedly. 'Now then, what can I do for you?'

'Half a dozen handkerchiefs, the silk ones. Don't seem to be able to get anything ironed round here. Three pairs of the lightweight socks, size eight shoe. Not the elastic tops. If there's only the elastic tops don't get anything. Ties? No, I'm all right for those.'

The major appeared to fall into a muse. Cleaver said: 'Anything else, Major?'

'Hold on, I'm thinking . . . Those American shirts. Has he got any left, do you know?'

'Well, he's probably got some more in by this time. He said he was getting some more in.'

'Make sure they're the same. The same as I'm wearing now. See? . . . You're not looking.'

'I am, honestly, sir. I know the sort.'

'Make sure the collar's the same. Get me three of them. Fifteen and a half neck.'

'Right.'

'Just a moment.' The major fondled his throat, his blue eyes bulging as he tried to see what he was doing. 'Better say sixteen to be on the safe side. I'll settle up with you when you see what you've got, OK?'

'Right, Major. Oh, by the way, I meant to tell you—'

'What?'

'A message came over the blower from Movement Control in Hildesfeld. Just an advance warning – there'll be a teleprint through this afternoon with all the griff. A platoon of the Montgomeryshire Light Infantry are moving into the area some time tomorrow and we're to help them find accommodation. They were supposed to be doing guard duty at one of the DP camps, but it closed down a couple of days ago and so there's nowhere for them to—'

'But it's not our responsibility to fix them up. They're not Signals.' Raleigh spoke with an anxious severity, as if, conceivably, the platoon referred to might turn out to be the one in which someone very dangerous to him was serving, someone who had seen him cheating at picquet or torturing a prisoner.

'I know, but that's not what they're on about. These people will come under the Admin Company in the ordinary way. It's just that – well, the Staff Captain in Hildesfeld seemed to think that with our knowledge of the area we could be pretty useful to these MLI types. Know where to look and save them time. Just lend them an officer and a sergeant for a day or so. Nobody at Movement Control who'd do and if there were they couldn't spare him. They're run off their feet there.'

The major hardly heard the last part of this. In the weeks since the war ended, even more since the larger part of the unit had gone to Potsdam, he had been possessed and tormented by dreams of triumph, renown or at least advancement. One of these, which he never visualized with full conscious attention, was about a local Nazi uprising crushed by him in a single prompt and ruthless blow. Another, disguised as an unuttered joke, involved the removal with ignominy of the CO as a chief executive of communications at Potsdam and the immediate substitution of himself: 'Where's Raleigh? Get hold of Raleigh. There's only one man for this job and that's Dick Raleigh.'

Dreams three and four engaged him more continuously, if less profoundly. Three he had taken what steps he could to bring to life. In the last month he had written three demi-official memoranda to the Signals general at Army Group headquarters. Their theme was that, if the war against Japan lasted long enough, there would probably be a role in it for a new full-dress Headquarters Signals unit, and that the body of troops at present under his command, admittedly miscellaneous but in a high state of training, could with advantage be used as the basis of such a unit. He himself, he had pleaded, could ask for nothing better than to stay on in uniform past the date of his expected release, indeed indefinitely, if he could be allowed to serve as its leader.

The first memorandum had been acknowledged with the utmost formality, the others not at all. As each day brought no word from Army Group HQ, and as news of Japanese reverses mounted, the major fell back increasingly on his fourth dream. This had been put into his head by the compulsions of military geography. The medium-sized village in which he and his men were living had turned out to lie within administrative reach of a smallish but important railhead – the one at Hildesfeld. The Movement Control people there were faced with the task of propelling personnel westward about three times faster than their resources allowed. The accumulating residue had to be put somewhere. The major's village and its environs were an obvious lodgment for it. The major had taken it upon himself to provide communications between the railhead and the tankless tank troops, the gunless artillery sections, the reconnaissance detachments with nothing in Europe left to reconnoitre – all those whom destiny or administrative whim had transmitted in this general direction.

If this situation continued, authority would have to recognize it. A different type of man from the major might have noticed an analogy with the experiences of an ex-colonial territory on the threshold of statehood. As things were he simply saw himself as an Area Commandant with a lieutenant-colonelcy to match. Only one officer of this rank was known to be living hereabouts, a youthful Engineer on twenty-four-hour warning of departure who was rumoured to divide his time between drinking schnapps in a farmhouse bedroom and driving round the countryside looking for more, this at a speed which suggested that death might remove him before officialdom could. Of the five or six local majors, inquiry showed that Raleigh was senior to three and had been around the place longer than any. 'Lieut-Col. R. W. Raleigh, R. Sigs' sounded authentic. So did 'Winkworth (West) Conservative Association – *Chairman*: Colonel Richard W. Raleigh'.

'All right, Wilf,' the major said. 'I'll take care of it. Was there anything else?'

'About the Shop again, sir. I take it it would be all right to get a few things for one or two of the blokes while I'm there?'

The major frowned. It was his major's frown, his responsibility-invoking frown, his slackness-detecting frown, his extra-duty-donating frown. He kept it on full for a while before he said: 'I'm not sure that's a very good idea.'

'Oh, I don't see why not. Things are pretty relaxed these days. We're not at war any more, after all. I can't see it doing anybody much harm.'

'I wouldn't go all the way with you there, old boy.

While the blokes have got so much time on their hands it's particularly important to maintain discipline. It doesn't help at all, throwing shoes and ties and what-not around indiscriminately. This is an Officers' Shop we're talking about, not a natty gents' tailoring establishment. Why do you think officers and men are required to dress differently? To emphasize the difference in their status, of course. That's quite fundamental.'

'I know, Major' – Cleaver was being uncharacteristically persistent – 'but it's going on all over the place, you see. Only yesterday I saw a couple of the lads on the switch-board wearing those jeep coats, the sort with the—'

'They're in Archer's lot; I've already had a word with him about it. There's a great deal too much of this all-chums-together spirit around these days and I don't like it. It isn't . . . healthy. Anyway, who were you thinking of getting stuff for?'

'Well, evidently Doll could do with a couple of shirts, and the Quartermaster-Sergeant was talking about a few pairs of shoes – he didn't say who he wanted them for – and then my batman was asking—'

The major's frown, which had almost cleared, came back again, but with a difference that indicated that thought of some description was going on behind it. 'That's rather different. Doll knows this sort of thing is a privilege and he's not the kind of fellow to abuse it. The QMS has done a first-class job for everybody at a very difficult time,' – and, the major might have added, a five-star *cordon bleu* crossed-knife-and-fork-in-the-Michelin-guide-type job for himself out of the petrol-hunger of a chain of civilians that stretched back as far as Arromanches on the Norman coast – 'and if he needs a pair of shoes or two I don't think it's really up to us to question it. As regards your batman – well, I regard that as a personal matter between the two of you. Batmen have always had these little perks – it's a tradition. Yes, that's all right, Wilf.'

'Thanks, Major.'

'You did quite right to tell me, though,' Raleigh said emphatically, leaving the other in no doubt about its being quite wrong not to tell him in the future, and picked up a sheaf of vehicle returns. He knew full well what was on them, for the transport situation, like much else, had remained static for weeks, but the small effort involved in putting common knowledge into due form helped to keep the sections on their toes, or at any rate off their backsides.

Cleaver cranked his telephone and after a moment said: 'Parachute Section, please . . . What? When was this? I see. Is anyone working on it? Well, let me know the moment it's back, will you? – I say, Major.'

Raleigh looked up as if he had been deep in the vehicle returns for a day or so. 'What is it?'

'The line to the parachute people's out. Looks as if I'll have to go and tell Winch myself.'

'Winch?'

'About the pay. We decided—'

'Yes, yes. Get Doll to send someone over. It's only a few hundred yards.'

While Cleaver again cranked his phone and spoke, the major turned over his in-tray a second time, then got going on his own phone. 'Give me the Signalmaster . . . Signalmaster? Signals Command Group here, Major Raleigh. Who is that?'

'Archer, sir.'

'Frank, what's happened to the morning summary of communications? It's supposed to be on my desk at nine o'clock.'

Seated at his trestle table in the commodious and airy barn that housed the Signal Office, Archer blushed. 'I sent it across, sir. Nearly two hours ago.'

This inadvertent reminder of how long after nine o'clock the major had presumptively begun his morning's work did not go down well. 'I don't care how long ago you think you sent it across, Frank, it isn't here.'

'There's only one thing on it, sir – the line to Para-Sec is down; otherwise—'

'I know that. That's not the point. You'd better have a look round there and then come over and talk to me about it. I want a word with you anyway.'

Sighing, Archer got to his feet and stretched. Inactivity reigned about him. A single teleprinter clattered away in one corner. A bespectacled corporal read a paperback novel in front of the wood-and-canvas rack in which transmitted messages were filed. The rack had been cleared at midnight and now carried half a dozen exiguous batches of flimsy. The two counter-clerks were playing chess while the orderly, an aged and delinquent Highland infantryman, watched them in wonder. The locations clerk was busy with his eraser, removing what must have been one of the last official traces of yet another defunct unit.

Archer raised his voice. 'Hargreaves!'

Peering anxiously, laboriously pinching out a cigarette, Hargreaves hurried in from the open air. His battledress blouse, instead of lying open at the top to reveal a collar and tie, was buttoned up and hooked at the throat; he must have been one of the last men in the British Army to avail himself of the recent sartorial concession. No doubt the older style made fewer demands on his time and energy. 'Yes, Mr Archer?' he said.

'You took the summary of communications across to Command Group, didn't you?'

'The what, Mr Archer?'

'That thing I gave you to take over to the major's office, you took it, didn't you?'

'Oh yes. Captain Cleaver was there and I gave it to him.'

'You're sure?'

'Oh absolutely, Mr Archer.'

'You'd swear to that?' Archer smiled conspiratorially.

'They're trying to make out over there that I never sent it. You'd stand by me if it came to a court martial, wouldn't you?'

Hargreaves looked worried. 'I don't quite understand, Mr Archer, but if there's any trouble you can count on me to—'

'Never mind, Hargreaves, I was only pulling your leg . . . Good show you put up last night at the parliament, by the way – I was meaning to tell you.'

'Oh, thank you very much, Mr Archer, how kind of you . . . You don't think perhaps it was a bit . . . extreme? You know, at the end.'

'Not a bit, you were quite justified. These people need to be talked to straight once in a while. You keep at it. Oh, and I thought that bit about Auden came in very well. I didn't know you were a fan of his.'

'I've just read a few of his things, sir.'

'I see.' Archer became conscious that he had been smiling rather a lot. 'Right, that's all, Hargreaves, thank you.'

'Thank you, sir.'

On Archer's table lay a letter he had been writing to a friend of his in Oxford, one who, like most of his contemporaries, was medically unfit for military service – a doubly fortunate shortcoming in the present case, for one of this friend's several neuroses forbade him to be ordered about. The letter was full of undetailed assertions of hatred and misery, unsolicited news about what Archer's two girl-friends in England had been writing to him, and inquiries about issues of jazz records. He put on top of it the Signalmaster's Diary – its sole entry for the morning read *0840 On duty F. N. Archer Lt* – and told Sergeant Parnell, the superintendent, where he was going. Then he donned his ridiculous khaki beret and left.

Outside, the sunlight was intense. Hargreaves was standing in the shade, leaning against the corner timber of the barn and talking to a switchboard-operator called Hammond, who among other things was Parliamentary

Under-Secretary to the Home Office. He gave Archer an inquisitive brown-eyed glance.

Archer went down the yard, at one side of which a dispatch-rider was dozing on a heap of straw, and crossed the cobbled street to the school building. He was thinking that the oddest thing about the major, or about himself, was that Raleigh's behaviour was getting funnier all the time without arousing any laughter in him, Archer. Take Raleigh's unconcealed delight whenever a new formation moved into the area and thus gave him another place to have a line run to and a telephone installed at, an amenity much resented by its beneficiaries, who would usually have spent most of the war too near a telephone and asked for nothing better than to remain incommunicable. The major had almost got drunk – he never did quite – on the strength of having foisted a special dispatch run and *a wireless link* upon a Displaced Persons Area Authority on the verge of closure. He seemed very near believing that stuff like this represented a serious and adequate role for a group that had provided half the communications of an Army Corps Group headquarters at war; he no longer excused the farce of having a Signal Office here at all by saying (untruly) that it kept the lads busy.

The same shift of attitude had taken place over his road. This boulevard through the camp area, too short to matter except in terms of the energy its construction absorbed and totally unnecessary anyway because of the dry summer, was about to be extended to other parts of the major's tribal domain. Archer foresaw himself doing further stints of uninformed supervision, watching the hardcore and rubble go down, scouring the village for more wheelbarrows, driving out to the Engineers detachment to borrow yet more. Hitler had been funny too, but you had had to live in Valparaiso or somewhere to be able to laugh at him with conviction.

A flight of green-painted wooden steps led up the side of the school. Sergeant Doll was sitting on them, evidently improving his tan. With the affability of a pub landlord at the entry of a notable big spender, he called from a distance: 'Good morning to you, Mr Archer, and how are you this fine morning, sir?'

'Oh, fed up,' Archer said unguardedly.

'Well, I'm not, sir, I don't mind telling you.' Doll made no move to get up and let Archer pass. 'I've got plenty to eat and a decent bed and no work and nothing to spend my pay on and nobody to bother me. I'm winning, sir.'

'Yes, you are, aren't you?' Archer, whose head was on a lower level than Doll's, noticed that the other seemed to have no hairs whatsoever in his nose. This had the effect of making his moustache appear, if not actually false, at any rate an isolated phenomenon.

'That was a nice little spot of bother at the old House of Commons last night, sir, wasn't it? Of course that fellow Hargreaves, he's unbalanced, isn't he? A lot of these Reds are, you know. There must be something in that particular philosophy that sort of attracts such people. He must be a perfect little darling to have in the section, Master Hargreaves. I don't know how you put up with him, sir, honestly I don't. I'd have got rid of him many moons ago.'

'Oh, he's not as bad as all that. He is an educated man, after all.'

'That makes it twenty times worse, sir, in my view. The corruption of the best is worst, I remember reading that somewhere. You'd be the one who'd know where it comes from, I expect, sir, wouldn't you?'

Archer looked up sharply, but Doll's eye was as bland as ever. 'It's Latin,' Archer said. 'I think.'

'No doubt, sir. It's really a pity Hargreaves made an exhibition of himself like that. Damaged his own case, I thought. Don't you agree, sir?'

There was a pause while Archer recalled what was perhaps his sole intelligently self-interested action since joining the Company: putting a half-bottle of whisky on Doll's desk last Christmas Eve. Ever since then the major, who tended to make a confidant of Doll, had found that his little surprises for Archer, in the shape of unheralded inspections of the Signal Office and the like, had an odd way of turning out not to be surprises after all. Rather late in the day, Archer was discovering a related principle, that the Army afforded unique scope for vindictiveness and that disagreement on apparently neutral matters often provoked such a reaction. He knew now that the Adjutant of the unit, who had of course gone to Potsdam with the others, had been that sort of person, selecting junior officers for troublesome duties less by caprice than by remembering who had most recently contested his opinion in the Mess, even if the subject had been literature or the weather. Sometimes a tendency to confuse names (surprising in so incessant an advocate of attention to detail) gave his selections an involuntary impartiality. After thinking about it for two years, Archer was nearly sure that a historic mission to collect a new type of line-transmission apparatus, entailing a journey three-quarters of the way across England and back in January and two successive nights in an unheated railway carriage, had fallen to his share because a second-lieutenant called Belcher, whom Archer hoped he did not in the least resemble, had a day or two earlier contradicted the Adjutant about *Alice in Wonderland*. But as the Adjutant got to know his subalterns better, such miscarriages of injustice had become rarer, not that this change had been to Archer's advantage.

Although Archer had never made any progress in finding out what Doll was like, he judged it unwise to risk diminishing the effect of that half-bottle by saying what he really felt about Hargreaves's outburst and thence, inevitably, what he felt about Doll's politics. The major's regime was doubtless drawing to a close, but its last days might well be marked by a fury of moral violence. Archer could not afford to irritate a friend at court, or anywhere else for that matter. He said decisively: 'Yes, he did go too far, much too far. I think he feels a bit cheap about it today. You weren't annoyed, I hope?'

'Oh no, sir, my back is broad. As I say, all he did was help my side. That Government'll fall soon, you mark my words. You were wanting to see the major, sir, were you?'

'Yes, I thought I might look in.'

'He's got Captain Cleaver with him at the moment . . . Ah, here is the captain now.'

Doll got up as Cleaver emerged from the doorway and descended the steps. Archer grinned at him; Cleaver was the one officer in the detachment whom he regarded with nothing but contempt – groomed for stardom by the Adjutant and finally rejected on the grounds of technical incompetence: a tremendous achievement. He had got his captaincy, though. 'Hallo, Wilf,' Archer said.

'Oh, hallo,' Cleaver said, getting into his tone surprise at being so familiarly addressed. He carried gloves and a short cane and looked more than ever like a British officer as pictured in a German army manual. 'The major's waiting for you.'

The major was looking out of the window. A cow wearing a large floppy hat had just run along part of his road (known to everyone but himself as Raleigh's Alley) and then turned off to flee up the lane past the wireless section's billet. From somewhere near at hand a loud silly laugh had floated into the air. Whether this was associated with the cow or not, the two manifestations combined to pique and depress the major. They formed for him a symbol of anarchy mounting, of discipline and seriousness and purpose melting away. He felt there was some connection here with the chance of a Labour victory at the polls. Apart from a few negligible wild men like Hargreaves and Archer, he had never met anyone who confessed to having cast his proxy vote for Labour. On a recent visit to the Mess at Hildesfeld he had made a point of questioning his hosts on the matter and had heard the same story. His wife's letters said that nobody knew of anybody in the whole town who was a Labour supporter and that everybody felt very sorry for poor Mr Jack, the Labour candidate. And yet the major was uneasy. Something monstrous and indefinable was growing in strength, something hostile to his accent and taste in clothes and modest directorship and ambitions for his sons and redbrick house at Purley with its back-garden tennis-court.

Somebody tapped on the door. The major called 'Yes?' and started speaking the moment Archer began crossing the threshold – a valuable foil, this, to his normal keep-'em-waiting procedure. 'Now, Frank, where's the summary of communications?'

Archer walked over to Cleaver's table and instantly picked up a duplicated form in pale-blue ink with manuscript additions. 'Here it is, sir.'

The major took it and went back to his seat. On the whole, he seemed mollified rather than the contrary. 'About this parliament business, Frank. I'm not at all happy about it.'

'I'm sorry to hear that, sir.'

'I'm seriously thinking of closing it down.'

'Surely there's no need for that?'

'That disgusting display of Hargreaves's last night. Couldn't you have prevented it? After all, as Speaker you must have some . . . And as an officer, you—'

'I don't think that anything but force would have—'

'Worst thing in the world for discipline. If the blokes get the idea that they can simply—'

'Oh, I don't agree at all, sir.'

The major's eyes narrowed. 'What?'

'It's a chance for them to let off steam, you see. They're off parade – rank doesn't count in there. Everyone accepts that. I mentioned last night to Doll just now and he obviously didn't resent it.'

'That's not the point. And if rank doesn't count, why aren't officers and WOs allowed to take full part, instead of having to sit out like that? I let you have your way there, since you were organizing the thing, but I never followed your argument.'

'Well, sir, rank doesn't count there really, but chaps may think it does. They might feel chary of giving, er, let's say Wilf Cleaver, a proper hammering when they wouldn't if it was a corporal from another section, or even their own.'

'Mm. I don't think the blokes are quite as stupid as you make out.'

Archer shrugged.

'Tell me, Frank, I've often wondered: why do you hang on to Hargreaves when you've had so many chances to get rid of him? Does the section no good all round, having a type like that in it. Bad for morale.'

'I just feel . . . he's more or less settled in there. He's not much liked, but at least he's tolerated. Anywhere else he'd probably have a much thinner time.'

'But good God, man, a Signals section doesn't exist to give a home to stray dogs and to wet-nurse people. It's supposed to be an efficient unit in a war machine.'

'Hargreaves can't do the Allied cause much harm now.'

'Perhaps I'd better remind you, Frank, that we're all still in uniform and that our country is still at war. We're not on holiday.'

Standing before the major's table, Archer shrugged again and put his hands on his hips. His eyes fell on a framed text that said: *Ich will mich freuen des Herrn und fröhlich sein in Gott.*

'Confidentially now, old boy, what's the matter with Hargreaves? Basically the matter?'

'That's very simple, sir. He doesn't like the Army.'

The major laughed through his nose. 'I should imagine very few of us would sooner be here than anywhere else. If a man isn't a cretin he knows it's a question of getting a job done. A very important job, I take it you agree?'

'Oh yes, sir. And Hargreaves is clear on that too. But

it isn't being in the Army that gets him down. It's the Army.'

'I'm afraid you're being too subtle for me, Frank.'

'Well, as far as I can make him out – he's not an easy man to talk to, but the way he sees it, people have been nasty to him in the Army in a way they wouldn't be in civilian life. The Army puts power into the hands of chaps who've never had it before, not that sort of power, and they use it to inflict injustices on other chaps whom they happen to dislike for personal reasons. That's the way the Army works. According to Hargreaves.'

'Don't stand like that, Frank,' Raleigh said, and waited until Archer had removed his hands from his hips and put them behind his back. 'Well, whatever friend Hargreaves feels about being in the Army, you can tell him from me to pull himself together. So far I've tried to keep the original Company in one piece as far as possible. When postings come through I've been seeing to it that they've got passed on to these new arrivals. But there's always plenty of call for blokes with Hargreaves's qualifications, or lack of them rather, and I can get him out of the way any time I want to. If there's one more bit of nonsense from him I'll see he's on the first available boat for Burma. Is that clear?'

'Yes, sir. I'll tell him.'

'And what's going on between him and young Hammond?'

'Going on? Nothing that I know of. They are friends. Hammond's about the only chap Hargreaves talks to.'

'Is that all he does to him? Talk?'

'I don't know what you're driving at, sir.'

'Oh yes you do, Frank, don't you try and bullshit me. There's something pretty unsavoury about that friendship, as you call it, if half I hear is true.'

'I'll go and fetch Hargreaves and Hammond now, sir, if you like, and you can fetch whoever's been telling you this and get him to repeat it in front of them. And me too, of course, as their Section Officer.'

'There's no need to take that tone, old boy. I'm simply telling you as a friend to be on your guard. You don't want a scandal in the section, do you? Hammond's a good lad and I shouldn't like him to get into any sort of trouble. If things turn out the way they might I'd consider him favourably for lance-corporal. Well, I suppose you'd better be getting back to the Signal Office. Sorry to have kept you, but this Hargreaves business has been on my mind rather.'

'Yes, sir.'

'Oh, before you go, Frank, any news of *Journey's End*?'

'The librarian chap in Hildesfeld says he'll do his best, but it's been out of print for years. The British Drama League in England are on the job now, apparently.'

'Good. I hope it comes through. It would be fun to have a shot at putting it on. Do you know it at all?'

'I'm afraid not, sir.'

'It's good stuff, you know, Frank. You'd like it. The best thing on the first war by far. Really gets the spirit of the trenches, the feel of what it was like.'

Major Raleigh stood on the steps of the farmhouse where the Officers' Mess was, trying to smell the lilac bushes. He was having a hard time of it. Competing smells included the one from the cookhouse bonfire, a mixture of rum and hot cardboard; the one from the henhouse where the Mess's looted chickens lived; the one from the piggery; the one from nowhere and everywhere that was apparently endemic to continental farmyards, about midway between that of a brewery and that of burning cheese-rind. As one of his own wireless operators might have tried to tune out interference, the major stooped and laid his soft nose alongside one of the pale clusters. It tickled, but he got something.

The voice of Cleaver spoke behind him. 'Are you all right, Major?'

'Of course I'm all right,' Raleigh said, wheeling round as he came upright.

'I'm sorry, I thought you were ill.'

'Well I'm not. Are you ready?'

'Yes, Major. Nobody else seems to want to come.'

'Did you ask them?'

'Yes, Major.'

'All of them?'

'Yes, Major.'

'It's a pity some of them couldn't have taken the trouble to come along,' Raleigh said, voicing a desire for his brother-officers' company that was to cool sharply within the hour. 'All right, Wilf, let's get moving. We're late already.'

The two got into the major's car, a saloon with faded checkerboard painting on the radiator and a cracked mica windscreen. Its only superiority over the major's jeep lay in the latter vehicle's having reached the stage of needing to carry a can of petrol, a can of oil and a large can of water whenever it went anywhere. And this thing was a piece of loot, too. While he pulled at the starter and the motor lurched over, Raleigh imagined his friends at Potsdam, each in a Mercedes with the back full of cameras, watches, automatic pistols, pairs of binoculars, crates of champagne and vodka and American whiskey, haunches of venison . . . Girls did not appear on the major's list; he considered that side of life much overrated. Before the car came shudderingly to life he had time for a surge of feeling, equally compounded of envy and righteous indignation, at the memory of a current rumour about a large RAF Signals unit which, ordered to return to England with all its stores and transport, and thus secure against Customs inspection, had stuffed every cranny with cameras, watches, automatic pistols – perhaps girls.

They moved out of the yard, with a grinding bump

when one of the rear mudguards, worse adjusted than its fellow, met the edge of the road surface. The sun was setting over the fields of rye or oats or barley or perhaps just wheat and there was arguably a fair amount of tranquillity and such about, but the major was beyond its reach. As he frequently said, it was people that interested him. The people interesting him at the moment were still the ones he knew at Potsdam. 'Funny to think of them all up there,' he said. 'Bill and the CO and Jack Rowney and Tom Thurston and all that crowd. And Rylands and Ben and Dalessio and Jock Watson. Wonder what they're all up to. Parties with the Russians and the Yanks and God knows what. All the big brass-hats around. The Jerries too. And . . .' – the major tried briefly to visualize what more might be on view there than other soldiers – 'everything. Of course I realize we couldn't all have gone, but I do wish—'

'The CO and the Adjutant tended to pick the crowd who'd been with them at North Midland Command.'

'Yes, I know they did.' A military Calvinist who had demonstrated to him his own non-membership of the elect, Raleigh spoke in a neutral tone. 'Not altogether, though. They took Dalessio with them.'

'I wonder why.'

'Rylands seemed to think Dalessio was indispensable,' the major said. Then, quite as if he realized that this was not the most tactful thing to say to a man whom all sorts of pressure had failed to get into Dalessio's job, he added: 'I wouldn't go all the way with him there.'

'I hear Bill and Jack and Tom are all majors now.'

'Yes. I'm particularly pleased Tom got his crown. He didn't fit in quite at first, I thought – a bit of an awkward cuss. But some time last winter he pulled himself together and started doing a first-class job. Co-operated for all he was worth.'

The car laboured up an incline past the burnt-out wreck of a civilian lorry, relic of the celebrations on VE night.

The cuff of a *Wehrmacht* jacket, charred and faded, hung out of the remains of the cab. Raleigh was about to comment adversely on this memorial of indiscipline, or of high spirits, but changed his mind and said abruptly: 'I'd give anything to be at Potsdam.'

'I'd have thought we were better off here, Major, with the staff off our backs at last after two years.'

'They're doing a job there, that's the difference. I suppose . . . I suppose I might still get the chance of taking the Company to the Far East. Depends how the war goes, partly.' The major was thinking as usual in terms of a Headquarters Signals unit, not of a mere company, and of a lieutenant-colonelcy, but he was too shy to tell Cleaver this.

'I didn't realize you were as keen on the Army as all that, sir,' Cleaver said carefully.

'Well, I've been doing a lot of thinking these last few weeks, Wilf. Serious thinking. First real chance I've had since 1939. I worked it out that I've spent half my adult life in the Army. Pretty shaking thought, that. I've got used to being in uniform. Hardly remember what it was like in Civvy Street. And from the way things are going it looks as if I might not care for it when I arrive there. If these Socialists get in—'

'I shouldn't worry too much, Major. However badly it turns out there's sure to be scope for, well, initiative and quick thinking and all the rest of it.'

'I hope you're right.'

The major parked the car in the Signal Office yard between an iron canister full of broken glass and a disused boiler stuffed with torn sheets. The two officers crossed the road to the school building and entered the hall.

Parliament was in session. As Raleigh led the way to the Visitors' Gallery, his shoes thudding on the greasy bare boards, an instrument-mechanic on the Government side was saying: 'We're going to build a decent Britain. Fair shares for all and free schools and doctoring and hospitals and no class distinction. The old school tie and the old-boy network aren't going to work any more. To make sure of that we're going to abolish the public schools and Oxford and Cambridge, or at any rate change them so that anybody who's got the brains can go to them, and we're going to either abolish the House of Lords or make it a thing you vote on, just like the House of Commons. It's undemocratic any other way. Some of us want to abolish the Royal Family for the same reason, but we're not decided about that. Personally I think that if you scrap titles and the Honours List and all that carry-on, then you can leave the King and Queen to stew in their own juice.'

The major's mouth tightened. So far he had refrained from interjecting more than a sentence or two into these debates, but after what he had just heard, and in this evening's intensified mood of discontent, he knew he would be failing in his duty to all sorts of entities – to common sense, to discipline both military and civil, to England, yes and to the King, why be ashamed of it? – if he refrained from extensive comment. His eye met that of Cleaver, who looked away instantly. The major waited impatiently for the Home Secretary or whatever he was to finish.

Interest in the parliament had fallen off from the moment of its inception. Deliveries of newspapers and magazines had recently improved in speed and quantity and the major suspected that access to civilian drink had likewise improved; he must get his batman to keep his ears open. Less than half the original members were in their seats tonight. The Opposition front bench lacked its Leader and its spokesman on Defence questions: Doll had declared himself finally disgusted with his fellow-MPs' frivolity – 'I think it's ridiculous spending a lot of your time and thought preparing stuff for a load of apes, sir, don't you?' The ministerial bench was even more thinly held, with the Lord Privy Seal (if the truth were known) risking court-martial by thoroughly fraternising with a nurse from the civilian hospital in Hildesfeld, the Chancellor of the Exchequer asleep on his bed with a three-day-old *Daily Express* over him, the Prime Minister himself with two of his mates from the Sergeants' Mess attacking something they vaguely thought of as gin in something they even more vaguely thought of as a pub on the far side of the railway yard. But the Foreign Secretary was in his seat, and the young man the major very precisely thought of as that official's boy-friend was in his.

The Home Secretary might have been thought to be drawing to a close, although, as the major reminded himself, you could never tell about that or *anything else* with fellows as unused as this to public speaking or indeed to *anything else* even remotely to do with the highly responsible and specialized and difficult task of running a modern industrial state. 'You heard the other week about how we're going to give the Empire back to the blokes that live there,' the Home Secretary was saying: 'well, we're going to do the same thing, so to speak, with Great Britain itself. The country belongs to the ordinary working bloke and by Christ he's going to be running things from now on. No messing.'

The major brushed his moustache with his knuckle and looked at the cracked and scaled maps which, in the absence of anything else that might blot out some of the clay-coloured plaster, somebody had pulled out of a cupboard and hung up. What a mess Europe had evidently been in in 1555, with all those hundreds of little countries, quite different from today, and how big Naples and Venice had been then. The major remembered enough German to wonder how there could ever have been *two* Sicilies. And again, who was Van Diemen and how had he filled in his time in Tasmania?

'Good enough, then,' the Home Secretary said. 'There are just three principles involved here: liberty, equality and fraternity. You'll remember that that's what the

French Revolution was about. Well, we're not going to have a revolution about it, that's not the way we do things in England, not violent revolutions anyway, with barricades and shooting and so on and so forth. But there's going to be a revolution nevertheless and nobody's going to stop us.'

He sat down amid varied applause from his own side. The major looked at the Speaker for the first time and raised a finger in assumed humility. Archer seemed to pretend not to have seen him at first, then, having looked round the chamber, caught his eye and nodded to him.

'I shan't keep you long,' the major said as he rose to his feet. 'But there are just one or two points I feel I ought to put to you, if I may. We're all equal here – we're all members for Arromanches and Bayeux and Amiens and Brussels and Mechelen and Tilburg and Münster and Rheine and all the rest of the bloody places, and we can talk to each other as gentlemen. We've been through the whole thing together. And the first thing I want to say to you is this. Everybody's done a first-class job, you have and I hope we have as far as it was possible to us, and of course the fighting troops, nobody can say what they went through . . . Anyway, sitting here tonight it just occurred to me that it would be an awful pity if we were to let one another down by forgetting the things that have made it all possible, the teamwork and sense of responsibility, and behind that the way of life we've been fighting for. We've always been a pretty good-natured lot, we British, and the fellows up here' – he raised his hand to shoulder level – 'and the fellows down there' – he extended his arm downwards with the hand still spread – 'have always got on pretty well together. Each has had his job to do—'

Hargreaves stood up and said: 'I spy strangers.' He spoke loudly but unemotionally, as if promulgating his occupation rather than delivering a challenge.

The major stopped speaking immediately and looked

towards the Speaker with an expression of courteous bafflement.

The Speaker's expression was of incredulous horror. He said: 'Er . . . Hargreaves . . . can't we . . . ?'

'I spy strangers,' Hargreaves repeated a little louder, gazing into space.

'Could I ask you to clarify that, Mr Speaker, sir?' the major asked good-humouredly.

Archer replied as if the words were being wrung out of him. 'I was reading . . . it's a formula calling for the expulsion of unauthorized persons from the debating chamber. The idea was—'

'Unauthorized persons? Smiling, the major glanced from face to face. 'But surely—'

'The thing is that officially only Members of Parliament are allowed to be present,' Archer said, more steadily than before. 'Anybody else is here on sufferance. *I spy strangers* is the way of saying you want to cancel that sufferance, so to speak.'

Raleigh still smiled. 'Are you ordering me to withdraw, Mr Speaker?'

'I'm telling you what the book says.'

In the pause that followed, the major again looked round the House, but nobody returned his look. He went on trying to think of something to say until it became clear to him that there was nothing to say. With a glance at Cleaver, who quickly rose and followed him, Major Raleigh withdrew.

Outside in the darkness he said: 'You drive, Wilf, will you? I want to think.'

'Are you all right, Major?'

'Wilf, if you ask me if I'm all right once more I'll . . . Anyway don't. Just shut up.'

'Yes, sir.'

'Well, you must be pretty pleased, Mr Archer, I expect, at the way things have gone.'

'Yes, I must admit I am, Sergeant. Such a thumping majority, too.'

'Yes, that did rather take me by surprise. I expected it to be a much closer run thing than this. Of course, being wise after the event, it's not difficult to see what happened. The Service vote did it. The lads have been in uniform all these years and they've had enough. Voting Labour's a protest. It's a way of saying you're browned off and want to go home.'

'Oh, there's a lot more to it than that, I'm quite sure. People are browned off *with* something, or rather somebody, a lot of somebodies. They're protesting *against*—'

'Well, you and I are never going to see eye to eye there, sir, are we? – not even if we discuss it all night. We might as well accept it.'

'Will you join me in a glass of whisky, Sergeant? If it doesn't seem too like drowning your sorrows while I celebrate.'

'Thank you, sir, I will. You've certainly got something to celebrate, and everybody else seems to be doing it, so I don't see why I shouldn't join in.'

Doll and Archer sat in the little sitting-room – all painted screens and wax fruit and clocks under glass domes – of the farmhouse that contained the Officers' Mess. Outside, a widespread uproar was distantly audible: shouts, the revving of jeep and motor-cycle engines, the braying of a trombone that was being blown through rather than played. Ten minutes ago what sounded very much like a long burst of light-machine-gun fire had come from the direction of the Signal Office. There was no reason to suppose that all this was a demonstration of Socialist triumph over cowed and silent Tories. Whether or not Doll was right about the motives which had prompted the return of a Labour Government in Great Britain, the local reaction to it tonight was largely non-political in temper.

'They're keeping hard at it,' Doll said, pointing out of

the open window to a sudden burst of flame somewhere across the road. It was brighter than the now hour-old bonfire in the billet area. A few figures could be seen in the light of the new conflagration, reeling in and out of the darkness like pantomime drunks. 'Funny how nobody seems to be interfering. The major's right about one thing, anyway. Discipline's going. Ah, thank you, sir.' He raised one of the glasses of whisky which the Mess corporal had brought in response to Archer's bellow. 'Well. A solemn moment. What shall it be? I give you England, Mr Archer.'

'England.' Not your England, Archer said to himself, not the petrol-flogging CQMS's England, not the major's England or Cleaver's England or the Adjutant's or the Colonel's or Jack Rowney's or Tom Thurston's England, but to a certain extent Hargreaves's England and absolutely my England, full of girls and drinks and jazz and books and decent houses and decent jobs and being your own boss. He said in a friendly tone: 'I wonder whether England's going to turn out the way you'd like her to.'

'Oh, I've no doubt she won't, sir. But that's not really going to concern me much. I shan't be there, you see. Emigration's the thing for me, as soon as I can fix it up.'

'Really? Where are you thinking of? Canada? Australia?'

'I think Africa, Mr Archer. A place where there's room for initiative and where a determined man can still make his way. Kenya, perhaps, or one of the Rhodesias. There's some scope there. No, I've been thinking about it for a long time and today's news really decided me. Taken a load off my mind, in a way. Funny thing, I should be feeling depressed, with the Socialists getting in, but I don't at all. Quite the contrary, in fact.' Doll drained his glass.

'How about another of those?'

'No, thank you, sir, I really should be getting along and seeing the major. It's what I came for, after all.'

'I'll take you up.'

'There is just one point you might be able to help me with first, sir, if you would.' Doll opened the buff file-cover he had brought with him. 'This posting advice. I expect you know how the major's got all that organized. He can send who he likes. Well, he's asked to provide eight bodies of various kinds. All signal-office personnel. They'll be entraining for the UK in a couple of days, twenty-eight days' leave, then the boat for Burma. I should imagine they'll all be joining the same unit out there. Now the major's been in a funny mood recently. Sort of withdrawn. Normally he'd nominate all these bodies personally, but this morning he gave me three names and told me to fill in the others myself. Not like him at all. Anyway, I was just wondering if there's anybody in your section you'd care to lose. Apart from Hargreaves, that is. He was one of the major's three, as you probably know.'

'Yes, he did mention it to me. Tell me, Sergeant Doll, is there a vacancy for a switchboard-operator on that list?'

'There is, sir. Two, in fact.'

'Mm. It's tempting, but I'm afraid—'

'Perhaps it'll help you to make up your mind, Mr Archer, if I tell you now that I wasn't going to bother the major with signing the order himself. He's got enough on his mind already. And of course any officer's signature would do. Yours, for instance, sir.'

Archer hesitated. 'He's bound to see the file copy.'

'Yes, sir, but that won't be until tomorrow morning, will it? And I was thinking of dropping the top copy off for transmission at the Signal Office tonight when I go back down. Get it out of the way.'

'He could cancel it and send an amended list.'

'Oh, do you think that's likely, sir? Major Raleigh wants to be thought of as someone who can take a quick decision and stick to it. It's like a moral code with him.'

'A good point, Sergeant. Very well, then. I think I'll nominate Signalman Hammond.'

'14156755 Signalman Hammond, J. R., SBO DII?' Doll ran his fingertip along a line of typing. 'Anybody else? Right. Now, if you'd just sign here, sir . . . Thank you, I suppose you'll be off yourself soon, Mr Archer, won't you, after what you were telling me?'

'I imagine so. Well, you won't be needing the major after all now, I suppose.'

'Oh yes I will, sir. That was just a routine matter. Something far more important has come up. There's a signal here from War Office telling 424 Wireless Section, 502 Line Section and 287 DR Section to stand by to move on twenty-four-hour notice. Half the Company. They've obviously decided we're to be broken up.'

'That's important all right,' Archer said. 'To the major more than anyone else, probably.'

'My feeling exactly, sir. That was why I thought it couldn't wait till the morning. I reckoned I had to let him know about it tonight.' Doll's eyes grew distant.

'He'd set his heart on taking the Company out East.'

'Oh, don't I know it, Mr Archer. That's the end of that ambition. I wonder what the next pipe-dream will be.' Suddenly getting to his feet, Doll roamed about the room with his hands in his pockets, an uncharacteristic bodily movement. 'It may surprise you to learn, sir,' he said cordially, 'that I'm by way of being a bit of an angler. Been at it since I was a boy. Well now, it used to surprise me very much at first how badly I got on with other anglers. Jealousy rather than congratulations if you managed to pull off something a bit out of the ordinary. No end of disagreements over red hackles and what-not. And a lot of boredom too. Now in one way you wouldn't expect that, sir, would you? You'd expect people who'd got interests in common to get on better with one another than the average, not worse. But when you come to think about it it's not so odd. Someone who's a bit like yourself can rub you up the wrong way worse than a chap who's totally different. Well, there's one obvious instance. I bet a lot of the lads in this Company hate their officers and NCOs a sight worse than they ever hated Jerry. They know them, you see.

'You'll have to forgive me for reciting you a sermon, Mr Archer, but this is a point about human nature that's always interested me. And it has got an application. I take it I wouldn't be intruding on your mental privacy, so to speak, sir, if I hazarded a guess that you regard myself and the major as pretty much birds of a feather?'

'I think that's fair enough.'

'Thank you, sir. In that case it may surprise you to learn that I can't think of anybody whom I despise as thoroughly as I despise the major. I know you hate him yourself or I wouldn't risk telling you this. You'll be leaving us soon anyway.'

Archer's puzzlement, which had been growing for the last five minutes, changed direction. 'But I've got personal reasons.'

'I too. Though they're quite different from yours. He's so sure he's better. But in fact he's shoddy material. Third rate. Not to be depended on. In many parts of the world over the next few years an important battle's going to be fought – largely against the ideas that you yourself stand for, sir, if I may say so with all respect. The major's going to be worse than useless to us there. To me and the people who think as I do. He's soft. He'll break. I can see him standing as a Labour candidate in ten years' time if the wind's still blowing that way. No principle. That's the one thing I can't forgive.'

Partly to throw off complacency at being taken into a fascist's confidence, Archer stood up briskly and said: 'I'll take you up to the major now.'

'Right, sir. I wish I'd been there to see him thrown out of that last parliament. Good for Hargreaves. And you yourself too, sir, of course.'

The muffled bang of an exploding petrol-tank reached them as they climbed the steep narrow stairs to the main ante-room. This had been created by the folding-back of folding doors between two former bedrooms and the importation of furniture from all over the house and elsewhere. Outside it was a tiny landing hedged by slender carved banisters. Archer left Doll here and went in.

The major was sitting in half of the curious high-backed double armchair, a favourite of his despite its clear resemblance to part of a railway-carriage seat. Probably he found it suited his characteristic activity, the having of a word, whether denunciatory or conspiratorial, with someone. He had been having one now, an earnest one accompanied by gesture, with the young and usually solitary lieutenant-colonel of Engineers whose thirst for schnapps had established him as a local personality. In his hand at the moment was a glass not of schnapps but of the Mess's whisky, a glass which, appearance suggested, had been emptied and refilled several times that evening. The colonel was rather elaborately accoutred with belt, holster, revolver and lanyard. Both he and the major, who likewise seemed to have taken drink, were dramatically illuminated by a many-tiered candelabrum that made great use of frosted glass.

Raleigh had interrupted his confidential word with the colonel to have a more public one with the Mess corporal, who was saying: 'About forty, I should say, sir. Well dressed. Quite respectable.'

'And where's this picture she says she wants?'

'It was in her bedroom when it was her bedroom, sir.'

'But it isn't her bedroom any more. The house isn't hers either, it's been requisitioned. It belongs to me. No, she can't have her picture. I don't care whether she painted it herself or not, she can't have it. Go and tell her so, will you?'

When he saw that Archer was near, the major turned his back as far as was possible without actually kneeling on his seat. The emotion he felt for the ex-Speaker of the now officially dissolved parliament was not military disapprobation nor yet personal anger, but sadness at the other's withholding of loyalty. All this and much more had been gone into at length the morning after Hargreaves had spied strangers. Archer had protested, with every appearance of sincerity, that the strangers could have been suffered to remain if anybody had thought to put forward a simple motion proposing this, and that nothing but general ignorance of procedure had brought about their exit. Raleigh paid no heed. In the course of a sad and objective appraisal of Archer's disloyalty he had recounted rumours about Archer's private life which, if repeated before witnesses and if the law of slander had run in the Army, might have been the occasion of awards in damages sufficient to buy and sell the contents of the Officers' Shop. Then, still avowing sadness, the major had announced that his duty to the Company forbade the retention in its ranks of anybody so provenly disloyal. In other words, it was Burma for Archer as soon as the major's pal at HQ could fix it. After that, the major had sadly shouted at Archer to get out of his sight.

Archer had, and as far as possible had stayed there. But now he had to get back into it for a moment. To facilitate this he leant against the sideboard (could it have been made of ebony?) and faced the couple in the double arm-chair.

The RE colonel, whose name was Davison, was not the kind of man to appeal to Raleigh. He was what Raleigh was fond of calling a disorganized sort of chap, meaning someone whose character had not been stripped down like a racing-car until nothing but more or less military components remained. But it was his policy to encourage colonels and such to be around. Colonel Davison, once acquainted with the volume and regularity of the Mess's liquor supply, had needed no encouragement. At the moment he was saying in his public-school voice (another selling-point for the major): 'But as I keep telling you, that's why the Army's so good. Because nobody could take the bloody nonsense seriously.'

The major came back with something inaudible to Archer, probably that he couldn't go all the way with the colonel there.

'Well, nobody with any sense, then,' Davison said. 'And that saves an awful lot of worry. Means you can start laughing.'

Again the major could not be heard, but this time he went on much longer. Davison listened, nodding steadily, his eyes on his glass, which he was rotating on the knee of his crossed leg. Archer's attention wandered. It came to rest on Cleaver, who was half-lying on a purple sofa reading an unexpurgated edition of *Lady Chatterley's Lover*. Archer had had a go at that too. General opinion in the Mess was that it ranked about halfway in the little library the batmen had been assiduously building up ever since the Company entered urban France: not so good as, say, Frank Harris's *My Life and Loves*, but clearly better than the available non-fictional treatments of these themes, vital books by Scotsmen with titles like *Married Happiness*. Cleaver laughed silently to himself, then looked quickly and furtively round without catching Archer's eye.

'It's all a joke,' Davison said loudly. 'The whole thing.'

The major saw Archer. 'Yes?'

'Sergeant Doll would like to see you, sir. He's just outside.'

When Raleigh had gone, Davison patted the space beside him. 'Come and sit down, laddie.'

'Thank you, sir.'

'Sir. Sir sir sir. Sir sir sir sir sir sir sir. Ha.'

From the way Davison swayed about in his seat as he said this, Archer concluded that he was not just drunk, but very drunk. 'Nice little place we've got here, don't you think?'

'Oh, delightful. Delightful. Your poor major's upset.

Have you been being nasty to him? Have a drink. Corporal! More whisky needed here. Crash priority.'

'I'm never nasty to majors,' Archer said.

'Aren't you? I am. All the time. One of the consummations. Compensations. What do you do in Civvy Street, laddie?' The colonel was perhaps five years older than Archer.

'I don't do anything. Not yet. I was a student.'

'Jolly good luck to you. I'm an electrical engineer. So of course they put me on bridges. But it's all experience. A very good preparation, the Army.'

'For what?'

'Everything.'

As they received their drinks, Archer became aware that an altercation was going on just outside the room, with raised voices and what sounded like part of a human frame bouncing off the door. Was Doll fighting Raleigh?

'Just about everything. You'll have learnt a lot in the last few years which will stand you in good stead when you get into the great world.'

Archer's mouth opened. 'You mean that this is what *life* is like?'

'Roughly.'

Doll called from the doorway. 'Would you come, Mr Archer, quickly?'

Archer hurried over, followed by Davison, who said: 'If there's anything to see I'm going to see it.'

Four men confronted one another in the confined space at the stairhead: Hargreaves, Sergeant Fleming, Doll and Raleigh. Whatever he might have been doing a moment earlier, Hargreaves was doing nothing now except being held from behind by Fleming and denounced by Raleigh. Doll stood to one side, his file under his arm.

'I didn't know anything like this was going to happen, sir,' Fleming shouted to Archer. 'He just said very quiet he'd like to see the major if he was free, to apologize to him about the parliament, and I said couldn't it wait till the morning, and he said, still very quiet, his conscience was—'

'You dare come here and say that to me,' Raleigh shouted through this. His soft face had a glistening flush. 'You dirty little homo. Can't leave a decent lad alone. Rotten to the core. I know what goes on in that billet of yours. I'm going to take you off that draft and have you court-martialled for . . . for filth. There are plenty of people who'd be only too glad—'

Cleaver stepped forward and caught him by the arm. 'Shut up, major. Pipe down, you bloody fool. Come back in here, for Christ's sake.'

The major shook off Cleaver's hand. The movement brought him face to face with Archer. A theatrical sneer twisted Raleigh's soft features. 'And as for you . . . Tarred with the same brush. An officer. Selected for his qualities of leadership. That's good. I like that.'

There was a pause. The moment it was over Archer realised that he should have used it either to help Fleming get Hargreaves down the stairs or help Cleaver get Raleigh back into the ante-room. He could even have told the major just a little of what he thought of him. But he spent the time quailing under the major's stare.

Panting a little, Raleigh took up a fighting stance in front of Hargreaves. At the same time Colonel Davison spoke from the edge of the group. 'That'll do, everybody.' Fleming's expression made Archer turn quickly. He saw with incredulity that Davison was leaning against the door-jamb and levelling his drawn revolver in Raleigh's general direction.

'Often wanted to use this,' Davison said. He was thin and very tall. 'Properly, I mean. Not just on pigeons. Well, better late than never.'

'Put that away, Colonel,' Cleaver said.

Davison grinned. 'Sounds as if I'm exposing myself. But I know what you mean. My turn now. Who's gonna make me?'

'Let's be sensible.'

At this, Davison collapsed in laughter. 'One up to you, by God. Funny, isn't it? – always turns out like this if you try to do anything. Chaps saying let's be sensible. Let's be that whatever we do. Oh, my Christ.'

Still laughing, he staggered through the group and ended up by the banisters, laboriously trying to fit his revolver back into its holster. The major swung back towards Hargreaves. Afterwards opinion was divided on whether he was really going to hit him, but Doll evidently thought so, for he bounded forward and shouldered the major aside. Raleigh collided hard with Davison, whose attention was distracted by his revolver and holster and who at once, with a single cracking of wood, fell through the banisters and down into the tiled hall. He landed with another cracking sound which made the back of Archer's thighs turn cold. Doll ran down the stairs, closely followed by Cleaver. Hargreaves said: 'I'm sorry, Mr Archer.'

'Cup of tea for you, sir. And the newspapers.'

'Thank you. Did you get on to the hospital?' Major Raleigh spoke almost without inflection, as he usually did these days.

'Yes, sir. Progress maintained. Too early yet to say when he'll be up and about again, but the concussion's definitely not as bad as they thought at first and the arm's coming along as well as can be expected after a complicated fracture.'

Outside, heavy transport could be heard toiling in low gear. 'What's that row?'

'That's 424 Wireless forming up to move out, sir. They're due at the railhead at fifteen-hundred hours.'

'I know.'

'Are you going down to see them off, sir?'

'No.'

'Oh, by the way, Colonel Davison sent you a message, sir.'

'Did he?'

'Yes, he did, sir. Thanks for the party and he hopes he wasn't a nuisance.'

The major screwed up his soft face as a motor-bike revved up in the road below. 'Shut the window, will you, Doll?'

'Right, sir.' The operation completed, Doll turned round and leant against the sill. 'Well, we've all been very lucky, sir, really, haven't we? Things might have turned out much more serious. By the way, I thought you were very wise not to go on with that idea of yours of having Hargreaves court-martialled. Very wise indeed, sir.'

'When I want your opinion of my decisions, Doll, I'll ask for it.' This tripped less well off the major's tongue than it might have done at another time. Only Colonel Davison's accident had prevented that last encounter with Hargreaves from degenerating into a serious breach of order. The persistence of this thought bothered Raleigh. He said wearily: 'And while you're here I'd like you to tell me in detail how Hammond got on to that list with Hargreaves.'

'I've nothing to add to my previous account, sir, but still. You asked me to complete the list at my discretion, right? So seeing Hargreaves's name there, and knowing that Hammond was his mate, I put him down too. We've always done that sort of thing.'

'Is that all you knew?'

'Why, of course, sir. What else is there to know?'

'How did Archer come to sign that message?'

'Well, again as before, sir, Mr Archer happened to call in at the Orderly Room and I asked him, as I might have asked any officer who was available. There were one or two things piled up and I wanted to get them off.'

'Did Mr Archer read it through before he signed it?'

'I really couldn't say, sir. Quite likely he had enough confidence in me not to bother. You've often done the same yourself, sir, and believe me I very much appreciate the implied compliment.'

'Are you telling me the truth, Doll?'

'Mr Archer will confirm every word I've said, sir, as far as it concerns him.'

The major sighed heavily. 'I suppose that's that.'

'I suppose so, sir. Actually, it's a pity we've lost Hammond, a very pleasant young fellow I agree, but it's not going to make much difference, sir, is it? There'd have been nothing for him to do here after the Signal Office closes down next week. I don't suppose any of us will be together much longer. Captain Cleaver and Mr Archer and the others on twenty-four-hour warning. You'll be all on your own here before very long, sir.'

'I'm looking forward to it.'

Doll almost smiled. 'Of course, it's Mr Archer who's come best out of this. Dodging the Far East after all. What a bit of luck that was, eh, sir?'

Something close to attention entered the major's manner. 'Dodging the Far East?'

'Oh, no doubt about it, sir. Even if he goes tomorrow it'll take him ten days to get home, the way things are. Then he'll go on twenty-eight days' leave, which'll bring him to the first week in September. And with his release due a month at most after that it wouldn't be worth anybody's while to put him on a boat. No, he's—'

'Doll, I don't know what you're talking about.'

'Really, sir? I'm awfully sorry, I was sure Mr Archer would have told you long ago. When was he telling me about it, now? Yes, I can remember exactly – it was the earlier part of the evening on which Colonel Davison met with his accident. Mr Archer and I went on to discuss the Election results – that's right – and then we—'

'All right, I don't want the story of your life. I asked you to tell me—'

'Do forgive me, sir – I've got this bad habit of letting my tongue run away with me, I know. It's just that the events of that evening are so indelibly impressed on my memory, sir, if you know what I – Yes, sir. Well, Mr Archer showed me a letter from the head of his college in Oxford, the Master I think he called himself. It said they were arranging his release from the Army and reckoned he'd be out in good time to go into the college when the term begins, which I gather is about the tenth of October, though no doubt you could put me right there.'

'But he's only been in for three or four years. You and I and most of the blokes have been in for six.'

'Seven in my case, sir; you'll recall that I was one of the 1938 militiamen. Yes, I know it seems strange, Mr Archer getting out so soon, but apparently this is something called the Class "B" Scheme – we had a memo about it a couple of weeks ago which I'll look out for you if you're interested.'

'Don't bother.'

'How funny Mr Archer hasn't told you yet. I expect he's waiting for a suitable opportunity, sir, don't you?'

'Get out and leave me in peace.'

'Glad to, sir.'

Left in peace, the major sat on at his almost-empty table. The bulk of 424 Wireless Station was evidently moving out on to the main road along Raleigh's Alley, making full use of that thoroughfare for the first and last time. The major's eye missed a letter from the British Drama League saying that *Journey's End* was not available. It caught an order informing him that with effect from two days' time the area of which he had hoped to become chieftain would be known as No. 9 Independent Transit Area and would fall under the command of a full colonel dispatched from HQ. He picked up a newspaper headlined *IT'S NO JOKE–IO TO LIVE IN TOKYO: 600 Super-Forts Blast Jap Heartland* and put it down again. The other paper contained a large Election supplement. He summoned the resolution to study the details of what he had so far been able to take in only as an appalling generality. Turning to an inner page, he read:

WINKWORTH (WEST)

R. Jack (Lab)	28,740
Maj.-Gen. P. O. de C. Biggs-Courtenay, DSO (C)	9,011
Lab majority	19,729

Labour gain from Conservative
1935: Maj.-Gen. P. O. de C. Biggs-Courtenay, DSO (C) 19,495; W. Mott (Lab) 9319: C majority 10,176

The major dropped his head into his hands. This, he supposed, was the bottom. And yet he felt a stirring of hope. Having sunk to the lowest depths his nature was capable of, he could not help seeing the future as some sort of upward path. Nobody and nothing in his immediate environment gave him the smallest reason for confidence. Doll, Cleaver, Hammond, Davison, Archer (whom he had tried so hard to train up as a conscientious officer), the Company, the Signal Office, chances of leadership – all in their different ways had turned out to be not worth depending on. But the world was wide. Bad things could happen and it all went on as before. The thought of his friends in Potsdam filled him with encouragement now, not envy. Much of what he believed in must survive.

And the guarantee of that was England. England had been up against it in 1940, in 1914 and no doubt earlier, with the Napoleon business and so on. She had weathered every storm, she had never gone under. All that was needed was faith. Despite everything that Hargreaves and Archer and the rest of them might do, England would muddle through somehow.

Ivy Day in the Committee Room

James Joyce

Old Jack raked the cinders together with a piece of cardboard and spread them judiciously over the whitening dome of coals. When the dome was thinly covered his face lapsed into darkness but, as he set himself to fan the fire again, his crouching shadow ascended the opposite wall and his face slowly re-emerged into light. It was an old man's face, very bony and hairy. The moist blue eyes blinked at the fire and the moist mouth fell open at times, munching once or twice mechanically when it closed. When the cinders had caught he laid the piece of cardboard against the wall, sighed and said:

'That's better now, Mr O'Connor.'

Mr O'Connor, a grey-haired young man, whose face was disfigured by many blotches and pimples, had just brought the tobacco for a cigarette into a shapely cylinder, but when spoken to he undid his handiwork again meditatively. Then he began to roll the tobacco again meditatively and after a moment's thought decided to lick the paper.

'Did Mr Tierney say when he'd be back?' he asked in a husky falsetto.

'He didn't say.'

Mr O'Connor put his cigarette into his mouth and began to search his pockets. He took out a pack of thin pasteboard cards.

'I'll get you a match,' said the old man.

'Never mind, this'll do,' said Mr O'Connor.

He selected one of the cards and read what was printed on it:

MUNICIPAL ELECTIONS

ROYAL EXCHANGE WARD

Mr Richard J. Tierney, P.L.G., respectfully solicits the favour of your vote and influence at the coming election in the Royal Exchange Ward.

Mr O'Connor had been engaged by Tierney's agent to canvass one part of the ward but, as the weather was inclement and his boots let in the wet, he spent a great part of the day sitting by the fire in the Committee Room in Wicklow Street with Jack, the old caretaker. They had been sitting thus since the short day had grown dark. It was the sixth of October, dismal and cold out of doors.

Mr O'Connor tore a strip off the end of the card and, lighting it, lit his cigarette. As he did so the flame lit up a leaf of dark glossy ivy in the lapel of his coat. The old man watched him attentively and then, taking up the piece of cardboard again, began to fan the fire slowly while his companion smoked.

'Ah, yes,' he said, continuing, 'it's hard to know what way to bring up children. Now who'd think he'd turn out like that! I sent him to the Christian Brothers and I done what I could for him, and there he goes boozing about. I tried to make him somewhat decent.'

He replaced the cardboard wearily.

'Only I'm an old man now I'd change his tune for him. I'd take a stick to his back and beat him while I could stand over him – as I done many a time before. The mother, you know, she cocks him up with this and that . . .'

'That's what ruins children,' said Mr O'Connor.

'To be sure it is,' said the old man. 'And little thanks you get for it, only impudence. He takes th'upper hand of me whenever he sees I've a sup taken. What's the world coming to when sons speaks that way to their fathers?'

'What age is he?' said Mr O'Connor.

'Nineteen,' said the old man.

'Why don't you put him to something?'

'Sure, amn't I never done at the drunken bowsy ever since he left school? "I won't keep you," I says. "You must get a job for yourself." But, sure it's worse whenever he gets a job; he drinks it all.'

Mr O'Connor shook his head in sympathy, and the old man fell silent, gazing into the fire. Someone opened the door of the room and called out:

'Hello! Is this a Freemasons' meeting?'

'Who's that?' said the old man.

'What are you doing in the dark?' asked a voice.

'Is that you, Hynes?' asked Mr O'Connor.

'Yes. What are you doing in the dark?' said Mr Hynes, advancing into the light of the fire.

He was a tall, slender young man with a light brown moustache. Imminent little drops of rain hung at the brim of his hat and the collar of his jacket-coat was turned up.

'Well, Mat,' he said to Mr O'Connor, 'how goes it?'

Mr O'Connor shook his head. The old man left the hearth, and after stumbling about the room returned with two candlesticks which he thrust one after the other into the fire and carried to the table. A denuded room came into view and the fire lost all its cheerful colour. The walls of the room were bare except for a copy of an election address. In the middle of the room was a small table on which papers were heaped.

Mr Hynes leaned against the mantelpiece and asked:

'Has he paid you yet?'

'Not yet,' said Mr O'Connor. 'I hope to God he'll not leave us in the lurch tonight.'

Mr Hynes laughed.

'O, he'll pay you. Never fear,' he said.

'I hope he'll look smart about it if he means business,' said Mr O'Connor.

'What do you think, Jack?' said Mr Hynes satirically to the old man.

The old man returned to his seat by the fire, saying:

'It isn't but he has it, anyway. Not like the other tinker.'

'What other tinker?' said Mr Hynes.

'Colgan,' said the old man scornfully.

'It is because Colgan's a working-man you say that? What's the difference between a good honest bricklayer and a publican – eh? Hasn't the working-man as good a right to be in the Corporation as anyone else – ay, and a better right than those shoneens that are always hat in hand before any fellow with a handle to his name? Isn't that so, Mat?' said Mr Hynes, addressing Mr O'Connor.

'I think you're right,' said Mr O'Connor.

'One man is a plain honest man with no hunker-sliding about him. He goes in to represent the labour classes. This fellow you're working for only wants to get some job or other.'

'Of course, the working-classes should be represented,' said the old man.

'The working-man,' said Mr Hynes, 'gets all kicks and no halfpence. But it's labour produces everything. The working-man is not looking for fat jobs for his sons and nephews and cousins. The working-man is not going to drag the honour of Dublin in the mud to please a German monarch.'

'How's that?' said the old man.

'Don't you know they want to present an address of welcome to Edward Rex if he comes here next year? What do we want kowtowing to a foreign king?'

'Our man won't vote for the address,' said Mr O'Connor. 'He goes in on the Nationalist ticket.'

'Won't he?' said Mr Hynes. 'Wait till you see whether he will or not. I know him. Is it Tricky Dicky Tierney?'

'By God! perhaps you're right, Joe,' said Mr O'Connor. 'Anyway, I wish he'd turn up with the spondulicks.'

The three men fell silent. The old man began to rake more cinders together. Mr Hynes took off his hat, shook it and then turned down the collar of his coat, displaying, as he did so, an ivy leaf in the lapel.

'If this man was alive,' he said, pointing to the leaf, 'we'd have no talk of an address of welcome.'

'That's true,' said Mr O'Connor.

'Musha, God be with them times!' said the old man. 'There was some life in it then.'

The room was silent again. Then a bustling little man with a snuffling nose and very cold ears pushed in the door. He walked over quickly to the fire, rubbing his hands as if he intended to produce a spark from them.

'No money, boys,' he said.

'Sit down here, Mr Henchy,' said the old man, offering him his chair.

'O, don't stir, Jack, don't stir,' said Mr Henchy.

He nodded curtly to Mr Hynes and sat down on the chair which the old man vacated.

'Did you serve Aungier Street?' he asked Mr O'Connor.

'Yes,' said Mr O'Connor, beginning to search his pockets for memoranda.

'Did you call on Grimes?'

'I did.'

'Well? How does he stand?'

'He wouldn't promise. He said: "I won't tell anyone what way I'm going to vote." But I think he'll be all right.'

'Why so?'

'He asked me who the nominators were; and I told him. I mentioned Father Burke's name. I think it'll be all right.'

Mr Henchy began to snuffle and rub his hands over the fire at a terrific speed. Then he said:

'For the love of God, Jack, bring us a bit of coal. There must be some left.'

The old man went out of the room.

'It's no go,' said Mr Henchy, shaking his head. 'I asked the little shoeboy, but he said: "O, now, Mr Henchy, when I see the work going on properly I won't forget you,

you may be sure." Mean little tinker! 'Usha, how could he be anything else?'

'What did I tell you, Mat?' said Mr Hynes. 'Tricky Dicky Tierney.'

'O, he's as tricky as they make 'em,' said Mr Henchy. 'He hasn't got those little pig's eyes for nothing. Blast his soul! Couldn't he pay up like a man instead of: "O, now Mr Henchy, I must speak to Mr Fanning . . . I've spent a lot of money." Mean little schoolboy of hell! I suppose he forgets the time his little old father kept the hand-me-down shop in Mary's Lane.'

'But is that a fact?' asked Mr O'Connor.

'God, yes,' said Mr Henchy. 'Did you never hear that? And the men used to go in on Sunday morning before the houses were open to buy a waistcoat or a trousers – moya! But Tricky Dicky's little old father always had a tricky little black bottle up in a corner. Do you mind now? That's that. That's where he first saw the light.'

The old man returned with a few lumps of coal which he placed here and there on the fire.

'That's a nice how-do-you-do,' said Mr O'Connor. 'How does he expect us to work for him if he won't stump up?'

'I can't help it,' said Mr Henchy. 'I expect to find the bailiffs in the hall when I go home.'

Mr Hynes laughed and, shoving himself away from the mantelpiece with the aid of his shoulders, made ready to leave.

'It'll be all right when King Eddie comes,' he said. 'Well, boys, I'm off for the present. See you later. 'Bye, 'bye.'

He went out of the room slowly. Neither Mr Henchy nor the old man said anything, but, just as the door was closing, Mr O'Connor, who had been staring moodily into the fire, called out suddenly:

''Bye, Joe.'

Mr Henchy waited a few moments and then nodded in the direction of the door.

'Tell me,' he said across the fire, 'what brings our friend in here? What does he want?'

''Usha, poor Joe!' said Mr O'Connor, throwing the end of his cigarette into the fire, 'he's hard up, like the rest of us.'

Mr Henchy snuffled vigorously and spat so copiously that he nearly put out the fire, which uttered a hissing protest.

'To tell you my private and candid opinion,' he said, 'I think he's a man from the other camp. He's a spy of Colgan's, if you ask me. Just go round and try and find out how they're getting on. They won't suspect you. Do you twig?'

'Ah, poor Joe is a decent skin,' said Mr O'Connor.

'His father was a decent, respectable man,' Mr Henchy admitted. 'Poor old Larry Hynes! Many a good turn he did in his day! But I'm greatly afraid our friend is not nineteen carat. Damn it, I can understand a fellow being hard up, but what I can't understand is a fellow sponging. Couldn't he have some spark of manhood about him?'

'He doesn't get a warm welcome from me when he comes,' said the old man. 'Let him work for his own side and not come spying around here.'

'I don't know,' said Mr O'Connor dubiously, as he took out cigarette-papers and tobacco. 'I think Joe Hynes is a straight man. He's a clever chap, too, with the pen. Do you remember that thing he wrote . . . ?'

'Some of these hillsiders and fenians are a bit too clever if you ask me,' said Mr Henchy. 'Do you know what my private and candid opinion is about some of those little jokers? I believe half of them are in the pay of the Castle.'

'There's no knowing,' said the old man.

'O, but I know it for a fact,' said Mr Henchy. 'They're Castle hacks . . . I don't say Hynes . . . No, damn it, I think he's a stroke above that . . . But there's a certain little nobleman with a cock-eye – you know the patriot I'm alluding to?'

Mr O'Connor nodded.

'There's a lineal descendant of Major Sirr for you if you like! O, the heart's blood of a patriot! That's a fellow now that'd sell his country for fourpence – ay – and go down on his bended knees and thank the Almighty Christ he had a country to sell.'

There was a knock at the door.

'Come in!' said Mr Henchy.

A person resembling a poor clergyman or a poor actor appeared in the doorway. His black clothes were tightly buttoned on his short body and it was impossible to say whether he wore a clergyman's collar or a layman's, because the collar of his shabby frock-coat, the uncovered buttons of which reflected the candle-light, was turned up about his neck. He wore a round hat of hard black felt. His face, shining with raindrops, had the appearance of damp yellow cheese save where two rosy spots indicated the cheek-bones. He opened his very long mouth suddenly to express disappointment and at the same time opened wide his very bright blue eyes to express pleasure and surprise.

'O, Father Keon!' said Mr Henchy, jumping up from his chair. 'Is that you? Come in!'

'O, no, no, no,' said Father Keon quickly, pursing his lips as if he were addressing a child.

'Won't you come in and sit down?'

'No, no, no!' said Father Keon, speaking in a discreet, indulgent, velvety voice. 'Don't let me disturb you now! I'm just looking for Mr Fanning . . .'

'He's round at the *Black Eagle*,' said Mr Henchy. 'But won't you come in and sit down a minute?'

'No, no, thank you. It was just a little business matter,' said Father Keon. 'Thank you, indeed.'

He retreated from the doorway and Mr Henchy, seizing

one of the candlesticks, went to the door to light him downstairs.

'O, don't trouble, I beg!'

'No, but the stairs is so dark.'

'No, no, I can see . . . Thank you, indeed.'

'Are you right now?'

'All right, thanks . . . Thanks.'

Mr Henchy returned with the candlestick and put it on the table. He sat down again at the fire. There was silence for a few moments.

'Tell me, John,' said Mr O'Connor, lighting his cigarette with another pasteboard card.

'Hm?'

'What is he exactly?'

'Ask me an easier one,' said Mr Henchy.

'Fanning and himself seem to me very thick. They're often in Kavanagh's together. Is he a priest at all?'

'Mmmyes, I believe so . . . I think he's what you call a black sheep. We haven't many of them, thank God! but we have a few . . . He's an unfortunate man of some kind . . .'

'And how does he knock it out?' asked Mr O'Connor.

'That's another mystery.'

'Is he attached to any chapel or church or institution or—'

'No,' said Mr Henchy, 'I think he's travelling on his own account . . . God forgive me,' he added, 'I thought he was the dozen of stout.'

'Is there any chance of a drink itself?' asked Mr O'Connor.

'I'm dry too,' said the old man.

'I asked that little shoeboy three times,' said Mr Henchy, 'would he send up a dozen of stout. I asked him again now, but he was leaning on the counter in his shirt-sleeves having a deep goster with Alderman Cowley.'

'Why didn't you remind him?' said Mr O'Connor.

'Well, I wouldn't go over while he was talking to Alderman Cowley. I just waited till I caught his eye, and said: "About that little matter I was speaking to you about . . ." "That'll be all right, Mr H.," he said. Yerra, sure the little hop-o'-my-thumb has forgotten about it.'

'There's some deal on in that quarter,' said Mr O'Connor thoughtfully. 'I saw the three of them hard at it yesterday at Suffolk Street corner.'

'I think I know the little game they're at,' said Mr Henchy. 'You must owe the City Fathers money nowadays if you want to be made Lord Mayor. Then they'll make you Lord Mayor. By God! I'm thinking seriously of becoming a City Father myself. What do you think? Would I do for the job?'

Mr O'Connor laughed.

'So far as owing money goes . . .'

'Driving out of the Mansion House,' said Mr Henchy, 'in all my vermin, with Jack here standing up behind me in a powdered wig – eh?'

'And make me your private secretary, John.'

'Yes. And I'll make Father Keon my private chaplain. We'll have a family party.'

'Faith, Mr Henchy,' said the old man, 'you'd keep up better style than some of them. I was talking one day to old Keegan, the porter. "And how do you like your new master, Pat?" says I to him. "You haven't much entertaining now," says I. "Entertaining!" says he. "He'd live on the smell of an oil-rag." And do you know what he told me? Now, I declare to God, I didn't believe him.'

'What?' said Mr Henchy and Mr O'Connor.

'He told me: "What do you think of a Lord Mayor of Dublin sending out for a pound of chops for his dinner? How's that for high living?" says he. "Wisha! wisha," says I. "A pound of chops," says he, "coming into the Mansion House." "Wisha!" says I, "what kind of people is going at all now?" '

At this point there was a knock at the door, and a boy put in his head.

'What is it?' said the old man.

'From the *Black Eagle*,' said the boy, walking in sideways and depositing a basket on the floor with a noise of shaken bottles.

The old man helped the boy to transfer the bottles from the basket to the table and counted the full tally. After the transfer the boy put his basket on his arm and asked:

'Any bottles?'

'What bottles?' said the old man.

'Won't you let us drink them first?' said Mr Henchy.

'I was told to ask for the bottles.'

'Come back tomorrow,' said the old man.

'Here, boy!' said Mr Henchy, 'will you run over to O'Farrell's and ask him to lend us a corkscrew – for Mr Henchy, say. Tell him we won't keep it a minute. Leave the basket there.'

The boy went out and Mr Henchy began to rub his hands cheerfully, saying:

'Ah, well, he's not so bad after all. He's as good as his word, anyhow.'

'There's no tumblers,' said the old man.

'O, don't let that trouble you, Jack,' said Mr Henchy. 'Many's the good man before now drank out of the bottle.'

'Anyway, it's better than nothing,' said Mr O'Connor.

'He's not a bad sort,' said Mr Henchy, 'only Fanning has such a loan of him. He means well, you know, in his own tinpot way.'

The boy came back with the corkscrew. The old man opened three bottles and was handing back the corkscrew when Mr Henchy said to the boy:

'Would you like a drink, boy?'

'If you please, sir,' said the boy.

The old man opened another bottle grudgingly, and handed it to the boy.

'What age are you?' he asked.

'Seventeen,' said the boy.

As the old man said nothing further, the boy took the

bottle, said: 'Here's my best respects, sir, to Mr Henchy,' drank the contents, put the bottle back on the table and wiped his mouth with his sleeve. Then he took up the corkscrew and went out of the door sideways, muttering some form of salutation.

'That's the way it begins,' said the old man.

'The thin edge of the wedge,' said Mr Henchy.

The old man distributed the three bottles which he had opened and the men drank from them simultaneously. After having drunk each placed his bottle on the mantelpiece within hand's reach and drew in a long breath of satisfaction.

'Well, I did a good day's work today,' said Mr Henchy, after a pause.

'That so, John?'

'Yes. I got one or two sure things in Dawson Street, Crofton and myself. Between ourselves, you know, Crofton (he's a decent chap, of course), but he's not worth a damn as a canvasser. He hasn't a word to throw to a dog. He stands and looks at the people while I do the talking.'

Here two men entered the room. One of them was a very fat man, whose blue serge clothes seemed to be in danger of falling from his sloping figure. He had a big face which resembled a young ox's face in expression, staring blue eyes and a grizzled moustache. The other man, who was much younger and frailer, had a thin, clean-shaven face. He wore a very high double collar and a wide-brimmed bowler hat.

'Hello, Crofton!' said Mr Henchy to the fat man. 'Talk of the devil . . .'

'Where did the booze come from?' asked the young man. 'Did the cow calve?'

'O, of course, Lyons spots the drink first thing!' said Mr O'Connor, laughing.

'Is that the way you chaps canvass,' said Mr Lyons, 'and Crofton and I out in the cold and rain looking for votes?'

'Why, blast your soul,' said Mr Henchy, 'I'd get more votes in five minutes than you two'd get in a week.'

'Open two bottles of stout, Jack,' said Mr O'Connor.

'How can I?' said the old man, 'when there's no corkscrew?'

'Wait now, wait now!' said Mr Henchy, getting up quickly. 'Did you ever see this little trick?'

He took two bottles from the table and, carrying them to the fire, put them on the hob. Then he sat down again by the fire and took another drink from his bottle. Mr Lyons sat on the edge of the table, pushed his hat towards the nape of his neck and began to swing his legs.

'Which is my bottle?' he asked.

'This, lad,' said Mr Henchy.

Mr Crofton sat down on a box and looked fixedly at the other bottle on the hob. He was silent for two reasons. The first reason, sufficient in itself, was that he had nothing to say: the second reason was that he considered his companions beneath him. He had been a canvasser for Wilkins, the Conservative, but when the Conservatives had withdrawn their man and, choosing the lesser of two evils, given their support to the Nationalist candidate, he had been engaged to work for Mr Tierney.

In a few minutes an apologetic 'Pok!' was heard as the cork flew out of Mr Lyons' bottle. Mr Lyons jumped off the table, went to the fire, took his bottle and carried it back to the table.

'I was just telling them, Crofton,' said Mr Henchy, 'that we got a good few votes today.'

'Who did you get?' asked Mr Lyons.

'Well, I got Parkes for one, and I got Atkinson for two, and I got Ward of Dawson Street. Fine old chap he is, too – regular old toff, old Conservative! "But isn't your candidate a Nationalist?" said he. "He's a respectable man," said I. "He's in favour of whatever will benefit this country. He's a big ratepayer," I said. "He has extensive house property in the city and three places of business, and isn't it to his own advantage to keep down the rates? He's a prominent and respected citizen," said I, "and a Poor Law Guardian, and he doesn't belong to any party, good, bad, or indifferent." That's the way to talk to 'em.'

'And what about the address to the King?' said Mr Lyons, after drinking and smacking his lips.

'Listen to me,' said Mr Henchy. 'What we want in this country, as I said to old Ward, is capital. The King's coming here will mean an influx of money into this country. The citizens of Dublin will benefit by it. Look at all the factories down by the quays there, idle! Look at all the money there is in the country if we only worked the old industries, the mills, the ship-building yards and factories. It's capital we want.'

'But look here, John,' said Mr O'Connor. 'Why should we welcome the King of England? Didn't Parnell himself . . .'

'Parnell,' said Mr Henchy, 'is dead. Now, here's the way I look at it. Here's this chap come to the throne after his old mother keeping him out of it till the man was grey. He's a man of the world, and he means well by us. He's a jolly fine, decent fellow, if you ask me, and no damn nonsense about him. He just says to himself: "The old one never went to see these wild Irish. By Christ, I'll go myself and see what they're like." And are we going to insult the man when he comes over here on a friendly visit? Eh? Isn't that right, Crofton?'

Mr Crofton nodded his head.

'But after all now,' said Mr Lyons argumentatively, 'King Edward's life, you know, is not the very . . .'

'Let bygones be bygones,' said Mr Henchy. 'I admire the man personally. He's just an ordinary knockabout like you and me. He's fond of his glass of grog and he's a bit of a rake, perhaps, and he's a good sportsman. Damn it, can't we Irish play fair?'

'That's all very fine,' said Mr Lyons. 'But look at the case of Parnell now.'

'In the name of God,' said Mr Henchy, 'where's the analogy between the two cases?'

'What I mean,' said Mr Lyons, 'is we have our ideals. Why, now, would we welcome a man like that? Do you think now after what he did Parnell was a fit man to lead us? And why, then, would we do it for Edward the Seventh.'

'This is Parnell's anniversary,' said Mr O'Connor, 'and don't let us stir up any bad blood. We all respect him now that he's dead and gone – even the Conservatives,' he added, turning to Mr Crofton.

Pok! The tardy cork flew out of Mr Crofton's bottle. Mr Crofton got up from his box and went to the fire. As he returned with his capture he said in a deep voice:

'Our side of the House respects him, because he was a gentleman.'

'Right you are, Crofton!' said Mr Henchy fiercely. 'He was the only man that could keep that bag of cats in order. "Down, ye dogs! Lie down, ye curs!" That's the way he treated them. Come in, Joe! Come in!' he called out, catching sight of Mr Hynes in the doorway.

Mr Hynes came in slowly.

'Open another bottle of stout, Jack,' said Mr Henchy. 'O, I forgot there's no corkscrew! Here, show me one here and I'll put it at the fire.'

The old man handed him another bottle and he placed it on the hob.

'Sit down, Joe,' said Mr O'Connor, 'we're just talking about the Chief.'

'Ay, ay!' said Mr Henchy.

Mr Hynes sat on the side of the table near Mr Lyons but said nothing.

'There's one of them, anyhow,' said Mr Henchy, 'that didn't renege him. By God, I'll say for you, Joe! No, by God, you stuck to him like a man!'

'O, Joe,' said Mr O'Connor suddenly. 'Give us that

thing you wrote – do you remember? Have you got it on you?'

'O, ay!' said Mr Henchy. 'Give us that. Did you ever hear that, Crofton? Listen to this now: splendid thing.'

'Go on,' said Mr O'Connor. 'Fire away, Joe.'

Mr Hynes did not seem to remember at once the piece to which they were alluding, but, after reflecting a while, he said:

'O, that thing is it . . . Sure, that's old now.'

'Out with it, man!' said Mr O'Connor.

''Sh, 'sh,' said Mr Henchy. 'Now Joe!'

Mr Hynes hesitated a little longer. Then amid the silence he took off his hat, laid it on the table and stood up. He seemed to be rehearsing the piece in his mind. After a rather long pause he announced:

THE DEATH OF PARNELL
6 October, 1891

He cleared his throat once or twice and then began to recite:

He is dead. Our Uncrowned King is dead.
  O, Erin, mourn with grief and woe
For he lies dead whom the fell gang
  Of modern hypocrites laid low.

He lies slain by the coward hounds
  He raised to glory from the mire;
And Erin's hopes and Erin's dreams
  Perish upon her monarch's pyre.

In palace, cabin or in cot
  The Irish heart where'er it be
Is bowed with woe – for he is gone
  Who would have wrought her destiny.

He would have had his Erin famed,
  The green flag gloriously unfurled,
Her statesman, bards, and warriors raised
  Before the nations of the World.

He dreamed (alas, 'twas but a dream!)
  Of Liberty: but as he strove
To clutch that idol, treachery
  Sundered him from the thing he loved.

Shame on the coward, caitiff hands
  That smote their Lord or with a kiss
Betrayed him to the rabble-rout
  Of fawning priests – no friends of his.

May everlasting shame consume
  The memory of those who tried
To befoul and smear the exalted name
  Of one who spurned them in his pride.

He fell as fall the mighty ones,
  Nobly undaunted to the last,
And death has now united him
  With Erin's heroes of the past.

No sound of strife disturbs his sleep!
  Calmly he rests: no human pain
Or high ambition spurs him now
  The peaks of glory to attain.

They had their way: they laid him low.
  But Erin, list, his spirit may
Rise, like the Phoenix from the flames,
  When breaks the dawning of the day,

The day that brings us Freedom's reign.
  And on that day may Erin well
Pledge in the cup she lifts to Joy
  One grief – the memory of Parnell.

Mr Hynes sat down again on the table. When he had finished his recitation there was a silence and then a burst of clapping: even Mr Lyons clapped. The applause continued for a little time. When it had ceased all the auditors drank from their bottles in silence.

Pok! The cork flew out of Mr Hynes's bottle, but Mr Hynes remained sitting flushed and bareheaded on the table. He did not seem to have heard the invitation.

'Good man, Joe!' said Mr O'Connor, taking out his cigarette papers and pouch the better to hide his emotion.

'What do you think of that, Crofton?' cried Mr Henchy. 'Isn't that fine? What?'

Mr Crofton said that it was a very fine piece of writing.